TO BE FRANK

A fictional memoir

MJ CORNWALL

Printed by BookPOD

First published 2022

ISBN: 978-0-6454923-0-9 (paperback)
ISBN: 978-0-6454923-1-6 (ebook)

Front cover art: Michael Fitzjames

Cornwall, Mark 1957-
Thring, Frank, 1926-1994 – Biography
Thring, Francis William, 1882-1936
Entertainment – Australia – History
Television – Australia – History
Actors – Australia
Film – Australia

NATIONAL
LIBRARY
OF AUSTRALIA

A catalogue record for this book is available from the National Library of Australia

For Ali and Paddy

TO BE FRANK

Seldom any splendid story is wholly true.

– Samuel Johnson

PROLOGUE

Oh, one is alright in a dreadful sort of way, having just had four toes off. On top of these liver function issues, and one's old pal oesophageal varices, all those throat haemorrhages. And the rest of it. Yes, pixie. One has had *fun*.

Never knew my old man, did you? No. Only Olive. My, er, *mother*. As a child, one saw him only now and then, this FT, as they called Frank Senior. Often in Europe. Oftener in the US. *Your father is away on business, Master Frank.*

The silent movies he shipped in from Hollywood for his cinemas *pulled more mugs than public hangings, Frankie my boy.* Before that, his handwound bioscope, bringing the first films ever made to the mugs out in the mulga, shaped his vision. And made me who I am.

About FT's sullied name. This work of snakes and toads took him at fifty-three. He looked far older. The drink. Salve for the fists and boots of slanders rained upon him since he created Hoyts cinemas back in the Roaring Twenties.

Fled home at fourteen. Learned magic tricks. From teenage conjuror the Great Dexter with a travelling circus midst the rotgut and brutes of Tasmanian mining camps, to tycoon in just ten years. Then fell, as do all who reach for the stars.

So here at one's own end, imperative I vindicate. FT had his shortcomings, but his punishers never tramped in his boots of holes and nails. They accuse him to this day of obliterating Australia's film industry of the 1920s, to serve selfish ends. But this pestilence came from elsewhere.

FT's dream, to create in Melbourne films equal to Warners, Fox, MGM, that dingo pack, was drowned in the Yarra in a sack full of bricks.

'Their libels extend to me,' I once told a young buck who shall remain nameless. 'The stuff of graffiti on a child's headstone.'

Yes. Some claim that one squandered the Thring fortune. In truth, much of it redistributed in ways far from their imaginings. Known only to benefactors, as one insisted. And that other stuff. Monster pervert. Molester of toddlers. Incontinence fetishist. Heard 'em all. Ah, yes. And dismissed as an actor of no flesh but ham. This account will see these critics eviscerated.

Would that satisfy thee, my liege? one asks oneself.

Not on your life, baby. *Let the games begin.*

CHAPTER ONE

'You could say one was born with a silver cock in one's mouth,' one nutshelled it to a young chum. One first saw what passes for daylight most Melbourne days on the eleventh of May, 1926. Sister Bennett's maternity hospital, Kooyong Road, Armadale.

Pampered rotten. Yet unloved, and cast as prince regent, heir to FT's throne of plastic sideshow skulls. For FT and Olive, theirs was the work of the First Thring Empire, not as custodial carers. Our household staff, the maids, our driver, served as one's *in loco parentis*. Foremost among them Nanny, by name as well as job description. Any virtues of winged heavenlies that one possesses, surely from her. *Hosanna.*

One's Grandma Harriet lived in too, until taken one day when I was eight. But she too hard as teak, hers the wicked vigour of the showie lifer. After all, her family's dosh had brought FT's schemes to life. I mean, why do you think he married a lump like Olive?

Yes, one was not unprovided for. One's model train set, a bigger network than British fucking India's. Lead *army men,* one's little soldiers, divisions enough to invade a toy Russia. 'The largest collection outside Buckingham Palace,' Olive would yap at her biddies-in-waiting.

For holidays, our weekender in the Yarra Valley. The writer CJ Dennis lived here rent-free but for when we lobbed for long weekends. Or our beach shack at Portsea.

For all this, FT and Olive were never fully accepted by the brainfallow bluebloods of Toorak. Olive, this warthog swaddled in sable and sapphires, laboured to be assimilated. But ours was a carny mob who'd plonked a Gracelands in their genteel midst. Worse, on the corner of Toorak and St George's Roads. Far above our gypsy station. FT built here 'Rylands.' Named after the family manse of Grandma Harriet in Somersetshire. At night, it looked like Bates Motel.

FT's bid to flee his Adelaide home, to run away with the circus, touring the mining hellcamps of Tassie as adolescent conjuror The Great Dexter, was brief. Soon fled home to Adelaide. Why, best left untold, one suspects. Then, a job as a cobbler's mate in Gawler, at the behest of his father, William, an alcoholic maltster at West End brewery between payday benders.

In Gawler, FT met plain Grace. Seven summers his senior. Uncourted by the bobbing cocks hereabouts. Ran a frock shop in the main street. *A going concern.* FT knew a good bunco when he saw one. Charmed her at the Gawler Theatrical Society with his magic tricks. Sweet-talked her into a double act for their Humorous Finale. Upped his age from 21 to 27 on their marriage certificate. Perhaps to mask his play. Gold digger dressed as toyboy. And what if he did?

'It's showbiz, Frankie,' Olive used to say. 'This is how the bloody dance goes.'

Back in Adelaide, FT had a bootmaker's shop in Mile End. For a time. Till the carnival called him, his magic act, ventriloquist's dummy, card tricks, and new glamourless assistant Grace. And a new gizmo. To the showie's bush runs they took a wooden hand-wound kinescope, to show the world's first flickering, soundless filmettes. Then more secure employ, as projectionist at the Gaiety Theatre in Zeehan, Tasmania.

'He stirred up a price war with the other cinema in town,' Olive told me. 'By the time FT was finished with them, bugger-all left of them but the head and hooves.'

Grace became with child. Yet agreed that he depart, alone, for Melbourne. There, to establish their own cinema and prosper, she and bub back in Gawler to join him in the big smoke anon.

Fresh off the train at Spencer Street, FT clocked an ad in *The Argus* for a picture show man at the waxworks in Bourke Street. There, the severed head of John The Baptist. Life sized renderings of PT Barnum's freaks such as the Pig Faced Boy. Axe murderers. Salome, naked but for beads. Psychotic bushrangers.

'The young hobyahs used to steal Ned Kelly's boots!' recalled Olive. 'But I fixed their cheese. My word I did. I nailed them to the floor!'

Here be ghosts too, was the word. In summer, Ned's wax head softened. Slid in increments down his shoulder. *Cripes, cobber. It's moving.* Manager Harriet Kreitmayer and daughter Olive did not discourage suggestible patrons. *The Waxworks is haunted.*

'The projectionist's job? Well, those jolly waxes no longer pulled heads, you see,' went Olive's recounting. She worked the ticket box. Untroubled by gentleman callers. Thick of neck and ankle. A safe pair of fists for snatching cash from the mugs. And romanced with ease. Harriet be moneyed, you see.

One's maternal grandfather Max Kreitmayer, toast of Marvellous Melbourne, had toured his first wax models, of diseased sex organs, round the gold rush boomtowns. This failed medical student from Munich, self-rebirthed as English gentleman, later prospered from a national chain of wax museums.

'Max also had a chain of families. One each in Sydney and Melbourne. Knew nothing of each other,' one's half-sister Lola told me. Made a packet from it, and his travelling shows. Boxing kangaroos. Midget wrestlers. Burlesque as saucy as could be got away with.

'It was said,' Olive once said, well gone in sherry,' that the old ram could pleasure a showgirl with a drink in each hand and not spill a drop.'

Max made foray into politics as Mayor of Collingwood. And was dudded by fly-by-nighters, mining sharpies. Rooked him of the lot. We never met. His appetites took him just after the turn of the century.

FT's courtship of plump Olive met a frost. You see, Grace now bore him a daughter, Viola, ever after called Lola. Mum and bub ironhorsed it across to Melbourne. But family life at FT's new house in Kew fast grew fraught. Grace and the little one soon rode the rattlers home, leaving naught but tears on a railway platform. FT shrugged and wired them money.

The Thring-Kreitmayer dukedom blossomed, the waxes punted to the ancestral manse at Prahran. The space at Bourke Street needed to create one screen, then a duplex, rebadged as the Star Cinema. Then, more screens. All over Melbourne. This enraged the fudds of JC Williamson's, the live theatre titans.

'Why, this jasper's stealing *our mugs.*'

They moved to buy him out. FT raised no fists – on condition they made him boss of their new cinema division. After all, he had contacts in Hollywood for the best new flicks. And they saw not his Trojan Horse.

FT silver-tongued JCWs into a cinema-building frenzy, to engulf all rivals. And bought out a chain of several small picture houses. Offered the owner, an aged dentist, a paltry sum.

'It's that or die in a price war for nothing, cobber,' one imagines him explaining. FT merged this new buy with JCWs cinemas. Called it Hoyts, the name of the little chain he'd just extorted.

'The fang snatcher, they say, expired atop a JCWs chorus gal, the deal sealer,' Melbourne impresario Garnet Carroll later apprised me. 'Or she atop him.'

To lay waste the remaining competition, FT now built the deluxe Regents chain, and more. Raised his stake in Hoyts to a controlling one with the tricks of a magician. *No one watches the hand that's not doing anything, Frankie.*

But tidings grievous now. Of Grace, taken by TB. FT shipped Lola across to Melbourne. Installed her in St Catherine's boarding school in Toorak. He and Olive could now wed, and did so, at Christ Church, South Yarra. No honeymoon. Why, they had an empire to build!

'Yes, we kept busy, by gum,' was Olive's recall. I'll say. Took them four years to conceive *me*, a scene too hideous to summon in the Times Square peep show of one's mind. And Olive took to infiltrating charities, for *entre* into Melbourne Society. Here be potential investors. Easily played ones.

FT acquired a business partner, Tom Holt. 'Travelling Tom,' they called him. His son Harold later one of our more useless Prime Ministers. A lucky imbecile all his life, that one. Well, with one exception.

An awkward ask for JCWs to induct a bush league roughnut into their old money otherworld, but they saw the nous of having FT inside their big top, not outside burning it down. Thus was he initiated into those dreadful Melbourne gentleman's clubs. The Athaeneum, the Savage, to golf at Riversdale and Sorrento, to mix it with the big knobs, so to speak.

At Rylands, Lola babysat me now and then. FT and Olive missed one's first words, *big clock,* for the flame mahogany grandfather piece at Rylands. They did notice when one repeated it ad nauseam as *big cock.*

FT made frequent voyages to LA, to Hollywood, for the latest films, and the gear to screen them. Spoke of Jack Warner and Zanuck as friends. It planted a seedling, nay fixation, that he might also make movies. Right here in Melbourne. Whatever it took.

'Under Prohibition, the Mob ran Hollywood, Frankie. Keen to buy any illicit liquor to be had.'

So went Lola's story that FT ran some bootlegging vis-à-vis his US safaris. The booze via midnight means in England and Ireland. The truth or not of it perished with him, but consider this. He a mere customer, queuing up with the rest of the world to beg Chaplin, Fatty Arbuckle, Laurel And Hardy silents. And yet FT did gain the *sancti sanctori* of the studio sultans, and their ears to his bids for co-productions between them. The Great Dexter indeed a magician. With perhaps bigger secrets than most.

Whatever it took. On that same day in August 1929 that Wall Street leapt off the unfinished Chrysler Building, JCWs flagship theatre, His Majesty's in Exhibition Street, burned down. Some of it anyway. Right after FT had bought fire insurance on the old gal. Make of that what you will. *I have.* The wily fucker talked them into using the payout to refit the Maj as a film production studio. They'd never have come at building one from the ground up, so...

However, the Great Depression meant that banks were gun-shy about lending for dreams. He had his film studio now, but making the buggers called for further moola. So FT, wait for it, sold off his fleet of

Hoyts cinemas to get the scratch.Yes. The lot. To the Tinseltowners; to wit, Fox.

Yes, pixie. He made them an offer he couldn't refuse.

CHAPTER TWO

Discharged yet again from the Epworth yesterday. Still not dead. The telly news not all bad, for once. Mandela headed for power in South Africa after almost three decades banged up. The Berlin Wall down. Oh, and the Oscars are on. One still recalls the 1959 awards. One was in *Ben Hur* as Pilate. It won twelve of the things. Every second fucker on the set bagged one. Except *me*. No great performance goes unpunished.

One no longer goes to the pictures. One does, however, know some of the stars. Like Anthony Hopkins, best actor this year for *Silence Of The Lambs*. Storied career, Tony, but really just a facsimile of Olivier. Larry's understudy back in our days together, you see. And his a too, too easy win up against, fuck me ragged, *Teenage Mutant Ninja Turtles*, *Terminator 2*, or *Don't Tell Mom The Babysitter's Dead*.

'This muck'll pull more heads than two free pies.' Yes, FT.

*

In the eye of that cyclone the Depression, one was chauffeured each day to primary school, Glamorgan Prep in Douglas Street by our driver, Ernest, in our Rolls Royce Phantom. Soon bored, one feigned illness to wag often. Began, with FT's OK if not Olive's, to tag along to their film shoots. A far, far better schooling.

'They don't like it, they can go to buggery.'

Their stars slaved at Efftee Films by day and in his stage shows at night. For just one wage. A hard road and such was Olive's charming appraisal of their lot. As a child I worshipped them, every one. Georgie

Wallace, the 'Boy From Bullamakanka', a Tivoli stager made movie star by FT in Australia's first talkies, a comedy god to me.

To make his pictures, FT also roped in for Efftee all the local indie filmmakers who'd gone broke after LA had applied a choke hold on him. You see, hundreds of silent features were made here once upon a dreamtime. FT and his Sydney rival Stuart Doyle used to run them all in their cinemas. Boffo box office. The Yanks heard of this via their 'distribution managers' in Melbourne and Sydney, in fact their corporate spies.

Screen US product only, see, FT was told, *or we cut off supply, wise guy.* So local movies all but vanished from Hoyts' screens. But for FT's films, he soft-soaped a pledge from Fox that they'd run them at the Hoyts hardtops now in their clammy fists. Or so he thought.

Efftee's first feature, the dire *Co-Respondent's Course,* was shot at Rylands and Portsea before His Maj was even refitted. Its director, well. FT thought he'd wheedled Fox into shipping out a top American as part of the deal he'd parlayed. This imbecile E.A. Dietrich-Derrick wore puffy jodphurs, a monocle, beret and jackboots. A tinpot Cecil B DeMille. Ran about fomenting havoc. One postulates that cocaine was involved. *Plus ca change,* pixie.

'He tried to make the gals go nude for the beach scenes,' Lola said of the Portsea shoot. Efftee leading lady Donalda Warne served E.A. a slap in the chops the equal of anything Cagney or Bogart could.

E.A. co-helmed three Efftee features, then vanished. The flicks, well, unwatchable. FT did not take this most Hollywood of hints. Yet, flashes of genius too.

'Look at this, boys,' he said to the crew one day. 'The date, scene, film's title here, in chalk. Camera rolls. Shout your take number. Clack this top bit down and Bob's your uncle. To line up sound and picture.'

Yes, pixie. FT invented the clapperboard. Then took it to LA *sans* patent. Whenever one clacked on one's own shoots years later, one had to stem the urge to weep.

'They numbskulled it with brandy from a dropper to get it to stay on its branch. May have glued it on, in fact,' was the word from Lola. FT loved MGM's roaring lion logo. So he did the same with a koala for Efftee films. Such are Aussie icons.

One had a pointless cameo in the second Efftee feature, *Diggers*. Offspring as Olive's vanity project, you see. For five year old me, a walk-on in pint-size French Foreign Legion uniform, with *Diggers* star Pat Hanna's daughter, also five. We toddled onto the French village set, saluted, and exited. Directed to hold hands, I spat in mine and grabbed hers before she could pull it away. Unhorsed the little bitch. Learned scene-stealing early, baby.

Efftee's third release, *The Haunted Barn*, was banned. All howling winds, ghosts of the murdered, escaped killers and casual slaughter by destitutes. Not a seed governments needed planted in the Depression's third year.

For the premiere of *Diggers* and *Co-Respondent's* in November 1931, FT borrowed Hoyts Plaza from Fox. Self in bespoke mini-tux, as ordered by Olive. The films ran for a week, unpromoted by Fox, to empty houses before they reefed them off. A cracked bell somewhere went *thunk*.

Ray Longford, who'd made a dazzling silent of the CJ Dennis bestseller *The Sentimental Bloke*, was now put to work by FT on a talkie remake; CJ himself for a screenplay. One was in this too, at Olive's whim. Directed to loll on a picnic rug in Fitzroy Gardens as The Bloke pursued Doreen across the path behind me. Before this even wrapped, Efftee began on *His Royal Highness*, another George Wallace turn.

Efftee's film editor was Lola. Now stepping out with Harold Holt, one of those adults to whom children, self included, take instant dislike. An item, this pair, in June 1932 at the premiere of *Bloke*. Fox consigned it to oblivion a week on. Then Donalda Warne, Efftee's biggest drawcard, quit.

'To try her luck on the London stage,' FT told Olive. He seemed devastated.

'Plenty more tarts like her out there,' sniffed Olive. She'd go grey in the face when the talk turned to other women in FT's life. All that time he spent abroad, you see.

So many ports, far from home...

Great commotion: FT in the front hall of Rylands with his dark timber and navy leather steamer trunk for the *SS Narkunda*. This tub bound for, er, London.

'To sell our catalogue to the Brits,' he told Olive.

'But Tom Holt could do that, FT,' she said. 'You have unfinished films here ...' Her voice faded as Nanny ushered me away. But for once the fat grey mare was right. Had Donalda entertained FT in ways Olive never could? Or did he have *other needs,* like me? One has pondered thus. Often.

We didn't see him for a year. Off in Great Britain and the Continent, he claimed in his letters that he was signing new stars. They never materialised. One never forgave him. Left unprotected from Olive's attentions, she circling me like a buzzard over battlefield dead. Made me attend school every day. Had Ernest deliver hot lunches there, for fuck's sake. Paraded me as trophy child at her Red Cross fundraisers. *Most* embarrassing.

In time, FT sailed home. Bought the Garrick Theatre in South Melbourne. Tissied up the Princess in Spring Street. One recalls the tradesmen carving *FT* at the top of the proscenium arch at the dear old Prinny.

'We'll put your initials on it, Frankie,' he said, 'so if it's lost they can return it to you.' And winked. Well, the letters abide. But an epoch since it's been mine to lose.

FT's plan now, to stage big musicals, rake in the cash, then turn these into feature films. But he'd changed. The reality of his spit 'n' shake with Fox must have hit home. He'd nick off from Efftee at midday, to the Occidental Hotel on Collins. For hours. Or all afternoon. Oft assisted by Ernest to bed.

'Your father is very tired, Frankie,' said Olive to my stares. There was, it seemed, nothing on paper compelling Fox to screen Efftee films on the screens now theirs. Oh, and if they'd been handjobbed by FT with sly grog, now no more need of *that* either. Repeal of Prohibition, you see. Yet he pressed on. As madmen do.

Efftee's first stage musical, *Collit's Inn,* opened just before Xmas in 1933. As an eight year old in the royal box with the twin mastodons one's parents resembled, unendurable. Every bastard there remarked on one's lineage.

'My word, FT. Little Frankie here looks just like you.'

Fuckers. If so, one resembled a great ape with a gob full of billiard balls. Still, *Collit's* sucked in the dosh for months. It was FT's casting: Georgie Wallace, with our then biggest, and I do mean biggest, singing star, Gladys Moncrieff.

Cashed up again, FT decided that his studio in the charred guts of His Maj wasn't up to musicals. So he bought the Wattle Path Palais de Dance on the Esplanade at St Kilda. He may or may not have been sober at the time. Spent large on pre-production for the film of *Collit's,* which was never made, and other new feature shoots, *Clara Gibbings* and *Streets Of London*. Neither pallid outing fared well.

At one point, to shoot establishing scenes for a film to be called *Sheepmates,* FT took off for the Flinders Ranges in his blue Packard. A full Efftee crew followed him in trucks and trailers. This with no screenplay yet. Nothing beyond that awful title. Out in the mulga for months, they wound up in Broken Hill. Here, FT vanished into the desert, with him a young pub cook. Most curious. The Efftee party found them dehydrated, near death, the Packard wedged into a fence post. It doesn't do to dwell.

Back at St Kilda, FT bolted single malts and heard not the chimes at midday. Deranged brainwaves proliferated. No-one was spared. To promote an Efftee travel doco on Far North Queensland, one was stood in the Regent's foyer wrapped in an eight-foot carpet python from

Melbourne Zoo. And the fucking thing didn't even match one's leopard skin loincloth.

Now Olive, the Giant Slug of Toorak, sent one to a place from which one has never recovered. Nor it from me. Melbourne Grammar produces cretins to rule over all, armed with naught but the old school tie. They'd do well to hang themselves with it. The navy blue uniform one loathed, and Olive had shirts made with Little Lord Muck collars. The old flabtower blind to one's humiliation. A son at Grammar de rigeur for a pleb on the make in Toorak, and all its stale hells.

One rolled up in the Roller to the grim sandstone pile on Domain Road, South Yarra. Boys stared. As well they might. We were herded into Grimwade House. One 'Dingo' Clark one's first teacher. Quite senile. One was too flash for him, and of low parentage. *Show people*, yet.

'What's your name, boy? Disraeli?'

He was anti-Semitic, a fad of the time. One was struck dumb.

'Boy! Where are your people from? Great Britain?'

'M-m-my grandfather was German, s-sir.'

'A Nazi then! Where in Germany, boy?'

'M-m-munich, sir. B-but...'

'*Hoh!* Catholic! Don't argue with me, lad. Hand, out!'

The cane sliced. The stutter didn't leave me.

Each day started with a spelling test. Often oral. One's s-s-stammer provoked more canings. The place was sports-mad, too. Best avoided. One found ways.

'Epsom Salts.' A pale boy called Ken. 'In warm water. Bolt it. Spew. In front of witnesses.'

Another little chap named Nigel loved to flash his little chap. One marvelled at his watery red eyes when one day he was sent to Matron, then home. Asked him how he did it.

'Wanna touch this?'

One had to, not without enjoyment, one concedes, to know. Toothpaste smeared just under the eyes. Thenceforth, one was spared when one's Bromby House risked all to pound other teams to mince, for the House football prize, the, er, Cock Cup.

But as you know, pixie, one didn't always fake it. Now and then I used to black out for real. Not diagnosed until years later. Still, once one became known for these, one's fake faints mostpart convinced.

'Now, boys,' said the master, 'you are on a tram, hanging onto a strap.'

Strange for an actor, one never made the cut for the school play, despite compulsory auditions every year. The class did a strange dance, one hand in the air. The master, well one could hardly call these mould-bound plodders teachers, saw me imitating this as the boys began to laugh.

'Silence! No, Thring, that's no good at all. What are you doing, boy?'

'I don't know.' And I didn't. 'I've never been on a tram.'

'Ernest, stop here. I won't run off this time. Just here.'

A master stood deluge-bashed in grey raincoat at the tram stop.

'Sir! Jump in!'

One continued the practice on a regular basis. He and others. Grammar's prefects, goon squads with canes, dared not come near me now. Yet one still jigged school when one could. *One had somewhere more important to be.*

At the theatres and studios, the actors and crew smoked, drank, read the *Truth* and *Sporting Globe*. Bet on the geegees with an SP bookie among their number. Played cards. Taught me how to cheat. They'd switch between voices of different characters as if possessed by succubi. One of them noticed one's stammer. Talked Olive into elocution lessons for me. Sixpence a session. The teacher's name, one never tired of enunciating. Miss *Badcock*.

'Half these rooms aren't being used, dear heart,' FT said to Olive as we roamed through the belfries and attics of the Princess. In 1935, Efftee Films dead in the water, FT was thrown a lifeline; a new radio license on offer. Fistfuls of gold no doubt exchanged under tables, and here we be. The Prinny's roofcaves would house 3XY, Melbourne's new stop on the dial, Tom Holt its general manager. Back then, a radio station as lucrative as a TV network. Here, one learned what makes showbiz tick.

And explode.

CHAPTER THREE

One's home here in Fitzroy, just the second in one's life, has its charms. And perils. A month or so back, en route to Bottlemart, one happened upon two lads. A smidge tipsy, one invited them home for a drink. *Well.* They stripped me naked. Bound me with an extension cord to a chair. One was gagged with one's black silk cravat. The louts hoisted one's cash and scrammed. Despite the discomfort of one's restraints, I nodded off, having necked two Nembutal with one's brandy, you see.

One's housekeeper Edith was horrified when she let herself in next morning and got the gag off. What could one say?

'I've just had the most marvellous weekend.'

In the stretched and hollow hours before dawn, one stares through insomnia's hard shimmer at the ABC's *rage*. Dross mostpart, but gorgeous George Michael, Farnham or Bette Midler are worth the wait. Yet the sonic Serepax of these times no less hideous than ever it was. This oaf Billy Ray Cyrus with his *Achy Breaky Heart*. And Mariah Carey should have been drowned at birth.

*

One was nine on the cusp of ten. FT announced that he was off to LA yet again. But this time, *con famiglia. I was bound for America!* I pointed at Olive.

'Does she have to come?'

Our ocean liner choofed across the Tasman. In Auckland, a sightseeing bus around the harbour. To gawp at seawater, after a week of naught else. In Fiji, we threw coins into the harbour for the 'natives' to retrieve by diving. A vile custom, one hopes since forbidden.

Just a frog in my throat, he said. But by Samoa FT could swallow only ice cream, the frog now more like a red-eyed hound. We crossed the Equator, making for Honolulu. A crewman, frocked up as King Neptune, gave us certificates to prove it. Then to San Francisco, whose 1930s skyline soared.

'It's like being in a movie,' gasped young Frankie. A Checker cab to Grand Central. The art deco train to LA. The Biltmore Hotel in Pershing Square.

'Shouldn't we see a doctor, FT?'

He waved her away. Wheezed like a car that won't start.

The sheer scale of the Warners lot at Burbank astounded. FT had a meeting here with Jack of that name. Warner burst out of his office with a short man, but the fellow all moxie for that.

'Forgeddaboudit, Jack, baby,' an unmistakable voice. *'Never happen, see...'*

'Shaddap!' said Warner. 'You'll hit the girls and *like* it.'

Wait on. The little guy is *Jimmy Cagney!* Jack turned to his secretary.

'That bum comes back, suspend him without pay.'

'Yes, Mr Warner.'

One adored Cagney. Even more after that. FT and Jack jawed while Olive and self waited in reception. *Went well*, said FT afterwards. Between coughs.

Olive's eyes were red. FT's, turned to stone. Back from the doctor, they didn't say why. No need. Yet the old man had the sack to box on, even dying.

Fox was next, those knaves who'd gypped him out of Hoyts. FT met with Daryl F. Zanuck. One came to despise this man. But here, a nine-year old cineaste fixated on a single whim.

'Can I meet Boris Karloff?'

'Sure, kid!' Zanuck was all falsetto exclamations. 'He's shooting here now! Can do!'

Boris? Well, the fucker was a bore. Talked only about cricket. Then FT started in.

Would Mr Karloff like to come to Australia? Mr Karloff offered vague assent. Then bounced us, ever so polite. As only an Englishman can. We barely noticed it was the bum's rush.

'Isn't this thrilling?' said Olive.

'Not really,' I said. Morbid at FT's prognosis, you see. To contract throat cancer in those times was, well…We'd been invited to the premiere of Shirley Temple's new film. Fox sent a limo. The flick, *Captain January*, at Grauman's Egyptian Theatre on the Boulevard. Olive made one wear one's Grammar uniform. With *shorts*, for fuck's sake. After the film, they lined us up to meet Shirley and mother Gertrude.

'Oh, my. From Australia. You speak English so well.' Shirley eyed me. 'And what's your name, young man?'

'This is our son, Frankie. He's a movie star too!' blurted Olive. 'What advice can you give him, Miss Temple?' Shirley's eyes were twin dead souls.

'Pay attention. Time is money. Do as you're told. Get it right first time.'

Monster mother Gertrude whisked her away.

One had one's tenth birthday at Gay's Lion Park in El Monte. Lions, leopards, panthers in an open air arena. A lion tamer did his thing. The al fresco dining area was ringed by caged, fetid felines, used in Tarzan movies and such. The staff brought out a cake. Sang *Happy Birthday*. Then FT coughed, a sound like a mad dog on a chain at midnight. *Whooosh*, it blew out all ten candles.

'He's not going to get better, is he?'

'You mustn't say that.' Olive turned her face away.

'Stop lying to me then!'

I bolted out onto the deck, taking the gangway steps two at a time, *clang clang clang, slip!* Hit the deck hard. The pain!

'Is your father unwell? What's the matter with him?'

Olive made me front the press alone at Station Pier in Melbourne. Broken arm in ship's doctor's sling and plaster. FT was stretchered off the *SS Mariposa* into an ambulance in which he and Olive roared off. I read out a statement from Olive and FT. Of deals done in LA and an Aussie filmbiz Renaissance. Naught of how he had just weeks to live. One's picture made the afternoon papers. One shook hands with an *Argus* reporter with one's one good mitt. Not unlike a dog.

To St Andrews hospice, East Melbourne. Morphine bore FT to quiet waters. Prayers from all lips but mine, already unbeliever, at bedside vigil. They rose to deaf skies and dead angels.

A BRILLIANT LEADER PASSES, howled the front page of *Everyone's*. The funeral, at Sleight's on St Kilda Road. At Burwood cemetery, icewinds off Port Phillip Bay whipped and scorned. A snickering incubus somewhere bid it rain.

Back at Rylands, those jolly Efftee faces, rearranged now by minds in mourning. Chalky, sallow. Scared. After all, many now out of a job. No follow-up came there from the shifty gnomes of Fox or MGM. Not ever.

And here, of all places, Lola let it be known that she and Tom Holt were engaged. He'd cuckolded Harold, his own son. Amusing in its own way, but FT's legacy now prey to this oily chancer. No divinity shaped my end. Travelling Tom had beaten God to the punch.

One's broken wing healed in time. Back at school, things not as bad as one had dreaded. A new Head, D.S. Colman, had axed boxing and cadets. Prefects' canes had been confiscated. And one didn't have to wear the school tie, but any one liked, so long as it was the colour of one's school House. One added to this a long scarf and cape, filched from the Prinny's wardrobe bays. Other boys of the arabesque persuasion copied me. But fathers were aghast at such raiment of the fop and Colman's other leniencies. *The man's a pansy, and no mistake!* He was run off by a jackal pack of old scholars.

'By the left, quick march! Left wheel! Right wheel!'

The next Head, Joseph Richard Sutcliffe. *Major*, he insisted. This from a pre-war commission, resigned at first wisp of Wehrmacht gunsmoke. So compulsory drill now, and cadets, the quadrangle and sandstone tower clock sole witnesses to our misery. For we were not soldiers. We were prisoners of war.

Then, deliverance. Olive had our family GP declare one unfit. Diagnosed hammer toes. One suffered no such condition, but not about to quibble. Olive, of course, had an ulterior motive. One was now dragooned for her charity turns, as daily handbag, a bonsai FT for this beminked and bejwelled vat of fat.

A causa di cio. Each afternoon, our Roller, at Grammar's front gates, Olive on board. On the back seat, one's formals laid out. Changed *en route* to event *du jour*. Just fourteen, yet looked of age. Height and bulk, you see, so no fucker said a word when one hoisted drinks from passing waiters' trays. These bunfights rather less insufferable if one was blootered. As you'd recall, pixie. *Non e cosi?*

One day at Rylands, our somnambulant Prime Minister Menzies on the wireless. As Britain was now at war with Germany, it was his *melancholy duty* to inform us that so were we. Olive poured sherry. To her, cause to celebrate. Stupid lump.

3XY burgeoned. One was required to join Olive the Bride Of Frankenthring for live broadcasts from the Prinny. One recalls that the Original Ballet Russe toured here in 1939. War broke out, so they couldn't go home. Hitler's U-Boats, you see. So she of course had them do a charity turn. One lured a young nymph from their number to one's hidey hole under the stage.
    'Speak English?'
    '*Nyet. Nikto.*'
    'I teach. Cock.' Demonstrated.
    '*Cork*', he smiled.
    'Hand.'
    '*Hunt.*'

Back at the apres-show party one pointed out Olive to him.

'Cunt.'

'*Kont.*'

Fast learner, that one. Yes. At war now. As were Olive and I. To end only when one of us perished.

One danced well the tango, foxtrot, the gypsy tap, as taught by the thesps of Efftee. As Olive's dancing bear, one whirled the hagdragons of Toorak round the parquet floor with expertise. For amusement, plucked the pods from some itchy powder trees in the Botanic Gardens. Rub them on your white gloves, then away you go. One's left hand on their frecklespeckled backs. They'd scratch all night after that.

Moonlings knew that a lad who could cut a rug like I was surely of the colours.

At Ormond Hall on St Kilda Road one night, a fellow shoved a note into my hand. Upstairs roped off, unused tonight. It was swift, we back steering cloven-hoofed harridans around to the detestable *Blue Danube* before anyone clocked our absence.

Look, about Olive's charity turns. They were not to aid the luckless, nor appease her long-fallow Roman Catholic conscience. She did it for herself. For 3XY, for the Prinny. For the Second Thring Empire, to plug our shows and broadcasts. So the sight of Olive scratching herself scarlet after our waltz, well, the least one could do.

One was Olive's toyboy for a knoll of offal called *A Cavalcade Of Empire Pageant,* with Hector Crawford's orchestra, in aid of Navy House. The old backfatter insisted on arriving early, that she might flap about, honking orders no-one needed.

'One made for the empty orchestra pit,' as I told it to a youthful consort some years on. 'Juicy Fruit chewing gum did a fine job of sticking together the pages of random music scores. Well, it was that or go mad. The *endlessness* of it.'

One was granted nights off only for her sherry circles. Vile covens of Toorak trophy widows at New Admiralty House in Collins Place. Ye gods. No wonder their husbands went first.

CHAPTER FOUR

One is nonplussed that Australians still puddle themselves at prospect of a Royal visit. Her Maj was out here a few weeks ago. Prime Minister Keating placed a hand on Herself's back, this to help steer the royal personage towards a fistful of fudds from our bunyip aristocracy. For this, he is today lashed by the Pommy rags as the *Lizard Of Oz*. It appears he rather likes it. As do I. Bert Newton asked me on one of his short-lived midday TV shows a few years back one's view of the Hawke government, which had recently consigned the Fraser regime to the fires down below.

'Oh. Very little.'

'What about the previous government then, Frank?'

'*Less.*'

*

The Sea Shall Not Have Them was a war film starring Redgrave and Bogarde. One recalls a group of us- Larry Olivier, Vivien Leigh, and self in Leicester Square with Noel Coward when he spied the cinema marquee for this picture.

'Well, I don't see why not,' he said. 'Everyone else has.'

Of course, that was some fifteen years on, but one's first contact with Coward was November 1940, in Australia. His first visit, to premiere his new play *Design For Living* and to perform at about fifty-nine thousand of Olive's Red Cross fundraisers for the British war effort. His first such at the Myer Mural Hall. A mob milled in Lonsdale Street hoping to glimpse him. Inside the closed store, Olive palmed things off shelves, a lifelong shoplifter.

The stage was draped in huge Union Jacks. On came The Master, white jacket and tie, green carnation, to cloudbursts of applause. Gestured to the pianist with his silver cigarette holder. Into *Mad Dogs And Englishmen,* the ad libs too blue for broadcast. Then, *Don't Put Your Daughter On The Stage, Mrs Worthington.* One was transfixed. *Here was who I wanted to be!*

At the Lord Mayor's reception afterwards, one was introduced. Speechless with awe, one drank. At fourteen, still a novice at pacing oneself. By dusk, blotto and bilious. Made it to the brasco just in time.

'Are you all right, young man?'

Coward stood hovering behind me. I rose from my knees. Most embarrassing. He proffered a silk handkerchief. *He had followed me in here.*

'Here, cockie. Keep it. I've been watching you. And you *me.* Haven't you?'

'Y-you're a w-w-wonderful p-p-erformer, sir,' I gushed.

'Yes, yes, of course. But *you're* more than just a pretty *face,* one hopes.'

'H-how do you m-mean, sir?'

'Come, come, boy. I knew the moment I laid my twinklers on you. Now...'

'I c-can't. I'm n-not old enou...' He sighed, smiled, creasing his face.

'Look, is your bum free tonight or not? I've been more than patient.'

Struck mute, I made off, mortified, just as a young man entered.

'Well, what have we here?' I heard as I fled.

At his supper show at Government House that evening, one couldn't bear to face him, but he smiled when our eyes met. *I perceive your predicament perfectly profoundly,* he seemed to say. As only he could have.

Olive had Coward do his thing for five thousand troops at Puckapunyal AIF base, plus paying civilians, proceeds to Red Cross. One had pals at Grammar one wanted to impress. Asked if one could invite them along.

'Certainly not. What do they think this is? A charity?'

Ah, the pals. Our tumbles were furtive, our elfin glade the Fern Gully in the Botanic Gardens. Made it quick. Masters and prefects prowled here. Cruising, one suspects.

You know, pixie, it turned out after the war that Noel's tour hadn't in fact been for Red Cross at all, but to entice Aussies into khaki, to battle for Britain. Olivier told me it was a tryout for a planned trip by Noel to the US, to beguile the Yanks into the war. This was all before Pearl Harbour, of course. But Churchill cancelled Coward's Yank swing. Larry and self were on tour at the time, on the Orient Express from Paris to Venice. Summer of '57.

'*Verum veritas,* baby,' said Larry. 'Winston saw that to petition flint and steel Yank generals with a mimsy might be, well, you know, ...'

I did.

There were bridge parties in the Brown Room of Myers to raise funds for the AIF Women's Association. Hosted by Olive. Quite insufferable. Then one day a lad who worked there spoke to me in the gents' rest room.

'Lipstick counter, Frankie. Saturday. Closing time.'

'Mother, I'm going to a matinee. Spencer Tracy. *Dr Jekyll And Mr Hyde.*'

I caught the Number 8 tram on my own. It was liberating.

Let's call him Troy. He parked me in a tearoom. One heard the midday bells, the hubbub of the store shooing out its Saturday customers. Nervous, one gulped Famous Grouse, courtesy of Olive's liquor cabinet, from FT's old Jensen silver hip flask. In came the boys, from departments various, and the window dressers. We were alone in the store now.

'Relax, Frankie, it's all locked from the inside. Give us a slug on that.'

'Oh, Frankie! You look like Barbara Stanwyck!'

One had on a white jacket, wide belt. And one was slim in ancient times. The skirt split down the front, and one a slink in dark tan gloves and heels. Troy, in a sleeveless blue number, struck poses like Bette Davis. Johnny wove among us in silk lingerie. We painted our faces. Booze went round. We paired off. The Myer Emporium was never the same for me again.

Another day, all of Rylands out for the day, the chums came over with a few borrowed outfits and a Myers fashion snapper of the nightling hue. One suited up first as Oscar Wilde. Then Noel Coward. Cigarette holder, white tie. Then silk, heels, lippy. I still have the photos, pixie. Any offers?

In late 1941, the RAN cruiser *HMAS Sydney* had its fatal run-in with the German warship *Kormoran*. A week later, Pearl Harbour. In Melbourne, power restrictions. *Brownouts* they called them. At moonrise, street lights off, and car headlights. This to conceal Melbourne from the air, and imagined imminent bombing by the Japs. Windows blacked out by blinds, black paper or paint. No end of motor accidents, but on cheerier note, illicit sex soared in unlit parks. Talk about stabbing in the dark. At Grammar, trenches dug and sandbagged, should Tojo rain fire from the sky. Air raid drills. Hideous hand-wound sirens, all that.

American sailors and GIs jammed Melbourne's streets. We might be safe from the Japs but the Yanks, quite another fistful of eels. Three women were murdered. A GI, Eddie Leonski, proved to be the *Brownout Strangler*. He was hanged at Pentridge.

'But your Leaving Certificate, Frankie,' said Olive. One had scraped through one's Intermediate exams, well, a representative sample of them.

'*Mama*,' I said, quite on purpose, given her hatred of any who spoke 'foreign' as she called it, 'I'm going to be an actor, so I won't need to continue...'

'*Francis,*' her voice now of red-eyed hellion within, 'you will finish high school. Or I shall withdraw your allowance.' And then the big finish. 'And I will cut you off with a *shilling*.'

She meant the will. Pigbag. Fucking Melbourne Grammar. Snob value. All that mattered to her. She had me by the cruets.

One has all one's life been a keen reader of newspapers. FT and Olive had them all delivered, you see, she to see her fucking picture in the social pages. And there in the *Argus* this day, an ad for a place called Taylor's College. Leaving classes, as adult education. *Aha.*

'It will be something that will make the papers, *Mama.*'

The Catherine The Great of Toorak was told that if forced back to Grammar, one would do whatever it took to get expelled. *What would the neighbours think?*

The Japs bombed Darwin one's first week at Taylor's, a greygreen hole in the wall in Flinders Lane, opposite the Australia Hotel. *Handy.* Pretty boys in the back bar, and the front bar, the snake pit we called it, *with good reason,* sailors and ex-prisoners up for a bit of the other. One proposed a lunch break drink to a bewitching classmate, let's call him Butch.

'How old are you, mate?'

'Twenty-three. Two large Remy Martin, straight, if you please.'

'Twenty-three? Prepared to sign a statement to that effect?'

One produced one's own Monteverde fountain pen, one's *other Excalibur.* No photo ID back then, you see. And one was tall, already thinning on top, and turned out in a well-cut suit. One's new pal turned out to be a two-pot screamer. *Luck's a fortune.* To the Bot Gardens, then, to answer the scream of the wild.

One typical afternoon, one had to go with Olive to 3XY as her foyer meet and greet monkey for a live broadcast at the Prinny. While she waddled about sticking gladioli in everything but her arse, one snuck up to the studios, of late declared off limits. Olive concerned about one mixing it with the tumblers and jesters, you see. Didn't like where one's thinking was headed in terms of career choice.

Upstairs, actors around a microphone. Yes, radio, yet the players were glammed up in tuxes or lounge suits and silk ties. The gals elegant in suits, feathers, brooches at the throat, hat brims so wide they collided at the mike. A mosaic of cigarette butts underfoot, some scarlet with lippy.

One was entranced. Went back every chance one got. Producer Alwyn Kurts cursed salty when things went tits up. The shows went live to air, or were pre-recorded on huge acetate discs, twice the circumference of LP records.

'Your mother will have my guts for garters if she finds you up here, Frankie,' said Alwyn. 'So if you hear her coming, best clear off to the brasco. Or I'll spifflicate you. Got that?'

One watched five actors do five eps of a series in one day. Twenty parts: Scots, Chinese, Indians, children. Drunks. At the end of each page, they dropped it, let it glide to the floor. Lit fresh gaspers they'd stuck behind their ears with bumpers of old. Blue moonstone fog hung, eye-watering. Here was my tribe.

'Your name's Gil. Born 12 December, '23. Got that, cobber?'

They were off to Scott's for a jolt one morning. One of them shoved his driver's license at me. One was shy, so drank fast. Told them I'd soon be joining their number. Several dozen times.

'Frankie!'

Oh, fuck. Olive. After Scott's, one had hoved on to the Australia. Now back at Rylands, it was *stop the room, I want to get off.*

'I have news, young man.' I swallowed brandy vomit. 'I know what you've been up to. There's nothing else for it. Frankie, you're going to be working at XY.'

'*Pftsv?*'

'Yes..'

'*Oh. Marvloushh.*'

'As a record boy.' *Eh?*

'*Recor' boy? But I wan' be an acto...*'

'You need to know how it all works, my darling, before we can promote you to a management position...'

I grabbed a jade Ming Dynasty vase. Threw up into it.

Olive of Gormenghast had received letters from Taylor's, you see, about one's ongoing non-attendance. So no more school. Now, a fetchworth's toil. *No special treatment,* her riding instructions to the 3XY brass. They dared not differ.

'Thring's my name. Fred Mogg is expecting me.'

Mogg being the General Manager, and knew me well. XY's front desk was at the side entrance of the Prinny. Here, a jane about my age.

'You think so, Frankie?' Damned impertinence! Yet I liked the kid's style.

'It's *Mr Thring*. I own the station.'

'It's Miss Cunliffe. But we're both pretty low on the rungs. Call me Joan.'

She smiled. '*Frankie.*'

'Kevin, get Frankie started, eh?' said Joan to this boy in the record library.

Fuck this. I *owned* this flea circus.

'You know who you're *talking* to here?'

'Yeah,' he said, meeting my gaze. 'The other record boy.'

One's *job*, if you could call it such, was to fetch discs for the station's announcers. Then return them to the library. But as with any peon in the Empire Of Thring, a second role in addition.

'Sound effects for the plays,' said Kevin. 'Footsteps; walk on the spot in that box of gravel. Doorbell and phone, this bicycle bell.' *Gring gring.* 'Revolver shot, this cap gun.' *Pap.* One had been enslaved.

'What if Mogg sees him there?' barked Kurtsy. 'You imbeciles think of that?'

Recording of a play was imminent one afternoon, and one of the actors still at Scott's, too munted to move. Kurtsy slung Kevin his car keys. 'Go and get him and stick him in the boot where no-one can see him.'

'Mr Kurts,' came a voice. Mine. 'I c-can play the p-part.'

He regarded me, sleepy-eyed. Apprehensive.

'Yeah, righto.' Pointed at my nose. 'But you fluff it and I'll fluff you, son. *Compre?*' Kurtsy got home that night to thumping from the boot of his car. And I to Rylands, with news for Olive. Of one's new job.

'It's called *Strange Library*,' said Kurtsy around the Woodbine bobbing on his lips. 'Tales from the world's library of the mysterious. Don't let me down, son. Go on, get.'

Five in our cast. We played phantoms, killers, grave robbers and their victims. Eps bore titles like *Lady Without A Soul* and *The Morgue*. One called *Listener In* magazine and we posed for their snapper, to go with a press release one wrote for the show's debut, just as one had seen FT do. Pulled a lot of readers and ears.

And the strangest thing. One fell into swoon for Joan the switch girl. Or *switch bitch* as I greeted her each morning. One had never felt this way about a doll. At weekends, we went to the pictures. *Kings Row, Casablanca, The Man Who Came To Dinner.* Or hired a rowboat if the weather was clement. Went out on the Yarra. And I'd make her take afternoons off mid-week.

'I own the station. No-one's going to sack my girlfriend.'

One used that word just to make her smile with her eyes. Sensational.

'Oh, Frankie. I'm not your girlfriend.'

'Of course you are. Now come on.'

I liked her too much to leave her be. As for The Other, well, the boygals of Myers and the Snake Pit would have to do. For now.

'Good evening, friends! Badness me, I nearly called you *fiends*. Of course you're not. Not *yet* anyway.'

One wrote some plays for XY. For *Devil's Holiday*, one's Satan a suave *bon vivant*, not a demented psycho. That's more of a God thing.

One was also assigned a Saturday timeslot. Midday to two PM. Music program. Classics. After that, Joan and I would meet in the city. A little drink on the air to embalm one's stage fright. On occasion poor Nanny had to take a tram to Joan outside the Ath or the Metro Collins to inform her that one was indisposed for the evening. Quite dreadful. One would learn the hard way the price of such insouciance.

'Mister Frank.'

Nanny, employed mostpart at Rylands as a kind of valet now, was calling from the tradesmen's entrance. 'A parcel!' One had to sign for it.

'Shit and bloody corruption.' One slit the package open to behold three live chickens. Except dead. The unknown sender thought one a coward for not taking on Tojo in New Guinea. *Getting the bird*, it was called. Not uncommon. One told the *Argus* and *Age* about it. Good ink for *Strange Library*, you see. And kept an eye out for deranged poultry farmers.

3XY's inhouse pianist, Dot Mendoza, was to helm a new kiddies' program, the *3XY Pals Session*. Assigned as offsiders Zell Manners, a Tivoli showgal, as Aunt Connie, and Yours Truly as, wait for it, Uncle Frank.

To kick off each show, we told a story, I the author of these tales. Laced 'em with double entendre, *the little bear worked the pump with both hands so she could fill her bucket*, to give the clinically depressed mums at home a giggle. On top of that, we ran a quiz, with real live little horrors in the studio. Padded out the remainder of our thirty-minute timeslot with songs and strange facts. One invented some ripsnorters.

Went live to air. Weekdays, five to five thirty. Prizes were donated by program sponsors in return for constant product plugs, this booty awarded for best riddles sent in by boys and girls. Gags with smutty subtext won every time, parental coaching rampant. Lubricated with Napoleon VSOP, one spoke on air of roosters as *cocks*, birds as *tits*. One day, on the subject of cats;

'Now, children, have you got a pussy?'

Dot made a face; *don't.*

'Look under your pussy if you have one, and see what you can find.'

Uncle Frank was never heard of again. Kurtsy moved me to a Friday night turn, *Youth Parade,* live to air onstage at the Prinny. Much tedium. Renditions of *Land Of Hope And Glory,* 10 year old girl saxophonists, all that cobblers, but some great satires on popular fables. For instance, one was a camp Sheriff of Nottingham in *Robin Snood And His Merrie Men;* a 'snood' being a woollen hat women wear, like a turban. The allusion, that both Robin and the Sheriff had a thing for dressups in

Maid Marian's finery. Such fun. One had found one's *metier*. Nothing could stop me now.

'Not to worry, my girl,' I said to Joan. 'One's fake symptoms, honed at school, will serve me well.'

OHMS on the envelope said it all. Exemptions not on. Well, it was wartime, after all. But you see, pixie, the AIF required medical grounds to punt mincers out of the Army, one had learned. Flibbertigibbet fakery *sans* observable illness wouldn't wash.

'I'm passing you fit.'

Fuck. They'd seen the sickly ponce act before. Five thousand times, by the look on this whitecoat's dial. I cursed Olive's hardy Bavarian genes. But one had not yet begun to fight. Meanwhile, Olive the Mountain of Mauve's pal Air Vice Marshal George Jones wangled one a berth in the RAAF. A safer bet than the AIF or RAN at this, the arse end of the war.

One's dress blues were an appalling cut. Had them altered at once, at American Tailors on Bourke Street. At a photo studio in Spencer Street, I gazed skyward, RAAF forage cap at forty-five degrees, mouth of a suckerfish. So *fey*. Inscribed one of the prints, for Joan, *To Flowergirl from Pansyboy*, our private nicknames. These days, gals like her suffer the crude soubriquet of *fag hags*. But in our day, they were styled *queen bees*, hence one's appellation for this loveliest of *amigas*. And her nickname for me, well, if you haven't jerried by now,....

'*Oi!* This cunt's got smokes!'

A hobyah loomed. One let the packet go, encircled as one was by killer apes.

'What's in the bag, cunt?'

One of them grabbed my duffel. Dug an arm in and came up smiling with a carton of de Reske.

'Hidin' 'em. Do that again, see what happens to ya, cun...'

'*What are you men doing?*'

An NCO. With two MPs, the feared provos.

'*No talking! Get in fucking line!*'

It was March of 1945. Ordered to muster at the MCG. Inside, Yanks filled the stands, including the Members'. How *dare* they. We non-Yanks, in tents out on the field. Ours indeed now a country under occupation.

At Spencer Street Station, young conscripts smooched sweethearts *sayonara.*

'We wish you fuck as we wave you goodbye,' said Joanie in gin-fumed whisper, and tongue-kissed me. The taste of Vickers agreeable, and public demonstration, in the interests of self-preservation, that one was a red-hot judy's man.

On the train, a poker game started. Mine. Butched up one's voice and manner. Won cigarettes, cash. Lost a few hands on purpose, of course, lest they twig to one's cheats. One's nickname evolved from *Cunt* to *Blue.* One's red hair, you see.

At Shepparton station, we were raused into trucks, then driven like livestock over dirt roads to the RAAF base. There, divvied up into squads of eight. Fatigues tossed at us. Boots also issued thus. Our octet assigned Hut AC2. All within its corrugated tin walls, nancies. Was it that obvious?

'Thing! Front and centre!'

Sunrise. The NCO, jabbing his finger at the spot where one must stand.

'Don't walk, fucknuts! *Move!*' Skullthrob from last night's brandy blinding. 'This man is his squad's *marker!* Every morning, he will fall in at this spot! The rest of you arseholes then fall in on his left, in order of height! Now –*squaaaaaad- fall in!*'

Down I went. One heard rather than felt one's head thwack the wet asphalt.

'This means war,' I muttered to myself. In sick bay, the MO dismissed one's history of fainting as a fabrication.

Next morning, as the NCO exploded into our hut, reveille blowing out in the murk, one was being sick, having bolted a tin mug of hot water from the showers, well salted. Toothpaste just below the eyes had stung them bloodshot.

'*Geddafugginmop!*' he bawled at dithering hutmates as I doubled over, dry retching.

'Thing! Sick bay! Go on, out of my sight!'

In the infirmary one had lain at dawn come the morrow, just before the sawbones came on deck, head upside down over the side of the cot, forcing a rush of blood to the skull. *Well, it's worked before.* The MO pulled the thermometer from one's gob.

'A little high. But you'll live. Go on, hop it.'

''ere, girls!' growled the NCO. Archaic .303 rifles were flung at us. Today, we were to learn the manual of arms, all that toss your fuckstick about business. Hopeless, the lot of us. So we 'butterfingers' were made to run around the dusty backblocks of Sunraysia, weapons held above heads, till we had coronaries.

But back at Hut AC2, provender! A tea chest, delivered by Ernie in the Rolls. Leg ham, pressed chicken, smoked oysters, caviar, table water crackers. Top shelf whisky and brandy. We fell to. One ignored Olive's letter. The chests came every few days. One shared it all, save some cigs and booze. These one stashed, for use as bribes.

'Thring's gone to sick bay, sir. Looked ruddy crook.'

Good lad. One had hid in the showers, which NCOs didn't inspect at reveille. Nor did they give sick bay a tumble. *So.* Quick sticks to the motor pool. There, a doze on sandbags in the back of a truck. The spanners here kept it zipped, *quid pro quo* swag, Scotch and gaspers. Sufficed for a few days. But then our lot was assigned to that very place, washing these same vehicles, then painting them in camouflage shades. One wonders if in later years anyone ever noticed all the somewhat expressionist, yet unmistakable, dicks and ballsacks.

'You have a hammer toe, Frankie, remember? Doctor says so.'

Olive insisted on visiting on one's first leave. Ghastly, but she came bearing a fresh care package in the Roller. And a letter from our GP.

'I don't care who wrote this,' said the MO. 'You're fit for duty. Piss off.'

Disconsolate. A big drink back at AC2 that night. Kept at it in the long silent night after the rest had flaked...

'Thing! *On your feet!*'

Thrown in the brig. One must have passed out some time before sunup, so one was comatose at reveille. Held forth with swearies at being shaken awake. Twenty-four in the iron, *clang*. Head felt as if impaled on a spike. Next morning, sick bay.

A surprise. A new MO. Where was the other deadshi....?

'The brass want senior MOs where they're really needed', he said. 'A lot of sick men in the repat hospitals. I'm a new graduate.' His tone softened. 'Let's see that toe.'

A moonling to be sure. And a medical discharge! More to it, of course. Seems that Olive had the Air Vice Marshal talk to the base CO. And wrote them both large cheques.

'For your favourite charity,' she said. Made out to *cash*. I blew the sentries a kiss at the gate. It was April 20, 1945. Hitler's last birthday.

Back at XY, such joy to see Joanie. One was full smitten. Got up to all sorts of tricks. No, not *those*. One would hide behind the modesty panel of her desk. Tickle her so she giggled while wrangling visitors and callers. Or stickytaped her phone down when she wasn't about. Then watch what happened when one called it from another. The Bourneville cocoa powder with which she filled one's coat pockets in revenge was worth it.

'Oh, Frankie, stop weeping. What would your father say?'

Five thousand gathered as if zombies to watch. The Regent, FT's first velvet and marble seraglio of cinematic satyrdom, devoured in a midnight fire. Little used now. A Yank-owned Hoyts on every corner, you see. But the land worth a motza. Yes, pixie. I think so too. Insurance job. *Fucking Olive.*

CHAPTER FIVE

One misses one's old column in *TV Week*. *A Piece Of Thring*, we called it. Telly nowadays, so many wounded animals. And no column, that one might gut and quarter this twaddle. Take *Neighbours* and *Home And Away*. Grotesque, and worse, identical. Or the game shows, like Ian Turpie and his cretinfest, *Supermarket Sweep*. Then *Burke's Backyard*, a gardening turn. Like watching grass die. Speaking of which, one's old pal Crackers, Ruth Cracknell, as senile senior in the ABC's *Mother And Son*. So unfunny it requires a laugh track. One's multi-facelifted protégé Bert Newton has the best show on telly right now. But in the morning, On Channel Ten. Twin heralds of career free fall. And that *makeup*. Good job they didn't call it *Wake Up With Bert*.

*

Every August during the War, Myers at Olive's command staged charity fashion shows for its new season, at the Myer Mural Hall. To liven up this near-death experience a bit, one suggested this year's theme, *Cavalcade Of Famous Lovers*, to the old fruit bat. Cast oneself as three of history's champeen ladypluggers, to accompany the gals on the catwalk. Lavish costumes tailored for the occasion. One's effete touches to one's Casanova and Louis XV raised smiles among display department head Freddie Asmussen and his window dressers. But one's Henry VIII, with six giggling gerts and an executioner, a lad shirtless and masked, whom Henry appeared to fancy at least as much as his wives, well. Freddie's boys sniggered till they blew cockmuck through their noses.

In the middle of all this, Japan surrendered. And one's turn at Myers was seen by a director from the tiny Melbourne Repertory company, Irene Mitchell.

'You're made for it, Frankie,' she said when she asked. 'The part is Henry VIII.'

'This is beyond implausible,' I said. 'This maniac living in the present day thinks he's Henry VIII and encounters six women he imagines to be his wives.'

Yes. Such was the deplorable setup for *Hal's Belles,* the first awful play by a pushy young chap called Ray Lawler.

'Well, Frankie,' said Irene, 'whose job is it to render it otherwise?'

Reeny, we called her, or Miss Mitch. My moon and stars. One owes her so much. One roped in Joanie to work on this turn, too, as prompt. And something else. The theatre was at Middle Park. A long trip home every night to Joanie's flop out at West Preston, with her job at XY come the day. Toorak somewhat closer.

'Stop the night here after shows, Flowergirl. Olive won't mind.'

She certainly wouldn't. Had hinted that we two should wed. *Nothing would delight me more, Frankie.* Perhaps hoped that a lass about the manor might shift one's gears in relation to *you know, the other.* Olive's craving for said consummation was no less than one's glee in denying it to that blowsy Hindenburg.

Opening night of *Hal's.* Olive, the Lady Bracknell of Toorak, front row centre, flanked by her crones-in-waiting. We made what we could of this thin gruel of a play. The Great Manatee Of Toorak elicited three curtain calls for me. *Just me.* Hand up, ordering, gesturing with white-gloved arms, monstering the customers to their feet for a standing O. Humiliating.

Backstage swept I, with one's selected retinue. Slimline Myers laddies. Joanie, very much one of the boys, joined us. Champagne awaited. One had also left a bottle or two in the females' dressing room. Olive, gliding around the foyer, encountered Lawler.

'So *marvellous!*' Came at him, hand out. He clasped hers, his head bowed in humble thanks. 'And he's only *nineteen years old!*' she honked. Meaning *me*. Then swept past, not one kind word to the author. Must have clocked a social pages snapper. Drawn to 'em as fat moth to streetlight, was Olive.

In the dressing room, we chirruped and tittered as the only other male from the *Hal's* cast, *not one of us,* cowered in a corner.

'Oh, Frankie! Look who's here!'

'Aaaah, Lawler,' I said. 'Wouldn't you know it. On the prowl for free champers. Can smell it a mile off.'

I poured him none as the boychums shrieked in mirth. God, one was a dreadful cunt back then. One is far, far better now. At being a cunt, that is.

'Neglected wives shouldn't worry, That's what God made sailors for...'

Kevin McBeath, the record boy from XY, was by now a good pal. As were radio luvvies from XY, 3DB, stagers from the Tiv, from all over the place. For Kevin's twenty-first, we all had to do a turn. One mimed to a Sophie Tucker song, Sophie a raunchy Mae West meets Bette Midler act of the 1920s and 30s. Joanie cued up the 78 RPM disc, and I shimmied on. Full Roaring Twenties drag, from Melbourne Rep's wardrobe skips. Blonde wig. Faceful of lippy, mascara, rouge, courtesy of Flowergirl. They loved me. *As did I.*

A return season of *Hal's* in December, for Gertie Johnson's National Theatre.

She and I did not hit it off. Squirty Gertie, as one called her, cast me not in further parts. Mattered not. Reeny's Little Theatre company more to one's taste. Radical, daring. A gateway to outrage.

The Little was in St Martins Lane, South Yarra. Tiny ex-church. Hundred and twenty seats. One's first turn here *No Other Heaven* by Perry Frame. Two parts to fill so one doubled, played 'em both. Common practice. Unpaid amateur theatre. Cattle always scarce. One's second part was very much against type. A quiet and lonely widower, for fuck's sake. But Reeny got me over the line. No easy matter with Olive there, front row stalls every bloody night.

Thank fuck Reeny and everyone played nice with her. Perhaps hoped the she'd write 'em a cheque to keep this company going. They didn't know her like I did.

'What's next, then, Reeny?'

'Got you down for a turn in May.' Two months hence. 'But don't run off, Frankie. I need you here, every day, right after you knock off at XY.'

'Miss?'

'To paint backdrops. Seek out props, sew costumes. Stagehand duties...'

Work? Here be monsters. All who trod the Little's boards had to slave in its galleys. This the dictum of Reeny's co-producers there, Brett Randall and son Peter. Odd pair. Matching berets and overcoats in most weathers, as if a bad mime act. Brett had known FT. The old man had given him free use of the Prinny's foyer on Sundays, when the theatre proper was closed, to workshop plays. It didn't take long.

'By gum, you look like your old man, young Frankie. Speaking of which, you're not short of a quid. You might consider...?'

He'd put it about that one was tighter than a first time rent boy if one didn't. *For drama tuition fees,* I told Olive, *Miss Mitchell. Private coaching.* Would never have got it otherwise.

My man in *Simpleton Of The Unexpected Isles,* GB Shaw's silliest play, was Pra, the priest. I designed the costumes, so my man wore an off-the shoulder, split to the thigh gown, beehive wig, and more lippy and mascara than Carmen the trannie snake dancer up in Sydney's Kings Cross. Faces drained of blood out beyond the footlights. A ripple of dry swallows. Splendid.

It was one's first play with Bunney Brooke. Some jane, this one. At different times in the army, homeless, a coffee lounge proprietress, tram conductress. Lovers of all genders. She'd king hit a woman as quick as she would a man. Yet gripped one's hand in the wings that opening night, we both shaking from stage fright.

Well, *Simpleton* shocked, but only the few who saw it. Then came *Acacia Avenue.*

'To bring in coin, keep the Little alive,' said Reeny. This asinine play had been both West End hit and a British film. Of course it had been. It was dreadful.

Joan became quite involved in all this carry-on. Did walk-ons, sewed and painted things, worked the lights and such. And roped in her mother, Edith, a gun seamstress. Her creations for our female cast looked stunning. Especially on *me.*

When not at the Little, one practised skills various at home, like slap. You know, makeup. Spent hours one day doing oneself up as one of Boris Karloff's grisliest characters. Still in it when Joanie came home from work. Well, waste not want not.

I jumped out at her from behind the drapes and roared. Poor gal screamed. Hared out the front door. One can only wonder what Toorak Road made of a woman fleeing down the footpath, pursued by Frankenstein's monster in embroidered smoking jacket, bellowing apologies.

For *Enduring As The Camphor Tree,* we were all Chinese, in mime. My man the villain, Lord Ku. Rehearsals, well, ideal prep for the run. For both, we played to nobody. Next up, *The Invisible Circus,* by a local, Sumner Locke Elliott.

'It's about a radio station, Frankie,' said Reeny, 'and,' *wink,* 'you're the station boss, my child.'

Well, then. My man JB Olliphant 'brainless yet self-important,' she advised. So one modelled him on Olive. Oh, yes, and how could I forget; that *other bit of business,* an after-midnight tryst at the Little - one had a key, you see- with *Circus* playwright, the winsome Elliott.

'All this cloak and dagger carry-on,' he said as he buttoned up afterwards.

'Oh, I don't know, lover. The dagger bit has its moments.'

We did a Melbourne Town Hall run of Dorothy Sayers' *The Just Vengeance* for Easter. All a bit sanctimonious. An irreligious airman, killed in action, can't enter heaven till he accepts Jesus as his saviour. Obnoxious, really. Paralleled news from the States. Blacklists. Hollywood people branded communists. Or outed as homosexuals. This madness would come here. As sure as rats on ships.

Reeny now cast me in *Skipper Next To God*. A freighter captain has Jews on board, fleeing Hitler. America refuses them, so the old seadog scuttles his own ship. Goes down with it, what's more. The US is forced to take the Jews as shipwreck survivors. One strove to make each customer in the audience feel as if my man the cap'n was addressing them, only them. Not so hard, given ticket sales.

Yes, there were turns at the Little when cast and crew outnumbered audience. But bushpig Olive came, to every play. Her hooting from the front row...in the theatre of my mind, my hands round her neck, squeezing...

For *The Macropolous Secret,* cast as Prus. Yes, the villain. And during the run, who could forget one's twenty-first, eh, pixie? Depraved and decadent. Well, after we got rid of Olive and her dowager cohort. Thought they'd never fucking leave.

Yes. *Olive.* Rylands was no place to entertain, er, birds of one's feather. One's 3XY work was unpaid. The Little an amateur company. No income from either. Ergo, no means to move out. So, rather than shallowgrave her on the grounds, one asked her for money, to do the only thing that her Anglophile mindset would abide. Sail for Britain, *do Europe* and slither one's way onto West End stages. Become one of these storied expats one heard so much about. Mostly from them, on their irritating visits.

Many couldn't afford travel abroad back then. There'd be envy afoot at the London Hotel in Albert Park, our regular luvvies' drinker, so one made it sound like I'd had it thrust on me. Told Frank Doherty, drama crit at the *Argus,* of a course 'on offer' at the Old Vic. To *Listener In* magazine, of an audition for RADA. To others, 'oh, the Shakespeare Memorial wants to look me over,' as if awaiting the gallows at sunrise.

Joanie and a few pals saw me off at Station Pier, all the streamers and razzamatazz they bunged on in those days when a liner left port. One did drop a tear, as we theatricals say. But the kip was loaded, one's pennies flung skyward, to fall where they may. Come in fucking spinner.

CHAPTER SIX

The 1992 Melbourne Comedy Festival must be desperate. At the Ath with Bea Arthur from *The Golden Girls*, Wendy Harmer and others, one is on the bill for *Humorists Read The Humorists*. To read from Dorothy Parker, Wilde, you know.

'Well, a bit disappointed,' I said when they asked at the run-through if everything was tickety-boo. 'I mean, one didn't have to fuck anyone to get on the show.'

*

Aboard one's maiden voyage abroad in 1947, one Robert Chisholm. Cast in *Collit's Inn,* so had known FT. A dismal twit. And quite unfuckable. One had tried, but the bastard just wouldn't be in it.

'Heard you were on board, Frankie,' he said. 'And how is your mother?'

'The same. Still a cunt.' He did a double take. 'And you should hear what she says about you, Bobby dear.'

Kept his distance the entire voyage. Mission accomplished.

'Alan! What are you doing here?' This one somewhat more seducable.

'Same as you, Frank. Off to London. Try my luck.'

Quite the luvvie contingent on this tub. This one, Alan Christie, former child star in FT's musicals. A dainty dish to set before a Thring. The boy's financials not up to First Class like oneself. So. To serve Master Cock, one ventured below decks, to the place of many serfs, the Cabin Class Lounge.

'Your luck's in, Butch,' I said. 'You see, one plans to start one's own company. Which means you may well be needed if...'

His cabin, so I could leave fast. His London contact details danced wild spiral as the gale across the deck snatched the paper as I released it from my raised hand.

An overnighter in the port of Singapore. One made for Bugis Street. *Boogie Street* as British sailors called it. The lurid showcase of trannie glam here quite overwhelming. And if you must know, one's first taste of gender-bender sex did not disappoint.

In port in Colombo, one did not leave one's cabin in what was then Ceylon, now Sri Lanka. Too many cocktails on the Promenade Deck *la luna* previous, you see. Dusky boys of ten summers could be had in this sub-continental fleshpot for a snip, it was said, but not one's go at all. An abhorrent and criminal practice. Of course, being both Australian and a public flamboyant, one has been accused of it on occasions innumerable. Without exception, by persons who themselves appear to harbour almost fetishist fascination for such horrors.

Genoa was one's first glimpse at *Italia*. One would return to this land anon, to play perhaps history's most reviled villain. Then Southampton come October.

Less than green and pleasant here, went my letter home to Joanie. *Grey and wan people queue at grey and wan shops for grey and wan meat.*

One's landlady in Hampstead a Miss Cavendish, seventyplenty. Of one's first post-war rations dinner here, one wrote it like it was. *Two sausages of wet bread and sage. Mash made of powder. A rhombus of processed cheese. Half a green tomato.*

Took walking tours of London. Goering's Luftwaffe and Von Braun's rockets had left it ravaged. Much of the result still remained. Jagged, broken walls of brickwork pointed, accusing, at the skies.

Come Xmas, a visit to the Creightmores in Brackley. One's cousin John and family. Had long since left Australia. The Kreitmayer name Anglicised to avoid internment during Hitler's War, you see. One saw snow for the first time. Couldn't contain my joy. What was *wrong* with me?

One skipped and sang through the stuff, spun one's umbrella like a Tivoli hoofer, one wrote to Joan. Never to Olive. Joan read her my letters. Quite enough for the old flabsack. One had vowed to 'do the Continent,' that arcane term for Europe back then, but only made it to Paris. *Ville de Lumiere* shimmered as it should. But post-war shortages of everything, bar hungry young men on the streets. One took shameful advantage.

'Robert Helpmann is playing there. Celebrated dancer, quite right too. Now an actor. Quite useless at that. But a compatriot, so...'

One explained to the Creightmores that it was imperative that one make for the Stratford-upon-Avon 1948 season. Aussie expat Bobby would be directed here in *King John* by the faerie queene of Stratford, Michael Benthall. One wrote to both that one was a producer who fancied touring the Stratford company down under. Well, I mean, they'd not waste time seeing *actors*. Benthall replied, but not Helpmann. This despite enclosing in one's letter to Bobby a traced outline of one's mutton shunter.

At full attention.

'You have thirty seconds. Begin.'

Camp as a tent show, this Benthall. So off I went, parts one had played in Melbourne. Othello, Herod. *Hut!* He cut me off.

'You said you're a producer, boy.'

'Er, I'm an actor-producer. Like Orson Welles, you see...'

'Actor? Never heard of you, cockie. Now, the producer bit, dear. Are we talking a tour of the colonies or...'

'Er... one was wondering if one might *audition* for *you*...'

'Oh. I *see*'. He beckoned, *come here, closer*. His old rammer squinted at me like a pirate king might at a cabin boy. *The things one does.*

'Well, then,' I said. 'Job for job?' He snorted.

'Heard yourself *speak*, boy?'

Oh, that. One's underslung jaw, *involuntary shibilansh on every shyllable*. Fucking born with it. Fucking Olive.

'Dear boy. Go back to Orstralia. I wish you well.'

'C-can we perhaps h-have lunch?'

'We just *have.*'

Swine! But I was not done. *Hamlet* was opening the season. Paul Scofield, a real actor, and Helpmann, playing the Dane on alternate nights. First night was Scofield. Bobby would be there watching, no doubt. Fucker needed all the help he could get.

At the Memorial Theatre foyer, Bobby hard to miss. Head like a rhesus monkey, that one. Ah! There he be, midst a circlet of slimline lads. I spread my arms.

'*Bobby!* Good to see you again!' To his chums, 'Can I borrow Bobby for a mo?'

Steered him away. He, popeyed at the temerity of this total stranger.

'Thring. Frank Thring,' I said. 'The *Melbourne* Thrings. I wrote to you...?'

'Ooooh, yes, of *course!*'

One's body language screamed tall teen flirt. 'Pon whom this sybarite might feast.

'So can I do an audition, Mr Helpmann?'

'You just did, lover,' he said, voice wreathed in insipid English morning sunlight. He wangled me a tryout with Tony Quayle, a new director at Stratford. Very military, like many who'd served.

'Front and centre, Thring. Where did you serve?'

I told him.

'Ah. Olivier's mob. Oh, well. Can't be helped. Right! Let's have you. Move!'

I did Herod's jewel speech from Wilde's *Salome*.

'Well, I won't say I don't like it. Stand at ease. Dismissed.'

'Well, if he didn't fancy it, he'd say so, Frankie. Full brutal.'

One was crestfallen. Helpmann, less so. 'Look, lover,' he said, 'go back to London, audition for parts in rep. I'll pull a few coats where I can, fetch up some bits and pieces for you.'

He meant well. But this would take five eternities.

Then, a brainwave. Back in London, I bought a typewriter. At a recording studio, a hole in the wall in Covent Garden, one paid to cut two short chats one called *London Letter*. Wry jibes of a man about town. A disdainful '*Oh. It's you,*' one's catchphrase to introduce each. Then had some 78RPM discs pressed. Shopped them round the BBC radio networks various, and copies to Helpmann, Quayle, HM Tennants the theatrical agents, others of this blood. Not Benthall.

Came back fuckall but the dead air of indifference. So one airmailed some of these records home. *My new BBC show,* I wrote. *Play it on XY.* No way to check back then. So Melbourne would believe one was on the wireless in Britain, you see. A grand illusion worthy of the Great Dexter.

But one remained hostage to fortune as Queen's Consort Of the Second Thring Empire. Olive now turned off the money tap. Summoned me home. The Lucrezia Borgia of Toorak had me by the giggleberries. I packed with dour heart.

*

Dreadful tidings. Nanny. While one was mid-voyage. *Nanny.* One shook as one wept. The funeral nigh unendurable. And our driver Ernest and housekeeper Margaret were now an item. Shacked up in the old stable out the back of Rylands, converted to what one dubbed a 'grannyfanny flat.'

In more cheery news, one was to meet Laurence Olivier and Vivien Leigh! The showbiz marriage of the decade were to tour Australia in May for the Old Vic, our new producer Garnet Carroll presenting at the Princess.

'Mobbed by peasants where'er they roam,' said Garnet. Larry and Viv apparently sought out post-show suppers at private homes, to escape this. Well, of course, Olive pounced. One wondered whether the Oliviers would make it beyond the soup course.

'Well, I based him on Hitler, you see.'

Such did Sir Laurence inform one at supper. By his *Richard III* was one spellbound at his squashed spider's gait, his yapping like the Fuhrer. And the sight of Vivien right there in front of us as Lady Anne, not on a cinema screen, well, dizzying, stuff, pixie. Others from the cast here, too. Peter Cushing with his wife Helen. And George Relph, with whom one would work much later, in a major motion picture as the Yanks say. Vivien, to one's alarm, played footsie under the table as she purred a question.

'And what do *you* want to be, young *man?*'

'I don't want to be, Lady Olivier. I am. An *actor,* good my lady.'

One bowed at the neck. Felt compelled to. Viv was garrulous, profane, all shrieks and giggles, and *trying to crack on to me.* Larry, however, clipped and distant. Exhausted, one suspects, knowing now what one didn't then about Viv. One would find out six summers down the line.

'They bill themselves as 'the Stratford-Upon-Avon Company', or 'specially selected from the Stratford Company,' said O'Shaughnessy. 'Preposterous, it is.'

A far lesser company than the Old Vic now sailed into Port Melbourne, to wit Irishman Anew McMaster and several woeful thesps. Total frauds. Well, Anew *had* performed at Stratford. Once. In about 1543, by the look of him. Yet every prancer in Melbourne was there for the tryouts for the support cast. For McMaster was from *overseas. Customers would flock.*

Few did not make the cut. Soon saw why. We locals, classed as amateurs, so no pay. This canny Paddy made a packet from this racket.

'Did someone say *closet'?* one whispered at the dress when Anew swept on for his *Othello.* North of seventy, naked save loincloth and turban. Blacked up head to foot. As if dipped in shit. The doughty Peter O'Shaughnessy was Iago, and Irene Harpur our Desdemona. Both starry fixtures in the 1940s Melbourne theatre scene. Alas, self cast as but a lineless super, an extra. But *Othello* has a principal cast of twelve. So when others fell sick or dipped out, one took on Cassio or Lodovico.

For *Taming Of The Shrew,* again one naught but mute stage-filler. But players left, tits in tangles at McMaster's dictatorial quirks. Enter one's Vincentio Of Pisa, well-respected sixtyplus moneybags. One's fey, foppish take turned a few heads. Recalling Larry's Adolfian Richard III, one's Vincentio a whole new look at Churchill.

'I met Bobby at Stratford,' I told her. 'We had a liquid lunch together.'

Sheila Helpmann, Bobby's sister, was in *Shrew* too. Our meeting here the genesis of a long friendship. And one's eyes fell on another bit parter. Awakened a great stirring amidships. One was too shy to make direct approach. So one started making faces at McMaster, behind the old dogberry's back, to amuse this lad that one shall call Dreamboat. A chippy by trade, he sawed and hammered sets together for productions around Melbourne, and had a small part in *Shrew*. One's facepulls made the boy laugh. But McFake noticed. *Oh, fuck.* He turned. One braced for notes brutal. But...

'Do what you like behind my back, lad. Every laugh's worth ten shillings.'

Advice heeded ever since. As for Dreamboat, well, a week on at the cinema, dress circle empty but for we two, one showed him that one was as good with one's hands as any tradesman. The film, Cagney. *White Heat.*

'Kenn Brodziak, Aztec Services.'

Short, loud, bearded. Extending his hand. A commercial producer, this one. Actors were paid, in other words. 'You know Sumner Locke Elliott?'

'Yes.' Recalling our tryst, our bit of business at the Little. 'Rather well.'

'He has a new play, boychik. Sold out season in Sydney. I plan to bung it on here. Need a local cast.'

Darling Reeny had put in a word. *Rusty Bugles* was set in a wartime ordnance depot in the Northern Territory. My man, Sgt Brooks, *il cunto di tutti cunti* in camp. The King's Theatre in Russell Street, dark for some years, would host *Rusty* for this rough old tart's refurbishment and grand re-opening.

'Some of you are confirmed bachelors, I'd wager.'

Director Doris Fitton, of Sydney's bold Independent Theatre, had us line up on the stage. 'None of my affair. But I keep losing people from this bloody show.'

In Sydney there'd been arrests, you see. Charges of 'gross indecency' in public toilets. 'So get your jollies off the beaten track, gentlemen, not on it. Let's get to work.'

And work it was.

'Mr Thring. One Charles Laughton in this world is enough. Base your man on someone else, please.'

'And, Miss, who might that someone b...' Doris looked up from her script.

'Someone you *know*.' *Isn't it obvious?* 'Where did you serve?' *Aaah.* I saw it now.

And so one did become the worst NCO at Shepparton RAAF base.

'Can we give him a prop moustache, Miss?'

'Does it help inform the character?'

'My word, yes. We used to call him Cockbrush.'

'Sorry to hear you're off, lad.'

To give *Rusty* my all, one must leave McMaster's low-rent circus.

'Now, ...' He rubbed thumb and finger together. 'My expenses.'

'Beg yours?'

'You signed a contract.' *What?*

'Or you can stay.' His gaze hardened. '*Lad.*'

Or a third choice. Got it done and scrammed. Left him open mouthed to the skies.

O'Shaughnessy found me at the Swanston Family Hotel with Dreamboat one Friday arvo. Along with the painters French, Perceval, a Boyd or two. Assorted potters, tumblers, thesps, bohos. Safety in numbers, you see.

'Thring. Melbourne Uni Drama Club. We're doing *Peer Gynt*. Reeny tells me you're the man. We need some masks, fella.'

Meant late nights and a key to their workshop. Alone with Dreamboat. At last.

'Coppers. Opening night is the word. Censor's coming, too.'

Just before *Rusty* opened in April 1949, one made a call to theatre writer Doherty at the *Argus*. All bulltwang, of course. He beat up a yarn of obscene language in our play and word of this getting to the fat blue line. Of opening night, a probable raid. An *Argus* shooter snapped pics of the cast, fondling our prop .303 rifles, grinning like blasphemers should. Ticket sales jumped.

First night, full house. Nine curtains at line-up. Out on the street, no coppers. Just undead whiskied-up molester priests and their blue rinse disciples. Ye wowser ghouls in dismal cluster.

A six month run, baby. Oh yes. Then we took *Rusty* on the road. First stop, the aforesaid Independent in North Sydney. The censors of Steamy City received complaints the moment we rolled into town. Well, you see, one does those livid greypates so well on the phone. And in fact newspaper stories of these prompted the real Censor to act.

They moved to close us down, so the run sold out, I wrote to Dreamboat. *We agreed to cuts in the language. Slotted them back in when the bed sniffers backed off.*

For our second run back in Melbourne, one had Dreamboat, Joan, the cast, everyone, write to the papers. Nom de plumes, of course. *Dear Sir. Saw that show. Filth!* Sold-out houses.

Olive had us do charity turns of *Rusty* at Repat Hospitals in the city and Caulfield. Maimed diggers jeered one's Sergeant Brooks. Yes. One was playing my man as one should. But one's first blue now with Dreamboat. No place in the cast of *Rusty* for him, you see. Well, he'd asked, and one promised one would talk to Doris, as cast members had left here and there. But one hadn't. You see, the boy, albeit delectable, couldn't act for toffee apples. Miss Fitton would've handed me my notice wedged in my arse if I'd talked her into it. And one had made one's pledge brimful of Glenlivet and with a bumful of Cupid's arrows. He slapped and I slapped back. Then he served me a faceful of fist and stormed off. What a ride we turned into. Think St Kilda foreshore. The Big Dipper at Luna Park. Engulfed in flames.

Rusty went bush now. Bendigo, Capitol Theatre. A dreaded 'bus and truck' tour. Six AM wake up after ten PM curtain and eleven PM bumpout.

Then drive all day till theatre ahoy. Bump in. Then tech rehearsal, one wrote to Joan. *After the show, bump out.*

One did one's best to avoid said bumps, but our stage manager a vigilant fucker.

'*Oi!* Lofty! Where you off to? Grab an end of this.'

Unwise. His bacon and eggs carpet-bombed with sugar next morning by, er, persons unknown.

His Majesty's, gilded citadel to the gold rush, housed our season in Ballarat, a frost-caked town in greyscape winter. Then to Coffs Harbour, Port Macquarie, Forster. Others. June and July roared by, screaming.

'England, Frank. I'm off.'

A reconciliation, and now this. Dreamboat reached for his Woodbines on the bedside table. 'Thought you could help out with the fare.'

'B-b-but why....'

'I could go places there,' he said. 'Here, well,..'

'But your future *is* here, laddie.' One slipped back into one's lilac lingerie, lifted from Georges on Collins Street.

'You said you'd get me a part in *Rusty*. Put in a word with Reeny. Talk to Brodsky...'

'Later, lover. Must rush,' I said. 'Kissy?' He swerved his face. No kissy. I had to go.

To meet Joan at the Waiters Club in Meyers Place. Spaghetti. Flagon red.

Autentico Italiano. In 1949, in drabglum Melbourne, *molto* snazzy. At the Metro in Collins St, for *Treasure Of The Sierra Madre*, one sat in the dark, puzzling. Dreamboat's plan to ship out, a gal one loved, but who couldn't meet one's, well,....What to do?

At the Menzies Hotel after the film, brandy crusters and a spat over Olive, upon whom Joanie doted, when I called her an old blurter. We sooked home to Rylands on separate trams. So on the outs now with both best friends. Going on tour never so welcome.

We boarded the *Taroona*, a pre-Empress Of Australia tub o' rust, for Tasmania.

By Devonport, one wrote to Dreamboat and Joan, separately, to mend fences, *why, the sea be five fathoms deeper from our throwing up.*

Then by rail in winter to Launceston. Too sick to drink. Not, however, by Hobart. Back to Melbourne now, tide in our wake slick with actor vomit, for the Southern Aurora overnight train to Adelaide.

First night at His Maj in King William Street was splendid, I wrote, but not of naughty fun among the cast. Yes. This sufficed at first. But I mean, the only fucks one ever craves are those one hasn't had yet, *c'est vrai?*

The footbridge, Torrens river, behind the university, was the whisper. Thence one swayed, Chateau Tanunda amidships for a bit of dutch. Harold Holt was in Parliament now, fuck knows how. Whenever we met, at Olive's wingdings, he'd hand me his card. *Harold Holt MHR.* Did it to everyone. Circled at first nights, parties and receptions like a shark with a gold tooth.

I saw two men throw a third into the river. Yet, in boozehaze, pressed on, full as WC Fields, enfogged, thus emboldened. They swerved heads at me.

'Who the fuck are you?' one said. The other flipped a warrant card at me. *Oh. Police. Fuck.* Too, too late to back out. *You're on, baby. Break a fucking leg.* I flashed a card under their torch.

'I'm Holt. MHR. Been at dinner with your Premier Playford,' I said. 'Sir Thomas. And your *police* minister. What's the meaning of this?' Saw their faces fall. 'Oh, fuck it. Just get out of my sight.'

They stumbled off, muttering. Only now one felt one's heart pounding.

'Come up here, mate, don't be frightened'. Turned one's attention to the poor drenched bugger. A professor of chemistry, he said. Dry clothes at his office on campus, and sherry. Mustn't have been the first time. Was most assuredly my last.

We are among savages.

The only thing one could write of our next stop, via the Nullarbor Plain. Three days on the Indian Pacific. In Kalgoorlie, with its two-sector mining town economy of grog and prostitution, *Rusty* played the town hall. Then in Perth, our stage manager announced a new Sydney run. One despaired of ever being free.

Back in Melbourne, a call from David Martin, he of the Tivoli circuit. Arthur Askey, 75 not out, Britain's best-loved wartime comedian, had sailed into Sydney with his show *The Love Racket*. In rehearsal, Askey didn't care for one of the local support cast. A vacancy yawned.

'Wait on, laddie,' I said. 'Is this a tour?' Dread rose within.

'Yes. The Tivoli's a circuit, Frank, you know that.'

One was about to say no. Just as Olive came in the door.

'David,' I said. 'When do we start?'

CHAPTER SEVEN

Peter Allen is gone. AIDS-related, howl the press, those agents of killjoy retribution. We met when the Allen Brothers used to do spots on telly in the early 1960s. Yes, we all knew. I mean, he dropped enough hints. All that *I Go To Rio* frou-frou. His bride for a time, Liza Minnelli. Judy Garland's daughter, for fuck's sake.One recalls their trip to Oz in 1968. And Liza, asked what she thought of Melbourne.

'Well, every city has its own colour, and Melbourne's is blue.' *Quite.*

*

Just as well one had left *Rusty*. It flopped in Sydney. Lasted two nights. And cast members were done. One for obscene exposure. A public lav in the Domain. T'other, sexual assault of a naval rating in The Rocks, also in a gents brasco.

'No class, yon Sydney lads,' I said to Dreamboat after a tumble. 'Harbour views from those establishments notwithstanding.'

'How soon can you leave, Frank? For Sydney. The Askey show.'

Just home from the pictures with Joan. David Martin calling.

'Beg yours? We open in Melbourne, David.'

'Yes, but Askey wants to rehearse in Sydney. Best get there quick sticks, lover.'

On The Spirit Of Progress, one could book a sleeper. And if a body meet a body ...well, gals and boys of the night known to work the interstate trains, you see. But as one took one's quarry, *oh shit; Dreamboat.* We had arranged to meet at the Windsor. One pictured him. Sallow, drawn. Waiting like Cho Cho San. Oh, fuck. Oh, well.

From Central, to the Tivoli on Castlereagh Street. Forgot about Sydney's weather. Overdressed. Sweating. Looked like I'd been pissed on by six elephants. Joan Davis, the producer, in the foyer.

'Mr Thring! *Finalmente!* Come along'.

They looked a weary mob. Askey not here. The Brits in the cast included his stooge-in-chief, Roy Royston. An overbearing boor. Buxom Val Tandy a good card cheat, one came to find. Audrey Jeans a fun gal. And then there was the local support cast.

'G'day, Fred. Charles Norman.'

Tall and talent-free, this one. Later big in Melbourne on kids' TV, as the stenchmost Funny Face Norman. And oh, yes, flirtygert Gil Johnson.

'Frankie, is it? I hope you're not just a pretty face,' said giggly Gil. 'Because you're certainly not that.' Joan stamped her hoof. He cowered. 'Sorry, Miss Davis.'

'Fetch Mr Thring his script,' she said, waving him away.

'Oh, if I must. This way, you long streak.'

'Ey oop! What's t' weather like oop there?'

They all fell about as the diminutive Askey took in one's lofty measure. To laugh at his tired gags was mandatory. As was due deference and disposition cheery at all times toward Arthur, his wife May and Anthea, their daughter. A family of despicables. They wore that hard-eyed misery peculiar to showies. Grinned like it caused pain.

The sketches, very much of their time. Obscenity could be prosecuted all the way to jail then. But gag writers found ways. Example, Arfur reading job ads aloud, in Scouser accent. With Spoonerisms.

'They want a *fook* and *cootman*.' Or explaining a new job to Val Tandy:

'If you've got what you need, where you need them, you can put your 'ands on them when you need.'

Cue busty Val. Places hands on tits.

'Yes, you've got the idea.'

Opening night in Melbourne, they gave Askey a standing O just for walking on. After the tiny stages of rep, at the Tiv, well, one had to shout to be heard. Not just by the customers, but upstage. Askey was half-deaf, you see. The need to repeat one's lines was signalled by him shouting 'You *wot*?' so it looked like it was part of the show.

At first night line-up, Askey beamed at the cheering, whistling, customers as we bowed behind him. And beamed, as ordered by May, a charmless termagant. Spoke with her teeth clenched together. Audrey Jeans had a tip for holding a trouper's smile fixed in place.

'Frankie, just look straight at the customers and keep mouthing *stick it in your arse. Stick it in your arse...*'

Curtain down. Arfur turned to us, his grin collapsed to scowl.

'Well, you fookers lift your game or I start dishin' out fines, right?' The last word came out as *rate*. 'Now. These knobs is comin' to first night party.' *Paatay*. 'First one I see with no smile on dial is off show, right?' *Rate*.

After Askey and the knobs left, things revved up a bit. Val Tandy strutted with her boobs out. Charlie Norman, a cartoonist, drew charcoal faces on them, nipples as noses. Audrey Jeans sang *Alive-Alive-O* while gargling beer. And one got giggly Gil smashed. Took him beneath the stage, *to show you something*. Well, pixie. He was three pints heavier when one was done with him.

Ten sold out weeks. After one matinee, Joan Davis called us together, *clap clap*.

'Mr Askey has been asked by the ABC to do a series of Sunday night wireless programs. Isn't that wonderful?' We slapped mitts together, *clapclapclap*. *Marvellou*...then realised. *Sunday*. Our one day off, theatres closed and dark on the Sabbath, *gone*. Such was enslavement on the good ship vaudeville for all who stoked its boilers. And I don't mean its female players.

May 1950. As North Korea's troops butchered a road into that peninsula's south, came *Racket* to His Majesty's in Brisbane. In the

Courier-Mail, one was lauded for one's turn as a senile 75 year old stooge, a 'delightfully nutty study.'

'Frank, Mr Askey wants to see you,' said Roy. In his dressing room, the little goblin slapped at the newspaper in his hand.

'You'd do well to remember 'oo they're comin' to see, lad. Comport yourself accordingly. Now fook off!'

Brisbane had its amusements. A marvellous jazz band, the Cane Cutters, for one. But a hotter kind of jazz an hour away at The Surfers Paradise Hotel. Theatre staff *in the know* invited me on a day trip. In the Birdwatcher Bar at Surfers, one advertised by one's choice of drinks - Tia Maria and milk, Bacardi and Coke, Barossa Pearl. Relief behind the surf club sheds. Then thoughts of Dreamboat, of Joan. And remorse.

South to Sydney in June for the Tiv run there. Shows kicked off at 7.30 PM. Six o'clock closing here. The mugs at the shows blotto, from sinking schooners with both hands from knock off time to chuck out o'clock. *Gerroff!* as we came on. *Get ya funbags out!* to Audrey and Val.

In the morning papers, North Korea had taken Seoul, and there was talk of The Bomb. We stayed at the Santa Fe apartments in Kellett Street, as travelling players did. Kings Cross close at hand for a drink at odd hours. Ginchy, seedy clubs galore. Also the Claremont Café. World's rudest proprietor, corpulent Walter Magnus. A role model for the public persona one had begun to craft. The El Dorado and Kookaburra cafes had queers on the cruise. The Hasty Tasty, Yank-style burgers. Abe Saffron's Roosevelt Club in Orwell Street offered topless showgirls. Scenic, baby. All this no big deal now. But for Frankie age 23 from turgid Toorak, in 1950, it was Times fucking Square.

The Cross also the first place one was bashed and robbed. Drunk, so one didn't feel much. Still, woke in fright next day. As a child, one had found a huge Bowie knife in FT's bag once. *Oh, your father keeps that*, Olive had said, *just in case.* Bruised and shaken this rainy morning, I bought one at an Army Disposals on George Street. *Just in case.* And in fact, as it turned out...but we shall come to that in time.

The shiner made one look like a one-eyed panda. The men of *Racket* mock-shaped up when they saw me, presumed one had been punching on. The women and wallies knew the truth. And said nothing. Extra slap hid it from Askey.

But, well, you know how it is. With a Black Bag full of Army knife, one again sallied forth. A mimsy from the Tiv stage crew had tipped one the wink about this beat. Here, a short, middle aged gent turned one's way.

'Are you fwee?' He had jug ears. *Fwee?* Oh. *Free.* Twice one's age. So no sale. But fun to be had. One slipped him a Harold Holt card. He looked up, most indignant.

'You're not Hawold. Where did you get thi... go away, clear off.' He scuttled to the kerb. 'Taxi!'

There it was in the *Sydney Morning Herald* a few days later. A story on the '49ers', newly elected MHRs in Canberra. Oh, dear. At The Wall, Darlinghurst, it appears one had met one of them. A future prime minister no less. But one doubted he'd run to tell Harold of meeting this impersonator while out cwuising for cock.

One gave the Wall a swerve when one noted its proximity to Darlinghurst police lockup, but there were other meetplaces. Like the Minerva Theatre in Orwell Lane, Kings X. The code, one wore green. A tie, socks or shirt. *The Third Man* the main feature the day one went. Engrossing. One almost forgot why one was there until the chap in the next seat, ahem, jostled one's memory.

From Sydney to Melbourne again now, then back to Brisbane. Three days. Three trains. Three gauges. Bar cars closed early. So, to fun with one's sleeper berthmate, a new cast member who shall remain nameless. Porters woke you at dawn with hot tea, so best be back in one's own bunk before that ugly hour.

We've lost our male lead for November, wrote Reeny. *Love Racket's* eastern states and last Adelaide runs were done. Perth now, last stop on this tour. Hmmm. One made an operator-assisted trunk call to Melbourne.

'Frank! Where are you? On the moon?' A bad line. We both had to shout.

'Adelaide! Same fucking thing! Listen, Joanie,...'

Feeding threepenny bits into a public phone in a red PMG box, I asked Flowergirl to tell David Martin that Olive was quite ill. One must leave *Racket* and return to Melbourne at once. Sadly, she wasn't, but you know, needs must. So 1950 ended well. Back at the Little, as the archvillain in *Shipwreck*. A tale of the Dutch East Indies ship *Batavia*. My man a murderer, sex slaver, cannibal, sodomite. Well cast.

Christmas. To Portsea with Olive. Obligatory. Inheritance in mind, you see. Lunch at the Holts' shack there, vile Harold now a minister in Menzies' musty government. At the beach, he ignored his latest wife Zara. Chatted up girls. Went out in rough surf. To show off.

'Frank, you know *The Man Who Came To Dinner?*'

Did I ever. Saw the film, with Joan or Dreamboat, several times. Each. So knew the part of male lead, obnoxious Sheri Whiteside. Reeny's production of *The Man* opened in January 1951. One cajoled minks and sables from Olive's collection.

'For the female cast only this time, mother,' to her alarm. For the set, Ming urns, jade vases, red velvet Louis XV chairs, also from Rylands.

One had fun, pixie, as you recall. In my man Sheri's wheelchair, one slammed on the brake whenever the actor steering one around began to push. Then one would release it, so we skidded all over the stage.

The young Joan Harris played sex-mad film star Lorraine Sheldon. Wore a skintight red dress. Had to be wrapped into it. Onstage, one rolled one's wheels over its train and sat there. If she moved, it would begin to unravel. The customers loved it. *Every laugh's worth ten shillings.*

Her character threw a book at me from atop a piano each night, and my man Sheri caught it. Seeking vengeance, she took to tossing it in such a way that I couldn't. One was made to look most clumsy. So next night she found that the book had been nailed to the piano lid. Not a jane to be messed with, she threw the only other thing on the piano - a priceless blue Qing Dynasty statuette of a dog, from Rylands. This I caught.

Two nights later, Joan hoisted the book aloft, having checked it wasn't hammered down, and hurled it. Confetti stuffed between its pages spewed out all over the stage. And a few shows on, well, she took her cue to sit on the onstage sofa-whence was hidden a whoopee cushion one had purchased at Bernard's Magic Shop in Elizabeth Street in the city. *Faaaarrrt !*

'Oh,' one said, still in character as Sheri, '*do you think so?*'

This was also one's first time working with the extraordinary Sheila Florance. She had a fatal weakness, one learned. So one night one faced Sheila in one's wheelchair, one's back to the customers, one's old fellow out, pockets pulled inside out as if elephant's ears. She laughed so hard she wet herself onstage. One called her 'Puddles' for ever after.

One paid for it, of course. At one point in the play, she shows Whiteside a photo album of herself as a young girl. One night she handed me the pix as usual. Cut and pasted onto its pages, nudes, from a banned naturist magazine. Overcome, one forgot one's line. *Dried.* Had to improv while wheeling over to prompt corner, that Flowergirl there rescue me.

'Well, someone fancied you,' I managed. 'Half those pages are *stuck together.*'

'Darling, a woman with a bottom like that could say anything!'

Brodziak now cast me as the Bishop Of Lax in a dire sex farce, *See How They Run*. Dreadful. Just one funny line in the whole thing. And not mine! So, then. To get all eyes on one's Bishop, one made him a stately homo. Onstage in cleric's mufti, one whipped out an emery board and filed one's nails. Made duckmouths to a hand mirror. Applied blush or lipstick. Well, one was building a profile. And imbeciles were swarming to see this goulash in Adelaide and Melbourne.

One weekend off, one went to Bendigo with Joanie, at Reeny's request. To do a make-up demo for 'Cover Girl For Victoria,' a modelling prize event. Rolled out one's rogues' gallery on self, assist from glam Flowergirl. Quite the comedy duo as we bewigged, dabbed, glued and painted up one's Frankenstein, Henry VIII, Lord Ku. Then in July, a quick call to Brodsky about *See How They Run*.

'Make it short, Frankola', he said, 'I'm bus...'

'As you wish. I quit.'

One was not for touring Sydney, Perth nor Hobart. 'Three of my least favourite state capitals, Brodsky. How *could* you?'

'How could I. Look, *schmendrick*. You can't work for me if you do this all the time'.

'Can I get that in writing, Kenny baby?' I said.

'In writing he wants it. Ah, *narish*. What will you do now?'

Well, one had thought about that. What followed, the best decision one ever made. And the worst.

CHAPTER EIGHT

'Mama, can I talk to you?'

She turned in dull surprise.

'It's time for a Thring to run a theatre in Melbourne again.'

One's inspiration, Orson Welles, his Mercury company. Well, Olive agreed to finance this tilt. Albeit with reservations. A small, affordable theatre only. And no scratch for paying actors. Amateurs only.

'I won't have you squandering your legacy before I'm gone, Frankie.'

One thanked her as a grateful son should, all the while thinking of a favourite film; *Arsenic And Old Lace*.

'Hear about Middle Park Rep, Frank?'

Met with Reeny at Cinders' Coffee Lounge in Collins Street to discuss it. Cinders banged down witch-brewed coffee with burnt raisin toast. Shuffled off in her black evening gown and gloves, worn day and night. 'The theatre's closed down. Can't meet the rent.'

'No surprise,' I said. 'Given the dreary piffle they insist on presenting.'

'Well, my child,' she said, lighting a Capstan Red off the one just sucked to the filter, 'there's the rub. A condition of the lease is that the theatre be used for plays. Spoken word only.'

'In your favourite colours, Mother. Chartreuse and navy,' one promised. Olive ponied up for the lease and to have this old playbox repainted. One kept from her a third shade one had in mind. Salmon, as in pink. Furniture to lux up the foyer came from Rylands. Most of this, lifted from Hoyts cinemas by Olive when FT sold them to Fox. One recalls Efftee actors press-ganged as removalists. Fucking ogress.

As names go, 'Middle Park Rep' as inviting as typhus. In the cold quiet of late night, waiting for the muse to strike, one sketched a stage mask. Half comedy, t'other tragedy. Hmm. Needed more. *Ah*. Two arrows embedded in the head at 45 degrees, forming an X. The mouth now half-smile, half-frown. An agonised twist, as at the instant of unforeseen, sudden death.

'The Arrow Theatre,' came one's whisper. Words crimson on black.

'*Salome* to open,' I told the *Argus*. 'Fruit and veg dyed red for guts. Red cordial syrup for blood. Costumes, brief and transparent as we can get away with.'

Wilde's play features a bloody suicide. A beheading. A murder by crushing with soldiers' shields. And Salome's seven-veil striptease. 'Something for everyone, baby.'

'One swears Olive's hair is a wig,' one sighed to Dreamboat. Lights out at the Arrow, post-midnight. We two bare bodkins, midst paint pots, tarpaulins, ladders. 'Nailed down. To constrain the *snakes* sprouting from her *skull*.'

One wanted to pay one's actors, to attract the best radio drama people and stage luvvies. To reap good box office, and a loyal company, staunch in lean times. But this Boadicea Of Toorak would not hear of it.

'Amateurs are free, Frankie. Keep it that way.'

She raised her hand, *be off with you*, one's audience at an end. Fucking *she-wolf*. FT had suffered a reputation as *a hard man with a quid*. One had no desire to acquire the same.

So one got around it, as far as one could, by skimming the box office take. As well as this, Olive never quibbled one's stated cost of sets, wardrobe, newspaper, radio and glass cinema slide ads and whatnot. Reached with flab-imprisoned forearm for her chequebook. Brash displays of wealth that would be reported in the social pages, you see. One embezzled by inflating the quotes one reported to her. Passed on the booty reaped to one's players. *It's showbiz, Frankie. This is how the bloody dance goes.* You said it, lady.

To massage Olive's ego, to Zara Holt's frock shop Maggs, in Toorak Village. Harold Holt's newest wife. Olive's favoured couturier. Ordered a surprise creation for *Salome*'s first night. Chartreuse and deep blue, to match the new décor.

'She's the same size as you, Zara. Circus tent.'

At rehearsals, Reeny wove from us mighty turns. Ron Field did marvels with sets and lighting, with assist from Dreamboat. One cast one's *inamorato* in a big part, to sway him from thoughts of England. And proposed a private celebration of his Arrow Theatre stage debut.

That Sunday, Rylands empty. Staff's day off. Olive out doing her Lady Bountiful bit all day. We popped some bubbly; then, on the goatskin rugs in the reception room...

'*Frankie!*'

Olive loomed over us. Returned early. What could one say?

'I'm afraid we've completely run out of champagne.'

One felt no concern. The silly flapdragon must have known since one was ten. That said, she now knew what Dreamboat looked like. *All* of him. And she'd be there, front row, for *Salome*'s first night.

'So you're blacked up, enturbaned, false beard. She'll never jerry it's you.'

This, the smaller part of The Nubian. Dreamboat sooked at his demotion, but one had no choice. At least Olive would never tell a soul of what she'd seen. She knew that if she did, some fucker would tip off the police, I told him.

'So fret not,' I said. 'And you keep *your* mouth shut too.' I adjusted his turban. 'Unless in private and as directed.'

'It's six inches too short!'

'Speak for yourself, darling,' I said to stage manager Ron Field. The Arrow opened on 23rd November 1951. Afternoon of first night, the stage curtain back from the dry cleaner's shrunk thus. Joanie and mother Edith supervising, panicked alterations, but we got there.

'Frankie! What's this?'

The foyer jammed, noisome. Olive made her entrance, in her décor-matching dress and opera gloves. Then saw the pink paint, glaring against sombre blue and green.

'Oh, that. The painters said we could have it at no extra cost. Talked me into it.'

Lola arrived, beaming. *Hello, Frankie!* The Creightmores in town too, visiting from England. And the cream, soured and curdled, of what passes for Melbourne society. Every first night at the Arrow had to be a charity turn, you see, this a further condition of Olive's largesse.

One had asked some young modern Australian painters, French, Boyd, and associates, to hang some works in the foyer, to tissy it up. Didn't sell one to the pinchfist society dorks. So one bought the lot, cheap as rough riesling. Soared in value over the years. Came in handy when one found oneself hard up. For rough riesling.

Just before curtain up, announcer Ron Field told the customers that they were about to witness *vice at its lowest and sin at its worst.*

'Oooh! This'll be good!' from front row centre. One prayed to Herod's gods, take her, now. A showstopper. *Is there a gravedigger in the house?*

From June Brunell, our Salome, Reeny Mitchell wrought a jezebel sorceress. And with lighting and gauze, June fooled 'em all into believing she stripped naked in the course of the dance. Encouraged in her daring by husband Helmut Newton, later celebrated and reviled globewide for his photos of mostly models, mostly nude. As Herod, one prevailed thanks also to our Miss Mitch. *More depravity, my child,* her daily rasping decree from the stalls at rehearsals, between fellatial drags on her Capstan Reds. And Dreamboat's Nubian left Olive none the wiser. At lineup, ten curtain calls, Reeny beaming.

Olive embarrassing, as ever. Still, her dough, so one paid her gushmost tribute at the after-show party. Dreamboat had to clean off and bolt, by the stage door, to avoid Olive. No party for him. He took it hard. Began to avoid me.

Stupendous notices from the *Argus* and the *Age* for our *Salome*. But bookings soon dwindled. Then, in the *Argus*, a letter to the editor from a 'Rod Cockburn' of Templestowe:

I am appalled at Salome at the Arrow Theatre. Obscene, this lustful play.

It pulled fresh crowds for a week. FT surely at one's shoulder when one wrote it.

Like every bloody thing else, the Arrow was closed on the Seventh Day. So, then. One decreed a Sunday night jazz club there. Booked Frank Traynor's band, who used to play at Athol's Abbey, corner St Kilda Road and Park Street, under the Domain Hotel there. Take you back, pixie? McBeath spun the discs. Lester Young, Thelonious Monk, Miles Davis. It was a jamboree for outcasts. Roll neck sweaters, berets, coloured socks. Hoisted from the girls' department at Myers, mine were rainbow, decades before the gay priders were onto it. An underage drinker who wore his bangs tucked up under a fedora to hide them from *poofter* bashers was a regular. Barry Humphries was yet to become Edna, Les and Sandy.

Dippy Zara Holt did a lot of the Arrow's costumes. Her hub Harold paid for it all.

'Oh, it keeps her busy while he's in Canberra doing whatever it is he does there,' said Olive. Indeed. Or *whomever*.

'It's not called the bush capital for nothing, sugarplum,' I said to Flowergirl, retelling Lola's tales of priapic Harold. 'His passion for *spearfishing* thus explained.'

'Renal problems,' said the whitecoat. 'She takes headache powders all the time. Bex, Vincents. Full of phenacetin. It's an opiate.'

Olive collapsed with acute lower back pain. Hospitalised. So one took instead Flowergirl for the premiere of Garnet Carroll's production of Shaw's *St Joan* at the Prinny, he now manager there. Well, owner. Thanks to scatty Olive, one came to find in time that we no longer held a controlling interest. Only the initials *FT* above the stage mine, a sniggering reminder for all my days.

'Frank Thring,' said Garnet, 'have you met John Sumner?'

This pale slim jim before me had been freighted in from Britain to rebirth the near-dead Union Theatre for the Uni of Melbourne. Best stage manager in England, it was said. Had worked with the Oliviers, among others.

'Oh yes, you're the Arrow man,' said this Sumner. 'Must get to a show there.'

'A pricey venture, running a playbox,' I said, fishing. *What was this fucker up to?*

'Oh, I plan to go professional,' he said. Oh, *fuck*. Pay actors. He'd *steal* them all from *me*. The Union thrice the size of the Arrow, and a prime location in the city. One was done for. I set to scheming.

'In Jonson's *Volpone*, the Sly Fox is a psychopath. Amasses gold by ruthless means. Fucks all the gals he can. I've based him on Harold Holt,' I told Joanie. Robin Casper Lovejoy, a Sydney boy borrowed from the National Theatre Ballet, directed us. And did the set design. He and I up late at night, painting the fucker. Alone, just we two, and, well... Dreamboat still sulking, not returning one's calls. *Any port in a storm, baby.*

The House Of Bernarda Alba followed the sparse crowds for *Volpone*. Robin directed an all female cast. No fucker came, so next, *The Man Who Came To Dinner*, also directed by Robin. We needed a crowd puller, and one knew the Sherry Whiteside part. Oh, and we stopped *meeting for sandwiches*. Fairies had begun to twitter.

Robin missed the first night of *Man*. Off to London and pastures greener, that very day. One held off weeping till he sailed out of Station Pier.

Man played well. Too bad so few saw it. Loveday Hills as Grace Blair wore a gown made by Edith. Cost a week's takings. The costumes and sets left nothing to be desired, sayeth the *Age* crit. I fucking *hope* not.

Via one's spies among Melbourne luvvies, news that Sumner had problems too. The Uni would only let him have their Union Theatre when they weren't using it, not year round. And *he* was getting cold feet, was the mail. Hmmmm....

He parked his aged Citroen outside the flats next door to Rylands. What the fuck was this Sumner up to? Got out of his car and went inside. Fuck me. He was my new neighbour! It happened to be his birthday, one of one's operatives at the Union had informed me. One took along a Yard Of Chocolates from Hillier's so the fucker would have to invite me in.

'The Arrow's too small. I need a big ship, boy. To pay people, you see.'

No fucking about. One offered him a paid job, running the Arrow. It would be a death blow to the Union. But the bastard didn't want to play.

'You need big box office to keep afloat and chart a course.' He was ex-British Navy. 'Or you're sunk.'

'A big ship, you say, John.' I stood up to go. 'You mean like the Titanic?'

'Oh, Frank. Some good news.'

Sumner was out in the street, bent over his broken-down Citroen. 'The Uni people relaxed their caveat.'

What?

'Yes. The theatre can now be used year round, for plays.'

Think fast, Frank. Olive out at bridge with a fester of crones, so I asked him in.

'How about this? I close the Arrow. We come over to you. My people and my dosh. A merger.'

Conditional on one's role as actor-producer, but he needn't know that- yet.

'Well, I might have to. You see, the Uni's not sure they can fund me now, boy.'

Oh. It was out of me before I could stop it.

'Look, you have the theatre, John. I'll get the money.'

'Why *not?*'

'Oh, Frankie. Why should this dreadful Englishman come and take all you've built up?'

'But when he suggested it, mother, I thought, well, the Arrow's a money pit, so his proposal is a perfect solutio...'

Yes, I know. Whatever it takes, eh?

'How *dare* he. Well, I'll fix *his* cheese. Not a penny. You'll thank me for this one day, young man.'

'It's bloody Olive, John. Said yes, then changed her mind. Can you believe it?'

'This is not good, Frank. I told the Uni people that we had a backer....'

We did not speak for three years.

For *Murder Without Crime*, the Arrow players did their best. One wonders how they might have gone with an audience. One was spared being cast. You see, Doris Fitton from *Rusty Bugles* was in a turn at the Prinny called *Black Chiffon* and offered one a part. Still, this had its own trials.

'You there,' a voice from the stalls. 'That won't do at all.'

Garnet's frightful wife, an ex-actress we called Pretty Kitty. Swaddled in minks, sat there day after day, kibitzing rehearsals. Had a red setter called Prince. Fed the mutt presentation boxes of James' chocolates as she harped on at us. 'People pay good money to see this.' Then one day; 'I used to be on the stage, you know.'

'Oh,' I said. 'Did anyone *notice?*'

'Mr Thring is Australia's one hope of an actor-manager like Orson Welles and Olivier,' wrote Doherty's in the *Argus*. Part of his stellar review of *Chiffon*. Forever one's champion, but the show flopped anyway. Then Dreamboat fetched up at the Prinny. Building sets for another turn here. One humbled oneself and begged audience.

'England?'

'This time for sure,' he said as one set down our drinks.

'What the fuck will you do there?'

'What I do here. And get some parts. I may not be much chop at it, Frank, but I'll never find out here.' He took a gulp of beer. 'And you know what, you're not so good at it yourself.'

He rose and walked out. After flinging the rest in my face. *Ah*. He must have heard about Robin. And others.

After *Man Who Came*, the Arrow staged another Kaufman and Hart, *You Can't Take It With You*. One did a walk-on in Act III. Just one line, pixie. '*Shaddap!*' After three nights, the cast was playing to seats.

MORONS!

Page One headline with photo, the *Argus*. Verbatim from one's speech, a dissertation on Melbourne's non-theatregoers, at a Meet Your Writers gabfest Reeny ran for local playwrights, all three of them. One's jeremiad of frustrations came from deep within one's heart. And deeper still from Olive's trove of Muscatel Sherry.

CHAPTER NINE

One cannot comprehend the allure of these portable phones. Big black brick thingamebobs. People babbling as if to themselves. And children twiddle their thumbs on hand-held little blue boxes called, ahem, Game Boys. The 'game' one saw at one's local Woolies over the shoulder of one brat consists of directing Batman and Robin to fight villains. The End. One wonders if they could fashion a model where one could compel them to do something else. Catwoman, The Joker, and the Riddler joining in the romp, unclad but for masks. Of course, one would need to operate it one-handed...

*

Come October 1952, the Arrow ran Wilde's *The Importance Of Being Earnest* midst bad tidings from Sumner's camp. He would be bankrolled by the Uni after all. In quest for regular wages, half the Arrow company defected. One lost heart. Quit one's part in *Earnest* as Algernon. Freddy Farley, already directing the thing, took on the part. Then Barry Gordon, playing butlers Merriman and Lane, fell ill. One had to jump in at five minutes to first night.

The Arrow's *Earnest* was not a smash. Usual reason. Customers simply wouldn't make the trip to Middle Park. Worse, Doherty in the *Argus* chided my butlers' winks and giggles to the customers. Who did I think I was, Harpo Marx? Well, one had no idea at that moment, in fact. Among Olive's effects from her most recent hospital stay, a bottle of Percodan. A painkiller. Compound of aspirin and oxycodene. Gordon's Dry Gin to sluice 'em down. Waste not, want not, baby.

For our 1952 Christmas turn, desperate for cash flow, we bunged on *Murder In The Red Barn*, a nineteenth century melodrama. My man, the villain, Corder. Top hat, cape, twirlable moustache. Surefire crowd pleaser, and a crowd, well, crowdette, did we command. They booed, hissed. Pelted one with peanuts provided in the Arrow foyer. One threw them back, too. They all seemed to hit Olive, in the front row.

We rehearsed Coward's *Present Laughter* by day. Did *Red Barn* at night. *Back to back* is what luvvies call this pitiless regime. Olive grew crook again too. Joanie was grand, doing what one just couldn't. Talking to her, sitting at her bedside. That's the kind of gal she was. Still is. So missed.

For first night of *Present,* Olive's charity do, she was here, if shaky on her pins. Joanie and I more or less held her up. She fucking insisted, as she'd invited the Victorian stunt doubles for the Royals, Governor Sir Dallas Brooks, and Lady Brooks. Well, it got our pix in the papers, but as usual, Olive snaffled all that night's box office for her charity thus blessed...

'They jack all the seats one could sell to pay you lot, Puddles,' one's lament to co-star Sheila Florance. Melbourne's luvvies often repaired apres-show to Sheila's. At her insistence, to her weatherboard slum near St Kilda Junction, off Punt Road. Open house, down and out actors cracking hardy midst the squalor. At one of these revels, a dreadful *faux pas*. One called Sheila's little son 'Blossom,' he having been awakened by the clangour of thespian shindig; laughter as of gibbons, songs belted out lusty. Arguments, stormouts. One meant no harm nor untoward intentions. Perish the thought. But Puddles was livid and let me have it.

One's shame next day, burdensome. The family not well off, so one slipped Sheila an envelope. Told her to keep it *schtum*. Then more over the years. A wonderful hostess. All the Seppelts Solero Sherry and Yalumba Four Crown Port in flagons one could keep down, and supper for all from steaming tureens. Oxtail soup or other slop du offal the complexion of mangrove swamps.

'I say place her in care, Joanie. She can get professional medical...'
We'd been drinking. Unwise.

'Throw your mother out of her home. Don't even *think* about it, Frank.'

'Well, you can get the fuck out *too* then!'

Well, then. To some flop in Hawthorn did Flowergirl flee. Bunked up with fucking *actors*. A new black hole in one's mind. Widening to chasm.

In February 1953, big news. The Stratford company- the *real* Stratford- were to tour here in June with *Othello*, starring Tony Quayle and Leo McKern. Peter Finch, whom one did not yet want to murder- more later on that- was also in it. Prompted a brainwave.

'Come April,' one announced to the loyal remnant of the Arrow company, 'Our *Othello!* We invite Melbourne to see ours first, then compare the two. Start a *feud* with these Stratford fuckers in the papers. *Voila,* a news story and we prosper full well.'

Ernest took ill. Didn't see out the month. One wept all day. Our housekeeper Margaret, now widowed. With us since the 1920s. No question of dismissing her, one insisted to Olive, now back in hospital. Too weak to speak, she raised a hand, all the assent she could manage.

One wasn't in the Arrow's *Ring Around The Moon*. Did the first night foyer meet and greet solo. They all asked about Olive. Fret not, was my advice. Didn't add that *I certainly didn't*.

'Frank!' She saw the flowers. 'W-what are these in aid of...'

'Oh! Flowergirl!'

Here we be, then. On the same tram. 'For Olive,' I said, offering the roses for a noseful. 'She's in Heidelberg.' *Oh my heavens,* said her face. 'Oh, she's alright,' I lied. Our conversation was cordial. In a bleak and frozen kind of way.

To play the Moor in *Othello*, not overmuch tasking. One knew the part from having endured McMaster do it for a fortnight of eight shows a week. Olive not about, so one pilfered from the box office to pay the cast one wanted, to poach them back from Sumner. And one had grown adept at forging her signature on cheques.

Never knew it would belt me as hard as it did. On Sunday March 21, a wet, moonless night, it was. Her only applause, a rustle of leaves whipped up by the wind outside the ward window.

Olive's funeral meant a visit to FT's grave at Burwood. Hers the neighbouring plot, you see. Chose not to tell Joan about it. Didn't want her upset. Tom and Harold Holt turned up. Lola. All those ghastly Toorakniks. The Efftee crowd the only ones it was good to see. At the wake at Rylands, one craved oblivion. Drank one's way there.

The old slapper had a shock for me in her will. No, not wedlock as a condition of bequest, a falsehood one's detractors have put about for years. Far worse. A cupboard barer than one had been led to believe. A fair whack of loot for Lola, charities various and surviving household staff. For self, a lump sum upfront, then endowments in two serves. Half withheld till one's thirtieth birthday. T'other, fortieth. In a dream that night, she told me FT had instructed her that I must 'keep the wheels turning on the river.' Then dismissed me. 'You can go now.'

Go where?

One could bear it no longer. Picked up the phone. For *Othello*'s first night, the last charity show Olive had teed up, a St Johns Boys Homes Hostel Appeal, one asked Joan to help one greet the foyerknobs.

'Oh, by the way,' I said. 'She's dead.'

One trod on her foot in the clinches. Bit her lip in mid-kiss, enough to draw blood. Moves one filched from Orson Welles, inflicted on his leading ladies. The *Age* called zesty Zoe Caldwell's Desdemona 'a revelation in shocked passion and horror.' So it worked. But one had to stop when Zoe threatened to quit.

It came to light that Dreamboat had not left town after all, unable to raise the funds. Well. Nothing else for it. One made *mea culpa* in a letter.

We met at The Maj pub in South Yarra. One promised him parts at the Arrow. It wasn't enough. The boy was upset that Joanie, not he, would be one's escort for Stratford's upcoming *Othello* premiere at His Maj. But it was just not done. Those society gobflappers, you see.

Dobbers, every one. The silly boy took it as getting the brush. Miffed all over again. Yes, all knew, one tried to explain. But none must see.

'Not unless you relish the prospect of prison bashings.' He hung up on me.

Well, the Stratford mob rolled into Melbourne. Blew our *Othello* out of Earth's orbit. Quayle's Moor slayed mine. Leo McKern's our Iago too. Keithy Michell, a dishy lad from Port Pirie in South Oz, was Ludovico. Peter Finch, Pommy migrant panel-beaten by publicists into knockabout Aussie, a passable Roderigo. Yes, pixie. All these Antipodeans at Stratford. Surely then my destiny also.

One threw a supper at Rylands for Quayle's mob. He hadn't forgotten one's audition for him back in '48. But one's joy diluted by other matters. Dreamboat's nose out of joint that he'd not been asked to this soiree. Joanie our hostess, the only socially acceptable option. Such were the times.

'Ah, digger,' said Quayle. 'I hear you played the Moor yourself a few months back. What Shakespeare have you?'

He was sizing me up for Stratford. One told him all the parts one knew. And rather more that one didn't. But one's mendacity would pay off handsome.

Morris West was a bad actor turned writer. To survive, produced cheap radio plays in a fetid studio in Smith Street in Collingwood.

'Job's for 3DB. Serial. Arthur Upfield book. *Man Of Two Tribes.* Know it?'

'Yes,' I lied.

'You're sure? Not everyone would want to play a...'

'I'm not everyone, baby.'

'Righto, then, I'll ink you in for Bonaparte...'

'Who?'

'Your character. You said you knew...'

'Oh yes, of course. Bonaparte. I'll re-read it.'

'You are quite mad. Should I black up? Like Al fucking Jolson? *Mammy!* This is fucking absurd!'

It was Bonaparte alright. But this Boney was a detective. An Australian. A *real* Australian, of Aboriginal heritage.

'Look, Thring, you don't want it, I'll call Noel Ferrier. I mean, what's the diff...'

'Is the job cash?'

Freddy Farley, a fine director and staunch Arrow man, had asked to stage a play of which he was most fond. Then Hoyts bunged on a return season of the Hitchcock movie, right in the midst of our ad blitz for *Rope*, for the duration of our run. Yes. That same Hoyts which one's old man had sold to Fox.

'Frankie! That lonely playbox of yours. I'd like to run this new outing off-Broadway, see how it goes...'

So it was Kenn Brodziak's *The Square Ring* for the Arrow. Yes, pixie. One now reduced to strumpet, renting out one's precious by the hour. One made it look for all the world like one was the producer, which of course one wasn't, to save face. Took a walk-on part, to gild this deceit. A thug called Watty. Ralph Peterson, who played Keghead to my Sgt Brooks in *Rusty Bugles* wrote *Ring*, also now a film, being shot at Ealing Studios in Britain.

Well, no fucker came. But at Brodsky's Prinny season of *Ring* that followed the Arrow run, every show was packed to the plaster angels. Location, you see. Meantime, we rehearsed *The Green Bay Tree* by Mordant Shairp, a subtle take on queers. Ran it the next month. It, er, stiffed. A relief in a way. You see, a thought inescapable had welled in one's mind and this latest fizzer left one with no choice.

'You might have told us, Frank,' they whined over beers at the London.

'I did. Don't you read the papers?'

It was all Melbourne's fault, one had declared in one's press release proclaiming the end of the Arrow.

'So what now?'

'Well, I'm off to England. Come along. If you *dare*.'

One used an address to the Plays and Playgoers Association to announce one's plan to start a Thring Theatre Company in London's West End. The details, one told the press, must remain confidential for now. One didn't add that as yet, there were none.

And in fact the Arrow's throat one spared, uncut. After all, one had paid rent on the place up to the end of the lease, so heeded the pleas of one's chums that they keep it afloat for as long as they could hold out.

'Well, the King of Thebes fucks his mother,' I said to her. 'Not his *grand*mother.' But she wouldn't be denied. This, one's last turn at the Arrow, *Oedipus Rex*. Sheila Florance as one's Jocasta, at her insistence.

One called Dreamboat, too. Offered him the part of Creon, but he made it known plain and curt that he was off to London, 'for certain this time', he said. *Not with you, Frank*, said his eyes, hard and dry. It was our last meeting. He didn't ask for the necessary, but one gave it him anyway. He fares well, one has heard. He sent no forwarding address.

One had fun as Oedipus. Murdering one's old man. Fucking one's mother. Taking up one of Joanie's outsize hat pins to gouge one's own eyes out. At run's end, one waited till dear Puddles, Freddy Farley, Ron Field, Frank Gaitliff, Flowergirl and all the rest had left the after-show party at Rylands. Then fell to sobs and shudders by surly light of dawn.

'Well, you see, he and his wife murdered his customers and she baked them in pies they sold,' one explained to Flowergirl, ignorant of this tale. We two greeted first nighters to *Sweeney Todd,* by the new Arrow Associates company, this one's last duty as skipper before leaving the ship. Gerts in the foyer dolled up in Victorian costume dished out peanuts for throwing, fruit pies for eating. One had suggested meat pies in seas of tomato sauce but Frank Gatliff, new Arrow boss, said no. One wangled Noel Ferrier his debut stage role for this turn. Gave Gatliff an envelope of the necessary to keep the Arrow alive, at least until it ran out. The ocean called me.

CHAPTER TEN

Prince Charles and Princess Diana have separated, it appears. What might the Windsors offer this abdicatress as fuckoff settlement? Wales, perhaps?

Daytime telly is now beyond surreal. Take these *Aerobics Oz Style* workout shows, to flog fitness merchandise bound to lose its lustre as fast as a new sex partner. Routines that can only be undertaken in candy-shaded lycra leotards, headbands and striped tights. The mugs, one presumes, spellbound. The lure, Buns of Steel. And these things called Thighmasters. *Straddle* one, they cry, for it will build strength.

'That's what they all say, baby,' I say, aloud at the TV. And this contraption the Abdomenizer looks like something you'd use to help a bull elephant dock its pizzle. Ah, the 1990s. *Next!*

*

Britain in 1954 was little changed since one's virgin foray in '47, save perhaps a new and violent youth cult. Teddy Boys. Zoot suits, drape jackets with tails, spiffy waistcoats. Tony Curtis coiffures to top it off. Oh, and cutthroat razors.

One found lodgings at Westgate Terrace in Earls Court. Others of the Arrow, companions in this venture, had already preceded one to London. Freddy Farley, Barry Gordon, and self had found our theatre, the Q in Kensington. West End stages, we'd learned, not for lease at any price. Not to our sort. *On your way, digger.* The Q, however, was skint. One's first offer was offer enough.

One had talked our director Freddy into also being our producer. A regular cash stipend, still warm from one's pocket, sealed it. Most welcome to a thesp with holes in shoes and belly. The best part, no more twenty-three hour days for I. And lo, Mr Frederick Farley's Season Of Australian Plays was born. And for our season opener, to pull the ghouls and perverts of London, the choice too, too obvious.

One found one's Salome in Agnes Bernelle, a singer at the Coleherne Hotel in Old Brompton road, this pub a hub for lads and lasses of the persuasion. She sang Brecht-Weill numbers, *Mack The Knife, Alabama Song* and had sass to burn. She'd scored a few parts in films, but it had dried up. And I pulled. No, not *her*. A sensational evening.

'Oh, Frank,' said Vivian Burnett, my Herodias. 'Leave some for the rest of us, eh?'

My Herod's face wore more lippy, rouge and mascara than the ground floor of David Jones. Not without purpose, one explained.

'Warriors have painted their faces to intimidate their foes forever. Scares the gizzards out of the customers, baby.'

First night, full house. Well, free tickets to every Aussie expat in London and gratis Veuve Cliquot in the foyer will do that. The Q Company's Sartre play curtain-raised for *Salome* as we togged up, midst stench of stale urine in the sink as per all British theatre dressing rooms. Most avoided backstage toilets.

'Crab lice, you see.' Geilgud's caution.

Just before curtain up, one snuck a peep at the customers. Saw a parched-looking fellow hobbling on sticks toward the front row. Vivian took a squint too, and gasped.

'Oh, crumbs. That's Speedy *Hobson*. Sunday Times crit. *The Iceman* they call him. Christ Almighty, Frank. Don't tell the cast. He'll put them right off their game.'

But ours was a well-drilled company. *Salome's* first night rolled out glorious. That said, at line-up, as we bowed and smiled, *stick it in your arse,* one saw Hobson's seat, vacant, its occupier gone. *Fuck. The Iceman goeth.* We celebrated full well anyway.

Next day's crits in the London papers, well, a mixed bag. *Herod's Dinkum Do* and other Ozphobic twaddle. Result, second night house half empty. The third, well…

'*Frank?*' Farley, from enmisted sonic distance. '*Have a butcher's at this.*'

Our third night, house a quarter full, one had drunk till darkest hour. Passed out on a sofa in one's dressing room. Now late morning, it appeared. Blades of pain, as of a halberd swung, split one's skull in twain.

'*Frank Thring plays Herod,*' read Farley from the newspaper. '*I've not heard of him. Some injustice here. Actors with no talent get long runs in the West End whilst Thring is this eloquent…*'

Well, pixie. Next thing we knew, we *were* on the West End. Thanks to Hobson, twelve nights at St Martins Theatre. And one made one's TV debut, on the BBC. Did Herod's jewel speech for *Curtain Up.* Filled St Martins for the run.

The 'Show Reporter' from the *Evening Standard* also called to do a piece on me. To make oneself easy to find, I told him *I look like Cesare Borgia,* Machiavelli's model for *The Prince.*

We met at a film premiere. My idea. A foyerful of producers, crits, journos, luvvies, you see. One was a head taller than most, in red and gold weskit. Red Mongolian beard, shaped as if by Hell's barber. Holding forth loud and clear on all things *me.* Who *is that man?* It was meant to be.

Then, oblivion. The plan post-*Salome,* to run *The Green Bay Tree, The Man Who Came,* and *Othello.* But *Green Bay,* well, cast outnumbered customers on opening night. There was nothing else for it. So one folded the Freddy Farley Q season, lest one wind up living in a park. And worse, word would reach home. It was all those fucking carrion crows needed. Well. Can't have *that.* Poured a G and T and picked up the phone.

'He calls them private auditions,' said Helpmann at a party at the Dorchester, thrown by right royal queen bee Princess Margaret.

'Young Frankie here acts, dear,' said Bobby.

'Oh.' Geilgud ignored me. 'And?'

'Oh, Johnnie. From Australia, this one. Rough *diamond. Very* willing.'

'Oh! From the colonies!' Drank me in with those old shogun's eyes. 'Come with me, boy. Come, come, do.'

And come, come one did. With regal imperium did one regard him from above as he bobbed and choked.

A private dinner with Geilgud last night, I wrote to Joan. *Paved one's way into this most magic of circles.* You know them, pixie. Geilgud, Quayle, Helpmann, Leo McKern et al. We dined at Caprice, Olivelli's, The Ivy, one's shyness held under in liquor lake till it bubbled and struggled no more. One made quite an impression, or at least was told so, one can't recall, at that actors' Camelot, the Garrick Club in Covent Garden.

'We saved you from being thrown out,' sniffed Geilgud after the Tullamore Dew did one's thinking out loud one evening. Oh, *really.* This from Johnnie. One's loose-tongued indiscretions castigated by he who'd been nicked in a brasco near Soho a few years back. *Importuning for immoral purposes* was what the papers called it.

'One avoids such on the job hazards by using one's loaf, darling Johnnie,' I told him. In fact, there came into being now a quite marvellous new police-proof beat one had conceived. At Brompton Cemetery near one's home, why, you could even bring flowers.

But one must now leave Britain. Money about to be released from Olive's talons, still growing in the grave.

Frank Thring is back from Great Britain, a successful season at his own Q Theatre in London, I typed on ship's stationery. *Acclaimed in the British press and on BBC television.* Straight off the gangplank at Station Pier, one sent out this press release. One's lilies not so much gilded as stuffed and mounted.

Didn't do much good. Sumner didn't return one's calls and no longer lived next door. Squirty Gertie Johnson's National Theatre cold to one's approaches as well. Reeny had something going at the Little but a distant four months hence. Then a rider approacheth, from unexpected quarter.

'Frank, I'm off to England for a bit.'

Doherty from the *Argus*. Asked one to take on his column for a spell. *Well.* One recalled *Hamlet* and his treacherous uncle. *Come, the croaking raven doth bellow for revenge.*

'We can catch up with all our pals at once,' said Joan as we did the RSVPs. 'You could use a jolly up, misery guts.'

Flowergirl, seeing one's dolorous condition, had proposed a party at Rylands.

'But poor Margaret can't handle all this,' she said of one's catering plans and the emerging enfeeblements of one's lifelong housekeeper. Joan suggested her mother Edith, our gun Arrow seamstress, as ideal for the task. She wasn't wrong. Indeed, Edith came to be permanent at Rylands, companion to Margaret's labours.

'It's okay, Frank! *Rela...,*' said Joan. Too late. One's Moet et Chandon all over this oik's face. He'd made a move on Flowergirl, you see. Then I pushed the fucker. Smack into several other guests. Everyone quite off their chops, so a brawl broke out.

'*I've called the police!*' Edith. 'Stop this at once and get out!'

Fuckers did, too. An Amazon, this doughty heifer. Not unlike her daughter.

'Joanie! Peta and Jimsy have invited us for dinner!'

Two of one's less frightful Toorak neighbours, you see. And Joanie was delighted at one's gift.

'Oh, Frank!'

One had been to Maggs frock shop and endured Zara Holt. A new red dress for my gal. And I told Joanie I loved her. Well, I did. In my own way. *In every way one could.*

A fabulous bash at the Petajimsy's. By sunup, most comatose, draped on the furniture or gone. Just two of us upright. The other, one of Freddie's flits, a window dresser. Our eyes locked. But the din stirred Joanie, flaked on a settee. Jerked conscious now, to see one *at it* with vim at the tradesmen's entrance of this moaning Minnie from Myers.

'*Frank!* What the fuck are you doing?'

'I'll give you three guesses,' I said. Giggling. Unwise.

Made our way home, trading slaps as we went. Rylands up the hill, dressed in saucy summer sunrise. A tram came clanking down Toorak Road.

'Help! *Murder!*' She hailed its bleary commuters.

'You want a tram? Go on then!'

Not thinking, one shoved her into the road. Just as a car herbed round the corner into her path. Oh *fuck*. Grabbed, pulled her back, which tore off most of her red dress. And the car. *Police*. They braked and leapt out.

'What you think you're doing, mate?' To Joan, 'You right, love?'

'It's alright, constable,' I said. 'She's had a few. Thought you were a taxi.'

'Ain't love grand,' said the second walloper to the first.

'Look, fellows,' I sighed. 'She has a lot on her mind.' Mimed a pregnant belly with my hands, *know what I mean?* 'Er, we live just here. You boys had breakfast?'

For a progressive dinner, each of several households hosts one course. Drinks at the dessert stop, tonight this being Rylands. One guest here, *oh fuck no*. A Grammar old boy. Prefect to boot.

'Aaah, Thring,' he says.

'Oh, yes, of course.' I, good and loud. 'Didn't I suck you off down by the Yarra?'

He went bone-white. 'Oh, wait on. That's right. *You* sucked *my* cock.'

He swung and missed.

'*Hey!*' Joanie king hit the fucker, *bang*. '*Deadshit!*'

A donnybrook ensued, stags and scrags. Edith not about this time to quell the riot. One answered the pounding door to red dawn and grim police. We shooed the drunks out. Made brekky for the john hops, same as last time. Then to sea of dreams on the good ship Nembutal, one's yellow submarines. Medicos wrote scripts that came in jars as big as an actor's head. Those were the days.

CHAPTER ELEVEN

Australians forever bemedal themselves for how fair they are, while demonstrating the opposite with bestial zeal. The papers today report that Lindy Chamberlain is to be compensated for wrongful imprisonment over the loss of baby Azaria at Uluru, the real name for Ayers Rock. Jailed for life in 1982. It's taken ten fucking years.

And our First Australians wait still. One small step here, in light of this Mabo case, reported with grudging ill-will in today's broadsheets. You know, *The Age, The Australian*, those drones embalmed in their own gravitas. The High Court now recognises our first people's ties to the land. One scans the death notices for Toorakniks taken by conniptions at the news.

*

Now to battle, bloody noses and crack'd crowns, as guest theatre critic for the *Argus*. First victim, *Charley's Aunt*, late December 1954, Comedy Theatre. Scorch-earthed it, baby, alongside a caricature of self by an *Argus* artist. Joanie thought it appalling.

'Oh, Frank! You look like a demon!' *If the cap fits, baby...*

At the Prinny, for *La Vie Parisienne*, they pulled heads with topless tarts, so to speak. Partial nudity onstage permitted in those frigid times- if the semi-clad remained immobile. The star, one Jean Sablon. A crooner, huge in America then. Made the girls cry upstairs *and* downstairs. Showgals posed behind gilt frames as he sang, they made up as portraits by Old Masters, which one reported as looking more like *Old Mistresses.*

Tits out. One wrote that breasts were bared as a dire necessity; to distract from what a load of pants it all was.

There was a new café in Exhibition Street, Café Mirka, run by the effulgent Mirka Mora. A hangout for artists, actors, bohos various. Mirka threw a party for Sablon and his pencil moustache. Joan and self fetched up. And Sablon fans. Drinks were flung our way for that *Argus* review, so we bolted, but one came to know darling Mirka very well over time. And would in time make some of Australia's best and worst films ever with her son, Philippe.

'My salad days, when I was green in judgment, and *cold* in blood,' I quoted to Joanie from that very play. We now braved an am-dram *Antony And Cleopatra,* a Squirty Gertie slopout, for the National Theatre.
     'Is there a doctor in the house!' I yelled during Act I. Yes. That bad.
     'Frank!' Joanie, trying not to laugh as heads swung our way.
     'We'll have to operate!'

'Frank. The *Argus* is on the blower.'
     Joan helped me inside. Plonked water and Vincents powders in front of me.
     'Terry from the copy table. Your yarn ready for the subs, is it, mate?'
     One had been shaken awake face down on Rylands' circular driveway. Bloody Sheila Florance and her all-night wingdings. Oh, shit. My *crit.*
     'Come on, Frank,' said Joanie, loading a sheet into the Underwood. 'Just talk and I'll type.'
     'Last night Cleopatra barged up the Nile and sank,' I croaked. Then passed out.
     The paper ran it as was. Just that one line. Then, that very day, immersed in one's grogsick daze, came a PMG telegram boy.

WILL YOU JOIN OLIVIERS AND SELF IN PETER BROOK
PRODUCTION OF TITUS ANDRONICUS? YOU WILL
BE SUPERB QUAYLE

Stratford. Olivier and Vivien Leigh! But how…well, you see, Brewster Mason, the thesp cast in this part, one learned later, had injured his foot. But one's foes in Melbourne need never know the wherefores of it. A dark joy spread through me.

A word to the *Argus* news desk, a fusillade of cold drinks on me, and *presto,* pics of self, plus Larry and Viv, for a Page Three story. *THRING TO CO-STAR WITH OLIVIERS.* Under this, one's crit of the Tiv's *Coloured Rhapsody.* Dreary Brit crooner David Hughes and a row of tits. One pronounced it dead on arrival.

'They did a lot with this souffle of a play', was how one tackled JCWs' pallid *Simon And Laura* at the Prinny. Its stars, Googie Withers and hubby John McCallum, were expat Aussies both biggish in Brit cinema, revered as two-headed god on their visits down under. And had sway in Britain. *Very* useful for the likes of self. So one crafted here a triumph of diplomacy. Disembowelled the play, full deserving, but not the players. It would serve me well.

Squirty Gertie's mob now bunged on *Twelfth Night* at St Peters Hall in the city, *in the grim graveyard of the taxpayers' money,* I wrote. One phoned one's piece in this time, as suggested by the *Argus* subs, this to better meet one's deadlines. A copykid or cadet at the other end got it all down in Pitman shorthand.

'Gertie's threatening to sue!'

The *Argus* features ed on the line, an excitable duffer. Something froze in my belly. But then, 'We sold out three editions! Going to an extra! Keep it up, son!'

They'd run one's crit on Page Three. A *news* story. No higher accolade in this milieu of ink that roars. They were deluged with letters calling for one's head, on platter or stake. *Veni vidi vici,* baby.

On March 9, to the Prinny for *The Merchant Of Venice.* The Gertie Show yet again. Joan and self took our seats. Enter Gertie, hovering in the aisle.

'Mr Thring. Miss Cunliffe. Come with me, please.'

'Surely you jest, madam. It's curtain up in five minutes,' I said.

'I'm afraid I must ask you to leave. The play will not start until you do.'

'What if I pay for the seats?'

'They're taken.' I stood up.

'Excuse me, everybody! This taxpayer-funded company has refused my offer to pay for tickets and is evicting us from the theatre!'

'Some dizzy in your fizzy?' asked our waitress.

We went off and drank 'Coke specials' at Val's Café on Swanston Street, ground zero for Melbourne's post-war *demi-monde*. Couldn't stop laughing. Val, tall and fearless in tailored mens' suits cut long, hair short, allowed one to use her phone to file this yarn. Eyeing Joan and all a-tingle.

'I'm the Page One lead!'

One started up an op ed show on 3XY on the strength of all this noise, *Frank Thring Speaks*. One would read out listeners' letters on air, these sour scolds of one's merry devilry. Ridiculed the fuckers with everything I had. Great sport.

For 1950's Moomba Festival, the National chose *A Midsummer Night's Dream*. Staged it in Fitzroy Gardens, *al fresco*. And banned me. Best we could do was listen from afar, under a towering river red gum tree. Joanie patted it.

'Why not write that you climbed up and saw the show from up there?'

'I love you, Flowergirl.'

The river red gum from whence one watched the show at safe distance from Gertie Johnson's fangs and claws was sturdy of bough. To one's surprise, the audience didn't use it to lynch both the cast and director of this abomination.

Sold thousands of papers. And fringe theatre groups now began to beg, via the *Argus* letters page, for one to crit their shows. *We don't care a hang what's said,* from Caulfield Rep. Ferntree Gully Rep promised *guaranteed no throw-outs* in a Page Three yarn, headlined *THEY WANT THRING TO TEAR THEM TO PIECES.*

'The Little White Cloud That Cried...' One all but couldn't hear him sing over the screams...

One swooned at the fabulous Johnnie Ray at the Palais in St Kilda, one of FT's showpiece theatres. Unremembered now, but then, a colossal star. Sinatra meets Elvis, entwining himself around his microphone stand *like a python with rickets,* I wrote. He dropped tears, lost his shoes onstage. Teenage girls wailed. And he was of the moonling hue. As he flung himself off the stage into those young women's arms, one pondered, *if only they knew...*

All too soon, Doherty was back. And one's victims? Just to squeeze lemon on the salt one had kneaded into their welts, one now starred in *The Prisoner,* with Reeny at the Arrow. A sold-out run. Gnashing of teeth and rending of garments all over town.

'Get married, dear boy, do,' Geilgud had said. 'They like a man with a bit of fluff on his arm.'

'Joan.' I reefed out the ring. 'Will you marry me?'

'What? Are you drunk?' She laughed as she spoke.

'Will you come to England, then?'

'And do what?'

'Same as me. Set it on fire.'

So one had fluff, if not wife. To put the Brit gutter press off the scent of *shirt-lifter.* Oh, and the police.

CHAPTER TWELVE

One did *Tonight Live With Steve Vizard* last night. Seven's 1990s salute to 1950s variety. Vizard on leave. Guest host, Craig McLachlan, from the twin execrables of *Neighbours* and *Home And Away*. Amiable but inept. One bit the poor lad's head off and spat it out. Studio audience adored me. Co-guest Molly Meldrum just sat there, useless as usual.

One enjoyed rather more one's turn last year on Nine's *Midday With Ray Martin*. Prompted by the compere, one told the live, well, live-ish studio audience of Viv Leigh's mental health problems. These near-dead duffers found this funny, so I rounded on them.

'No good *giggling!* Most of *you* are halfway round the *bend!*'

Gave half of them a stroke. With any luck.

'What would you like to do now?' asked Ray of one's ambitions.

'Go *home?*' I suggested. Told him that the floor mikes reminded one of one's first husband; that I had my *own* lethal weapon, as per that new Mel Gibson film. And of one's thespian peers, this;

'Well, you see, you're either a tiger or a pussycat.'

'Which one are you?'

'Not a *pussycat*, baby.'

Front page all over Australia next day. *BIZARRE TV APPEARANCE: FRANK DOES HIS OWN THRING, VIEWER OUTRAGE.* One didn't just steal the show, pixie.

I sold it to the devil.

*

'Oh, the Hammer Horror man,' said Freddy. 'All those those vampire films, yes?'

Waiting for the *SS Arcadia* at Southampton when Joan and self docked on 3 July 1955, four weeks voyage from Melbourne, were Helpmann and Farley. Stout fellows! Gave us a lift to our temporary billet, Peter Cushing's pile.

'Yes,' I said. 'Cushing's touring down under, so I offered a swap for Rylands. One just hopes he doesn't turn into a bat at night and fly around shitting all over the place.'

Cushing's flat was in Kensington. Tres swish. Alas, no crypt nor coffin in the cellar.

'Three *big* parts,' he said. Flared his nostrils. Gave me his *Olivier eyes*, I called them.

'I've seen *bigger*, Butch,' I said.

Stratford's playbill that year, *Macbeth, All's Well, Twelfth Night* and *Titus*. One was not the only digger here. He of the three big parts Keith Michell was MacDuff, Orsino in *Twelfth* and Paroles in *All's Well*. Fetching Trader Faulkner, son of Aussie silent film star Jack, was Sebastian opposite Viv's Viola in *Twelfth*. And Kevin Miles, one knew from the Little. Good and intimidated so he knew his place in one's company. But all bowed now as Larry and Viv entered the room.

'Ah, Thring, laddie,' said Larry. 'From *Melbourne*, yes? I remember.' A knowing glance. 'Geilgud tells me good things.' *I bet he did.* 'A fine Saturninus you'll be, Wallaby.'

Viv was agush at meeting me again. And seemed to fancy Joan to the point of carnality. Vim to the brim was Viv. Well, when not sobbing behind locked doors. Took us a while to jerry why.

The Oliviers took us all to see Redgrave. *Tiger At The Gate*, at the Apollo. His co-star Diane Cilento, a bewitching banana bender from Brizzie. We'd meet again several summers on, in Roma, she ill and imprisoned by a psychotic husband.

'Orson, you big prince!' said Viv. He addressed us over his shoulder while pissing in the dressing room basin.

'Mark these days, ye of Stratford! They are the greatest of your lives!'

At the Duke of York, we saw Welles in his own *Moby Dick-Rehearsed*. One will never expunge memory of Kenneth Williams as a sailor, shouting 'He blows! He blows!' And Joan Plowright as Pip the cabin boy, on her knees, forming herself into a crucifix between Orson's legs, mouth agape.

Larry and Viv hosted us for *Moby* too, with Quayle, Michell, and a dark plump boy of twenty-seven who tittered. By name Peter Brook, director of our *Titus*. Fellow castee Alan Webb, Noel Coward's catamite for a spell, came as well.

Backstage, Orson ate with both hands. Yet tossed his chicken hunks aside to plant a kiss on Viv's mitt. 'My dear, you *still* with that bum Olivie...oh, Larry! You're here!'

One liked *Moby* so much that one's wine at supper asked Orson if it could buy the Australian rights. And Viv invited Joan and self to Sir Larry and Lady Olivier's country estate for the weekend. Well, commanded.

We met at Durham cottage, Viv and Larry's London flop. Followed their limo, plated *VL0-1*, chauffeured by the sainthood-worthy Bernard Gilman, to Notley Abbey. Larry's mediaeval key opened Gothic oak front door to suits of armour, heraldry, a Great Hall. Fireplaces blazed. Drinks served by butler. Dinner, candlelit, at midnight.

'How does Larry afford all this?' I asked Quayle. This meant as accolade.

'He doesn't.' *Oh. I see.* 'Viv's the breadwinner. He hasn't had a hit in years.' Yawned. 'And she's only free because she was fired from her last picture.'

One dared not ask.

Next evening, Viv and actrines Angela Baddeley and Max Audley took a dip in the river. Naked. Larry's mood somewhere between maudlin and punchy-drunk. Peter Finch was here, you see.

'Viv's latest paramour,' Webb told me. 'One of them, anyway. And,' he said, 'Viv has stolen Finchy from, er, *Larry*.'

Olivier left us now, to roam the grounds. 'To stroke the trees and talk to them, as usual,' said Webb. Quayle saw my face.

'Not to worry, digger,' he said. 'It gets worse.'

Cushing was due back from Australia, so Joan and I rented a flat in Albert Bridge Road in Battersea. Borrowed rings various from friends to slip on our fingers, to fake it as hub and wife, or they'd never have given us the place. Such were the times.

First day of rehearsals and *oh fuckety fuckety fuck*. At Sloane Square station, one took an express up to Stratford by mistake. *Not good, Frank.* Just past Stratford station, watching it flash by in horror, one pulled on the emergency cord. The train wailed to a halt. One not given to sprinting, *ever*, yet dashed across the fields to the Memorial Theatre. Brook did not abide latecomers. So in I went, on my toes, arms out, a *tai chi* flower move. World's biggest bearded ballerina.

'It's alright, darlings, I'm here now.' Got a huge laugh, as intended. Brook threw the stare of a thousand cuts my way, but had a bigger problem on his hands.

'*What are these trollops doing here, Larry?*'

Viv was enraged that her Notley nudist pals Maxine and Angela, *ex-Larry joyrides, the pair of 'em*, Alan Webb had told me, were cast here. She seemed just now aware of this for the first time, even though.... Oh, never mind. One learned that summer that in true madness there is no method.

Viv calmed down at the sight of comely Trader, who she insisted sit next to her for the cast meeting, to annoy Larry. Then, at our first read-through, she snarled at Larry as might a succubus from hell's red caverns.

'*So you brought your nostalgia fucks with you!*'

Brook ordered us all to our dressing rooms.

'At the double!' affirmed Quayle. 'Move!'

'Flowergirl, we shall have to buy a car.'

Brook did chip one for one's tardiness that first morning. In alto whisper, far more chilling than a parade ground blast. One had obtained one's driver's licence, *never mind how,* just prior to sailing out of

Melbourne. So one bought an Austin A40 Somerset and took to driving up to Stratford on Monday mornings, and staying there at the White Swan overnight as and when required for rehearsals. If one was called for Fridays, Joanie caught the train up for weekends.

But one was not a confident motorist. One Monday morning, in Banbury en route to Stratford, one lost one's bearings and panic took over. Took one's hands off the wheel and screamed...

Locals milled as if sedated mental patients. A bobby arrived on a bicycle. A Stratford season program, one's photo just below Larry and Viv's, impressed and mollified the copper, a film fan. Tow trucks hovered, tipped off by local shopkeeps, one supposes.

'Joan. Hello. I'm in Banbury but I'm alright. You need to start taking driving lessons right away.'

'What?'

One called from a phone box near the scene.

'I mean, what breed of simpleton builds a road with a wall at the end of it?'

'Oh. You've pranged the car.'

'That fucking wall in Banbury. I mean they should do something about it before someone gets kill...'

'It's a T junction left and right there, Frank. Why didn't you just...'

'It's costing three fortunes for the parts and repairs.'

'For the car or for you?'

No plans to return to Melbourne in a rush. So one bought the pile at Westgate Terrace where one had lodged back in '54. Joanie and I lived on the first three levels. Leased the top two flats to tenants. Living in sin we be, of commission perhaps. But most surely not of emission.

'And Larry's gone round the twist, of course.'

After rehearsals one day, Quayle took the support cast for drinks at the Black Swan, the *Dirty Duck* as Stratford locals had it. He had news. Finch and Viv were shacked up in a hotel here, the Pen And Parchment, Viv having abandoned Larry and their suite at Avoncliffe, the Georgian pile where they were lodged. And Viv had plonked a framed picture of

Finch on her dressing room table. But both Larry and Viv had form, of course. Maxine Audley, our Goth queen Tamora in *Titus* and I often fed the swans on the Avon in rehearsal breaks, to escape the Oliviers' forever wars. Here, Max told of her own fling with Olivier.

'But I'm unusual among their lovers, darling. I only ever went to bed with Larry.'

So small wonder Larry was fuming at Finch. Then at a twilight picnic thrown by Viv for the cast, Finch fetched up, at her invitation. Larry seethed and caught the look on Webb's face. Had Quayle and others grab him.

'Get his shirt and trousers off. *All of it !*'

Oh, dear. Poor pale Webby in his French silk lingerie. Larry cackled like a warlock. Bade they toss him in the Avon. The rest of us cowered. Glanced away lest Larry lock eyes. *Sploosh.*

'Is Viv all right?'

Joanie said it first. Neither Larry and Viv's *Macbeth* nor *Twelfth* shone. Larry blamed director Geilgud. But the real cause, Viv not up to it, any of it. Larry should never have forced her into this. She was *unwell* in ways psychiatric and unfathomable to us. But, as is the brutal way of these things, others paid in blood for it. For Viv's flat and brittle Viola in *Twelfth,* Stratford directors Geilgud and Glennie Shaw stuck Viv's leading man, Trader, in the frame. At the Old Thatch Tavern, Trader held court, the very picture of the Bard of Avon's *map of woe.*

'Hopeless, mate,' of Viv onstage. 'Not even *there.*'

He'd been demoted to a super, a spear-carrier, bumped from playing Bassianus, a major part in *Titus.* But in fact, said Trader, there was a secondary reason.

'You know, Geilgud told me I was very pretty when I came here. But I did nothing. And yesterday Glennie Shaw said there was a way to change his mind about this turn-up. But I'm not for turning.'

Poor boy. Career *suicide.*

Enter messenger with two heads. A stage direction for *Titus,* Shakespeare's goriest play. In one scene, my man, Roman emperor Saturninus, learns rather too late that he's scoffing a pie, its filling the flesh of his own sons. The day of the dress, madly busy, one hadn't eaten and so, quite famished, started in on the pork pies being used for this scene as props. Thus distracted, one missed Larry's cue and chomped on, despite having just been told by his Titus of the meal's contents. One heard Brook say something. Mouth full, one pretended to hear. Nodded and took another bite. Then he raised his reedy voice.

'Frank, I wouldn't go on *eating* that! It's not very *nice!*'

He lasered me a glare. As did Larry. One thought of Trader's fate. *Oh dear.*

'Five minutes,' Paddy O'Donnell, our stage manager. 'Onstage, please, Sir Laurence, Lady Olivier, Mr Thring.'

Opening night. So proud Joanie was here. One thought of Dreamboat, too. And a mite woebegone that FT was not here to see it. Olive, well, ...

Well. Twelve curtains at line-up. All teeth and smiles all round, of relief as much as triumph. *Stick it in your arse. Stick it in your arse...*

'The naysayers now brought to heel, and will make obeisance accordingly,' proclaimed Larry. At the first night party, yes, on the Avon's banks, Sir Noel Coward remembered me from 1940 in Melbourne.

'Wallaby! Your Saturninus. You took a five star cunt and made him a sixer. Commendable. Commendable.'

As good as it gets from Sir Noel, albeit he appeared to no longer crave one's pleasure carnal, what with other youthmeat to be had here. Among other stars bright and queenly, Helpmann made the scene with a retinue of three boydancers. Later on, he, not they, pranced about in a leopardskin jockstrap. And Butch Quayle called one aside for a quiet word.

'Turn down your man a notch, digger. That Larry win the day, you see. As you were.'

Oh. So one painted over one's mad emperor with pale Gainsboro grey. In the reviews, one went all but unmentioned. Just as well. Had one been lauded, well, one recalled Alan Webb hauling himself out of the river in his drenched ladies' unmentionables...

'Wallaby!'

Viv, her arm in Joanie's. 'You must marry this young beauty.' Michell, behind them, gagged on his Moet.

'And think of the press!' said Viv. We brayed feigned laughter. Thought it but a jest, a Viv whim. Not the directive we came to see that it was.

After what Geilgud and Shaw did to him, Trader started picking on Webb. Declaiming loud that life would be easier *without all these poofters about.* Very Australian threats of *I'll knock your block off* and the like.

'So why come to me about it, baby?'

Webby and self had enjoyed some swift mutual relief aboard an empty barge on the Avon. Thus he thought us friends. So, incumbent on one now to help out a mate, if one may put it that way.

'Follow me, cockie,' I said.

One had practised one's throwing skills on trees across the years. The *choonk* into the frame of Trader's dressing room mirror, the hunting knife from one's Black Bag launched from behind his back, captured his attention.

'The P-word. Drop off, Butch,' I said, deep and soft, flanked by Webb, 'if you want to keep your tongue in your head.'

'*Piss off!*'

Well, Trader was a hard nut from Sydney, after all. The 'Trader' nickname, from stealing bootleg whisky his old man used to cook up in tin bathtubs during the Depression, to swap it with schoolmates for marbles, schoolboy currency as valued as tobacco in prisons. Still, he left Webby alone after that. Er, unlike oneself.

'She never stops. So what the fuck now, Pansyboy?'

Viv had been pestering Joanie further. Then Larry yanked me into his dressing room one day.

'Do it, laddie. The press, your profile.' His face darkened. 'That's why we *all* do it. Well, that and the *other* bit of business. *Comprenenez-vous?*'

Then someone told the London *Times* that one planned to ask for Joan's hand. One suspects Larry. You see, the story was all him. Pics of he and Viv, plugging the Stratford season and tour. *But also oneself, writ large, and seen by all the world, favoured in this glorious company.*

'Frank, are we doing the right thing?'

'Well, yes, you silly tart. I love you.'

On October 15, 1955, readers of the *Times* learned from the births, deaths, marriages and such columns, of the wedding of Joan and self, on Tuesday November 22. And in the process, that we two were unwed, *yet did abide at the same address.* In that gelid time, in that nation of shopkeepers, well,.... Larry's idea, you see.

'Remember your Emperor Tiberius, Wallaby,' he said. '*Let them hate me. So long as they fear me.*'

Marriage. *Me.* Yes, I saw flashes. Yellow eyes. Monsters in the jungle, left and right. Yet slashed on.

'Make a noise about the gown,' said Viv. Joan had written home to Melbourne cutter Hall Ludlow and ordered a coffee-shaded, ruched silk number.

'It might not arrive on time!' we shrieked at the press. And sure enough, the *Daily Mail* social pages set to running daily updates as to the fucking thing's progress, making much of Joan's stories of trundling out to Heathrow each day, there to bide forlorn. She of course did no such thing. Until the day when the *Mail's* social columnist made appointment for an interview. The dress was arriving that day, we'd been informed, so one sent Joanie off in a taxi and lay in wait for one's prey. This correspondent would report that she arrived at midday as agreed, to find one having breakfast in bed.

'The full English,' I said when I answered her knock from the upstairs window.

'Sadly, not the *other* kind. Well, apart from the *sausages.*'

One threw on a black velvet robe over one's daffodil yellow pyjamas and received her in the drawing room. Gave her a scoop, baby. We'd been told that the dress would be ready for pickup the previous evening, I explained, but that it had, like so many other airmailed packages, been forced to the back of the processing queue, behind the incoming livestock.

'Animals, I mean,' I said. 'They come first, one is informed, so one supposes that Joan is still waiting for the snakes, dogs and monkeys to have their passports stamped first.'

Well, Joan made it back from Heathrow with garment and without being stomped by elephants, hippos and rhinos. Viv insisted on a sneak preview.

'I told the press the stars will be there,' she said, clapping herself. 'And told the stars that the press will be.'

And laughed like the Weird Sisters.

'Oh, Frank. I wish Olive could be here.'

'*I don't.*'

One sometimes wondered about Flowergirl. Picture Olive, a walrus a-braying in mauve shantung, in amongst *this lot.* Talk about pearls and swine. So here we were.

At the Church of the Holy Trinity, Stratford, Olivier gave the bride away. Viv, matron of honour. The Stratford company entire attended. With Helpmann, Peggy Ashcroft, Coward, Cushing. Geilgud, who spoke of one as 'the many splendoured Thring,' all the statelies of Brit film and theatre. Press in hordes. Larry nominated Trader as one's best man. *Bonza* for the task, declared Sir Laurence. A fellow *digger* and all. Trader and self hardly cobbers after recent standoff. But went without saying that neither of us dared demur.

'Well,' I said, garrulous on pre-nup tots of Belvedere,' you're even more gorgeous than the bride, dear!'

Flowergirl and I stood at the altar, on the very graves of Shakespeare, his wife Anne and daughter Susanna. But as we left the church as queen and wife, one spied a young thesp most fetching. Yes, pixie. A grand farce.

Just as hoped. At the vestry, a confetti blizzard. Pics for the newspapers, choreographed by Larry. Him kissing the bride, him dashing confetti over us, oh, and later on, Larry, sorry, *Sir* Larry as the papers called him, proposing a toast to the bride.

'You know, *Sir* Larry,' I said, all these newsdogs about, *too good to let a chance go by,* 'perhaps you could invoke the noble and traditional privilege of the lord of the manor and mount and service the bride as well.'

Half of Stratford lined the walk from the church to the reception at the Welcombe Hotel, to gawp, then milled about like the walking dead outside. The *Daily Express* ran a double page feature on this vaudeville pasquinade. And *Sir* Larry called me an 'agile wallaby' in his speech. As well he might, given later events.

'Syb!' said Larry. 'Anything going for Wallaby here?'

Among Larry's pals at the bacchanal into which the reception fast devolved, loomed here Sybil Thorndike, grande dame of Brit stage and cinema.

'Russell!' she yapped at her less famous brother, not unlike whistling for a dog. He'd just scored the part of Smee in the annual *Peter Pan* run at the Scala, he said.

'They haven't cast Hook yet, you know,' was his further intelligence.

'Well, there you have it, Thring,' said Syb. 'I'll have a word with Jack Hylton.'

Ah. *Pan's* producer, a commercial theatre czar.

'I mean, you look like you were *born* a deranged pirate child molester.'

'Oh, Frank. What have you done?'

'Well, what did you *think* I was going to do? There's nothing else for it, you see, and that's that.'

At Avoncliffe, choicest flop in Stratford, one had booked a suite for one's wedding night. A bit surprised at Joan's reaction to one's choice of a twin rather than a double. If anyone knew me, it was her. Of one's *manly duty,* he called it, Olivier had advised *just close your eyes and think of Montgomery Clift, laddie.* But one had been engulfed by dread, and believed my Joanie would understand. She didn't.

'The bugger's too old,' said Russell. 'We're about to tell him.'

The old queen who'd played Hook in *Peter Pan* since the First Ice Age was one Lionel Gadsden. The run, a season in London, then tour. Syb had put my name up, so the fix was in. One cancelled our honeymoon trip to Paris. Rehearsals, you see. In one's glee at bagging the part, one didn't notice that Joan had all but stopped speaking to me.

'Say, Frank. Funny accent. What part of England you from?'

'Longcockshire.'

John Fernald, *Pan* director, was oblivious, as Yanks are, to double entendre.

'Hmm, don't know it.'

'Frank,' said Joan *in that tone of hers,* when one bowled home from *Pan* rehearsal one evening, 'I can't do this. I think if we get an annullme...'

Then the tears came.

'No need for that', I said. 'Darling, you know who I am. You always have. I work at night. And this tour, well, it comes with the job.'

'*But what am I going to do?*'

One was tipsy, weary, irritated. And a selfish fucker, high spirits now despoiled. So it came out unfiltered.

'Well, why don't you have a fucking affair?'

The slap in the chops she dished out was a stinger. And the kick in the shins. *Oof.*

'I mean, I can't live without you, even if we are, er, incompatible in certain regards,' one gasped through wet eyes and hot pain. 'So I don't mind a bit if...'

I grasped at a second thistle. 'Have you thought about getting into the game?'

'What's *that* supposed to mean?' Her hand raised again. Well, her fist.

'You know, a job. As an agent, or manager. You've got what it takes. And we're well connected. *More* than well.'

We wept together. Even tried to conceive a child that night. You can guess how *that* went. But no beating around the bush, as it were, in regard to the work proposal. One called around. HM Tennants, Hyltons, agents and managers various. Set up appointments for Flowergirl with all these dreadful people, Binky Beaumont and such. The outcomes of both one's suggestions to save our *lavender marriage* as they called such unions back then were, well, unexpected.

CHAPTER THIRTEEN

'Well, I said yes because I'm between pictures, fella, and I didn't have to blow the producer to score this part, so here I be. What about you?'

For *Peter Pan*, Peggy Cummins in the titular part. Tiny, blonde, tough. Irish as they come. Hollywood film noir like *Gun Crazy*, Ealing comedies, she could do it all. We got on like the Great Fire of Rome. And one had the company of succulent boys various as one's pirate crew. Crusty Lionel Gadsden, he bumped as Hook, was re-cast in a tiny role, Checko, to soften the blow. Yet went for me, red in gum and claw.

'An overthrown old queen, brimful of seethe, passing comment on one's imaginary shortcomings in rehearsal, simply won't do.'

One laid out one's woes to director Fernald, but he cared not for my qualms.

'He makes a swell understudy should misfortune befall you, Frank, so...'

And the *exertion*. Leaping about. Swordplay. Swinging on ropes. One had to duel cutlass to cutlass with Peggy's Peter. She half one's height, a quarter one's bulk.

'I shall hold back, yet look as if going in hard,' I said to Peggy at rehearsal.

'So to speak.'

Pan opened on Boxing Day 1955. The audience, for one's trespasses, kiddies mostpart. They were bad enough, but the brats in our cast were products of stage mothers. Needed shaping. So, one tripped them up on entrance or exit. Elbowed them in the head when drawing sword. Or, *woops*, rammed into them a-swingin' on the ropes. Fun at first. But after a week, the *taedium vitae* relieved only by mishaps. The best of these when the Lost Boys and Wendy, twirling round above us on flying wires, became entangled. They had to drop the curtain mid-scene and unravel them all.

'Oh, come on, Butch,' I said to the stage manager, glaring up at them.

'Can't I just swing by on a rope and cut them down?'

'Well, I'm afraid we're looking at permanent damage to that ear, Mr Thring.'

One's Hook was also blown up by a prop bomb twice a day for four months. Yes. Thus did the whitecoat decree. *The things one does.*

Long nights at the theatre with nought but slugs of Courvoisier stashed in the wings for solace, one ministered to one's boredom with one's prop hook. Pulled at the back of people's tights as they went on. Stretched them as far as one could, then let 'em go, *snap!* Well, someone must pay for one's misery.

Rolled home late each night to an empty house. Joan even later, if at all. *Well.*

My idea, after all. So best not ask, that peace be upon the rubble of our wedlock. In happier news, she'd been taken on by HM Tennants, *la prima* production company and talent agent in Britain. Secretary to begin with. Learned luvvie-herding as she went. One suggested a whip and a choker chain.

We toured *Peter Pan* mid-January to April of 1956. Liverpool, Manchester, Dundee, Aberdeen, Edinburgh, and worse. By train, for fuck's sake. Our only relief from two shows daily came when Peggy's hubby Derek drove up on Friday nights. Took us out on our day off, Sunday. Balmoral Castle. Ruins of Roman forts and baths. Culloden, Hadrian's Wall. One recalls them well. The distilleries, like the Macallan, Glenlivet, others - in part.

At supper in Glasgow, one whined about always being cast as a man 2,643 years greater than one's real age. Peggy talked one into going on a diet with her.

'A lot easier if you're not doing it on your tod, fella. Skip that breakfast lard and just one glass of wine a day. Down to your fightin' weight in no time at all, at all.'

Murder, but one has slimmed down, went one's letter to Joanie. Didn't add that certain chaps were giving one a second look. Nor what resulted therefrom. And a few weeks on, one's Captain Hook breeches fell down onstage, mid-duel with Peggy.

'Behold!' I roared as I thrust my jockstrapped pelvis at her. 'I always keep a spare *sword* handy, boy!'

In Aberdeen, Peggy's hubby took us out to Glenfiddich distillery in Dufftown.

Next day, well, Gadsden had to jump in as Hook. All one heard after that was how marvellous he'd been. I mean, I did it day after day. Our little customers inert in terror, pissing in their smalls. Yet not a syllable of acclamation. Such is showbiz.

'I think you've had enough!'

Knocked his glass out of his hand. *Smashtinkle.* At one's welcome home party, some flit gone in champers told me they'd seen Joan with Finch at the White Tower, a *chi chi* London eater. And he was here!

'Frank?'

'Enough of my popskull and enough of my wife's cunt!'

'Whoa, steady on, mate...' Finch had his hands up, not his fists.

'Think of the cocks you could suck in Hollywood with no *teeth!*'

I swung. He ducked and fled. Joanie ran after him. Our guests made their excuses and left. Joan returned, weeping. One retired to one's own bedroom, unravelling.

'Why Finch, Flowergirl? Of *all* people! Not fucking Finch!'

Joanie reminded me as she packed that it had been my idea.

'I didn't say *Finch.*'

'Well, who, Frank? The milkman? Johnnie fucking Geilgud?'

'It's just that – it's just...'

Finch. A screen star, not just some johnnycock. *Everyone would find out, including the press.* 'Finch! All that fucking! Small wonder his head hasn't caved in!'

Joan took refuge with pals, from the maimed cave monster one now resembled.

'Rehearsals in June at the Vic Pal. Then the out of town tryout. Brighton in July, for seaside holidaymakers,' said director Richard Bird. Oh, fuck it. Anything to get out of that house. The play, *Doctor In The House*. Sir Lancelot Spratt my man. Hylton's had liked one's Hook, so here I be.

Graham Greene's *Brighton Rock* is called a 'novel of sin and redemption,' but at Brighton with this ghastly play, sin was all one sought. Met a lad there, a stagehand.

A revenge fuck, you see. Yet pondered naught else but how much I missed her.

'I think it's for the best, Frank.'

We opened at the Vic Pal in Westminster. Opposite Victoria Station, you know the one, on 30 July. Joanie called. She'd found a flat, she said. In Trebovir Road, at the other end of Earls Court from Westgate Terrace. Well, then. She wasn't coming back.

For *Doctor*, a young Edward Woodward was the lead. Diminished me with his flair and the alluring look of a rough trader, so the least one could do was cough or sneeze during his lines. All of them. Fucker's hated me ever since.

'Hylton's wouldn't give blood if they could charge rent for it, Frank,' said Dickie our director when one quizzed *Doctor's* lack of scene changes from hospital ward to lecture theatre to students' pub, as per the book and film. You see, we had just one set. Hence, one's man Spratt had to visit the rookie medics in their digs for every scene.

A big ask of the customers, to suspend disbelief at such absurdity. So one made him queer, to explain a professor's unlikely pop-rounds to a cluster of grotty male undergraduates. One's stylings wrought big laughs, so Dickie didn't interfere.

'You said you wanted children!'

Joan had reminded me of this not long after our wedding. Well, I had. While drunk. 'Well, I still do, even if you don't, Frank, so...'

'Well, go and get them somewhere *else!*'

This exchange now made front page in the red top tabloids of England and Australia. Well.... *Doctor* was near its end. No job beyond that. One's profile needed servicing. Just as Larry had said.

'Frank! McCallum here! How are you, old bean?'

John McCallum, this Queenslander self-rebirthed as more Brit than the Brits. Well, it was a struggle to stifle one's mirth. *I know the truth.* One had written to the McGoogallums, suggested a catch-up. Lunch, at Caprice. This pair back in London now for film parts at Pinewood and Ealing studios.

'Mayhap they could swing *you* a role or two,' I said to the mirror as I trimmed my beard the morning of our luncheon. And they knew all about one's marital tempests.

'Well, how could we not,' said dear John. 'These stories in all the papers. Who *tells* them these things?'

One said nothing to that, but wept soundless over the veal cutlet with truffle butter for one's lost Flowergirl. This no pretense. Googie bade one spend Xmas with them. Perhaps in the interests of suicide prevention.

'Joan, please don't hang up. Westgate Terrace. It's yours. Free. All of it.'

Time ploughed on to February 22, 1957. Our marriage annulled, by Joan, on grounds of non-consummation. Not strictly true, but yes, we'd not managed feature-length fuck, nor happy ending. One drink had led to another, and two wrong numbers later...

'Frank, are you alright?'

'We can swap. I'll take Trebovir Road. How soon can you move?'

She'd have an asset, you see, and income from the tenants. I still call her Christmas morning, every year since that one, 1957. Gets one through that longest of days.

One yearned for home. Not an option, however. No more inheritance ackers until May 11, 1966, one's 40th birthday. This treasure clamped in cold bank vault iron till then by wish and whim of that oom-pah band with tits, the late Olive.

'Frank, it's Joan.'

Oh. One was now ensconced in her little pad in Trebovir Road. Something must be in need of repair at Westgate Terrac...

'Sumner has brought *The Doll* here. Lawler's new play.'

This was *Summer Of The Seventeenth Doll*, all the talk in Melbourne, one had heard.

'Would you like to go? Sumner asked Larry and Viv but Larry can't. Viv asked if we'd like the tickets, so I...'

'Oh, Flowergirl. Why don't you and Vivvy go?'

They were still pals. One couldn't face Sumner. Nor Lawler. Joanie, come to that.

'Viv at any first night is far better for its prospects than Thring,' I said.

One sent Viv and Joan gift-wrapped Cristal and crimson roses. To Sumner, teetotal, a box of Guylian pralines and one's best wishes for *Doll*.

Then Joan, praise her name, organised for Sumner and self to dine together at Westgate Terrace. Reconciliation was effected. One took along something for him to have a butcher's at, too.

'*Moby Dick Rehearsed*, eh, boy?'

'They asked me to do it, but one is so busy.'

Elucidate, I said.

'Colony Room, cobber,' said McCallum. 'Tonight.'

In Dean Street, Soho. A squalid belfry. Sheltered producers, homos, directors, pill pushers, transvestites. I called it the One Stop Shop. Bile-green walls. Leopardskin stools. Bamboo screens, plastic palms. Proprietor Muriel Belcher a *Jew cunt bumper* in her own words.

'Frank, this is Don Chaffey.'

A younger *me!* Gingernut, tall, beard, weskit. His screenplay, *A Question Of Adultery*. One took them to dinner, Kettner's in Romilly Street. The part McCallum couldn't do, a Mr Stanley QC, barrister. *Right up one's dark and stormy alley*, as Bobby Helpmann used to say.

The purpose of *Adultery* was to rebirth fallen matinee idol Anthony Steel, Chaffey explained at a read-through with one's co-star Julie London, she of *Cry Me A River*. A sultry *chanteuse*, a thousand smoke-wreathed nightclubs in a single voice. Steel was late this day. An agreeable likeness to Olivier, one observed when he made the scene. Bar his bruised face and skinned knuckles, that is.

'Other fucker started it,' he said.

'And finished it, by the looks,' said Julie.

These film johnnies don't fuck about. Straight to makeup, wardrobe and shooting after one read-through. My man's cross-examination of Miss London provoked tears - for real. She thanked me afterwards. Ah, well. A step up from making poor Sheila Florance piss herself.

'You free for the summer, digger?'

Summoned by Quayle now, for Stratford's annual Euro tour. A reprise of *Titus*. One celebrated. To Brompton cemetery, where elfin chaps paid respect to those gone to the light, by gloom of night. Well, one is so busy at work, you see, constable, ...

CHAPTER FOURTEEN

'**O**h, fuck. How *could* you?'

Sumner called. He's writing a book. Coming here tonight. Dinner, cheffed by self, one proposed. Yes, pixie. One still conjures in *la cucina*. He wants to check a few facts. One needn't worry. Far too much an Englishman to say what he really thinks. Let alone confess any of his bastardry, nor his joyrides with actrines across a hundred seasons. No betrayals. No sex. Be lucky to sell three copies of the fucker.

From what one sees on the telly and out around Fitzroy in these strange and miserable Nineties, fashions have sunk to depths where lurk antediluvian sea monsters. Girls in all-denim suits. Jacket, trousers and denim *vests*, for fuck's sake. Or those bib overalls. And those *perms*, pixie. They look like electrocuted poodles. Then there's this fucking *plaid*. Jackets for women, baggy pants for men, who also favour hair five sizes too large.

'An entire generation,' one said to Roland when he called to check if one was still alive, 'pays good money to dress like Ronald fucking McDonald.'

*

'You're a long way from home, boy,' I said. 'What possessed you? You don't look like you're any good at this.'

Rehearsals. A new Aussie here, Michael Blakemore. Good looker.

'Well, I finished third year med, Mr Thring. It wasn't for me. So ...'

'Quite,' I said. 'I do hope you're more than just a pretty face, cockie.'

Got nowhere. Still, worth a try. And young Blakemore really did go places later on. Webb was still in the *Titus* cast, despite what Larry did to him.

'Viv hasn't aged well,' I said, aghast at what one beheld.

'No, cockie,' he said. 'From Helen of Troy to Sid James in drag.'

'This *bitch!*'

Viv to Larry, of Maxine, our Goth Queen Tamora. 'On tap here so you can fuck her!'

Well, some things hadn't changed.

'Get the boy *out* of here!' Peter Brook. He meant thirteen-year old Dave Barry, as Lucius, grandson to Larry's Titus. Poor kid. Maxine whisked him away, one suspected to get out of Viv range herself. That left Larry. A ziggurat of blue and gold cartons of cigarettes served Viv well. His own brand, 'Oliviers'. Lending his name to a brand of gaspers. Well, anything for money. He stood inert now as they were flung his way and bounced off his back. Quayle jerked his head at me, *get her outside*. For one was now become the company's Viv wrangler. Why, one shall never know, but the sight and sound of Thring calmed her shredded seas.

Outside the theatre, Viv swooned in one's arms.

'Oh, Peter,' she moaned. Peter? *Finch*? Oh, fuck. Should have killed that cranny hunter when I had the chance. Would have saved a mint of trouble. I looked down. Viv was asleep. Larry signalled from the street, *hurry up, Wallaby, bring her here*. So one carried her to their driver, Gilman. Thinking of Finch and slow torture in soundproof bluestone dungeon.

'Can you write, digger?' Quayle. '*Plays And Players* want someone to cover the tour. There's a quid in it for you.'

Well, why not? It was read by producers and casting agents, you see. FT smiled up from deep in Dante's circles.

Like a drunk you don't want to talk to, one's 30th came along. Viv threw a bash. New boys in our cast most desirable, but one's gargoyles within, unchained by finest French and barbiturates, rose up snarling. Such lads were of late less attainable, one had recently come to learn. Borne of this resentment, Moet-stoked ridicule did one serve them. Foolish. No birthday fuck for Frank.

'Best come along, Wallaby. You may come in handy.'

Viv dreaded planes, so Larry had one join he, she, Brook and Maxine at Heathrow. Spare seats, you see. Quayle, although a Stratford director, had elected to drive across to Paris and for the whole tour. Had a new model Aston Martin. Couldn't wait to road-test the fucker. He took along the grande dame of our cast, Rosalind Atkinson, reprising her part as Nurse, given her own terror of flying. Brandy doused one's own jitters. And washed down the Relaxa Tabs.

From Orly Airport, a taxi to meet the company's train at Paris-Gare de Lyon.

At Le Train Bleu restaurant and bar, we waited. And waited. Larry went to investigate. This major star could go anywhere and not be recognised, with just a hat or glasses. Brook and Maxine made for our hotel, at one's *sotto voce* suggestion. To pre-empt Viv going off at Max and stabbing her eyes out with a cake fork.

'Fucking Frogs!' Larry was back. The *gendarmerie* had detained our train, in rail-melting heat. Searched it on suspicion of drug smuggling. Or of being British.

At the Sarah Bernhardt Theatre, Viv's French fans swarmed.

'Scarlett O'ara!' Cameras flashed, albeit these days she looked more like Hattie Jacques. And Larry's smile as if fashioned by a funeral director. But our first shows in Paris, *mon dieu!* The acclaim at line-up, breathtaking.

'Where are you *going*?' she'd shriek at any who tried to sneak out after dessert.

Viv took all of us out every night, until 4 or 5 AM, on Stratford's tab. The expense gave the directors the horrors. Maxim's, Tout d'Argent, Cafe de Paris. Grand at first, but...you see, she suffered from manic depression. Bipolar disorder as one gathers it's called these days, just as 'problems' must now be bowdlerized as *challenges,* or 'being sacked' as *let go.*

'Larry is a good fuck, I'll grant him that. But a selfish man,' whispered Maxine as we waited for our cues in the wings one night. 'This tour is all about him. He's making Viv do it because she's the bigger name, pulls the customers. But in no condition to...'

She heard Larry coming and tailed off.

'Fred! Love how you chopped off Larry's hand.'

Kirk Douglas had joined us at supper after seeing *Titus.* And now sought one out.

'Oh, thank y...'

But that was Quayle, not me.

'I, er...'

'I'm making a picture, Fred. About the Vikings.'

You see, pixie, Quayle was blacked up onstage as Aaron the Moor. But now, cleaned off, Tony and self looked much alike. Both had faces like a fat woman's arse, so...

'I'd like to give you a part. You see, a mad king in my picture chops a hand off too.'

Should I tell him?

'I, er...'

Oh, fuck it. Go with it.

'Splendid! Er, whose hand, old chap?' Yanks love this Brit shit.

'Pal of mine. Tony Curtis.' My face told him. 'You're persuaded, then.'

A Hollywood movie. Fuc...

'OK, then. My people will be in touch. Oh, and Fred, not a word, huh? I'll have all these fine Brit actors pestering me all night!'

He chuckled as he spoke. A rusty, squeaking sound, an irritating mannerism.

'Don't worry, old man,' I said, looking over at Quayle. 'Not a chance.'

Ah, Viv's all-nighters. Naps backstage and even on it became the norm. My man had scenes where he reclines on couches. To doze off, well, irresistible. Larry, half-mad by now, giggled when this happened. Blakemore as the Roman captain was deputised as 'Frank's wake-up call' to rouse one from said snoozettes.

'Larry, you tell her. It's the entire fucking company or nothing.'

The delightful Marie Bell of Comedie Francaise had invited Larry and Viv for a Seine cruise. But Vivvy was off with the bad fairies that day, and I don't mean me, baby. So, then, to Mme Bell's dismay, forty of us boarded a craft designed for about half that number near the Eiffel Tower. Past Notre Dame, the Louvre, the Palace de Concorde we cruised. Then Viv vanished. Poor Bernie Gilman, the Oliviers' driver, was blamed.

'Where *is* she, Gilman?' demanded Larry. 'Help him out, would you, Wallaby? There's the chap.'

Well. One had noticed with concern, only part-numbed by Dom Perignon, our vessel just missing other craft and the pylons of *Pont Neuf, Pont de la Concorde* and more as it cruised along. So as suspected, Gilman and I found Viv in the wheelhouse. Nude. Piloting the boat. The skipper to her rear, hard at it. Gilman, with remarkable poise, said we'd been asked if would she come and sing for us? He'd done this before, it appeared. One wrote it up for *Plays And Players* thus:

We passed under some bridges rather precariously only to be told that our helmsman for the last ten minutes had been Vivien – steering our course as she did for the tour...

'Auditorium! Right now! Move!' Paddy Donnell.

'Eh?'

Looking like the contents of a mental hospital, all bathrobes, hairnets, faces feral in greasepaint, we filed into the stalls. Olivier swept onstage in black tie, but made up as Titus, all tan skin and silver wig. The face of a Soho strip joint king.

'Our host, M'sieur Paul-Louis Weiller, bids us be joyful. For he hath bestowed upon Lady Olivier, mark ye what follows, the Legion D'Honneur!'

We sprang up, applauded. Dared not do otherwise. Viv entered stage left, in white chiffon, looking not quite sure where she was. Richest man in France, this Weiller. Air France and Texaco. He'd lined up this bauble so he could hang out with Viv, you see. Your *Plays And Players* correspondent wrote it up like this :

...like a lovely girl receiving her prize...tears streaming down her cheeks, and ours too...

Well, they were. Our delirious giggles muffled by clapping hands. *A shiver of seals skylarking for dead fish* came to mind. Weiller asked Larry, Viv and six of us to supper. You can guess what followed. No small task to pacify Vivvy and rejig this beano for the Fifty Zombies Of Stratford, nodding off into our bouillabaisse.

For Larry's 50th, our last night in Paris, the theatre manager came on with a *gateau* at line-up. Olivier blew out the candles with defiant vigour. One kept one eye on Viv, she seething at all the cheering for Larry. The other on the cake knife.

Larry and Viv had a huge domestic in public. Our first Venetian meal at Antica Trattoria Posta Vecie, with *la bella vista* of the Grand Canal, ruined.

'Quick, before Viv sees us!'

Next day, to flee this tempest, one took the ferry to see the glass-blowers of Murano Island. They created eight wine glasses for me. *Blown by hand*, one would verify at Rylands whenever one produced them to serve drinks.

'*Get out of my light!*' Larry hissed. So as one spoke one's lines, one moved. '*Not off the fucking stage!*' through his teeth. Yes, first night at Teatro le Fenice a fiasco. Exhausted, we missed cues, forgot lines. In Act II, Larry, as Titus, in a scene with just Viv, as Lavinia, whose tongue is by now cut out, a prop bandage across her mouth.

TITUS: O here I lift this one hand up to heaven...

LAVINIA: *Unt!*

TITUS: ...and bow this feeble ruin to the earth. If any power pities wretch...

LAVINIA: *Ucking unt.*

TITUS: ...to that I call!

LAVINIA : *Unt!*

'*Dio mio!*'

Half-dead by daylight, sleep-deprived midnight to sunup, and one had run out of Bennies, Dex, Obetrol, Relaxa Tabs, even Nembutal. But hark. Brown bottles of pills had Webb in the folds of his toga.

'Crave thee nuggets or pixies, dear?'

'Both.'

One's swift and supple hand his just reward. Well, it was that or the other. And one was watching one's weight.

'Puss has her tits in a twist,' said Larry, as we waited to come on. 'I'm toning my Titus down. Too much on top of the other.'

'The other, Sir Laurence?'

'Yes, Wallaby. Three, four times a day she wants it...'

He was trying to fuck their marriage back into life, he explained. And to this end,...

'Look, could one ask a favour, baby...'

Hidden in Larry's wardrobe, one peeped through the louvre doors. He couldn't, er, perform without an audient, you see. Well. *Larry gave it his level best, as always,* one thought, as if writing this up for *Plays And Players. Then, the most curious thing.*

'Stick your finger up there,' he commanded Viv. '*Do* it!' She did it. And that did it. She uncoupled herself. Straddled his chest. Rubbed his leavings on it.

'Come on, Larry. *Dessert!*' He sighed.

'Oh, Puss. Must I?'

Viv huffed and made for the bathroom. Larry lifted his head my way. Jerked with thumb and head, *out.*

'O Wallaby, I beseech thee,' he said. 'All this tumbling with Puss. Sharpens one's appetite. Prithee?'

Viv's mother and daughter were here and had taken her for a gondola ride. Larry had begged off, pleading illness. One was taking late breakfast in the dining room. Well. One doesn't argue with one's leading man. Ever.

'Is this a dagger I see before me, Wallaby?'

'A broadsword, good my lord.'

'Behold this stale promontory,' cupping his in his hand. 'A tragedy,' he sighed, 'that such a great actor should be cursed with such a small cock.'

To this day, one has no idea who watched *us* from the wardrobe.

In Belgrade we were met by a gnome from the British Embassy, plus troupes of Yugo officials. Our hotel, *molto grande*; but the jukebox in the cafe had just two records, Harry Belafonte's *Banana Boat Song* and Bill Haley's *Mambo Rock*. The only such machine here in Marshal Tito's Yugoslavia played them night and day.

In our dressing rooms, armed goon squads, Tito's 'secret' police. The stage declared perfect vantage for an assassin's shot at the Marshal up in the royal box, and so…Roman soldiers, nobles in togas and Goth warriors shoved through Tito's *lumpen* thugs backstage, cursing, to get onstage in time for our cues.

At interval, Tito asked to meet us. He wore more suntan pancake than any of us, bottle-brown hair, blonde highlights. On a heavyset man of 65. Tailored powder blue uniform. Diamond cufflinks. Larry introduced Quayle, the latter still blacked up as Aaron The Moor. Mentioned Quayle's service with Tito's partisans. Tito was confused, staring at this man in blackface. Quayle scratched off a smidgeon, to show the pink underneath.

'Take your clothes off, Tony!' Viv. 'That'll fucking clear it up!'

We got her out of there before *she* did.

Rosalind Atkinson rode in Quayle's Aston Martin no more. One suspects his driving had aged our company dowager ten years closer to

124

her Maker. Thus was one offered a lift to Zagreb. Well, anything to slip the Viv Express. One feared only for one's new Venetian wine glasses in a car steered by this leadfoot, so carried them in one's lap.

'This is a DBR2, digger,' said Quayle as he drove. 'Like a DBR, but bigger. With a multitube.'

'Yes, I've heard,' I lied. 'You know, Butch, ...'

'Engine's a DBR4. 3.7 litre straight-6. Di Dion rear suspension...'

Dog tired, one dove into one's Black Bag for bombers and Remy. Good night, nurse...

'You alright, digger?'

Quayle, from far away. The car on a forty-five degree angle. Dust in the air. We'd been rear-ended by a truck when he braked too late and hard to avoid a cart full of hay drawn by a bullock. Quayle had words in Yugonese with farmer and truckie. Terse ones. Turned to me.

'How much cash have you, digger?' Farmer wanted compo. The truckie would give us a lift to Zagreb. For a fee.

'What about the car, Butch?' I said.

'Insurance. Be stripped by tonight. I'd say by this chap.'

One still held the box of wine glasses, intact, unbroken. A miracle.

In Zagreb, a state dinner. Eastern bloc types, faces of toads. Speeches toasting us, of which we fathomed nought. Then Viv rose and raised her glass.

'This is the most boring fucking evening of my *life!*'

We went berserk, falling about. Bellowing with laughter. The Balts, uncomprehending, followed suit, in shouted assent, *ja, ja!*

Later, Viv vanished. Last seen in a green silk number. Matching emeralds and eyes.

'Puss hasn't returned,' said Larry at breakfast. And a matinee in two hours.

'Sir.' Quayle. He all but saluted. 'We'll have to cancel and....'

He was cut off by Larry's raised hand as a car pulled up outside. Viv fell out. Dress muddy, ripped. Emeralds gone. Larry guided her to a table. Placed a tray of breakfast in front of her. She hurled it against the wall. A shard of china bounced off one's face.

The matinee went ahead. Olivier came to the 'ocean speech.' Only Viv, as tongueless Lavinia, was onstage.

'I am the sea...' Olivier.

'Silly *cunt!*'

Our Lavinia handless as well as tongueless, with bandaged stumps, but had somehow ripped away the prop bandage across her mouth.

'CUNT! CUNTY CUNT!'

Three in the morning. Gilman and self found her in Maksimir Park near our hotel, moonlit and nude. Persuaded her back to the hotel. Now come morning, she refused to board our train to Vienna.

'I can't stand it,' said Larry. He'd had the huge police chief, Otto someone, frogmarch Viv from the hotel to their car to the platform. Otto picked her up. Plonked her on the train. She king hit him, bestowing a royal purple shiner.

Europe's hottest summer in decades, but all quiet on the Orient Express...

'You can't fuck a *dead* woman, Larry!'

Maxine dashed past our compartment, in mauve silk undies a trannie would die for, one noted. Pursued by Viv, naked.

'I'll chop your *tits* off! He won't want you then!'

Viv threw chunks of bread at Max as she went, tearing them from a loaf. Young *Titus* cast member later a cyborg spy in *Alien*, Ian Holm, was just departing the brasco.

He grabbed Max. Pulled her in. Locked the door. Viv stomped starkers back to her car. Quiet. Then... *Vivien! No!* Larry. We heard a window smash, then Viv flashed by again. Clothed this time.

'Stop the train! My *makeup* case!' Larry appeared in our car. One was playing poker with Paddy Donnell.

'Get me another compartment, will you, Paddy?' We Heard Viv coming back. Larry scarpered.

'*WHERE IS HE?*' Viv loomed. Enter Thring, arms wide in welcome.

'My darling!'

One became Finch. Made a face one didn't feel. Well, that is an actor's job, after all. 'I've missed you so.'

She fell into one's cradle. One sugartalked her to sleep with words no sane person would believe.

Later, the train had to stop at a railway cutting in the mountains. A huge drop on one side. Viv disembarked without telling anyone, to take in the view. No one noticed her gone, so the train rolled on without her. Had to shunt the fucker back to pick her up when her absence was noted.

'Lady Olivier will not be joining us on stage in Vienna tonigh...'

Spontaneous applause burst from our ranks. Quayle was livid.

'*As you were!*'

The nimble Rosalind Atkinson doubled as Lavinia and as Nurse. Customers at Vienna Burgtheater somewhat miffed at Viv's no-show that night, of course. Yet this turn the best of the tour. A telling result.

To get to Poland, we had to cross Austria, Hungary and Czechoslovakia. Armed guards, barbed wire, watchtowers. Had to fill out forms at every border. Everything from date of birth to, odd for communist states, religion. At one checkpoint, Viv and I looked at each other. Those merry eyes of mischief came back for a flash, and, pens poised, we shouted as one.

'*Druid!*'

Our accom in Warsaw, The Hotel Europjski. All Old Continental gloom and grandeur. Shows went well here. Even a laugh on opening night. You see, Larry had come back on each night after curtain with a speech, in the language of that nation.

Tres bon in France. *Molto bello* in Italia. Even his Serbo-Croat passed muster. Here, well, Polish speakers heard him say not that he would like to thank them, but *I would like to fuck you all very much*. Poland's military-communist party elite laughed their ample guts out in this state of starvelings.

'We're going on a picnic!'

One heard Viv heading for our dining room, too late. No time to hide. *Oh, Christ.*

We rumbled along now, on a bus onto which we'd been ordered, to some lake outside Warsaw. One drank hard from FT's old silver hip flask. Passed it round. We were a morose company.

'Everybody! Come on! Let's have a swim!'

Olivier sat, arms wrapped around knees, like a man expecting a beating. Viv peeled it all off and swam out into the lake.

'Come on! Join me!' But then, 'Oh! It's freezing!'

Then her face crumpled. She grabbed her foot.

'Fuck! Fuck!' Claret flowed from her heel. One sprang up. Wrapped a picnic blanket round her.

'Vodka, Frank,' said Blakemore as he crouched by Viv's side, examining the cut. 'Got a clean hanky?' One did. A black silk one, redolent of cologne.

Aaarrrgghhh! from Viv as Blakemore sloshed the wound with Belvedere Pure.

'Glass,' he said. 'Needs sutures.' He called to Larry, who hadn't budged.

'Sir. She needs a doctor.'

I'll say.

Homeward bound. The Czechs searched our train from nave to chop. Then uncoupled the trucks carrying our costumes and sets! Quayle and Paddy Donnell jumped off to talk to them. Were ordered back on, at gunpoint. Paddy somehow got the gear back just in time for our London run at the Stoll.

'Rehearsal is cancelled!' Quayle.

Eh?

'Move out, five minutes!'

Then, a clanging noise. Viv, a bell in her hand. Larry trailing. Looked undead.

'We're going to save the St James!'

Luftwaffe bombs, you see. This theatre unsafe now. Chalked for demolition. Yet Viv bent on a mad bid to prevent this. She and Larry had once played there, you see.

Newsdogs circled. Viv proclaimed her cause righteous as we milled along most miserable, a forced march up Whitehall to the House Of Lords.

'Sir Laurence, Lady Olivier, we are graced.'

The Usher Of The Black Rod, through clamped teeth and rictus grin.

'We would meet with the peers of the realm, Black Rod,' said Viv.

'Off you go, everyone.' Larry to the rest of us. 'It's you they'll want to see, Puss.'

But Viv gave the Rod the slip. Made for the Stranger's Gallery. There, she tried to address the House Of Lords itself. *My Lords!* Black Rod's flunkeys whisked her out before her dress and what lay beneath came off. They'd heard the stories.

Maxine had avoided this protest. Back at the Stoll, Viv demanded to know why. Showered Max with sailor-strength abuse. Then trod on the hem of Maxine's costume as she turned away, causing it to rip.

Still and all, the run was good. The final show superb. Perhaps our euphoria that it was over. Yet we legged it to our dressing rooms after line-up that last night. Costumes off, exit stage door, *hastus maximus*.

'Wallaby! What's the rush?'

Viv stood in the doorway.

'We're going back to Notley for the greatest party of our lives!'

Oh, no, no. Then, the moodswing.

'Don't even think about running off! I'm *WATCHING YOU! All of you!*'

Every fucker was there. Coward. That poison elf Cecil Beaton. You know, the photographer, costume designer. Both of us eyeing the same boymeat, so hot hatred on sight. Syb Thorndike, Robert Morley. The freshly damed Peggy Ashcroft, Geilgud. Helpmann and his boys. McKern, Michell. Viv kept changing outfits, this for serial addresses to us from the top of the stairs. Conquests, well. One wasn't even in the race with all these cock hounds about. One reached for champagne and yellow subs....

'Please sir, time to get up.'

Face down on a rug. Slapping the top of one's hand, Hester, the Notley caretaker. The day pallid, drained, like the light had spent itself venturing too far from the sun.

At Trebovir Road, thumping on the door. *Fuck*. Threw on a robe. One's face all tusks and snout. A big drink at the Spartan Club the night before. Turned to the lad. Gestured, shoosh. *Get in the fucking wardrobe*. This a police knock if ever one were heard. Opened the door. To a telegram boy.

NEED YOU FRANCE NOW FOR VIKINGS STOP KIRK

Odd. One had been told one wasn't needed for weeks yet. Seems the Norwegian Olympic rowing team hired for the Viking longship scenes had downed oars. Wanted more money. Kirk The Hothead fired them and struck the set.

So plane, then train to Dinard in Brittany, a beach resort for Euro cafe society, or *jet set* as they came to be called. High and mighty they be. Yet cushioned on aught but hot air.

CHAPTER FIFTEEN

Out in the street, a car radio is playing *I Will Always Love You*. A Whitney Houston song. No doubt to become the *lumpenproletariat* wedding theme of choice before this year is out, for unions of bellowing louts and bawling widgies which will collapse within a single circle round the sun.

'Well, I throw the pills up as often as not; so what fucking good is medication if it...'

'The nausea is your liver, Frank, not the tablets. So is the itching, and lack of appetite. For food, at least,' says one's new GP, eyes askance at one's Liquorland bag. What to do? If one tries another of these health Hitlers, one will only hear the same. No scripts for sleepers! A world gone *mad*. And the same at all the others one has tried.

This year, 1993, marks forty years of 3RRR, one's chum Lucille Rogers told me yesterday. One was there to record some station promos. Their annual parade, one is informed, is to feature a large Thring. Atop a car, in *papier mache*, a pink Humpty Dumpty in VYI sunnies. Clad in black, collar to shoes. Escorted on both flanks by prancing youths in pink and gold togas.

'One would love to be there, baby,' I said, 'but just between us, one can't be seen in public. I mean, look at me. I'd scare your crowd off the streets.'

*

The Russians launched Sputnik 1, the first ever satellite, just as one arrived in France for *The Vikings* shoot. Our location, Fort La Latte.

Built a thousand years ago. At the Hotel San-Michel, one was to meet co-stars Kirk, Tony, Janet Leigh and Ernie Borgnine. Oh, and a saucy one called James Donald.

'M'sieur Douglas is indisposed.'

The concierge to one's enquiry. Well, it was late. And Kirk liked the ladies, Larry had said. So best not disturb. Four's a crowd.

A jingle jangle dawn. No sleep. One's nerves at prospect of meeting Tony Curtis and Janet Leigh, the hot ticket Hollywood couple. One was first to arrive at the breakfast room. It simply wouldn't do to front late.

'Ah, Thring. Been working with Larry and Viv, I hear.'

James Donald the first of the cast to join me.

'And lived to tell the tal...', I began, as Tony Curtis appeared, bushy-blackbearded. One rose to greet him.

'Get the fuck away from me!'

Oh. Behind him, Janet Leigh.

'Miss Leigh.' One bowed at the neck. 'Frank Thri...'

She ignored me. Rounded on Tony.

'So get another broad in this part,' she snarled. 'So you can fuck her!'

'Hey, think what you like, cupcake.'

'Hey, loveboids!'

Ernest Borgnine now, also bewhiskered. Turned to me, hand out. 'Ernie. How ya doin'?'

'Fred!' Kirk Douglas. Shinyfaced. Beardless. Hair a frightful butter shade of blonde. Curtis rounded on Kirk.

'You told us all to grow beards, *schuyster*. But *you* don't got one *yourself*.'

'Well,' chuckled Kirk, 'I'm the producer. I have to meet all the LA people, the money, and...'

'Ah, baloney.' Ernie. 'He just wants to look younger than everybody knows he is. Right, old man? Not so hot in a grey beard, huh?'

It was tense. I turned to Janet.

'So why haven't *you* got one?'

Here in France, one was but an extra, as my man King Aella's castle is stormed by Vikings. Kirk baby watching us, as a green mamba might a rat. The director was Richard Fleischer, but Kirk stood at his right, behind the cameras, interfering.

Don't mind admitting, pixie, that one was shy of these stars. But Janet soon warmed to me, as judies do to witty queers. Even Tony began to smile now and then.

And one was a hit with their little daughter Kelly, too, she appearing in a couple of scenes as, well, a little girl. One pulled all of one's Georgie Wallace pratfalls and faces, to her giggling delight.

And speaking of *children* on the set, Kirk was producer *and* the male lead. So always looking to save money *and* make his part bigger. He *kibitized* Tony, Ernie and self at our table reads. Most upsetting. After each run-through, Kirk jumped right in.

'Any of this we don't need?'

Asking actors which of their lines they'd like to sacrifice. Good luck with that, baby. Yielded naught but silence thick as the smoke from a burning witch.

'Well, take another *look*. Again, please, everybody.'

All of us lost lines before week's end, by decree of Kirk; and save Kirk himself. Indeed, in a two-hander scene one had with Tony, Kirk even said *he* should do it, not Tony.

'But Kirk, your man has far less to avenge on mine than Tony's,' one reasoned.

'It doesn't make a lot of sense that...' *I saw his face and stopped.*

'Frank's right, Kirk.'

Fleischer. Kirk baby backed off. But his eyes said it all. He liked not my *goyim* gall.

'Hey, Lord Fred. Walk with me. Tried this shit?'

Tony lit up. One realized he was thanking me. One's virgin joint on the sea-bashed cliffs of Brittany triggered a coughing frenzy. One stuffed one's spleen back down. Croaked one's gratitude.

'Spot on, baby.'

One was with the second unit. Today, one's mad king Aella pulled alarmed faces at imagined Viking hordes invading his castle. Meanwhile, the first unit shot the battle. Extras as archers copped a Kirk pep talk after two dull takes.

'Act like real archers or I'll get people who will!'

It worked. All too well. Curtis was hit by a blunt-tipped stage arrow. Took to bed on doctor's orders, in shock and aslosh with painkillers and sedatives, nursing a bruised, bloodshot eye.

'Kirk says he'll shoot with doubles if Tony doesn't heal up,' Janet told me at dinner. 'The *schmutz*.'

She wept, but one suspected not over this. Their marriage was finished, you see.

Janet knew of Tony's fling-a-ding-ding with Gloria DeHaven during the shoot for *So This Is Paris*. And Tony had told me how he envied his pal Sinatra, single of late and 'free to *schtup* any *shiksa* he pleases.' They would stagger on across this permafrost of dead romance, punctured by suicide bid and fluff on the side for several winters and one baby more, Jamie Lee, till neither could further endure it.

Of Tony's injury, wild rumours emerged in the press. Tony had lost an eye. Kirk had fired Tony, or would use doubles. At the evening meal, Kirk most vexed.

'I'll look like a *golem*, a body without a soul, if I ...'

Ernie Borgnine and self made for the bar. Here, in assumed names and voices, we'd called the Paris bureaux of the London and New York papers the previous night. After a puff of pot, now laughing too hard to even order drinks.

To Geiselgasteig Studios in Munich now, for interiors. Kirk had used this place before to shoot his splendid *Paths Of Glory*, Stanley Kubrick in the chair.

'Boy, did I get a deal on this place.'

Chuckling. That *annoying* quirk that all but drove one's hands to his throat. Yes, well. There was a reason our hotel, the Bayerischer Hof, was so cheap. Hit by Allied bombers, so beset now with the clamour of workmen's repairs. Scaffolding all up the side where Kirk's 'bargain' rooms were. *Our* fucking rooms. One could not possibly welcome, er, gentleman callers here. Not with prospect of stout labourers at one's windows, copping an eyeful of one, er, entertaining.

Kirk's family made landfall in Munich as we rolled in. A wondrous woman, Kirk's wife Anne. Her fluent Deutsche would come in handy. To palliate one's privacy concerns, one moved to the nearby Vierjahrzeiten Hotel on one's own coin. Had a quick word to slinky James Donald.

'Discreet and out of sight. The back stairs. There's a *service entrance*. And upstairs, baby, well, two *more* of *them*.'

Here also in Munich, a delightful surprise, one's Stratford pallie Maxine Audley. Kirk had cast Max after seeing our *Titus,* as Enid, a Northumbrian queen. Max and self a hit with everyone. Regaled 'em with tales of life with Larry and Viv. Well, some of them. Others best left unsaid.

We were graced with a visit to the set one day by another movie star, too. Just three films to his name. Hotmost in Hollywood right now.

'Mr Douglas, sir. Mr Curtis.' Miss Leigh for Janet. Called me *sir*. On a three day pass from his army base here. With a very young 'actress,' Vera something. And two imbeciles, Red and Lamar, his bodyguards. Elvis charmed us all. Well, save Curtis.

'Fuckin' hillbilly *narish*. Copped my whole schtick. *Schlmiel!*'

'Splendid. More terrifying,' one agreed. For the wolf pit scenes, Fleischer deemed filmgoers would only hear them howling, never see them. Then Kirk saw the dailies.

'No, goddamnit, we must have shots of some.'

Well, wolves could be had, said the Germans. How much did you want to spend, Herr Kirk?

'Spend?'

Kirk had his wife Anne ask some extras, in Deutsche, 'Got a dog?'

The German Shepherds that made Kirk's cattle call cut were made up as wolfesque as could be managed. Silver dust for grey lupine fur. But no-one could get the fuckers to growl or snarl. To Anne, Kirk said, ask the crew if they have cattle prods, jiggers. *Ja, ja, wir haben diese.* But all this did was make the poor mutts cry.

'I want snarling, not weeping!' yelled Kirk. At the dogs. Then a voice from among the crew. Anne translated for us.

'You want them to get mad?' said the oldest prop man at Geiselgestag. Probably knew Attila. Strips of wool soaked in methylated spirits were jammed, er, under their tails. It worked. But all you see in the film is their heads. Need I say why?

The crews at Munich, extraordinary. Huge sets knocked up in a flash. Meat halls, throne rooms, cathedrals. For one scene, one had just a single line.

'Bring me his head!'

They built the dungeon for this in a day. One marvelled to the English-speaking best boy for the key grip, of how they did it all so fast.

'Well, why not?' he said. 'They ran Auschwitz.'

The death of my man was at the hands of Tony Curtis. He squeezed my face and pushed, and one fell on mattresses just out of shot. These in lieu of the wolf pit into which it appears my man has plunged. But it didn't play well at the dailies. So next day, Fleischer had Tony thrust a flaming torch at me when I tumbled. To avoid one's beard catching afire and one's face being flame-grilled, the crew held a large, thin sheet of glass between us. The result, sensational.

Yet when one saw the final cut some summers later, they'd fucking cut it. Censors decreed it too violent. This in a movie where a hawk takes out Kirk's eye, drunken Vikings toss axes at a girl bound to a wheel with her blonde tresses nailed to it, and my deranged king lops off Tony's hand with a broadsword. You tell me.

'Scream like all the hell-bound doomed, darling.'

Speaking of that last, one suggested that Janet, also in this scene with Tony and self, do thus as one swung sword. She did. The full skullbuster. Did it again two years later in a film called *Psycho*.

'Fred,' said Kirk, on one's last day on set, 'you know the story of Spartacus? I need a Roman senator type. My next picture. Larry said to ask you. He's in it too.'

Well. *Gratius tibi*, Larry.

Back at Trebovir Road, so fatigued from *The Vikings,* one slept for most of a week. A handful of Nembutal between bouts of repose as close to dead as it gets. Put you under good and proper, these little yellow submarines. Small wonder they were nicknamed such.

A letter by airmail one day, *par avion* as per the blue sticker thereon, from Melbourne stage colleague Freddy Parslow. Seems Sumner had left the Union, for a director's job. The Elizabethan Theatre Trust in Sydney. *Hmm.* The Trust was bankrolled by taxpayer coin. One had no jobs on here Britside now. One could nip home. Wheedle out of Black Jack the ackers to stage Orson's *Moby.* One well into one's letter proposing same when...

'Frank? Sheldon Reynolds, Rediffusion. Max Audley told me about you...'

Darling Maxine! A TV job! Only a shitcom as one calls them, but a big one, baby. *Dick And The Duchess* was an *I Love Lucy* knockoff, huge at both ends of the Atlantic. My man on Ep 21, a Mr Wembler. Juror. Delaying a verdict. Enjoys too much the perks for sequestered juries. Would that one could stay the hand of the Reaper thus.

CHAPTER SIXTEEN

'**F**uck *you!* How can you be more beautiful than *me?*'
A Burmese cat the culprit, one of many Viv had. Puss was asking for me. *Of course,* I said. Larry had called. One's leading man. *Jump to.*

'When would be a good ti...?' *Now,* he said.

One arrived to Viv screeching at pussycats. All forgotten as she fell into my arms. We popped bubbly. Played charades. Viv asked me what one was up to. Did one have *anything going...*

'Well, off home for now. Producing Orson's play. Doubling as leading man and director. They insist. So yes, rather a full dance card...'

'Well,' said Larry. 'Tarry not overlong among the gum trees, Wallaby.'
A wicked smile.

'Go on, Larry. Tell him.'

'I've put you up for a film, baby.'

'*Oh.*'

What could one say...

'Thank you both so much...w-what's it called?'

'*Ben Hur.*'

On a Qantas Super Constellation rolled Thring to Oz. Three sunrises long, this trip. Brainswoggled, one checked into Sydney's swish Australia Hotel on Castlereagh Street. One's mission here, to see Sumner about *Moby.* To fashion one's white lies to the Oliviers into reality.

'Well, the day that one fucked Tony Curtis in a castle is a memory that abides.'

With such confections did one reel in radio johnnies my pals and chums of the colours Sydneyside. None of the good stuff on air, of course. Spoke of *The Vikings,* and one's upcoming roles in *Spartacus* and *Ben Hur.* Did radio bits on 2FC, the ABC station, and the commercials 2CH and 2UW.

'Well, Vivien's thing is threesomes. And mixed doubles,' I said when he asked. TCN9, Australia's first TV station, had been on the air now for three months. One called Clyde Packer, elder son of Sir Frank, Nine's monsterboss. Clyde was the producer of a daytime show, *Tuesday At One.* One also did his womens' show, *Thursday At One,* while one was about it. Clyde was an imposing fellow. A likeness to silent comedy star Roscoe 'Fatty' Arbuckle. A thought one kept to oneself.

'He says he was on the toilet, Mr Packer. Wants you to run it again right now.'

Clyde looked at me. *See what I have to put up with?*

'Tell him we'll run the race on the telly again after the show, not during,' he said to his secretary. 'And just ignore him, darling, if he tells you you're sacked.'

He lit a cigar. Offered me one. Poured brandies and shrugged. 'The old man's horse won at Warwick Farm. Kerry?'

Clyde held up the Remy Martin XO, *you in?* to his younger brother.

'You know I don't. Haven't you got any fucking Fanta?'

Kerry had trouble reading at school, it was said. Old Sir Frank assailed him, in company, as the 'family idiot' and 'boofhead.'

'Your old man was in the game, Frank,' said Clyde. 'What was he like?'

'Hard to say. Hardly ever home. And he went just after one's tenth birthday.'

'That a fact?' He pondered this for a tick. 'Half your ruddy luck.'

This TV jazz was magic. One was blitzed with calls from the paper press after one's turns on the little grey screen. Had to stage a press conference at one's hotel, in the Emerald Room. Yes, pixie. One had become an international star. And these fuckers couldn't wait to claim the credit for it.

'Thring here. I have a message here to call Mr John Goffage.'

'Yes, this is he. We should knock heads, Frank. Boil a billy, swap a few lies.'

The voice, as of a circling blowfly, familiar. 'You're as big as the Trocadero, I hear.'

'Look, sorry. Who is this? What do you want from m...'

'It's Chips Rafferty, old son. Of whom you may have heard.'

Ah. Australia's best-known and least talented film star. But why...?

'John Goffage is my real name, digger. I'd like to have a yarn. What say tomorrow? The Astra.'

Sydney people. Assume that you know where they mean, with just one meaningless reference. A weird mob indeed.

'Astra?'

'Best pub in all of Bondi, no risk. And pies as big as your head.'

'Frank, this Lee Robinson. Our director. And moderate drinker. Much to my disconsolation,' said Chips.

'Frank.' Offered his hand. Beard, like me. Linen suit.

'Where did you serve, Frank?' said Chips, eyes narrowed. Not hard to read his thoughts. Best butch up.

'The RAAF, mate. The bloody Brilliantine Boys,' I said.

'Well, whacko the diddlyo! So did we, didn't we, Lee?'

Chips sculled his beer. Snake-eyed me. *Now you.* One choked it down. Nearly gagged, but made it.

'Your Wally Grout, cobber,' said Chips. He meant shout, as in round. Wally Grout being Australia's wicketkeeper at the time. 'Come on, Robbo,' he said to Lee, urging him to upend his KB Cold Gold. 'That's three weeks old. You wouldn't let a boong drink that.'

Yes, pixie. Chips was a man of his times.

'Your script, Blue.'

At their Bondi Junction studio, on Ebley Street, once FT's rival Stuart Doyle's Cinesound film factory. Chips chucked a screenplay at me from across a set dressed with barrels, fishing nets, lanterns. Buccaneer's accoutrements.

'Your man's this fella Gar.'

One had agreed six schooners in. We'd start right away. Tomorrow.

'Piccaninny daylight,' said Chips.

Flaming Sword was a pirate yarn. Characters called Poggy, The Captain, Blind John. Chips the lead, Long Tom. The cast, a queer mix of locals, shall we say, plus the usual import for star power. Back then - still now - the only way to get films made down under. You know Terence Morgan, pixie. From the Brit TV series *Sir Francis Drake*. Laertes in Larry's film of *Hamlet*. We'd met when he came out with Larry and Viv in '48. We compared memories of the Oliviers fair and foul over monster serves of steak and chips at North Bondi RSL.

Bang! Three beers hit the table. Chips loomed.

'Sink that, you bludgers.' Winked at me. 'Let's teach this Pommy bastard how to drink, eh, Blue?'

Well, I fixed his cheese. Every time it was 'my Wally Grout', I ordered 'two schooners and a U-Boot, thanks, love.' This last, beer with invisible and tasteless shot of vodka in it. Poor Chips never did find out how a pair of theatrical types summoned up the sack to scull him under the table.

'Whaddyareckon, Robbo?'

Chips worked fast. After a take, just one, he'd clock Lee with outback killer's eyes.

'Well, I, er...' Lee was a quality control man at heart.

'Frank?'

'Well, Chips, I thin...' As was I, but...

'Too right! Print it. The mugs love this stuff. Next!'

Chips had to leave us to it for a few days. Shooting a cinema ad for British picture theatres, to entice England's cold masses to migrate to Oz. The 'ten pound Pom' scheme. Cat away, Lee did retakes and re-shot some pick-ups for stuff that Chips had waved through. But on his return, Chips bailed me up at the Rat House, Bondi Diggers.

'Now Lee is a fussy fellow, Blue. These directors, they...look, here's the ticket. Do it the same way every take. Don't change a jolly thing. They get the message soon enough. My word.'

Your Wally Grout, said his face. Watched me scull when I brought them brimming from the bar. Then the rest of the cast turned up. Wally Grouts all round. In the De Luxe cab back to one's hotel, one bade the driver pull over. Vomited a keg's worth out on to Oxford Street.

'I was in New Guinea. With the fuzzy wuzzies. And the Dutch East Indies as was. And you?'

My scenes for *Flaming Sword* done, Chips decreed we make for the Tea Gardens Hotel in Bondi Junction. Beered up and keen to talk of war, he was. And details of one's RAAF service.

'I, er, can't, Chips, mate,' I said. 'Official Secrets Act, old fellow.'

I tapped the side of my nose. Saw a glimmer of envy. He'd been in the RAAF Revues, you see. The entertainment corps.

'Been around the world since then,' he resumed, heedless. 'Done a spot of droving. I was having a grog in a bloodhouse in Darwin. Cove made me an offer. Matter of providence, I suppose.'

It was all rather like a postcard from a boring relative on holiday in some place devoid of anything.

'Been on the pearl luggers too. You'd have to be a mug to live in the big smoke, by crikey. But out under the stars, a few blokes...' I tried to respond, but...' swapping yarns. A mug of billy tea.' He stopped. 'You don't say much, do you?'

Then slapped my back, hard.

'Ah, good-o! That's why I like it out in the mulga, Frank. I go troppo down here in town. Everywhere you go, some big note merchant. Yabbering on about himself...'

One made it out of the *Flaming Sword* shoot alive. One has never seen it. With any luck, nor has anyone else.

'A suggestion. To cut costs. Cast it in Melbourne. Rehearse there. Then a run here in Sydney. Then a season back there,...'

Met with Sumner at Romano's, on the corner of Martin Place and Castlereagh. He couldn't wait to run *Moby* in Sydney for the Elizabethan, he said.

'Very well. But early days, boy. Don't go off half-cocked.'

'Fear not, John. It will hail in Hades before one is *ever* half-*cocked*.'

'Well, Bert, you know, when Larry and Viv are in your corner,...'

Back in Melbourne. On the wireless and the telly with tales of *The Vikings, Titus*, the imminent *Spartacus, Ben Hur*. Noel Ferrier had me on his Friday night show on HSV7. Gra Gra Kennedy now doing *In Melbourne Tonight* just three times a week. And behold. A new boy on my station, 3XY.

'How did you get this job?' I asked him on air. 'You're not very good at it.'

Young Bert Newton was sensational, in fact, as we would all come to see. Speaking of boys, at the Australia Hotel, one was hoisting a Barossa Pearl, admiring lads gathered about me, when I heard the barmaid's call.

'Frank Thring 'ere?' Thrust the receiver at me.

'Thring, you cunt!' came a voice from the earpiece.

'Ah, Gra Gra. How are y...'

'Don't say my name in a public bar! Especially that one!'

Alas, poor Kennedy. Everyone knew our biggest telly star was a swish. But wished they didn't.

'Well, don't call me at one! What do you want, baby?'

'Same as everyone, Podge. A hot root, a cold beer and a good lie down. I want you on my show tonight.'

'Sorry, chum. Already did Noel.'

'Yes. Lucky no bastard watches it. Come on, Podge...'

'Have you heard the boy Newton? On XY? You should get him. On your show. As a double act. If you take my meanin...' Awkward silence.

'Can't see it myself.' Ah. Scared of being upstaged, one suspected.

'Suit yourself.' I'd tortured him enough. 'What time do you want me?'

He did get Bert, of course. You know the rest.

'Get out,' I said.

To Freddie Asmussen's one had ventured for New Year's Eve, in deep blue of dusk. Now, Day One 1958, hot noon, one near death.

'But, Mr Thring.'

At one's side, this urchin pale and sticky, that one must have enticed home.

'You said I could stay here and have private acting lesso...'

Oh, Thring, you bumstruck fool...

'But you have *had* them, patch. Last night, how to do a *love* scene. And now,' I said, 'for when you need to drop a *tear*. Now be *off* with you.'

Pushed taxi money into his mitt. Steered him out the front door. Then found oneself quite overcome. Dizzy. Black patches, white dots danced before one's eyes...the floor came up and socked it to me.

'Any vertigo? Spinning sensation? Fainting?'

The blackouts, semi-regular since one had been a child. Couldn't be just the booze. One's doctor was away. His locum a woman. A scope, cold and shuffling in one's lughole.

'Hmm. Labyrinthitis, I'd say. You had mumps, chicken pox,...?'

I had.

'That's how you got this, then. Cochlear nerve damage. Sleeping problems?'

'I have medication for that.' She checked my file.

'So I see. Best give that a rest.'

Oh, no.

'And your drinking too. That's why you can't sleep.'

A clear message. Action this day. Find a new doctor. Or two.

CHAPTER SEVENTEEN

'It's for the Actors Benevolent Society.'
Reeny asked one to do *The Strange Case Of Dr Jekyll And Mr Hyde* for their 1958 fundraiser.

The first night, we used a fog machine for the first time. Too pricey to hire for rehearsals, you see. But the fog rolled into the front rows. Coughed like they'd been gassed on the Western Front. And as one's Jekyll in one's lab, we'd planned to use dry ice to induce bubbling and steaming from the prop test tubes, beakers and such. But that which had been promised, not here!

'*There's no dry ice,*' I hissed at the stage manager in prompt corner. She found it in the fridge backstage while one improvised. Handed it to me from the wings. Her end wrapped in newspaper. Mine was not. Damn near burnt my fingers off.

'Some bitch just handed me the Glacarium!' I screamed. Meaning the edifice that now housed the St Kilda ice skating rink. Prior to that, Efftee Films for one mad flash of time.

One night during the run of *Jekyll,* one was full as a fairy's phone book from pre-show settlers. The door to the set wouldn't open. So I went behind the fucker. Here a hole, for the set's fireplace. Stuck one's head through that. Did the scene from there.

Kept on even when the Mr Hyde eyebrows fell off. Then the cable came from Hollywood.

FRANK THRING REQUIRED FOR BEN HUR CAST MEETING FEB LONDON PLEASE CONFIRM SAM ZIMBALIST MGM

Darling Larry! One made the horror flight, or should one say flights, to the UK. The dreaded Kangaroo Route. Four days of it. Melbourne to Sydney to Darwin. Then Singapore for an overnight stopover. Here, there be treasure.

'Girls too. But you can always tell the boys,' Helpmann had confided over supper at the Tung Tai, Stratford's only Chinese eater. 'Far more gorgeous.'

'Have to be, cockie,' said Coward. 'To fool those British sailors.'

All outdoor bars. Tiger Balm Bar. Bamboo Lounge. Cocks in frocks, on me like mosquitoes. Chose two. Showed them what one wanted.

'Oh. You *poo'ter*', said the little one.

'You pay more.' The rather bigger one.

Calcutta to Karachi, then Cairo. Stopped the night at Shepheard's Hotel on the Nile. A tourist bus to the Giza pyramids, at city's edge. A tense time. Egypt's bolshie President Abdul Nasser wanted to merge with Syria. Create an Arab oil superpower, you see. Stick it to the Yanks. You'll recall Eisenhower's reaction, pixie. Russians backing Nasser's play, all that *fol de rol*. Now, several decades on, the Gulf again thunders and boils. The telly news tells me that one Saddam Hussein, installed by the little gnomes of Washington, has invaded Kuwait.

At the Auberge des Pyramides club, at one time second home to the dissolute King Farouk, one craved a youth. But that meant going out on the streets. Not on. I mean, one looked both British and American. So after losing at rigged blackjack, one repaired to one's suite, the thick hush of solitude at midnight. Come the dawn, unslept, the final leg. To Tripoli, then London.

They said little to me this first day, one wrote home to Sumner. *But one soon learned that this merely reflected the magnitude of their hangovers.*

MGM had premises in Charing Cross Road. In the dressing room, one froze, quite stunned. Here before me, the prevailing pantheon of British cinema. Jack Hawkins, Hugh Griffith, Finlay Currie, Terence Longdon. And George Relph, who'd toured down under with Larry and Viv back in '48.

Hawkins. How like a god in *The Cruel Sea* and *Bridge On The River Kwai*. They bantered. Of drinking games. Of aces, diamonds and hearts. Of blood sports and *if you're going to buy a fucking car, go British!* Parleyed and parried and threw on white dressing gowns. Towels round their necks, like boxers before the bout. Knew the drill. One followed them to the fitting room.

'Up on the dais, please, Mr Thring.'

I jumped up. What stars had stood here before me?

'Thring.'

Hawkins, in full Roman general's uniform, hand thrust out sideways. 'Olivier said to look out for you.' He gripped his tunic. *Look at this.*

'This fucker's too short, isn't it?'

His cigarette nodded up and down 'tween his lips as he spoke. One thought it prudent to agree. 'I knew it. I will *not* act in a fucking *cocktail* dress!'

'Give it here, Jack.'

In one's Black Bag, needle and thread. Force of habit from one's touring days. Tossed him the Courvoisier I had in there. He caught the bottle one-handed. Smiled round his Marlboro. The ice broken, nay melted.

'Fuck me, Taffy,' said Jack. 'You look like you stuck your head up someone's jaxie!'

In makeup to shoot our costume stills, Hugh Griffith, blacked up to play Shiek Ilderim. Blue eyes set in a Vegemite face.

'No, boyo. Taffy was but passing by. Was sucked up his bum, isn't it.'

Winked at me. To Jack: 'You see, boyo, you were sucking the laddie's cock so hard that ...'

Both bellowed laughter. Hugh turned to me.

'Thring, is it?' He addressed my dilly bag. 'Ah, Black Bag. We meet at last. I thirst.' He placed an Arabian kaffiyeh on his head. Gestured like a fakir at Black Bag. Clapped twice. 'Open sesame.'

It was ten in the morning. I was among friends.

'They still haven't cast the leads. No fucker wants it.'

This from Jack. We were at that steakhouse, you remember, pixie. Just off Berkeley Square. 'Brando's turned 'em down. Burt Lancaster.'

'Rock Hudson too,' said Terry Longdon.

'And all *those* boyos all after Paul Newman did,' said Hugh. One dared not voice it. Was this also the reason *we* had been cast?

'The Excelsior.' Coward's tip. 'The only hotel in Roma.'

Yes, miles from Cinecitta where we'd be shooting. But then, Cinecitta was fucking miles from all Roma's wonders. The Ex was right on the Via Veneto. Close to Doney's, for breakfast. Handy to the Colosseum, the Pantheon, Piazza Navona, Vatican City, all that jazz, for virgin sightseers like self.

'And a hop, skip and jump to Harry's Bar. For Prosecco and peach juice. Good after sex,' Larry had said.

'Or before.' Helpmann.

'Or during.' Coward.

'Welcome to you all,' said Sam Zimbalist at our cast meeting. 'I can tell you that talks are still in progress...'

'*No one's returning their calls.*' Hawkins, interpreting in one's ear, *sotto voce.*

'...but we should have some great news about our male leads very soon.'

'*Abbott and Costello are thinking it over.*'

Zimbalist a producer straight out of Central Casting. Suspicious hue of inkblack hair. Lips in pout of a purple matching the bags under eyes, and a Presidente, those cigars the size of a stick of dynamite.

'Now, the book. Willie will tell you where we're at.'

Wyler, this great director, stepped up. Tiny fellow. Face of a shah on a huge head.

'Thank you, Sam.' He held up a copy of the script. 'Well, the studio likes it.'

'*The studio loathes it,*' whispered Hawkins.

'But it needs a fresh pair of eyes.'

'*They've sacked the writers.*'
'A little polishing.'
'*It needs a total rewrite.*'
'I have an open mind on it.'
'*I haven't read it.*'

No expense spared on these sets, to make them as historically inaccurate as possible, went a new screed to Sumner. *Domes atop buildings in first century Jerusalem. Just 500 years before the dawn of Islam.*

And then there was my man Pilate, fitted out in purple togas. Too bad only Senators in ancient Rome were entitled to wear said shade, not provincial governors. But I wasn't about to tell anyone. I mean, one looked such a catch.

Yes, a ropey script. But we fell to regardless, for table reads. Wyler and Zimbalist hovered as we waded through stillborn lines; Hawkins, Longdon, Currie and self. With Italian actors standing in for our yet uncast leads Judah Ben Hur and his nemesis Massala. Then, trouble.

'Frank. A word,' said Willie. Sam at his shoulder, puffing on his Brobdignagian stogie, hands-free. *Pilate is a problem*, said Willie as we stepped outside. Sam all stony indifference, a hitman awaiting the nod.

'So, er, what can I do?' I said. Willie smiled up at me like a poison goblin.

'Improve.'

Sam slapped my back. Grinned. As if wishing one luck. At one's hanging.

'Oh, that,' said Hawkins when I told him. 'They do that to everyone. Are you playing your man as you think you should?'

In Harry's Bar we were, somewhere betwixt the sixth and the ninth drink. I nodded. 'Well, fuck all that, Thring. Just give 'em Laughton or Ustinov.'

'Nothing of one's own? But...'

'It just confuses the fuckers. By the way, heard about the leads?'

'Hi. Charlton Heston.'

Hard crush on the shake, let you know who's boss of the wash. Pulled my arm toward him with his other hand. 'Larry tells me good things, Frank.'

'W-well, thank y-you, Mr Heston,...'

'Please. Chuck.'

He swerved to Wyler. Bent forward, as if to address a midget sultan, to Wyler's one good ear.

'Willie, I have to learn to drive this damn chariot.'

Chuck, like Kirk, chuckled as he spoke through his teeth. *Why do they all do this?*

'So two hours a day on table reads, and four on the track. Oh, and Sam. The guy playing Simonides.' He chuckled. 'Lose him.'

'Heard bad things?'

'Get Sam Jaffe.'

'Sure, Chuck.'

Well, pixie. One knew now which arse to kiss first. Saved one a trove of bother.

You see, there were so *many*.

'*Gubernator!*' he boomed. At me. As in 'Governor', as in my man Pilate.

'*Auroram!*'

Good morning. In fucking *Latin*. One groped in the dim and musty cellar of long ago lessons. Ah, there it is.

'*Illo est.*'

It is. Hoped it made an impression. For one stirred hot and hard below decks, a shudder of lust when Wyler introduced our new writer, Gore Vidal.

'So,' I said, 'What's he like?'

Stephen Boyd, our second male lead, playing Massala, had made landfall in Roma.

'Golf. Loves it,' said Terry Longdon. 'As do I.' Clamped his teeth on his pipe. 'We're off to play a few holes next week.'

'Holes, eh?' Jack, lighting a Dunhill off its predecessor. 'Any minge in his life?'

'A handsome boyo,' said Taffy. 'Be knocking 'em back with his driver, isn't it?'

'I'd say his putter,' said Jack, looking pained. 'Has he got a piece of fluff?'

'Liz Mills is her name,' said Terry. 'Older woman. Rather plain.'

So, then. A *beard*. This Boyd was camp as a wigwam.

'Gubernator! Like your new lines?'

'The scorpions and holy prophets can't get on without me, there it is.'

One quoted from Pilate rewritten by Vidal, my man despondent at his posting to arid and hostile Judea. He'd bailed me up at the Cinecitta commissary, as one fetched a Samson-strength *macchiato*. Hungover, you see. Sloshed Armagnac into it from one's flask.

'Gorino!' An Italian gent, elegant pinstripes, stocky build, hailed Vidal.

'Frederico!' To me, *'Alora, Francisco Thring, mio amico, Frederico Fellini.'*

Fellini regarded me, hands out.

'Ah, bene. Tu scrittore? Attore?'

'Io Ponzio Pilato,' I said. *'Al suo servizio.'*

They both laughed. I asked Fellini about the film he was making here.

'Ah, si Signore. La Dolce Vita.'

A useful introduction. 'Fred,' as Vidal called him, lived on the Via Margutta. *Molto* hospitable. Marvellous parties there. Scored a lad for a tumble more than once. And the most glam young women one had ever seen.

'Surely fashion models. So elegant,' I said to Lex Barker, an erstwhile Tarzan in Hollywood, now cast in *Dolce*. 'One sees them all over Roma.'

'Oh, them,' said Lex. 'They're the whores.'

As for Lex and I.... *Well, what do you think, baby?*

'This damnable picture. The story's built on sand. Two inseparable boyhood friends meet again as adults. Then suddenly hate each other's guts. Won't rest for an aeon of screen time until the other is dead.'

Vidal spread his hands. *I ask you.*

'Ah,' I said. 'But it can be refashioned to make perfect sense.'

'Do tell,' he said. I signalled for more *Prosecco.* One had invited him as one's guest for dinner. A *trattoria* where he and erstwhile companions such as Tennessee Williams, *the Glorious Bird* as Vidal styled him, had once with their custom favoured.

'I shall. Well, you have these two rugged bucks, you see. Very, *very* camp.'

I had his full attention now.

'But they can no longer be lovers as was, Judah decides. After all, Massala is now a Roman commander. Judah, well, the fucker is now prince of his people. Rough and ready recreation out of the question. Massala is heartbroken. But Judah, immutable. Why, if anyone finds out that they were once...'

I pretended it was his idea. 'That's what you mean, isn't it?'

His eyes lit up.

'You just bought yourself a night on the town, pilgrim.'

'Say it ain't so, Gubernator!'

I followed Vidal down the Via Veneto.

'*Si, il povero,*' I confessed. Young men. On the streets. Starving. Sometimes with wives, infants in prams. I thought everyone did it.

'I hope you don't overpay them out of guilt,' he sniffed. One had, but spoke not as he swept aside a beaded screen. An odour like a hospital's. Here, a room hung with Turkish rugs. Dust-encrusted hookah on a low table. A fat man in a fez. Vidal glanced at me. *Alas, this day Vidal carries no cash.* One fished out a sheaf of lire. Vidal paid the fez, who motioned us to proceed. In the next room, young men. Reading newspapers. Drinking dark wine. Some slumped, dozing, groggy.

'Just point,' said Vidal.

'Opium,' he said afterwards. Hence the clinic aroma. 'From Afghanistan. The French connection. Sex and drugs, *Gubernator.* Roma's economy would collapse without them.'

He walked off. Waved but didn't look back. '*Domani!*'

May 20, 1958. The shoot upon us. A giant arena, to simulate The Great Circus Of Antioch. A practice chariot racing track next to that, where Heston and Boyd trained every day. Twelve thousand Romans at Cinecitta's gates at five AM today. Penniless, desperate to be extras. Eight thousand made this unkindest cut of all.

The cameras rolled on my Pilate's entry, flanked by gorgeous Italian extras. The gals too. Smart as paint. Terry Longdon, one's centurion Drusus, chimp-rolled, as a soldier should. One's Pilate sashayed. It was intoxicating. Well, for the first twenty takes.

'The bathhouses, Gubernator. Tonight's the night.'

So now, for this rookie sybarite, Vidal's idea of a good time in the Eternal City.

'By the way,' he smiled. 'How many have you had?' *They always ask.*

'Oh. I've lost count.' Waved a hand as if at a blowfly. *That should fix his cheese.*

'I haven't. Over a thousand by my twenty-fifth birthday.'

Bastard. 'I'm thirty-two now. And not a bit tired.'

I, thirty-one. Somewhat fewer. *And he could tell.* One's *envy.* Green and bitter as limes.

At the bathhouse, wicked romping. Quaffs of Ruffino Orvieto Classico eased one's trepidation, but it bode wise to keep one's head above the waterline. Later, glowing and spent, to Bricktop's for Veuve Clicquot. Bricktop, the former Ada Smith, was a jazz singer, vaudevillian and club owner in Paris, Mexico City and here. Luck was in. She was in town tonight. Gilded our ears with her marvellous *St Louis Blues.*

'You recall my notion,' said Vidal, recalling my notion. 'Ben Hur and Massala as lovers. Well. I rewrote their lines to suggest just so. Then went to Boyd. Told him to cruise Heston when they shot it.'

He raised his brows.

'And it seems someone has wised to it, and told Wyler.'

'Oh,' I said. 'Oh dear.'

'Oh, no. It's perfect, Gubernator. I *want* MGM to fire me. They'll have to pay me out. Go back to novels, say heart and mind.'

Wobbled his head a little as he spoke. As he did when pleased with himself. Which was often.

'Aren't you playing Pilate that way too?'

'*OK. Pontius Pilate, everybody. Slowly look to your right.*'

Willie called the shots from the chariot track with a megaphone, he so small the thing was half his size.

'*Pilate, Drusus. Slowly look to your left.*'

Then days of *nada, niente,* just sitting in that stadium in full costume while directors and crews fiddled and faddled. One poured Ballantine's into purple metal beakers one had bought. Matched one's toga, you see. Ice from a thermos. We were chided for this by Megaphone Willie, and for smoking. Not authenticity-ready for takes, you see. On one occasion, we braced for '*Action!*' Then this from Wee Willie's bullhorn.

'*Would Pontius Pilate please remove his sunglasses.*'

We had awnings for shade. The eight thousand extras, none. They commenced to fainting in impressive numbers. Ruined takes. As did temperamental equipment, and changes to script mid-production. *Well, then.* As one would be here far longer than expected, one checked out of the Ex. Rented a place on the Via Sistina. More discreet. To shower with a friend, as it were. Or friends.

The actors' eater of choice was Otello on the Via della Croce. And one went there for more than just *mangiare.* You see, across the street, there was a shabby trattoria where all the out of *work* actors ate. So for these wan fellows, the likes of I were a possible conduit to work, you see. Increasing seldom did one awake alone come soft pink Roman sunrise, its dawn chorus of church bells and Vespas.

Wyler hid behind my Pilate's backless throne.

'Frank, I'll direct you from here, *OK*?'

Then spent an hour yakking into his walkie talkie. Boredom and brandy, well...

'Frank!'

'*Hmpft?*' I jolted awake. A headache ringed my skull.

'On three, I want Pilate to stand up and look to his left. One, two, thr....'

One rose with imperious toss of head. Brandy, beakers, ice cubes, sunglasses, bottles of tablets, fell from within one's toga for all to see, and bounced, tinkled and rolled around at one's feet. Terry Longdon, smashed on one's Grand Marnier, laughed like a kookaburra.

'*Cut!*'

Then, Willie's voice at one's ear.

'Don't worry, Frank. *It's only money.*'

Best avoid doing that again, one has been cautioned by other support cast, lest they cut one's scenes or give one the flick and re-shoot with a double, went one's letter to Joan in London. Indeed, not a few were necking Dex to stay chirpy on this bloody stadium set and elsewhere.

'*White crosses,*' said several, the street name for this amphetamine divine, as they proffered fistfuls.

'Frank,' said Andrew Marton, first AD. His hand out. *Gimme.* Took Black Bag from me. Willie had said no more about one's *faux pas,* but it was plain that one was on notice. But the Dex served well. One was jumping like popcorn. So the brandy miniatures one had taped to one's thigh under one's toga came in handy. To the brasco in the break. Gulp 'em quick. Calm the heebie jeebies. Necking firewater in a tiled toilet, a wave of homesickness for Aussie pubs rolled in. Then the rain came. And stayed.

'They won't fire you, Thring. Nor I. Can't re-shoot now, not with all they have in the can. That stadium will take fucking days to dry out. We'll call each day. Check if we're needed. Fuck 'em.'

He talked me into it. We roared down empty autostrada in Jack's Silver Wraith, in episodic showers.

Vesuvius dozed hazy across the bay. We checked into the Excelsior on the Via Partenope. Right on the Napoli seafront. One obliged beggars at first, but Hawkins stopped me.

'Fuck, Thring. You'll start a riot. Or they'll follow us and slit our throats.'

Naples was home to the *Camorra,* he explained, the local strain of the *Cosa Nostra.* We drank Campanian wine. I, *Lacryma Christi,* tears of Christ. Jack, a *vino rossi* man, the *Agianico.* Food, shellfish pastas various, *al fresco* at tables on cobblestones amid snarls of scooters.

Pompeii was thirty minutes' drive from Naples. Twenty with Hawkins at the wheel. All buildings in the ruins, it seemed at first glance, had served two purposes. The second as whorehouse. Baths, taverns, gyms. Murals and mosaics of couples and more hard at it. Carvings and pictures of cocks everywhere. A symbol of power in that place and time. And these dicky birds not exactly to scale, shall we say.

'The *Rione Luzatti,* Thring. The poor quarter.'

Half-shickered, one did not register the alarm one should have. Hawkins loved a wager. 'You're good with cards. Come on.'

Easy to find a game. Had enough Italiano between us to ask around. But tense. Hawkins paid handsome to have their *uomini* guard his Roller. The *ragazzi* running the game cheated. No surprise. One let them win most hands, of course. It was alright, one's *Lachryma Christi* below decks decided.

Until we got back out on the streets, that is. Two lads jumped out of an alley. Slammed Jack to the ground. Didn't see me, clad in black as one was. *Soldi!* they demanded of prone Hawkins.

'Hey!'

Me. They turned. One of them laughed at me.

'*Avere una faccia da colo.*'

One had a face like an arse. Well, then. Drew my knife from Black Bag. Thrust it at them.

'*Che cazzo?*' What the fuck? They took off.

'Fuck, Thring,' said Jack. 'Didn't know you had it in you.'

'They'll be back, mobbed up,' I said. '*Andiamo va!*'

'Hawkins? What brings you here?'

Standing before me, a favourite author. Had a house here, to write. We'd taken the ferry to the island of Capri. 'It's not the best time, Jack.'

'Oh, come off it, Greene. Thring here is your biggest fan.'

Which I was. Saw the first draft of *Our Man In Havana* that day. We got back from Capri that evening. Doleful news. We'd been called back to Cinecitta.

'Off the picture, dear boy. They sacked him,' said George Relph, *Ben Hur's* Emperor Tiberius, of Vidal. They'd shipped in yet another writer, Kit Fry, author of *Venus Observed* and other plays one had bunged on with Reeny at the Little and at the Arrow.

'What for?' I said. 'This bloody screenplay's been polished more times than Casanova's cock.'

'It's Chuck Heston,' said George. 'He's complained. Wants rewrites. Says his lines for some reason make him sound like a sissy.'

Shot a major scene now, one's speech after the chariot race now, to victor Judah Ben-Hur. Chuck at his best here. Lineless, motionless. Saying nothing, doing less. *To paraphrase Caesar Augustus,* went one's dispatch home to Freddy Parslow, *Chuck came to Rome as an actor of wood. And left it as one of marble.*

Our scene at the villa of Jack's Quintus Arrius took seven eternities. One's Pilate, Chuck's Ben Hur and Jack. Days in costume, loitering like stuffed dummies on the set, while they shot a dance performed by what the script called Nubians. In fact, Les Ballets Africains from Paris. The boys, dark skin, near nude, oiled. Most arresting. One's toga poor concealment for one's excitement in mid-section.

'Signore Franco!'

Thumps on my door. Carlo, one's driver. *Che cazzo?* Squinted at my Citizen watch. 6.15 AM. But this was one's day off. Just as the bedside phone rang.

'Frank?'

Oh, no. Andrew *fucking* Marton.

'Frank, Willie wants to shoot some pickups today. How soon can y...'

Felt like about to pass out. Last night, a boffo soiree at Fellini's. Now within one's skull, all the punishments of the Underworld. Dispensed as only its king, pitiless Hades, can.

Taffy Griffith was in the next makeup chair, sparkling.

'Oh, dearo, boyo! Bonkers, it is!' as he espied one's troubled condition. 'Come, Pilate. Follow hither.' He grabbed my arm. 'For relief is at hand, it is.'

'Okay, keep your thumb on that for just a minute.'

Dr Max Jacobson withdrew the syringe. Hair rose on one's neck, head, arms, legs...

'Just a vitamin energy cocktail.'

One roared through the morning. Later, the Doc hit me up again. One had joined a club exclusive yet near numberless- the patients of Doctor Feelgood. The cocktail, a tincture of Vitamin B, *plip*, in an ocean of methamphetamine. And away we went, all jaws and eyes of moray eels.

'Frank,' said Longdon, just back from his second 'quite dreadful' *Carry On* picture in London. 'Bad news, dear chap.'

'What? They've stopped making Dexedrine?'

'Your friend and mine, Diane Cilento, chum. In the clinic in the Vatican. TB, old cock, is the word. Heard about it from Kenneth Williams.'

He smiled and looked away. 'I gather you two chaps know each other.'

'*Buon pomeriggio*,' I said. '*Ponzo Pilato!*'

About me swirled a violet velvet cape, liberated from Cinecitta's wardrobe.

'To see *la Principessa* Cilento!'

'*Va via!*' shouted this crone at the reception desk.

'Go away? Not on your life, baby!'

Then this nun at Clinica Morelli clocked one's four bottles of Roderer. Their clinking in Black Bag betrayed one as surely as the kiss of Judas.

'Autio! Pazzo!' she shouted.

'No, I am not mad, madam. I shall not harm y...'

After an eternity of this dance, *dopo qualche tempo,* one was at last let in to see Diane.

'Oh, Podge,' she smiled. Then tears. It all came out, the brutalities of her husband, that ogre Volpe. 'Doesn't want me working,' she said. 'It's a wog thing.'

As the Roderer worked its wizardry, we dissected the issue and one proposed a solution. Then heard nuns at the door, eavesdropping. So one started to make loud kissing noises, groaning and panting. *Oh, baby.* She joined in. *Ugh! Oh! I'm coming!*

'AARRGGHHH!' I roared. Yanked the door ajar. Three nuns fell into the room.

Dr Feelgood's pep shots afforded boundless energy, one must concede. Volpe was out today, Diane said. We made fast to her place. Here, one paid off little Giovanna's nanny, far more than she was owed- but *questa nonna* now out of a job, after all.

At the airport, one booked their flight to London.

'You can stay at Trebovir Road.' Told her where the spare keys were hidden. 'And here's cash for the necessary.' She baulked. 'Go on. Take it, take it.'

Felt good about oneself. For a change.

The German actor Claude Heater, playing Christ here, could only be filmed from behind and did not speak a line, the producers apprehensive that the Vatican might damn the film for blasphemy, direct Catholics to boycott the fucker. So this scene of the Saviour's trial had one's Pilate harangue, demand answers, *quid veritas,* 'What is truth?' and all that, to no response, to this Messiah's awful mute stillness. The tension, the silence, the suspense thus created between my Pilate's pronouncements, wrenching and searing. We felt it even as we shaped it. A flash of cinema sorcery in the making.

Then they cut the whole fucking thing but for my man washing his hands at meeting's end. Such is Hollywood-on-Tiber.

'They did the same to me, Thring,' said Hughie Griffith. 'And to Longdon and Hawkins, isn't it.'

En route to our respective last scenes, we encountered one another crossing the vast and cooling autumnal plains of Cinecitta on the Vespas provided. 'It's Chuck's picture, boyo.' Asked with his brows, *do you understand now?*

Quite. The leading man not to be upstaged – and this Heston, well, impossible not to. Ah, well. One's final scene now. Chuck and self, as it happened. A two hander standoff, post-Christ's crucifixion. *It's Chuck's picture.* Well. I knew something that Chuck didn't, baby. Vidal had given me all the good lines here.

'And something else,' he'd said, a wobble of his head. Chuck's lines as written by Vidal compelled Heston to blub and quaver at all that had befallen his man Judah. Mine, to respond as the immutable force of Imperial Rome. To counsel him, as if parent to child throwing tantrum, *not to crucify yourself on a shadow such as old resentment or impossible loyalties.* No contest, baby.

'Frank Thring leaving the picture, everyone,' said Willie.

A standing O did they bestow. Yet despondency rolled over me now. Most others here going straight from this shoot to their next, but oneself not so favoured. So best keep busy some other way. Qantas had a London-Sydney route via Rome. Sadly, the stopovers also included Athens, Karachi, Delhi, Bangkok, Singapore, Jakarta and Perth. Close to dead and home at last, one called Sumner.

'Now,' I said. '*Moby.* Where were we?'

CHAPTER EIGHTEEN

In Australia, success abroad is licence for the nation entire to brand one as up oneself, unless one returns bemedalled or with fistful of cup or shield for sporting exertions. But no matter. One was good 'talent', as the TV johnnies say.

Hosts of calls did one field. To guest on *IMT* with Gra Gra, Bert Newton and Mary Hardy. The wireless on 3DB with Ferrier. The press one indulged by inviting them to Rylands for Melbourne Bitter, served in one's pewter tankards. One did the dailies, you know, *The Age*, *The Herald*, *The Sun News-Pictorial*. Magazines like *Everybody's*, *Womens Weekly*, *TV Week*. In fact, the print media, in noisome desperation, were lying in wait on one's arrival. Asked straight off the fucking jetstair at Essendon Airport what one thought of *Ben Hur*, one couldn't resist.

'Loved *him*. Hated *her*.'

Asked one's galpal Mary Hardy to New Year's at Freddie's. You know, pixie, Mary was a ton funnier than any male on telly. But the bull-necked boys' clubs of Seven and Nine would never give this vixen her own show. Appalling. Of Freddie's wingding, she asked if there'd be men there.

'Oh yes, baby,' I said. 'No shortage.'

At Freddie's, a troupe of boys from Sydney, the cast of some hideous JCWs musical turn here. Despite Mary's local TV, theatre and radio profile, they knew her not. No national networks back then, you see. One of these flits, well gone in Pimms Number One Cup, came to believe that Mary, with her trademark turban, nut-brown voice, brunette bob and salty ways, was, well...

'Show me your *cock*, darling.'

'Eh?' said Mary. 'Fuck off! Show me your cunt!'

'Let's get that wig off, bitch!'

He whipped off Mary's turban. Grabbed her very real hair. She grabbed his very real balls. Banshee wail shook the moon.

All this sent our host Freddie into a terrible tizz, so one had to reef her out of there. Revellers on the street clocked us. *Frank! Mary!* Such is local telly celebrity. To their nearby party were we begged attendance, *oh come, please do.* Free champers, *quid pro quo* for our showbiz tattle. Mary made up even better stories about various TV talking heads' sex fetishes than I. Then found she two cocksmen of swarthy cast, her favourite, and vanished. The moon, full and bright, compelled one to hove back to Freddie's for a lad. Ah, that fleeting perk of fame. To score without tears.

'I am unwell. Leave me.'

One's head a snake pit in flames. By midday's hot grey light, I roused the sticky flake at my side.

'But,' he said, 'you said you would...'

Oh, Frank. Not again. One bid him dress. Wrapped oneself in embroidered green robe.

'I'll have a word to Sumner.'

Downstairs, herded him to the door. 'For a taxi.' Shoved the necessary at him.

'You can go now.'

'Frank! You still alive?'

Mary on the staircase. *Oh, that's right.* She'd brought those two bucks back here.

'Where are Butch and Butch?' I enquired. *Christ,* it was *hot.*

'Oh, them,' she said, naked save turban. 'Bolted and bolted.' She shook bottles. Found one that sloshed. Gulped from it.

'Oh, there's news, by the way. Cuba. Fidel. Rolled into Havana a few hours ago.'

'Hmmm.'

One couldn't help notice, in her unclad state, quite a jungle downstairs. Took to calling her Blackbeard for a time.

Melbourne was invaded in January 1959. Gregory Peck, Ava Gardner, Fred Astaire and Tony Perkins here to shoot Stan Kramer's *On The Beach*. Nevil Shute's novel had been set in one's home town. So. Motion pictures shot in Melbourne. Yankee stars. Aussie support cast and crew. Stories by Oz-born writers. FT's vision made flesh.

Sightings round town. Greg Peck dining at the Menzies. The Society Italian at the top of Bourke Street hosted Ava and Sinatra. Frank out here on tour, you see, and attempting reconciliation with his now ex. And crowds bunched and buzzing wherever scenes were shot. At Frankston station, some hobyah called out to Astaire, *give us a few steps, Fred*. He did too, right there on the platform.

But Ava, well. Dried during takes. Slipped over during one. Her *fuck this* and *cocksuckers* lent extra tang to the seaside air. Thick ears were likely dispensed all over Melbourne that night as kiddies from among the mobs regurgitated Ava's epithets.

'The Union want me back here, boy. To save it from going under.'

The plan was to run *Moby* in Sydney first, then Melbourne. Then, without notice, Black Jack fetched up in the town he'd forsaken. His former baby had foundered under their new director, he explained, bunging on strange plays no-one went to see. Wal Cherry, who'd replaced Sumner, thought Melbourne was ready for Brecht and such. *My dear fellow*. In 1958, they still weren't ready for fucking Sophocles.

'Buddy Holly's dead. Richie Valens. And that *Chantilly Lace* fella. Plane crash.'

At a meeting of the Union which Sumner called to explain the tumult and his reinstatement, Mary Hardy arrived, tardy and flustered. Tearful. With shocking tidings.

'Well?' said Mary. 'Anybody going to say anything?'

Sumner looked up from stroking his forehead.

'Is that any excuse for your being late?'

'Frank, it's Rod Lever here. From *TV Week*..'

The editor of a top-selling mag. One's response, *why the hell not?* One's *TV Week* column started around March of '59. One called it *A*

Piece Of Thring. One's *TV Week* column oozed its first around March 1959. It would be a long and turbulent marriage.

One arranged to meet with Sumner at his dreadful office at Melbourne Uni, to discuss *Moby* and other matters. Several flights of stairs. No lift. Opposite the Ewing Gallery, a forlorn artspace often open but unattended. Students liked it for a quickie. Sumner's eyrie but a small desk, rusty single bar radiator. Grey filing cabinet. Faded sofa. Mock Gothic windows peered down at a humming, chunting aircon plant.

Some king. Some castle.

'You're in films, boy. We can't afford film stars.'

One was offering to join the Union as one of its ensemble, you see.

'Not an issue for me, Butch.'

His veins. Blue deltas beneath film-thin skin. Surely got by on photosynthesis some days. 'Pay me what you can.'

He was distracted. He'd left his wife Karis. Caught romping a rookie starlet from the Union, a bit of squish on the side. Now he be sleeping *here.* Said he'd think about one's overture as a couple across the way groaned to a messy photo finish.

'Very well. You know *Arms And The Man*, boy?'

Luncheon. Amiconi's, West Melbourne. Some stared. I'd told Black Jack that one's movie shoots each year would be in the Northern summer. So, free otherwise for plays here. He gave me a part in this GB Shaw, another in Kit Fry's *Venus Observed*, and a run for *Moby* in the Union's Christmas season.

Neither of us ever said it, but he took one on board only because one's film star name might flog seats enough to keep the Union from the morgue. I was Sumner's PT Barnum mug-puller, you see. His Feejee Mermaid, his Jo Jo the Dog Faced Boy, his Chang and Eng the Siamese Twins. *Every crowd has a silver lining* a Barnum maxim, his freak shows testament to that. One's duty was clear.

'Is this gaggle of the undead the best you've got?'

Thus one addressed Sumner and his idea of a top-shelf cast after our first day's read through of *Arms*. Well, yes, one had been spoiled of late.

Still, this mob was familiar, a comfortable fit, for all their shortcomings. Frank Gatliff was here, back from his own odyssey abroad. Freddy Parslow, part of the Melbourne am-dram scene for several eternities. A *frisson* of Richard Burton in his fetching looks. Got him a long way.

'No need to fall back on talent,' I said of him to Sumner. 'And just as bloody well.'

Also here, from all the way back to the Little, Melbourne Rep, the National with Squirty Gertie, Sumner's *Trojan Women,* I called them. Dot Bradley, Lyndel Rowe, Moira Carleton, the rest. Just one problem.

'Just what this play needs, baby,' I said to this moppet. 'The moment you come on, everyone else looks so much better.'

Sumner had recruited this fellow Lewis Fiander for the Union. Late of Sydney radio dramas. Granted, pretty enough to *eat.* But useless here.

'You're supposed to *play* the part. Not fucking *read* it,' one felt compelled to explain. Worse, he snubbed one's RSVP to Rylands, to 'work through our scenes together.'

One *knew* he was of the colours, despite flimsy cover of a wife. Well, then. No choice.

One would take Sumner's perky wooden puppet and render him sawdust.

For *Arms*, my man was Sergius. A rowdy roughnut, just back from one of those forever wars in the Baltic states. For one's moments, one recalled returned soldiers on Melbourne streets after Hitler and Tojo's Wars. My man scratched his crotch. Spat on the ground. And one pretended to urinate on the spot in outdoor scenes, delivering lines back over one's shoulder as one did so. Sumner, ex-British Navy, thought it good.

Full house first night for *Arms*. I should fucking hope so. One did a heap of press and radio for it. And daytime telly, that flat, dull grey milieu. Personified by *In Melbourne Today*. Housewives, hair in rollers, half-belted by lunchtime on Vickers Gin from cracked teacups, tuned in to a young Bert Newton to forget.

We rolled on to Kit Fry's *Venus Observed.* The setup here, preposterous. My man, a Duke. Planning a third marriage. Choosing from women selected by his son, who has, it is presumed, field-tested their, er, hidden charms. Our director not Sumner but one John B Trevor. And one was lumbered with Fiander again, as the Duke's son Edgar.

Then there was Patricia Kennedy. She'd haunted Melbourne radio and theatre since the fucking Iron Age. The whisper, that arrests of queer thesps around town had been down to this toxic termagant. She'd failed to have their Actors Equity union cards revoked so they couldn't work, you see, so instead dobbed them in to the coppers for no crime but dalliance. A lifelong celibate too, it was said. No wonder. Now this rosary-wringing harridan, a decade one's senior, cast as siren after whom one's Duke is meant to lust. God spare me. Justice must be served.

'Is my man meant to be a drunk?' one enquired of director Trevor one day.

'What in blazes do you mean, Frank?' One pointed at Patricia.

'Well, why else would you want to fuck *that?*'

She bid Sumner sack me. He'd none of it. One was a drawcard, you see. I backed off, at Sumner's entreaty. *For now.*

'There shall be gory reckoning for this foul deed,' one told the mirror as one trimmed one's beard. You see, pixie, Sumner chose to follow *Venus* with *Rape Of The Belt*, a tedious burlesque of the ninth labour of Hercules, namely to steal the belt of the queen of the Amazons. The part of Zeus, made for me.

'Yet he casts this popinjay Fiander!' one barked at one's reflection.

On *Belt's* opening night, I'd had a few belts myself. Came on the stage just before curtain up. Thanked the customers for their support for our *Venus*. Then, despite not having been asked to, introduced *Belt*.

'*I* thought it was *dreadful*. But *you* might like it.'

Sumner steamed backstage. Reminded me that I was not director of this company. One's Martini and Rossi retorted that neither was *he* its *star*. No matter. *Belt* closed after a week, an unloved and deserving flop. One needed most of its cast free anyway, for a show far more important.

'A woman? Playing a boy?'

'Orson cast Joan Plowright,' I reminded Sumner. 'And we have someone here in Melbourne who will bring the house down.'

Mary Hardy was one's only choice as Pip the cabin boy for *Moby Dick – Rehearsed.*

All over telly and radio, loved by all. Talent that sizzled. And as one owned the rights, one insisted that one play Ahab. Sumner demanded that one cast Lewis bloody Fiander. So I gave the fucker the part of Ishmael.

'Little more than a chorus, a narrator, really.'

This as I tossed him a script at the cast meeting. 'So even you can't fuck it up.'

He was not without ability, but humiliation in front of one's peers is a marvellous motivator. Frank Gatliff doubled as the Chaplain and Starbuck, as Sumner had stymied one's plans for a big cast.

'This isn't Stratford, Frank. I can't afford it.'

So, then. One bid others double as well. Anything for respite from his ghoulish hovering. Our *Pequod* crew, George Ogilvie, Robin Ramsay, Fred Parslow *et al*, had skills we put to work. George played guitar, for instance, so he led the sea shanties. Of Freddy's *talent,* well, the shreds that comprised his costume amounted to very little.

'They're paid every week, so they work every week.'

'But....'

'There's your starting point, boy.'

No parts for females in *Moby,* but use them one must, Black Jack decreed. One found ways. Dot Bradley bowed a violin to suggest the sound of whales. Lyndel Rowe pounded a bass drum for suspense. Marion Edward banged a spanner on a 44 gallon drum for ships' bells. And better singers than the boys, so one had them join in on the sea shanties.

'You scrubbers give it a choral quality,' I said. Swerved to the lads. 'As opposed to a singing *dog* act.'

Opening night. Cast onstage, in silhouette. Immobile and mute as the customers drifted in, as per Orson's turn. Knew not what to make of it. Fell to chatter. We darkened the houselights to hush their babble. Then Lewis Fiander spoke.

Call me Ishmael. We were off.

When one's entrance came, one stormed on as Welles had in London. Ferocious, booming. Much narrowing of eyes, knitting of brows. One played Welles playing Shakespeare, you see. Bits and pieces of his Othello, Macbeth, Shylock. One's Actor-Manager playing Ahab roared at the cast to *stand six feet back and do your damndest.* Shook a fistful of broomstick as a harpoon. Whooshed it about above their heads. They learned fast to duck. Well, most of 'em. And Mary Hardy as Pip, the cabin boy osmoting into madness and death, well...people who were there still talk about it.

Play's end. Silence in the stalls. *Jesus wept,* I thought, *we've completely fucked i*...then spatter of claps. Like firstborn of rainstorm. Climbing to a tide. Stamping now, stalls to gods. On their feet, a roar...

The critics raved in tongues of fire. And so they bloody should. Bar one. A young Phillip Adams wrote in puerile jest that one was such a leviathan talent that one should have played the whale. He'd keep. *Moby* the best thing one ever did. That *we* ever did.

'Well, one's ancestors were Kreitmayers from Munich. Can't get much more German than that. You've come to the right place, baby.'

The ABC made TV plays inhouse back then. Producer William Sterling cast me in *Treason*, of the failed plot on Der Fuhrer's life. Brian James, The Gentleman, we called him, and Junie Brunell, one's Salome way back at the Arrow, were Col von Hoffaker and his lover Else. And self, one Karl Albrecht, one's first and last Nazi.

Being the ABC, they ran it in January, the entire nation at the beach or the bloody cricket. But being the ABC, they also repeated it so many times that in the end, half the country saw it whether they liked it or not.

Meantime, the Australian premiere of *Ben Hur* loomed. Chuck Heston said to be flying out for it. 'Twas much hyped. By me. On telly, the wireless. You see, it helped to fill the Union for *Moby,* night after night. Absurd, really, but there it is.

A record run for *Moby,* January to March 1960. Herograms, too, for *Treason*, to *TV Week*. One letter, signed 'Clancy.' Most worshipful.

170

Turns out it was Jackie Clancy, from HSV7's trove of unfunny comics. Fishing for praise from *A Piece Of Thring* for his lamentable stylings, no doubt. So one sent a cheerio in one's next column, to a fellow who *calls to mind the Hunchback Of Notre Dame with a home perm.*

Oh, Christ, pixie. Aussie TV back then. Full as a tick with undead vaudeville. *Top Of The Town, Bandwagon, The BP Super Show,* 'variety' they called it. Singers, dancers and comics, all hatched from identical gooey pods. It was lonely work, shaming this pestilence in *TV Week.* Yet one failed to eradicate it. The offal on offer to this day proves it.

Near the end of *Moby's* run, came there karmic wrath for some past crime. One awoke to one's right foot hot and swollen, all the hues of the red end of the rainbow. Hennessy's and Vincent's Powders cut the pain from wail to throb. My Ahab's one-legged hobble never more convincing onstage.

'Cellulitis,' pronounced one's new GP. Well, one of them. 'Bugs get in through this broken skin here. All this smoking and drinking doesn't help, Fra...'

'Can you just write me a script so I can go *home*?'

'Home?'

Three days in germsville be one's sentence. Freemason's Hospital, East Melbourne. Purgatorial, pixie. Well, bar the intravenous painkillers. Elixir of all the angels; Raphael, Gabriel, Michael, Uriel. And Lucifer.

CHAPTER NINETEEN

The divine Ella Fitzgerald played Embers jazz club in South Yarra, one recalls, the same day that US President Kennedy decreed a naval blockade of Cuba. GTV9 filmed it for their prime time stinker, the *BP Super Show*- but only after one urged them to do thus in *A Piece Of Thring*. *Besides that*, one wrote, *this program offers little more than sideshow silage*. French acrobats The Dandinis, Sing Lee Sing's contortionists, all that dross. All wrangled by former circus ringmaster and sideshow magician from West Virginia, Tommy Hanlon Junior. Of Tommy's game show, *It Could Be You*, the less said the better.

For the Sydney *Moby* run, it was all aboard the Spirit Of Progress at Spencer Street station, destination the fabled Elizabethan Theatre on King Street, Newtown. Well, we might have known. Sydney's customary dismissal of anything Melbourne sniffed at us, fangs bared. Customers were few. So we pushed one's Hollywood profile a bit.

'Here by popular demand, the star of *Ben Hur*, all that frogshit. Can you help us out, baby?' the gist of one's calls to one's wireless and telly pals in this rank and sultry burg. One scattered a flutter of milk-white lies on Sydney ABC radio 2FC and on ABC TV. Clyde Packer at TCN-9 had me on, of course. And we did Australia's first ever breakfast TV show, *Today* on ATN 7 with Ray Taylor. Not much to it, really. Rip 'n' read cable news straight off the clattering Telex machine, recited on air by Ray between a *Crusader Rabbit* cartoon and Australia's first ever TV soapie, *Autumn Affair*, a fifteen-minute dose of televisual typhus.

Our *Moby*, yes, mixed success here. But there were compensations. A lot of 'round midnight time up the Cross, for one thing. Ray Taylor, self, Mary Hardy, Freddy Parslow, Gaitliff, Robin Ramsay. Other hardies.

Made the scene at El Rocco Jazz Cellar after the show almost nightly. And just as often, several nightspots on, wound up at the Mansions Hotel, bleary all over as the rooster cockadoodled. Then Ray would peel off, straight his morning TV show. The rest of us, to an early opener.

We took in the Staccato Club, Australia's first strip club. Also the Taboo, the El Bongo, daddio, the Afro Cuban. Scenic, baby. But pricey liquor. Smuggled in our own Clelands Liqueur Brandy and such, purchased at those Sydney wine shops. You know, with the Orlando Wines sign. Rummies bunched outside, waiting for it to open. Or actors. Then back in Melbourne, a cablegram and the shock of one's life.

LOVED YOU IN BEN HUR ARE YOU FREE MAY FOR SPAIN TOP SECRET MOVIE PROJECT WITH NICK RAY STOP BRONSTON MGM

One had first heard of Sam Bronston during the *Ben Hur* shoot. American tycoons various, the greediest and meanest of 'em, had dirty fortunes untold stashed in Spanish banks, as tax dodges. These had been frozen by *El Caudillo,* the despicable despot Franco. The old tyrant declared that these funds would be freed only if spent in Spain. Bronston a canny one. Shot the very first of the 1950s blockbusters, *John Paul Jones,* in Madrid, bankrolled by these blackmailed Yank investors. And get this. Bronston, one came to learn, was a nephew of Leon Trotsky. The *irony.* One's chum Peter Cushing starred in *JPJ* between his vampire movies, with Bette Davis, Robert Stack, others. And Cushing had put in a word for me with this Bronston.

Just one niggle. One still hadn't heard from Kirk Douglas of when we might start on *Spartacus.* Then, saw in one's airmailed *Modern Screen* magazine that production *had* begun in Spain. Oh. *I see.*

So, at this, the cable from Bronston, one's endampened spirits took wing of archangel. And his choice of director, fuck me dead, *Nick Ray!* He'd directed Bogart, Joan Crawford. James Dean, in *Rebel Without A Cause.* Chuck Heston was due in Melbourne for the *Ben Hur* prem.

'Well,' one told the press, 'Chuck will have to make do without me.'

'Yeah, well, you should see the other bitch,' she said through a fat lip. 'And her bit on the side.'

Bunney Brooke, between beating up lovers, was directing *Frenzy* for the National at St Peter's Church Hall on Eastern Hill in the city. Mary Hardy, also cast, roped one in. Christ, Bunney was a trial. All this *acting is breathing* twaddle. And yes, pixie, the *National.* One was surprised to be asked, given one's trespasses against Squirty Gertie and all. But, well, one was a *name* now. So. Forgive and forget. Well, forget.

Bronston's secret script came via airmail. Well, no wonder the fucker was under wraps. A million-volt shocker. *King Of Kings* by name. Oh, dear. A remake of Cecil B DeMille's silent epic, you see. Jesus of Nazareth on the big screen. The very concept being proposed, the Saviour to speak and cinema customers to look upon His face, most controversial.

'Scowls and scolds from the best dressed transvestites of the Vatican and other vexatious vicars must surely follow,' I said to Mary Hardy.

'The turnstiles will be spun off their gudgeons, of course. The mugs love this Jesus muck. But the dialogue,' this to Sumner when he dropped by one afternoon, 'well, not so much dead on arrival. More in a tertiary state of putrefaction.'

Bronston's notes were vague. To do what one had done in *Ben,* said his letter. So, then. Pilate. *Again.* One trawled my man's pages for one's moments. Yes. There were none.

From that essence of misery, Essendon Airport, one flew to Australia's only international terminal then, Mascot in Sydney. From there on Qantas to an overnight stop in Bangkok. Fuddled. Wearied. But Mr Cock not a bit tired. Led the way, off a tip from Helpmann.

'*Sa wat dee khaaaaa...*you wan' *harp harp?*' from a painted Siamese trollop. Half half, she meant. You know, a bit of upstairs then downstairs.

'God, no, you silly bitch. *Katoey,*' I said, the word Bobby H had taught me.

'Ah. Ladyboy. You go Chinatown.'

I go Chinatown. Made it quick, choppy chop. *Rib reng,* as the Thais say. Early flight come the dawn, you see.

At MGM in London, a bony jasper called Cledwyn reefed his tape measure out.

'Okay, lover. Got your inches done,' he said.

'That's it? No makeup test, stills, all that carry-o...'

'No, dear. Locals make the duds in Spain. We pay them. Franco insists,' meaning the ursine fascist dictator. 'We just design the bloody stuff.'

One took him swift and brutal in Graeco-Roman grapple.

'Getting into character, baby.'

'Frank Thring! Over here!'

On the jetstair at Madrid's Barajas Airport, the summer wind wrapped itself around me. Calling to me, a short, round man. Silver hair swept back. Bronston, with a Rolls Royce Silver Cloud and driver. *On the tarmac.* The ground crew offloaded one's bags, right off the plane, into the Roller. No Customs, no passport stamps. He clocked one's bemusement.

'No problem, Frank. *El Caudillo's* a pal.'

We breezed out of the place like we owned the bastard. *A pal,* repeated Sam as he poured drinks in this long grey limousine. One a trifle queasy at the thought as we rolled into Madrid. Wherever one cast one's gaze might conceal clusters of mass and unmarked graves.

'Frank, meet Phil Yordan.'

This was Bronston's co-producer and writer. Panda patches around his eye sockets. Hair, bottle black. *A face that orders executions.*

'Frank,' said Yordan, 'here's a rewrite.'

Lobbed it at me as if one's unsatisfactory homework. Some hours and a dinner later, at long last alone in one's suite atop the Castellana Hilton. Took the only course one could, bedrowned by now in enveloping gloom. A handful of Nembies, one's mellow yellow ferry to the underworld.

'What are you *doing* to my *movie?*'

Nick Ray dull-stared me. A face mean and blank. One right on cue with Pilate's line here at our first day's table reads. And yet...

'Frank,' said Hurd Hatfield, 'that's *my* line.'

*Oh. What the fuc...*Bronston leapt in.

'Oh, sorry, Frank. Er, my error, Nick. I forgot to tell Frank that we'd re-cast him as...'

Nick deaf to this. Eyes gone hard. Wired on more than his breakfast vodka and orange, to be sure.

'You're *Herod*,' said Nick. '*He*,' flinging fingers like a kick chorus line kick at Hurd, 'is Pilate. You're *Herod.*'

'Nick,' said Bronston. 'This is an oversight on my part...'

'This limey,' said Nick to Sam, pointing at me, 'is *trouble.*'

Next day, Nick called *cut* mid-scene. Bid me take a walk with him outside.

'Herod. Tell me about yourself.'

The fucker was deranged, this much clear. One best play along.

'I'm not a real king,' I said. 'A mere puppet of the Romans...'

'No, not *that.*' *Fuck, what now...?* 'Are you happy just to fuck your wife?'

'No.' Now to drop the fucker on his head. 'Nor other women.' I arched a brow. His eyes widened.

'That's it! *Yes!*' He walked in circles, muttering. 'Herod is a frustrated homo stuck in a loveless marriage...'

'Sounds like a Hedda Hopper column,' I said.

'Leave her to me, Herod. Nothing my swift and noble cock won't fix.'

Hedda, Hollywood's queen bitch of the scandal sheets, was seventy-five at the time. One had heard that nutty Nick was profligate with the pork sword, but...

One's man Herod was the son of Herod The Great, played by Gregoire Aslan. Thirty films under his belt had he.

'All as evil foreign types,' he smiled. 'Get used to that, my friend.'

The set, a throne room. Expat Aussie Ron Randell, ex-Tivoli song and dancer, as Lucius, a centurion. Self in black wig and maroon cape, as if a starter for *World Championship Wrestling*.

'People,' said Nick. 'You have any idea how much I lost at the track yesterday?'

Whistled, *oh boy*. Lit a Salem. All day long, he quoted at us, apropos of nothing, from *King Lear* to Nieztsche and back. Thought I had my Herod right, but ....*Cut!*

'Herod Antipas. Walk with me.'

One was led around the set and the studio beyond for fifteen minutes as he babbled.

'Macbeth. You are Macbeth.' I nodded. *Yes, of course, now I understand.* 'Yes. Or Oedipus. Kraft-Ebling, too. Psychopathia sexualis, sadism...'

Whatever you say, baby. Best, in one's experience, to concur with a vodka-infused, amphetamine-stoked, omnisexual gambler. He led every fucker on the set off for these walkies. One day, an extra with no English. This poor drudge the beneficiary of Nick's epiphany that *the ancient Romans built in Cinemascope!*

Thank the god of wine I packed it. Reading Wilde's Complete Works on set while Nick dithers. A dispatch from the Front, to Sumner. Frozen into Rodin's Thinker catatonia one day. A rambling, spittling Moses to our lost tribe the next.

In this script, after the boy baby slaughter he orders, Herod Senior collapses. Heart attack. Did someone say *deus ex machina?* My man his son sweeps in. Plants his arse on the tyrant's throne. His father, unable to rise. Pleads, *no, no, please...* I push him back with my foot. Gently. Tentative. A bad seed child, experimenting. The old man slumps. Perishes in silence. My Herod, indifferent. Just as Gregoire and self had planned it. Marvellous.

'No. *No*, Herod. I want you...'

Nick mimed, arms flung out. Palms up, '...do that.' Never lost for words except when he needed them. 'And, er, bare your...' Showed me his teeth. Pointed at them. 'And, ah, a big....'

Shot his foot out. He meant *kick*. One must have looked as one felt.

'Is there a problem, Herod?'

He was known to throw actors off pictures at first whiff of insolence. So with a sigh unseen and within, his wish, my command. Can't look at it even today on the telly re-runs at Easter...

'I'll kill him,' sneered Hurdy Hatfield.

'Well, let me fuck him before you do, baby.'

Our Jesus, Jeffrey Hunter, was now among us. Hurdy miffed that the part hadn't gone to *him*, he fumed here upon our maddened sheets. One had returned dishy Hurdy's glances on the set, you see, and, well, ...

Bronston bunged on a bash to welcome our stars, such as they were. Namely, Jeffrey and the talented and overlooked Robert Ryan, our John The Baptist. Nick Ray fronted in a Bond villain's white suit and unnecessary eyepatch. *You tell me.* Had his arm wrapped round Jeffrey all night like an anaconda. One can only conjecture on the priapic brutals forced on the boy.

'The life of Christ is a story about young people,' Nick declared. Jeffrey was thirty-five, but his Messiah would come to be pilloried as *I Was A Teenage Jesus.*

'Eyes by Sinatra,' one's aside to Hurdy. 'But can't act for a pie with peas.'

Former child star Brigid Bazlen, our supposed Salome, brings to mind not slut, but Mouseketeer, one wrote to Mary Hardy. *This whole thing, an abomination. Send whisky for the walking wounded. Shotguns for the rest. The band is playing Nearer My God To Thee and there aren't nearly enough lifeboats.*

Scene: Night. A palace balcony. Our Salome shouts at the Baptist, preachifying in the street, to hit the bricks.

'Herod, get behind her,' gestured Nick. 'Get a hold of her arms like you want her.'

But Brigid's remonstrations came out like Shirley fucking Temple scolding a puppy. So one squeezed hard on the inside of her elbows, where it hurts most. To get her seething. Breathed on the back of her neck. Snapped her elastic waistband. All one's old stage tricks. She now hated one's guts. As her character *should.*

Nick's current wife Betty Utey, a gun Hollywood choreographer, flew in from LA to coach Brigid for her dance of the seven veils. We draped languid and damp, in Madrid heat in full costume under white fire of studio lights as Betty shouted Brigid her moves from off-camera.

'Bend! Kick! Weave! Kick!' Fruitless.

'Our temptress wiggles like a speared *fish*,' I said. To fire her up a bit. Nick dropped to his knees to talk to me reclining on my couch.

'Herod, can't you drool more at Salome when she shakes her....' Then froze.

'That's *it!*' Now he chopped the air with his hand at head height where he crouched. 'From now on, I want the camera at *this level!*' The day wasted, road-testing this whim.

'It'll be boils and frogs next,' I shouted to my Herodias, Rita Gam, over the roar of the rain. No roof on this sumptuous set, so the fucker entire drenched and flooded. And we, shooed off to other scenes in less waterlogged locales.

For Hurd and self, Pilate and Herod, a steam bath. Together. What this suggested to moviegoers doesn't bear thinking about, but there it is. Beset by lights, cameras, boom mikes and crew. Randell's centurion Lucius returns from the Sermon On The Mount, disguised as Jewish commoner, and reports. To we two, near-naked, oiled up under blaze and glare. Gave us the horrors, pixie. To douse our trepidation, breakfast of Cava, Spain's brusque yet elegant riposte to Gallic champagne. One's loincloth as if a nappy on a giant baby. But soused on Catalan bubbles, one no longer cared.

'You see the moon. You know it's there. But you don't know why. See?'

I nodded, just to shut Nick up. One's best pass at it this day, yet failed to satisfy. Read-throughs, you see, for Herod's showdown with Christ. Nick curled into foetal ball for a time eternal before he spoke. Muffled, his arms wrapped round his head.

'Herod, swing by my pad tonight. We'll hash this out.'

To Nick's pile in La Florida, Madrid's Toorak. A valet led me past many rooms, to one dark, save for shimmering glow. *Flamenco Sketches* by

Miles Davis purring and chortling on the stereo. Candle flames wavered. Here was Nick, naked. With another, likewise. Dancing cheek to cheek.

'Oh, Herod. Drink?'

Oh, dear. The other nude, *Hurdy.* Nick read one's mind. Well, some of it.

'Betty's out of town. On another picture.'

As if the most normal thing in the world, and, well, in Hollywood, it is. They threw on robes now and we worked on the scene, Hurdy standing in for Jeff Jesus.

'Baby, I think you've got it,' said Nick after countless identical read-throughs.

'I need to go play some poker. Fuck some poontang. You two boys enjoy yourselves.' We did. Poor Hurdy. Yet one understood. Showbiz, pixie. *Whatever it takes.*

'Action!'

One circled our Christ, the wooden, nay ossified Jeffrey Hunter. My man bids him take a clay vase. *Turn it into gold.* Then, to *make it thunder.*

'Cut! Herod! Movies *move.*'

Yes, pixie, yet again. Nutty Nick steered me on a silent stroll round the set. Pointed or waved at random cast and props as we went. *You see? You see?* Then spoke.

'See? Do you see, Herod? You're sitting on a keg of dynamite!'

Twenty takes on, he was still not happy. *Then it came to me.* Orson to Larry in Paris, on playing tyrants.

'Well, old man, when my man goes mad in *Citizen Kane,* he summons not the tempest. No. Throws things around like an *infant.*'

Rigatoni fragments had pelted one's face as he spoke. Occupational hazard of dining with the Great Auteur. But no matter. I had my moment.

'Action!'

I took up the vase. To Jeff, *turn it into gold.* Then, having told not a soul, one made a toddler's silent fury face. Dashed the clay vessel to the floor, hard, *BANG!* Everyone jumped. Smoke-thick silence. I picked up a shard.

'*It's still made of clay.*' Whispered. Voice breaking. A devastated child.

'Cut! Herod, what the hell was that supposed to b....'

Rita Gam started applauding. As did Randell, Jeffrey Hunter, the crew. The extras. One's cape swirled as one rounded on Nick.

'My keg of dynamite, *baby.*'

The set for Herod's palace was now usable again. At a banquet, my man drunk and ogling stepdaughter Salome. Wife Herodias oozes suppressed rage. Rita, a fine actress, could seethe with her eyes. In weighty costumes, bar Brigid in a few billows of ice-blue gauze, we sweated till we squelched. Extras fainted, ruining takes. For one's wine-gilled Herod, one pulled off some fabulous pratfalls and trips, learned from Georgie Wallace back at Efftee Films as a kid. But Nick, well, ...

'Not cinematic enough. I want the air to *move.*'

'Budgerigars. Five hundred of 'em.'

Nick pointed up at a huge gold globe hung from the ceiling.

'Now, Salome, as you finish the dance, pull this,' showing her a gold rope. 'It splits open the globe. The birds fly around the set...'

Well, she yanked, but the budgies didn't budge. So the crew fed an air hose into the thing. *Action!* Birdies were blasted at walls, drapes, the floor, many so hard that they bounced off. Little dead green and gold fluffballs fetched up all over the lot for days afterwards. Gruesome testament to the madness of Emperor Nick.

His scenes done, history's most miscast John The Baptist Robert Ryan took us out on a spree. A torrid and bibulous excursion. In the end, our numbers down to Ryan, the quite mad Rip Torn, our film's Judas, and self. Ryan said *we godda go to La Venencia,* propped up by his forehead as he peed against a wall. Bob, quite the civil rights activist, explained that this tavern had been a hangout for Republican soldiers during the Spanish Civil War.

'A drink to their memory, boys. Their bold stand against fascism.'

'Americans! Over here!'

A sad-eyed, greybearded man arose.

'Why, Mr Hemingw...' I managed.

'Papa, call me papa. Get me a drink, limey.' Seems he knew Bob. 'Ryan! Who are these bastards?' Bob explained. A round of *Rioja* and *Albarino* one fetched from the bar. Then one's drink caught Papa's eye.

'By the *stem*, gringo. By the *stem!*' One was holding the glass full in one's hand.

'A code, you ignoramus. If you held your wine glass the way you are, you were a Franco *spy!*'

He was here on a story. *Life* magazine. Pamplona, the Running Of The Bulls. Rip had a camera that he now reefed from his bag.

'Oh, man,' he said. 'I gotta get a picture of this.'

'*What?*' roared Papa. '*Are you mad?* They'll call you a Fascist spy in here. Don't make me break that thing. Or your goddamned head.'

'Somewhere out there,' I said as we lined up one morning, 'a pirate wants his treasure back.'

Four weeks into the shoot, we were yet to be paid. Then Sam fetched up this day with carpetbags, yes, pixie, carpetbags, each full of every stretcher case currency in Europe. Lire, pfennigs, pesetas, drachmas, francs, were ladled out. Not a happy sign. Further, we were evicted from the Hilton and tipped into a two-star pit in the guts of Chueca, Madrid's Times Square. Oh, and one had had a tiff with Hurdy, so he and self were off the boil. It was the first time one paid for sex with fistfuls of trans-Euro spare change.

Bronson now learned that he must cut *El Caudillo* in on the box office action for *King Of Kings*. Or – well, a madman general, capable of anything. At the same time, a battalion of Franco's troops, our paid extras who'd been dispatched here whether we asked for them or not, were marched off the set. Spanish workers had gone on strike, you see. Came now riots, terrorist bombs, arrests. In the middle of all this, an airmail letter from Hugh Griffith. He'd bagged an Oscar for *Ben Hur* and so now much in demand.

I'm in Israel, boyo. 'Exodus' with Paul Newman. And when that's squared away, 'Mutiny On The Bounty.' Larry O, Ustinov and Laughton have all said no to the Bligh part. So I've put in a word for you, laddie.

Taffy, you marvellous Welsh bastard! one aerogrammed in response. And sure enough, *KOK's* first AD Sumner Williams called me at our new hotel, The Regina, which we'd all taken to calling The Vagina.

'Frank, LA wants a test of you.'

On a sound stage at Chamartin Studios, one let rip. Saturninus. Pilate. Herod. Parts kingly and vicious.

Weeks hence, news made its way to Madrid of how one had fared. This on the same day as a visit from Norman Banks, one of those detestable moustachioed roving Australian reporters.

'Oh, I don't need the money,' when he asked why one took on job after job playing history's most loathsome varlets. 'It's not even work, really. One has a certain affinity for these brutes. And I mean, it's all rather relative. In this picture we're doing here, I chop the Baptist's head off. I kick King Herod as he dies. That's pretty hard to top.'

'I hear you weren't even sure of your part when you arrived.'

Who told this cunt? It was fucking Bronston's fault. But for one to say so of one's producer and benefactor, just not on.

'Well, it's a ten thousand mile trip from Melbourne to Madrid, you see, Norman. Yes, one had played Pilate in *Ben Hur.* So somewhere over the Indian Ocean, one got it into one's head that one was doing so again. But I'm glad I'm Herod. I'd be jealous of whoever did if I wasn't.'

'The Bligh part for *Bounty.* Went to Trevor Howard. Not you.'

Wonder who'd leaked this. Then realised. They're actors, baby. So fucking ALL of them.

'Ah. Well, Norman, MGM said I was a perfect Bligh, you see.' *Pause for effect.*

'But not me. Couldn't see it myself.' Spread my arms, *c'est la vie.* 'They just couldn't talk me into it. So Trevor it was. And nobody happier about that than I.'

He opened his yap but I raised my hand, *pray silence.* 'Had I done it, people like *you* would brand it but a pale Mr Laughton or Sir Laurence. No matter what I did.'

'Are you tough on your own performances?'

'Oh, Norman. How *could* I be?'

King Of Kings was done. The phone rang as I packed.

'*Oh. Sam.*' What could he possibl.....

'Stay right where you are, Frank baby. Need you for a new picture.'

'Beg yours?'

'We start shooting right away.' He was calling from LA. One didn't ask. Probably best. 'I'm on the next plane.'

'Hurdy! *Et tu,* baby?' *Oh, happy da...*'

But he met not my eyes. So. Another suitor. The little *bitch.* Bronston threw a cast dinner, for those of us pressed to tarry in Madrid, at an eater specialising in slaughtered game, called Horcher. At Puerta de Alcala, the sole surviving gate of the Old City wall.

Yordan rose to speak. The film would tell the story of El Cid, who battled Spain's Arab overlords in the 11th century. My part, Al-Kadir. The baddest black hat. Well, turban. But fuckall to do while waiting for our leading man Chuck Heston. He was still busy on a film in LA, Sam said. Nothing else for it. Time for a holiday.

Ah, Gibraltar. Luncheon for one. The Wisteria Terrace of the Rock Hotel...

'*Thring!*' Jerked from one's reverie, Orson Welles loomed over me.

'Have you produced my play yet?'

He meant *Moby.* He'd just stomped out of post for *Touch Of Evil* in LA, the film he'd been working on with Chuck and Marlene Dietrich.

'They won't cut it my way. Meddling philistines!'

He was here, he said, to scout locations for a film of *Don Quixote.* And CBS wanted a teleplay of *Julius Caesar* from him.

'What Shakespeare have you, Thring?' One spouted the first lines that came to mind.

'*Cowards die many times before their deaths...*'

'*Outstanding!* Get over to LA. It seems I have my Brutus. The best part in the play, you know. I wouldn't give it to just any bastard...'

'Oh, Orson, I'm sorry.' *And I was.* 'One has this film in Madrid...'

'Disregard it! Shakespeare is the work God *made* us for, old man.'

He signalled for more wine. Having drained one's bottle, unbid.

'Yes, this *El Cid*, you mean,' he said. 'Yes, yes. They offered me a part. Arab warlord Ben Yussef.' He scowled. 'With my face veiled! I said I'd do a voice-over and they could shoot with a damned double. They said no. The hell with them.'

Orson made short work of his huge luncheon order, enough for he and two companions, the film stars Keenan Wynn and Eva Gabor. He claimed they'd be joining us and so ordered for them, but they never showed. Repast demolished, he stood up, 'to go turn wine back into water, old man. Our unprepossessing mortal conjuring trick.'

One waited; and waited. Orson was a gifted magician, you remember, pixie. Indeed, his disappearing trick a specialty. The bill was, shall we say, impressive.

'So, folks, we have to shoot all Sophia's scenes first,' said Bronston. La Loren, our just-signed female lead, was with child, you see.

'And she's not happy with the script,' said Yordan, with a deathglance at new writers Frederic Frank and Ben Barzman. As if his deplorable screenplay was their fault.

'What does *not happy* mean?'

This from our director, Tony Mann. Bald. Visage of a man trying to survive to the last reel of one of his bullet-riddled Westerns. Or war pictures. Or gangster flicks.

'You tell me,' said Yordan. 'We have twelve weeks, is all we know.'

'Well.' A voice of red sand and badlands dust. 'Best get to it.'

Table reads. Herbie Lom's Ben Yussef harangued we warlords to kill more, more often. We responded in kind. Scene done. Books down.

'You men kill in cold blood,' said Mann. 'The thing is, not one of you sounds like it right now. Set it right. Or I'll give your lines to a man who does.'

But it was Yordan's dreadful script, you see, not us. Yet as we went on, lines were torn from us. Given to Herbie. It morphed into a monologue to mute statues. Then Yordan lobbed with new lines from his writers, they presumed chained up in cages somewhere. Mann slung these to Herbie too. We did it again. Well, watched Herbie do it. My man, the fearsome Al-Kadir, now reduced to trembling butterball, going by changes elsewhere in the script. But my scenes must be *mine.* I fell to plotting.

'Oh, Tony won't be directing you', said Hurdy. Yes, quick as one's first fuck, he'd been cast aside by his fresh meat. Silly boy. Over brandy alexanders at the Castellana's lobby bar, his sob story in that regard, and come daybreak, *here we be...*
   'He's just told Sam he'll only direct Sophia and Chuck. First ADs will do the rest.'
   Fuck.

'She's getting paid more than him,' Hurdy told me. 'He's just found out.'
   Just days after Loren joined us, there was talk of either she or Chuck leaving the picture. 'So he's only giving half a performance, he's announced. Flat, robotic.'
   'Oh,' I said. 'How can they *tell?*'
   Sophia had also insisted that while the action takes place over twenty years, makeup were not to age her one jot. Looks as absurd as it sounds. Ah, motion pictures. Hurd finished on *Cid* soon after. Left without a goodbye. Don't they all?

On one's days off, to Madrid's wonders. The Royal Palace. The Prado. Basilica de San Francisco. One randy eye out, for *hombre joven* open for business. T'other for muggers. The two often worked in concert, you see.
   Meanwhile, Heston so broiled about Sophia's paycheck, he wouldn't even face her on camera. They had to shoot him looking at stand-ins for their two-hander scenes.

'Those two?' said Tony Mann out of their hearing one day. 'Like shooting a goddamned lumber yard.'

Now to Peniscola. Yes, that really is the name of this walled and ancient burg stunt doubling for mediaeval Valencia. Yordan came to one's suite the night before the shoot. *Knock knock.*

'Frank?'

His voice from without, Dracula summoning a valet. One was naked. Opened the door good and wide. 'Oh! Oh, Frank, I'm sorr...'

'About what, dear boy? Do come *in.*'

'Er, Frank, I won't keep you. Tony Mann will be directing you tomorrow.'

Well. Wondrous tidings.

'Now, Frank.' Looked away as he spoke. 'About your Al Kadir. He needs to be more, er, *sinister.* How, that's up to you. So, well, um, see you at sunrise.'

The fucker. They hadn't shot a frame of me yet. The subtext here, one could be sent packing and replaced with ease. Producers do this all the time, to mortify supporting cast into lifting their game. *More sinister. How the fuc...* Then one recalled Max Schreck in *Nosferatu The Vampyre,* one's favourite silent flick.

'What have you done?' said Yordan. But Tony Mann shrugged and nodded approval.

'Works. One mean hombre.'

'*Kill them! Run them down!*' screams one's Kadir at his troops. He flees- but is trapped on the city walls, 'tween mobs of vengeful Valencians. Tony went with one's proposal here. No riotous assembly as per the script. Instead, they fall to a hush, seeing they've snared their prey. One's cleanhead skull, self-shaved with cut-throat razor after Yordan's visit last night, did the rest. A dummy me was flung from the parapet by extras. I supplied the scream.

On a freezing hillside, Peniscola our backdrop, Herbie Lom's Ben Yussef ranted at we evil Arab warlords to upscale our kills. Took three days and all the pep pills and brandy one's belly could hold. Seconal, *reds* as the

Americans in cast and crew called them, erased all memory of the five-hour drive back to Madrid.

From Peniscola, to Torrelobaton, in the hills outside Madrid, for one's al-Kadir to watch his men lose a battle to the Cid. AD Yak Canutt had shot the *Ben Hur* chariot race. An action man. Had time only for stunts and derring-do.

'Not my department, baby,' I told him. So one sat one's horse for days, waiting for Yak to say 'Lean forward, alarmed by what you see, Frank,' and such. One was about to suggest at lunch one day, as one opened a second bottle of Valdepenas, that they use an extra. Then realised, well. They *were*.

One's only scene with Chuck Heston loomed. Cusp of autumn and winter now. Cold as fucking Pluto outdoors. My man is taken hostage early in the film. Franco's troops loitered, costumed as mediaeval Spanish rebel soldiers, staunch to the Cid.

Yes. Fascist legions cast as freedom fighters. The latter, thin on the ground. They'd murdered all the real ones hereabouts.

It meant a tax break or some such Bronston-Yordan lurk. Herbie Lom and self were sent off to to shoot our two-hander scene in Rome, for fuck's sake, at Cinecitta. One was packing for the flight when the phone trilled.

'*Francois.*'

Winsome Genevieve Page was cast in *Cid* as the King Of Spain's sister. We had no scenes together in the film, but had met, and discovered a mutual passion for jazz. Miles Davis was in town, she said. 'Join us, *Francois, mon frere.*'

Her hub Jean-Claude was here too. The gig, at El Berlin Jazz Club. There'd be a queue longer than a Proust sentence. So she dolled up like La Loren. Headscarf. Fly's eye sunnies. We men in suits and shades even darker than hers. *Bodyguards*, you see.

'*Como sabes que esto es?*'

Do you know who this is? Jean-Claude convinced the doorman. A fistful of *pesetas* from stony mute me scored us a ringside table. A superb set from Miles, this his immortal sextet, with John Coltrane, Cannonball Adderley and Bill Evans. After the show, Genevieve and Jean-Claude made for our hotel. Self, well, Madrid an all night long kind of town, so one chose to box on. A fateful decision.

Swaying up a side street, Isabel la Catolica, to the Gran Via, five AM... *a thud in my chest.* On my back, on the cobblestones.

'*La bolsa! Damelo!*'

He'd high-kicked me to the ground, I realised. Planted his boot in my chest. One so drunk that one wasn't frightened.

'*Dinero! Plata!*' Money. Very well, then...

'*Por supuesto,*' *of course*, I managed. Reached into Black Bag. *Ah, there it is.*

'*AAAARRRGHHHH!*'

Up on the Gran Via, a movieland touch. A vacant taxi. Still dark, so any blood on a black suit unseen. The desk clerk, *gracias a Dios,* on the doze. Elevators *sans* attendants at this hour.

Rent my clothes to shreds. Washed self and knife. A cab to Chamartin Studios. Gate sentries knew me. Pre-dawn arrivals quite the norm. To the props bays. Dropped the blade into a wicker skip full of the buggers.

At Barajas Airport, in the brasco. Going from stall to stall, took ripped shards of ex-suit from Black Bag. Flushed. Breakfast, *el desayuno* at the coffee shop. Slugs of Manzanilla *con* reds at the bar, to stop the shaking.

Roma. Taxi to the quiet shades of a suite at the Ex. Here, More reds. Tumbledown to slumber, as if to the undiscovered country that awaits us all.

On the set at Cinecitta, one's shaved skull glared at people. As intended. Then some fucker decided that it gave one too much menace and Herbie's Ben Yussuf must dominate. So they stuck a white turban on me. Now I resembled a Florida dowager, fresh out of the shower after tumble with toyboy. *Bastards!* So to subvert things, one cruised Herbie for our scene. No one jerried. All there in the final cut, pixie. *Heh heh.*

'Frank. Have seat. I have a good news and a bad news.'

Michal Waszynski, Bronston's executive fetchit, had called me into Chamartin.

'I think you mean bad and worse, Mike.'

'Is good joke, Frank. I laugh,' he said, not laughing. 'Frank, soundtrack is bad. Electrical current here *straszny*. You must London go. Re-record dialogue.'

One stifled a whooshing sigh of relief. I'd come here expecting to be arrested.

'Oh. I see. So what's the other bad news, Mike?'

'No, this is a good news. New picture. Sam want you.'

He pushed a script across the desk. *The Fall Of The Roman Empire*.

'Orson! What brings you to this sonic Belsen?'

Two days on, just finished dubbing at MGM in London and here he be as one tried to exit the lift. I swear the fucker was stalking me for free luncheons.

'A voiceover narration, old man. For that cockamamie Jesus picture of yours.'

'*King Of Kings?* Whatever for?'

'Why does *Henry V* have a chorus? Why, to have us believe that here be greatness, for some clamhead is telling us so, in sonorous tone. I said five grand. Half for the job, half for my name in the credits.'

'And?' *Fuck, that was all I got for the whole picture.*

'Well, I'm doing the talking. But pig-ignorant filmgoers will wonder eternal just who that velvet-voiced bastard is. That vapid boy Hunter as Jesus.' He shook his head. 'Guess they need the gravitas. To stop 'em laughing at the poor sap.'

'Yes. Fuck, what a Christ.' I turned to go. 'But Christ, what a *fuck*.'

It got around faster than pubic lice. Thus has the myth spread for decades that I, Thring, whambammed Jesus of Hollywood. Well, it's nice to be remembered.

'Thring, you cunt,' he smiled. Graham Payne, his live-in flooze, showed me around while one's host mixed the drinks.

'You look all done in from the flight, Frank,' said Payne. 'Come and have a swim. It's just behind that wall.'

'Oh, and cockie,' said Coward, handing one a *Spritz Veneziano,* 'nudity is mandatory.'

Firefly Estate was once the pirate Henry Morgan's. *You must come visit in Jamaica, Wallaby,* Sir Noel had said. So here I be. His Caribbean eyrie roomy and awash in light. That Scott 'n' Zelda palm court ambience he seemed content to inhabit forever. Paintings by Coward himself of previous guests. A flawed Churchill pouted at a haughty Katy Hepburn. Olivier's eyes bored into one's back. Noel's Marlene Dietrich, an ice-faced Isolde.

A stone hut had been built on the estate by that rapscallion Morgan the Pirate, well, privateer, really. As a lookout.

'To get the drop on Spaniard brigantines. Well, any bounty-bearing dago vessel sailing the Spanish Main was fair game,' said Coward. 'Morgan had a license to plunder, signed by the British governor of Jamaica, *quid pro quo* a slice of the action. But I've converted it to something far more useful. A wet bar, cockie. Anything one could desire. Save rough seadogs and dusky cabin boys.'

Evenings, we sipped white rum here as luminous insects danced attendance. Noel handed me a spliff. From the banana plantation on the estate next door, he said.

'Best with rum and tonic chasers. And bumsex.'

'A heart attack, old boy. Right in the middle of ruddy ed conference at the *Times.* They told me to take some time off, so here I be.'

One was asked to lunch with Noel, Payne and our host, at the latter's lux villa. Goldeneye he called this pile, just down the road from Firefly. He took his pipe out. Pointed with it as he spoke. 'They want to film my books, Coward. What say you? Worth the horror?'

'Well, they'll destroy them, goes without saying. But you're paid twice for the same job, so...'

'Your stuff's *made* for cinema, laddie,' I said. I'd read *Casino Royale, Goldfinger, Diamonds Are Forever*. And who better than Yours Truly to play a Bond villain if...

'I've got a new one on the go, Thring,' he said. Passed across a manuscript. 'I look forward to your critique.'

I looked down at the title page. *Thunderball. By Ian Fleming.*

'*Well?*'

Fleming, two days later. 'Come on. Full brutal, Thring. Out with it.'

'I don't like the black hat. But I want to. A murdering jewel thief. A thought, if I may. He should perhaps rob only the jet set, themselves reprehensible. Hence deserving.'

He nodded, *right you are.*

'And his lair. In the Bahamas, with a pool full of sharks...' I clicked my fingers.

'I have it. A pirate's eyepatch. Why, never revealed. An unknown, violent past. And so now,' I said, 'a badfellow fit for film.' *In which one might be cast as this very chap.*

'The other boy made me do it, sir.'

Alas, it raised not the smile sought. Payne, back early from a shopping run, caught Noel and I at it. Well, it was at Coward's bidding. But, yes, one also doesn't wait to be asked to leave.

CHAPTER TWENTY

Maxine Audley is dead. One fumbles to open this cask of Coolabah Riesling, parblinded by tears. I saw her in that Helen Mirren series, *Prime Suspect*, just a few weeks back. One raises the very goblet, from *The Vikings*, from which we'd sipped.

'Cheerio, Max,' one whispers in deepening eventide. *Or perhaps, see you soon.*

A new radio station has bubbled up from the swampdepths. 3EE has been rebirthed. Well, exhumed. You see, it's the ghost of that once mine, 3XY. Poor old XY. Once Melbourne's top rating rock and pop station. Stymied by the advent of FM in the 1980s. They stripped XY of her advertisers in a price war. Then her listeners. Bought the smoking remains and closed her down. Months of cold silence on that old spot on the dial followed. Now in 1992, she is resurrected as conduit for vapid pop hits of best-forgotten yesterdays. Sonic Mogadon, pixie. One had sold off one's interest long ago. Thus spared bedside vigil at the old tart's last rattle.

*

After so long abroad, Melbourne in 1961 at once alien yet over-familiar. You know, pixie. That eerie sense of displacement that befalls the Aussie traveller returned. One had not seen a lot of Rylands since 1955. Here, safe haven. The old gal still redolent of Margaret's furniture polish, the aroma of Edith's cooking.

'The cost of living has risen somewhat,' one observed. Handed them envelopes crammed with cash. 'So for you two old choppers, pay rises. Backdated.'

Nothing going for now. Glad of it, truth be told. In green suede dressing gown purchased in Roma, one worked through Xavier Herbert's *Capricornia*, sitting in a huge bay window at Rylands. It looked out on a huge magnolia planted by FT. And for all of its glories, this effervescence of pink and white flowers was an invader from north of the Equator. As per the villains of Herbert's novel, their pageant of brutalities wreaked upon the First Australians. The story prompted memory of Olive, and a Day of Mourning protest by Aboriginals in Sydney. Australia Day, 1938, it was. One was twelve. Saw the story in the papers, and expressed at a bridge night a cheer for their cause.

'Oh, Frankie,' she snorted. 'Look, if they don't like it here,' she huffed, 'they should never have come!'

'Did you really fuck Jesus in Hollywood, Frank?' Mary Hardy on the blower.

'Can I have his number?'

Word gets around, like I said, pixie. Mary asked one to do Friday *IMT* with she and Ferrier, to pull a few viewers. Gra Gra Kennedy, the main compere, had been grinding his teeth about the ratings – *their* ratings, not his. So one must give aid and succour where one can. To plug that, one set up an interview with *TV Week*. Some wireless as well, you know, 3AW, UZ. One's own station XY, of course. One spoke to most of Melbourne, one way or another, of both one's new Friday *IMT* turn and the *Fall Of The Roman Empire* shoot next April. And war stories of *King Of Kings* and *El Cid*.

Then a cable came.

HESTON   OUT   EMPIRE   SHOOT   POSTPONED
BRONSTON

Well, yes, one kept this to oneself. And lied without shame to *IMT* viewers about one's fees for *KOK* and *El Cid*.

'Oh, baby. One can't find a *sack* big enough to *hold* it all.'

One took part in their weekly sketch, the *IMT Friday Night Players*. Noel and Mary featured, along with Gra Gra's 'favourite little druggie' as he once called her on air, Toni Lamond. Freddy Parslow fetched up too, doing his superb, well, Freddy Parslow. At drinks for cast and crew back at Rylands, one suggested a weekly solo spot for oneself.

'A crit of the week's TV,' I said. 'From an armchair, in embroidered smoking jacket.'

Their ratings rose. The freak show was back in town.

'Frank, it's Rod Lever from *TV Week*. How would you be?'

One also resumed *A Piece Of Thring*. Told readers of the imminent *Roman Empire* shoot. Left out the bit about Heston bailing. Also that one had been airmailed the script. And the horrors within. The torpid words of Phil Yordan peeped up from its pages as if begging for a quick death.

In the middle of all this, a call from one Gloria Payten, a sassy young talent agent based in Sydney with ICS. Hmm. *I'll give you the big tip, Frankie, my boy; no middlemen,* FT had said. Yet she was persuasive. Dangled the prospect of TV and film work for fees they'd never offer *me* upfront. And she could snare me more of it than I could, she also a casting director, you see. But one reserved the right to book direct, as it were, for theatre turns. One didn't want to price oneself out of this most impecunious of markets. It later became apparent, of course, that one's diffidence in that regard cost one a Matterhorn of gold. Ah, well. *Ars longa vita brevis.*

'*The Guardsman,* Frank.'

'Oh, for fuck's sak...'

Fucking Black Jack. Our luncheon at Florentino now ruined. *How could you?*

'It fills theatres, boy. Our subscribers aren't coming like they used to...'

'I know how they *feel,* Butch.'

'And I'll need you for this Ionesco play.' His eyes braced for one's reaction. 'Where people turn into rhinoceroses.'

'I see,' I said. 'Sounds like Channel fucking Nine.'

Back at *TV Week*, of Seven's *Sunnyside Up*, one wrote that their singers looked like a Pekinese dog told to practice deep breathing. *One wonders whether someone should be standing by, cupping their hands to catch their eyeballs when they pop out.* And of the compere, toad-eyed horse race caller Bill Collins, that *he comes across as though delivering a funeral oration; his own.* Well, it sold magazines, you see. Lots of 'em.

But look, pixie, it wasn't all putrid. *Consider Your Verdict* was world-class telly. Made by Crawfords for Seven. They gave scripts only to the actors playing judges and barristers. Those cast as defendants and witnesses had to ad lib. Made them look petrified, ambushed. Capital idea. A first-class recommendation in A *Piece Of Thring*.

Earned me a part in the thing, as a QC.

ABV2's drama unit made some awful stuff, but not John Mortimer's *Call Me A Liar*. This teleplay had turned one's head for an array of reasons. One of them, a sprite among its cast. One must call him Antinous, after that Greek boy, the emperor Hadrian's lover. He was also fetching up in turns at the Union of late. Gleaming was this whippet. Quite mad, too, one would learn, and epic appetite for liquor and pharma. But...*I must have him.*

Darling Vivien Leigh came to town in August, Helpmann directing her in an Old Vic tour. Viv and Larry had divorced two years back. Larry, of course, had married Joan Plowright. In Viv's thrall now, a new handbag, young Jack Merivale.

'A real tonic for Viv, that lad,' said Helpmann when I called him. 'But not fooling anyone with that beard, those glasses. A score of summers her junior. Brimful of spunk.'

'As is Vivien much of the time then, one assumes,' I said.

Vivvy still played teenage Viola in *Twelfth Night*, despite being thirty in scrubber years too old. Less manic now. But in her state, could no longer learn new parts, and so...

'One has worked with Miss Leigh before,' I said. 'And loath to impose on her while she's resting before the show.'

Met Helpmann with this boy Merivale, at Jimmy Watson's Wine Bar in Lygon Street in Carlton, to tee it up. After the prem of *Twelfth* at Her Maj, one hosted the cast at Rylands for supper. And one invited Mary Hardy, Sumner and his incumbent wife. And, yes, young Antinous. To impress the boy. That he might, well, you know...

A splendid evening. Vivien, playing charades as only she could, spilled sherry on a goatskin rug. One has never had it cleaned. And she had a request.

'Wallaby. I would so love to see a local play while I'm here.'

The One Day Of The Year was on at Russell Street Theatre. One kept Viv's visit secret from all but Sumner. Asked Antinous along. And Mary Hardy, so that oneself and this young buck didn't look like what it was. *Not in public. Just not on.* After the show, a private reception one had organised at the Embers jazz club in South Yarra. *One Day's* leading lady Bunney Brooke managed not to swear or punch Viv in the face. Nor vice versa. One hocussed Bunney's drinks, you see. Two nuggets crushed to powder. She slumped into a chair with a beatific smile. You're welcome, Black Jack. Glad to be of service.

The telegram boy looked away. One was nude, you see. One's custom at home come summer.

LOREN, BOYD, FOR FALL OF ROMAN EMP ARE YOU
FREE NEXT APRIL SPAIN BRONSTON

'Oh, if I must.'

TV Week insisted on an interview when I told them. One threw a blue and gold silk robe on when Jack Ayling came to one's home. One gave Aussie TV two cheeks full of verbal shotgun swandrops, for not making more TV drama the way the Yanks and Poms did. It fell on ears of tin.

It was time. You recall Rylands as was, pixie. One cleared it of Olive's mud and guts paintings, ornaments and furniture. Those gauche ebony elephants and such. Kept the good stuff. You know, FT's purchases abroad, genuine Louis XV pieces, Ming and Qing Dynasty artefacts. What the Salvos didn't want of Olive's chattels, an offering to the Lord of Misrule. The bonfire waved at me.

The rooms at Rylands were lined with dark timber panelling in shades of shit and treacle. One had the lot removed. Gorgeous brickwork underneath. Alas, no hidden troves of FT treasure. On the bright side, nor any skeletons.

'Ceilings, skirting boards, window frames, the hall. You sure, mate?'

'*All* of it.' Waved my hand at it. 'Paint it *black.*'

They must have thought I was Count Yorga, Vampire. For one wall of the reception room, wallpaper, watered gold silk. Floor to ceiling mirrors at each end, should one get lucky on the animal skins underfoot. The kitchen's drab vanished under orange and black, Sinatra's favoured combo at his Palm Beach pad, Chuck Heston had told me. Bathroom, black with red and white fittings and features. One's tiny boyhood bedroom, whence one still reposed, black all over. *Window panes while you're at it, mate, if you would be so kind.*

The area alongside the east wall of the property no longer corralled FT's old blue Packard, the family Roller, nor Olive's Riley. So one decreed a swimming pool here. In what feature stories forever after reported was an *unusual shape.* Not a bit of it. Fifty percent of humanity sport appendage in those contours.

One served up, or had Margaret serve up, bountiful morning teas and hot lunches for the tradesmen. With cold beers aplenty. And in the middle of all this, Margaret found a large portrait of Olive and hung it in the hall. Under that, on a small table, she plonked a vase of white gardenias.

'What is thi... I seized it. 'It will burn this very *hour!*'

'Leave it, Frank,' she said. 'or I'm off. Clean your own bloody house.'

She placed flowers here daily. Until she, like them, wilted. And breathed no more.

'I'm so sorry I'm late.'

A willowy lad. His first day at the Union. Sumner's eyes burned black, fuelled by his fetish for punctuality.

'My hotel's not the b-best,' this faun gibbered. 'I had to handwash a shirt and...'

'Oh, dear boy,' I said, reclining in the prop throne built for the show now in rehearsal, 'bring your shirts and come and stay at my place. My housekeepers would be delighted to launder them, and...'

But yon pup looked apprehensive.

'No, thanks!'

Well, then. He must be punished. At rehearsals, one walked all over his lines with one's own, booming and snarling. Oh, and offered damning notes on his work – in front of fellow castees. But the fucker kept trying to pretend he was *one's equal.*

'Morning, Frank! Hi!'

I kept walking. In one's *own domain.* Insulted by this imp and no penance offered. And one's *thirst* unslaked by cheeky Reg Livermore from Sydney. *I shall break him on the wheel yet,* I vowed.

Sheila Florance was in *The Guardsman* too. Magic oftimes, but forgot her lines. We had to improv our way out when she dried. One had to play nice. Sheila was also a floor manager at the ABC. Performing in teleplays there, one at her brutal mercy.

Back at the Union, no two shows of *The Guardsman* were the same, thanks to Sheila's dries. Oh, and pieces went missing from young Livermore's costumes each day. The boy needed blooding. To dart hither and yon in a flopsweat, seeking out these misplaced items or last-minute substitutes, just the ticket.

'Character-building,' one said to Clem McCallin, a Brit expat thesp one's co-bully in the Razzing Of Reg. Sumner fumed at the boy. Just as hoped. Still, Young Reg was good. *Too good* at times. Now, if he'd had the nous to move into Rylands, well, ...

'We have Larry and Orson's imprimatur,' one's assurance to the press, for our own Melbourne stab at their hot new play in London, Ionesco's *Rhinoceros.* Of course, one hadn't spoken to either. They ran the yarn big. Pics of Larry, Orson and self. But ticket sales stayed slow. So, then. Called the newsdogs again. At Melbourne Zoo, one climbed into the rhino enclosure. Asked the beasts how one should play them. A move right out of the FT playbook. Scored us a big run on the TV news. But *Rhino* was a play to be endured, not enjoyed. The customers, thin on the ground.

'Come see the show,' I sighed to director Wal Cherry at a near-empty matinee.

'And stand *out* from the fucking *crowd*.'

'You must be *mad. Me?* As Macbe...?'

'Ah, careful, boy, bad luck to say its nam...'

'Haven't said yes yet. Don't see me as Dracula either.'

'Well, you should know I'm not asking you on the basis of your performance in *Rhino,*' he said. *Ouch.* The fucker cut people in half with that.

'Oh, alright. We go forth and make shows that make dough,' I sighed, 'or there be no dough to make shows.'

'My *Drac* will be a Falstaffian glutton,' I told her. 'A world first.'

Whether she liked it or not. Very trad, was *Dracula* director Moira Carleton. Came from JCWs musicals, TV soapies. Competent. But as deep as a birdbath. Sheila Florance was cast too. As ever, we piled back to her humpy in St Kilda, any night we cared to. Drunken thesps roaring, weeping, fighting, all the hours of *la luna*.

'Oh, Sheila!' I'd squeal when one of her cats jumped into my lap. 'Your pussy has laddered my stockings!'

Moira was a bit cold on this idea at first, but one went ahead anyway. One deployed fake blood for *Drac.* Spat it, or let gushes go when one 'bit' others. But never let on as to when this would happen. Never knew when they'd be splattered, you see. Their whining to Moira one disregarded when she came to me with plea that one back off a smidgeon.

'It keeps them on edge, as their characters should be,' I said. Clem McCallin joined again in sporting with young Livermore for this play, too. But no matter what we heaped on poor Reg, he never cracked. Not once. *Bastard.*

For New Years' Eve, one hosted at Rylands. All the janes and johns of Melbourne showbiz. Great happiness. Sheila F gave us her *Summertime.* Gal had pipes. In the kitchen, we two, the last not felled of sixty starters, had final showdown drinks. Dawn peeped, appalled, through the window.

Back at *Drac,* one took to adding white vinegar on the sly to the fake blood of others. Their onstage gagging, priceless. But the *Age* called one's Drac a house guest who's outstayed his welcome. *Well, fuck them.* We filled that gummy old crone the Union for weeks.

One kept up one's TV bit on Friday's *IMT* with Ferrier, Hardy, all that mob. Straight to GTV9 after curtain for *Drac.* Be mad not to. Telly types. Reliable abundance of Nembies, Dex and reds.

'Me? It's like Orson Welles as fucking *Tinkerbell.*'

Black Jack unmoved. Yes, Thring as Thane Of Cawdor in his Scottish Play might shift tickets, but...

Sheila Florance was one's Lady Mac. Moped around day and night *in public* in a frightful black wig with plaits. Filched from the St Martin's wardrobe.

'To get into character,' she squawked. Oh, and speaking of frightful, Bunney Brooke was Lady McDuff. But Sheila's part did she sore covet.

'Bunney, you're already Mrs McDuff *and* doubling as a Weird Sister,' said Sumner to her bunched fists and jutting jaw.

'And good at it,' I said. 'You play a witch like you've been one all your life, dear.'

At a safe distance, of course. You know, given stories of her decking a man at the Tote Hotel in Collingwood. Or holding a girlfriend over the balcony of a fourth floor flat in Footscray. By the hair.

'Frank. Louder, please.'

But I'd seen Larry's Thane at Stratford. *Most overdo it,* Larry had said. *So you're buggered by Act III when you really need the energy.* But Black Jack, well, ...

'You're not commentating lawn bowls, boy. You're plotting regicide.'

The real problem? The fucker was half deaf. But one stood firm. A moonwhite hand gestured glum surrender from the gloom of the stalls. Meantime, dippy Sheila harped on about one's costume. She'd rubbed filth on hers to get it *more Dark Ages,* she said.

'But I'm a king, you silly slag,' I said. She grabbed my hands.

'Clear nail polish? In mediaeval Scotland?'

For opening night, one came in to find one's costume smeared with dirt. *Well, then.* Her face that night when she sat in a puddle of water for the banquet scene, priceless.

One checked oneself in our only full length mirror backstage. Livermore, playing the murdered king's son Malcolm and addicted to this looking glass, hovered, in fur boots, coat and hat. I raked him with my eyes.

'Ah. An Eskimo *rent boy.*' He ignored it.

'You look great, Frank.' He did a model's twirl. 'How do you *really* think I look?'

'Well, if you want to look like Sonja fucking *Henie*, go ahead.'

Sonja was an Olympic skater and film star. She and Hitler, mutual fans. Despicable.

'And did you know,' I said, 'she *fucked* every *man* with whom she *ever worked*.'

'I'll rip ya throat out and bite your head off before you hit the *deck,* slut!'

On Sheila's dressing room table when she came in and turned on the light, a cow skull. Her scream split our heads in twain. The culprit, Bunney, wailing at her now. Still fuming that she wasn't Lady Mac, you see. Others restrained her while I shepherded Sheila away. And yet, I walked in on Sheila a few days on, her back to me. Grinding her teeth to Sumner. About *me.*

'I think he's forgotten he isn't hamming it up in Hollywood now.'

I see. I made off.

'Do you have to shower spit all over me every time you open your yap?' wailed Sheila at line-up that night. A move one learned from Tony Quayle. Makes co-stars flinch and twitch onstage. Puts 'em in their place. But one couldn't be angry at Sheila for long. One made up for it by mouthing her lines to her when she dried. We'd have been there all night otherwise.

'*Frank!* I *never* thought I'd see *you* play the Thane!'

To one's aghastment, some real actors saw the show. Syb Thorndike for one, she out here on tour.

'Nor I, Syb, by my troth.'

Zoe Caldwell, now a TV star in England, here in *St Joan* for the Adelaide Festival, fetched up as well.

'I like it, darling.' Her smiling fib a pleasant sunset pink.

'Well,' I said, 'we must thank young Mr Livermore here.' A languid hand flicked his way. '*He* makes us *all* look good.'

Now, in *A Piece Of Thring,* one wrote of cataclysms. HSV7, in early '62, axed all their panel and variety shows. The lot. Dorcas Street, South Melbourne, Seven's HQ, *had to be hosed out.* Then they hired all the people GTV9 had just fired. *Talk about keeping it in the family,* I wrote. It was like a hillbilly sex party, pixie. *And yet, a diamond from all this sludge,* came from one's two-fingered hunt and peck clatter. A new program on Seven, *Daly At Night.* Seven signed Jon Daly, one of those Yanks then infesting Aussie telly, after Nine punted him. Viewers wouldn't cop locals, the execs insisted back then. Gra Gra Kennedy proved them dead wrong, yet they persisted with shipping in these failed Vegas lounge acts and worse.

Daly was a cut above. The rest of this Yankfest, the cast of lamentable Tommy Hanlon Junior. And Larry K Nixon, his teeth and manner suggesting parentage of Red Riding Hood's wolf and a fucking draught horse.

Gra Gra was huge because he took the mick out of things, including advertisers' products. Daly's brief was to do likewise. This, declared Seven, would steal Kennedy's viewers from him. *Daly At Night* premiered in March 1962. The launch at HSV 7. One was invited, but was failing in our Scottish Play at the time. Sent regrets and French champagne.

At first, *DAN* didn't click. So one gave Daly a bucket in *TV Week*. Plus a few suggestions. *And they listened!* Daly persuaded Seven to do it more like the *Jack Paar Show* from the States. One had seen the Paar show on British telly. Met him at a party for BBC TV luvvies in London.

That's the ticket, one wrote in praise. *A show for our times, not some Edwardian music hall turn. Kennedy better start looking over his shoulder.* One had to hang up on Gra Gra when he called. Swearing in a most unladylike fashion.

'*Daly At Night* comes on right after *Sunnyside Up,*' one opined on the *Noel And Mary Show* on 3DB, 'the latter about as sunny as a plague of locusts.'

This vaudeville throwback gave *DAN* grief from the off. Daly's turn took money from *Sunny's* budget, you see. Its crusty Tivolidians dumped shrill on Daly in the press. *The mood at Seven like a moonshiner's feud* was how *TV Week's* readers heard of it. Jon Daly threw buckets at *Sunny* on his show. The press beat it up. Result, more viewers for *DAN*. A canny carny, this Yank.

Daly At Night was made at HSV7's Fitzroy Teletheatre, a refitted derelict cinema once FT's. On the new *Panel People* segment, Daly and his offsiders, harmonica whiz Horrie Dargie, songstress Vikki Hammond and others took on Melbourne's pompous archbishops, any politicians who were game, mad fitness guru Percy Cerutty in his sandshoes and whites, Toorak socialites, shifty entrepeneurs. But the panellists were not crash hot, a bit wet. Daly needed a red-fanged inquisitor, to set him apart from the rest of the *glutinous morass that comes from the one-eyed monster,* one wrote, this to see if it got past the *TV Week* subs' desk of all-day drunks. It did.

Well, blow me down if Daly didn't ask me to be his sidekick on *DAN*. Jack Ayling did a piece in *TV Week* about it, pics of one's signing on with Daly's production company, DYT. At the presser, Daly did his somewhat derivative mental defective comic bit in a multi-coloured golf hat.

'Well. If Jon is Melbourne's Jerry Lewis,' I said, 'that must make *me* our Dean *Martin.*'

'Sorry for all the horrors you're about to see. Playwright's trick. A hook. Sucks the customers in every time.'

One suggested we open each show with what one called The Apology. Pitched a few other ideas too.

'Get Vikki to do the weather. Horrie to read the news.'

'They don't know how,' said Daly. 'Why...'

'Precisely, baby. So they'll fuck up. Like Kennedy fucks things up. Gary and Gertie Gogglebox of Coburg and Footscray fucking love it.' The network did too. At first.

The set for *DAN* was cheap. A long table. Chairs on one side of it, facing the giant Marconi cameras gliding round on black and white check studio floor.

'A *Last Supper* setup,' I said one night to the panel. 'All these men. Out on a *date.*'

Christians complained in shoals. Of their rage did paper boys bellow in the streets. Just as one had planned. Ratings, you see.

Much of the time on *DAN*, we winged it. No team of writers here like Jack Paar. We had *one*. David Sale contrived a singing dialogue between Daly and self to open each show. With canes and straw boaters, we worked the old Gallagher and Shean routine.

'Oh, Mr Daly.'

'Yes, Mr Thring.'

'Have you seen the mess that JFK is in?'

It never worked, of course. We messed up our lines despite the floor crew holding up idiot sheets for us, behind the cameras. Wild flights of improv, to make each other laugh on camera. You see, the mugs love it when it all comes unstuck. David was poached by the *Mavis Bramston Show* and later scripted Ten's sordid sex soapie *Number 96.* Depraved mind, that boy. Commendable.

For our interview guests, one went in *hard*. To a celebrity Melbourne car dealer, one asked if his motors were good as getaway cars for bank jobs. Of a morals campaigner, if she had any children. To her yes, *Oh. How on earth did that happen?*

'We get a lot of these, viewers. Ruling their imaginary kingdoms *with a rod of putty,*' I said one night, ripping into Bob Santamaria. A distillation of many miseries, this fellow. On a mission to inflict them on the rest of us. Poor Santa. Face of a bald ventriloquist's dummy and voice to match. A Catholic morals fetishist. Had a fifteen-minute Sunday morning program on Nine, *Point Of View.* Airtime gratis courtesy of Sir Frank Packer. Spoke of how the world should be ruled, as a Vatican-spooked serfdom.

None were spared on *DAN.* Not even ye gods of Aussie Rules footy. Lou Richards easy meat on our segment *Pick The Teams.* Chunnering on about who'd win that weekend. He was wrong as often as not. One made much of this, to rile him up.

'How the fuck did you manage *that?*'

Jon Daly knew him from his LA days, it seemed. Out here to promote *How The West Was Won,* one of those all-star epics, crammed with every name in Hollywood. You know, to distract from the script. Jon called Henry Fonda direct at his hotel. Got him for *DAN* over Kennedy over at Nine. Gra Gra livid, as we stole his viewers that night.

But Channel Seven didn't want me anywhere near Fonda. Teed it all up without telling me. A pre-record, just he and Daly in HSV7's 'interview studio' at Fitzroy Teletheatre. And yet I, co-star to galaxy of Tinseltown great and good. *And* Chuck Heston. *Omnia gloria labilis* indeed. For some, even more fleeting than others.

We knew we must be rating for *DAN*, what with the Fonda coup and one's provoking Niagaras of complaints, you see. Thought we'd be toasted at the next meeting with the Seven bigknobs.

'Daly talks about America, not Australia,' Seven's producer Norm Spencer read from a sheet. 'And Thring talks about what sounds like reproductive organs.'

He took his glasses off. Pointed them at Daly and I. 'Now you two fix this up or I'll fix you up. Oh, and we want a real sheila on the show. Not like that old moll Vikki. A teen. Girl next door type.' He slid his glasses back on.

'Big tits, looks an easy root. With me?'

'She's a pal from LA, Frank,' said Daly in his odd Mickey Mouse voice. 'Got a great gimmick.' He winked, *chk chk* with his teeth. 'Can't say any more. Secret.'

She flew in the very next day. Came and saw the show, after we'd dined next evening at the Savoy, the 'Saveloy' as she came to call it. To Rylands for afters, still going at six AM. A trouper, this brassy femme, and *of the chosen*, partial to genders other than the opposite. But what was this *gimmick?*

'My name is Betty Bobbitt. I'm from Big Bear, Pennsylvania, and I really want to be in show business.'

Her first night on air. In cardigan, dowdy skirt, flat shoes. Prop spectacles held together with a Band-Aid, brunette wig in a topknot. A simpleton. Wardrobe by charity bin. *What the fuc...*

'Okay, kid,' said Jon, glancing in alarm at the camera. 'Show us what you got.'

On a harmonica, she assaulted us with a dire *Oh Susannah*. Stomped her foot out of time as she went. *Then I jerried. Brilliant.* A fame-seeking *imbecile*. TV infested with such. Doing a Norman Gunston, you see, but ten years before his time. One played along.

'You want an audience, darling, go and lie on the tram tracks in Swanston Street.'

'Doesn't he like me, Mr Baily?'

Jon of course was in on the gag. One sighed. Rolled one's eyes to camera.

'My dear girl. Did you get lost on your way to Channel *Nine?*'

The *Age* and the *Sun* went Page One. *WHO IS BETTY BOBBITT?* HSV7 choked with viewers' letters. Railed at this 'mental defective,' the charming label of the times. And yet, not as single spies but in battalions, lured from Kennedy's *IMT* to behold.

Betty's songs, *DAN's* musical director Arthur Young at the piano, or with Horrie Dargie's band, were train smashes. The sound of five cats on a fence at midnight.

But her fame came at a price.

'Keep up that persona everywhere you go, kiddo,' said Daly. 'Never do interviews out of character.'

'In fact,' said DYT's ad boss John Tilbrook, an oaf, 'don't go out at all.'

In those days, male TV execs did not make suggestions. They gave orders, in particular to female talent. It was appalling. Poor Betty. She loved Melbourne's cabaret scene, the folk clubs, the satirical revues. You know, the Treble Clef Club, or Tikki and John's in Exhibition Street, all those red velvet murkpits. So one tried to make up for DYT's *diktat* by throwing parties at Rylands for her. She adored one's cats Dracula, Tiddles and Squeaky Weasel.

'It's *fur!*' I heard her squeal one night from the hall. One had commissioned a second WC installed there, for the convenience of guests. It featured a fitted fake fur toilet seat.

'Oh, *that*. One of my *servants* ran it up,' I said, indicating Edith, who rolled her eyes. And a fib to taste. 'When one of the cats died.'

'Mr Thing! I'm in a play!'

I looked across the Panel People to Daly.

'Make it go *away,*' I said, fluttering my hand at Betty.

'No, really. Do you know the Arrow Theatre, Mr Thing?'

'Know it? I *started* the faaa...p place!'

Almost but not quite saying *fuck* on TV. I did it first. Kennedy stole it with his 'crow calls' later. Pulled viewers, the sad fuckers living in vapid hope that one day...

Yes, Betty was indeed in a revue at the Arrow. Sendups, current events. She and her co-stars did a bit from it on the show. Came there complaints, in quantity. Baby, we were the talk of Melbourne.

But Norm Spencer didn't like Betty. Desirous to fixation of poaching Nine's viewers, he craved Nine's stars. In particular Princess Panda

Lisner, and her asinine *maaaaaaarrrrvellous* catch-phrase. Wanted to fuck her, one supposed.

'But all these complaints means a lotta people are watching, Norm,' said Daly.

'Yeah, but we don't want them. We want Kennedy's.' Madness.

After an all-night shivoo with Betty and others, one stirred at midday. The sky, dull, mute. Saturday. No show tonight. *Fuck it.* Reached for the jar of Nembies...

Awoke; recalled, mortified. Dark now. Very late. *Oh, shit.* Daly had organised a party for one's thirty-sixth. *Today,* at the DYT office in Bourke Street. So. Chocolates and champagne for all. Sent 'em on their way in a fleet of Civic taxis. One kept aside profusions of both for just such. One's default apology. Often.

'Frank? Daly is ill. Can you compere tonight?'

A great show. At ad breaks, one stole glugs from one's Cognac Paradis hidden behind the set. Nerves, you see. Afterwards, party at the DYT office. One had been dropping Drinamyl of late, purple hearts they were called. Mix with spirits and...one fell about, one was told. Smashed into things. Wondered what one had said. Dared not ask.

Then two things happened. The Cuban Missile Crisis, that chilling end of days standoff, Kennedy and Khrushchev. Far more troubling, *DAN's* ratings dropped. You see, Jon Daly's former GTV9 partner Ken Delo was back from the US, and appearing on *IMT* with Gra Gra. Viewers had adored Ken as much as Jon. And now the two men, never enemies, started hanging out together, with their wives, snapped by the press at the prem of *The Sound Of Music,* that sort of thing.

'We want the old Jon Daly back.'

Norm at our next meeting with the Seven cave monsters. He meant the GTV9 incarnation of yore, the double act with Ken. 'Not all this hanging shit on people.'

He gestured at *DAN's* choreographer, Joe Latona. 'You people have a new producer. Joe?' Daly looked appalled. We all were.

'It's not working, Jon,' said Joe, a kindly fellow, and not without ability, but...

'So leave it to me and I'll...'

'Turn us into the *BP Super Show?*' I said. 'For fuck's sake, Joe...'

'No-one's talking to you,' said Norm to me, but looking at Daly. 'Oh, and no more play dates with Ken, mate. You two are at war. With me?'

When the networks impose their own producer on an independent show, it's curtains, pixie, as you know. Haven't got a clue that they haven't got a clue. We had to find other ways to pull viewers, keep ourselves from being axed. And fast.

JCWs and Kenn Brodziak were planning to stage the hit 40s musical *Out Of The Frying Pan* at the Princess. So one called Brodsky. Proposed the cast of *DAN* for it. He was keen. Saw a quid in it. But couldn't get the backers. Could have saved us, but...

One night, talking to Daly, one mentioned the Union's *Drac* and *Mac*, in particular the jolly fun with the fake blood.

'Oh, Mr Thing!' Betty. 'I love Shakespeare. Can I do some with you?'

'Yeah, why not?' said Daly. Oh, *must I?* But I liked Betty, so...

'What Shakespeare have you?'

One invited BB for a run through at Rylands, just she and self.

'Well, the Scottish Play, the dagger scene, for one,' she said. *Oh.* The gal was *versed*.

I mixed us both a Bloody Mary. But then, *oh dear.* One had crushed a purple heart into one's own refresher as per one's custom of late, but, too late, one realised, had *given it to Betty by mistake.* Wobbly on her pins, the poor poppet had to lie down. One felt dreadful. To this day she must think one slipped her a mickey, to take unseemly advantage, or as a psychopath's sport. Well, after that, I had it coming to me.

'Is this a bucket of *blerrrd* ah see before me?'

On a *DAN* set, Betty, in her hillbilly voice, togged up as Daisy Mae Scragg from Al Capp's comic strip *L'il Abner*. A grinning Daly plonked a prop wooden bucket on to our prop mediaeval table.

'Why, worthy Thane.'

Splort! One copped a mooshful of Kia-Ora cordial and Rosella tomato sauce from said receptacle. *I might have known.* One retaliated, slammed a handful of this gloop into Betty's face. The studio audience shrieked like caged monkeys.

'Why did you bring these daggers from the place?' from her bespatter'd Lady Mac.

'They must lie there. Go carry them. Smear the sleepy grooms with blood.'

She smeared some muck over my head. *'Like this.'* One kept one's composure, feigning dignity. As slapstickers must.

'I am afraid to think what I have done,' I said to camera. Then rubbed some glop in Betty's hair. The customers incontinent with squealing delight by now.

'Inpirm of furpose!' spurted sauce-coated Betty with Spoonerific mispronunciation. ''Tis the eye of childhood that fears the painted devil.'

Exeunt. *The things one does.*

Yes, pixie. We tried everything. Betty, also a gifted pianist, tried playing Chopin's Minute Waltz in under a minute, Daly with a stopwatch. Some other comedy piano stylings too, as per Victor Borge or Dudley Moore. And we had Betty and Vikki, sometimes Mary Hardy, do show tunes medleys. Yes, even the deplorable suggestions Joe Latona put before us like so much *hospital food*. Well, we tried. To little avail. Daly, harangued by Norm, now blamed Betty for our bad ratings.

'I'm sick of it, Frank,' she said over drinks with self, Vikki and others at the Savoy one day. 'You know, there's this group at the Treble Clef. Really fab. So I asked DYT to audition them. But Jon said they were no good. Had no future.'

'Hmmm. What are they called?'

'The Seekers.'

DYT now had the *DAN* cast record a comedy LP. Daly's idea, but Joe Latona insisted on larding up the comedy 'bits' with musical numbers. 'A publicity hope,' Betty called it. Fucker didn't sell. Radio wouldn't play it.

Betty and Vikki despaired now, fearing the chop. To cheer them up, one sent them some Roderer. The card, from a certain city bookshop. Twin Michelangelo's *Davids*. One upside down, hand cupping the other's scrotum. One inscribed it thus: *If girls can have a ball, have one with this.*

'Frank? William Sterling at the ABC.'

Came one's way a part in a teleplay, *Light Me A Lucifer*. By John O'Grady, he of *They're A Weird Mob*. One was - and about time, too – cast as Satan. Wife Lilith, sultry Lynne Flanagan. One's old stage pal Joan Harris here as well, Lyndel Rowe too, and Wyn Roberts. This last fucker a fixture of Australian telly. *Homicide, Neighbours, A Country Practice, Prisoner*, and those confusing films of the 1970s like *Picnic At Hanging Rock*. One's object of desire, Antinous, also had a part. Indeed, my lovely boy's casting a condition of one's own.

A trite but amusing plot. The Beast complains to his agent that not enough Aussies are being sent to Hell. Taking the initiative, Lucifer travels aloft to Sydney to *stir the pot*. Hi jinks ensue, mayhem wrought by Satan and Lilith encouraging lust and abandonment in the suburbs. Yes, quite dreadful.

'But such is one's vocation,' I explained to Antinous one late night at Rylands.

'It's like sex partners. You just have to work with what you've got. Or go without.'

'Geezus! Who told you to do that, Frank?'

'It looks more, well, Beelzebubian, baby. Isn't that what you want?'

One had dyed one's hair black. The producer in a tizz. One hadn't sought his leave, you see. 'Don't get your tits in a tangle, Butch,' I said. 'Just trying to help. And take it from me. This tub of swill needs all it can get.'

The shoot went as these things do aboard Aunty ABC. Platoons of pointless producers, flocks of flouncers dashing hither and yon. Much ado about fuckall. One was driven to seek refuge from this faffing about, via the contents of Black Bag. Quite the find, advertised in *Women's Weekly* alongside a puff piece about Rylands. Just the ticket, this Ben Ean Moselle.

'Frank? Wrap that round yourself.'

Now, the PR presser to pimp the show, self in Satan's cape, with Lynette in Lilth's all-white outfit. And also starring an eight-foot carpet python from Melbourne Zoo.

Just as FT had compelled one to do in the window of the Regent, so so long ago.

'No need to shit yourself, mate,' said the khaki-clad wrangler as the thing tightened its grip round one's arm. 'We took its teeth out.'

'Well,' I said. 'No *wonder* the fucker's got so far in *showbiz*.'

In November, a delightful surprise. An invite from Diane Cilento. Her second wedding, to a rising British film star. Before one left town, an interview with *TV Week* to talk of this. It sold oodles of the thing. One spoke also of *DAN*. This, to petition the surviving remnant of our viewers not to forsake our burning, sinking ship as Gra Gra's Channel Nine fighter planes minced us to shreds.

'Do you think you use too much double entendre?' asked one's interlocutor.

'I don't think I use enough, Butch.'

'How many rebukes from Seven this year?'

'Oh, I think three times,' I said. 'A week.'

'*We want to sell you to Nine,* they told me, Frank. *You have a great future,* they said. *Just not on this show.*'

On the eve of one's flight, a sobbing Betty called. Ordered to a meeting, they'd ambushed her. The star of the show. Unconscionable. Was I next? Should I cancel... oh, fuck it. Fuck *them*.

In Gibraltar, all very 1960s, pixie. Diane's bridal gown several colours, none of them white. The groom a thug in a brown suit. Moustache to match. And she eight months gone, all boobs and bump.

'Don't open it with your thumbs.'

One took the Tattinger from him.

'Grab it with your hand, you see. Like this. And twist, then lift off.'

How they ever fashioned this uncouth drone Sean Connery into James Bond is beyond one's comprehension.

'Theatrical agent! What a gal.'

One caught up with Joanie in London to toast her new job. Dined at the Ritz.

'And how's my husband-in-law?' She'd remarried, you see. And had been tasked with a new talent.

'The agency lumbered me with him, Frank. He's staying at my place till they get him sorted. He's a full-time job. My other clients are complaining. What shoul...'

Succulent young balletomaine Rudolf Nureyev had just defected from the Soviet Union, you see. All the talk in the news. And a needy sort. As prima donnas are.

'Oh, for fuck's sake, Flowergirl. Can't you *see?*'

'See *what* exactly, Frank?'

Not best pleased. One braced for a slap but held up one's hand, *if I may.*

'Your boss is a fool to hand you this. And you not to see it. This Rudy. He's going to be a massive star. Don't you see?'

I put my hand over hers and leaned in.

'*Make him your sole client.* Leave that idiotic agency.' I fumbled in Black Bag. 'Here. Stop blubbing and get yourself set up.'

Take it, I said when she demurred. I forget how much. *Please.* One felt euphoric at being able to help her. Sad, too. One's little bird had flown away. The leaves of one's magnolia at Rylands whisper'd from across the sea. *You can go now.*

'Close the door, Frank.' *Oh. I see.*

'*Daly At Night* has a big future. No doubt about it. That said, we feel that...'

A tram dinged out on Bourke Street. I stood up. Walked out without a word.

CHAPTER TWENTY-ONE

'So it's come to *this*. The tightrope aflame of insolvency.'

Our subscribers at the Union liked the same fare over and over. Rather like dogs. As a result of our bold adventurism, said Black Jack, the company was broke. So yet again, one was emotionally blackmailed into *The Man Who Came To Dinner*.

Fred Parslow cast here, outdoing his even his last turn as Fred Parslow. With the versatile Finno, Jon Finlayson, and feisty Lynne Flanagan from *Lucifer*.

'Ah,' I said to Sumner of this gaggle of greensleeves. 'Fresh *meat*.'

Yes, pixie. New recruits, to be tested in our *Man Who Came* by spectral Black Jack. Like Ellie Ballantyne, later Meg in *Prisoner*. And the nascent Simon Chilvers. Cast here as Bert Jefferson.

'Cursed with the corpse that is Bert, eh?' I said. 'Go on, get it in you.'

He took a slug of one's Tolleys TST brandy.

'Fret not, Butch,' I said. 'Sumner does that to everyone. Bad parts. To see what you do with them. Assess your potential,' I lied, 'for greater ones. Go forth and dazzle'.

Well, he didn't flirt back. But we became lifelong friends. One also met here the brilliant polymath Alan Hopgood. Amazed at one's daily taxis to and from rehearsals.

'It's alright for you, mate,' he said. 'We get around in old bangers, can't get a park, can't afford a chauf...' His marriage just gone *kaput*, so his sauce one forgave.

'What do *you* spend on registration, insurance, *petrol?*' I inquired. Ha. I had him. 'Well, there, you see, I'm way ahead of you lot.'

His man here Beverley Carlton, a nod to Noel Coward. And Alan, well...

'Dear boy,' I said. 'I *know* Coward. Let me show you.'

And I did. The royal wave entering rooms. Dusting the carnation with his fingers. The slow blink. One hand held out limp, for greeting. Next day, Hopgood did Coward to a tee. Sumner noticed and approved. *Don't mention it, Hoppy.* Not a chance of the other with this one. An incurable taste for the best and fairest sex.

Of Paul Karo, one had seen this elfin delectable in sundry ABC tellydramas. Here, cast as John the fucking butler, poor lad.

'That the best you've got, boy?' Sumner could smell fear.

'W-well...w-what would you like me to...'

'That's your problem, boy. That is why you are paid.'

'W-what don't y-you like about i...'

'Nothing. There's your starting point.'

'Don't mind that sadistic shit. Does that to everyone.'

One commiserated with young Paul at day's end.

'Come, boy. You need a drink.' *The word was that he swung both ways.*

Back at Rylands, giant goblets of Mateus Rose.

'Oh!' I remembered. 'One's column is due.' Flicked on the AWA in the corner. Bid him take his ease. On the sofa. Next to *me*.

'On with the telly, then,' I said. Raised a brow. 'Seeking *prey*.' On came *The Samurai.* Japanese. Bad dubbed English. One went to change channels...

'I speak Japanese, you know,' said Paul. 'I love their culture, their...'

'That's *it*, my boy!'

'That's what, Frank?'

'Your lifeless John the butler. As a *Japanese houseboy.*'

The little fucker loved it. We workshopped it for a bit, walked through his scenes. Watched some telly for one's column. Had Edith prepare dinner for two before she went home. Where the little sprite managed to fit all that booze, one shall never know.

'You know, baby,' I said some drinks later, 'you can be *my* houseboy if you want.'

It was midnight. One sat on the floor at his feet. He gently brushed my hand away.

Oh well.

The cast for *The Man Who Came* is enormous. And all those entrances and exits. Offers a director few opportunities for the cast to double, you know, play two parts.

It meant that divine Antinous was also cast. Ah, Antinous! *How like an angel in apprehension.*

'But that young buck likes the ladies. Older ones, with money,' was the mumble on the molly grapevine.

'He's an actor, for fuck's sake,' one's riposte. 'Even a prancer like *you* could manage a spot of lady-tupping if there was a quid at the finish line.'

Another of the Union company, a very married, very closet flamboyant, had a beady on Antinous too. One tried to dissuade. Souped-up tales of the boy's fondness for the chickadees.

'Nonsense,' said Mr Closet. 'I relish the challenge.'

'You're on. Not a chance, baby.'

Fucker. But one knew his bind. Such be our cross, rough hew it how we may.

Our run of *The Man Who Came* saved the Union. Packed that rough old moll of a theatre to its chandelier dust for weeks. Months. And one had *fun*, pixie. As you know, my man Sheri is confined to a wheelchair for much of the show. One night, Carmel Powers, as my man's nurse, Miss Preen, somehow slipped and tipped me out of it on to the stage. Felt Sumner's eyes burning blisters in our foreheads from the front row. One glanced up. Whispered to her, loud as one could.

'Now this will just have to be our little secret, won't it?'

The customers laughed their tonsils out. *As did the boy Antinous. One was playing to him, you see.* One even threw a cast party just to get him to Rylands. Like a lot of thesps, the lad was domiciled in reduced circumstances. One reason, it was claimed, why he flattered and rode flabby matrons. Warm roof over one's head and a cellarful of wine. This night, he drank too much. Had to be put to bed in the guest room. And no, not a finger did one lay upon him in such state. For one craved his love. All of it.

'You can stop the night anytime, silly boy,' I told him next morning when I fetched he and his hangover coffee and aspirin. 'And you don't have to *sing* for your *supper*.'

Oh, and in the middle of all this, *Daly At Night* was axed. One sent flowers. Daly showed his viewers on his last night. A funeral wreath.

'Well, one had to turn them down,' was how one spun it to *The Age* when they called. 'One's first fealty is to one's home town and her prime theatre company. And one's word is one's bond. An unfortunate clash, but there it is.'

One had heard not a word from Sam Bronston about *Fall Of The Roman Empire.* Then in one's airmailed *Photoplay,* a story on Sophia Loren, cast in *Empire* with Alec Guinness, Stephen Boyd, James Mason, and, *oh,* Anthony Quayle. Tony as 'Verulus.' Quayle had been cast, it read, after Bronston saw him in *Lawrence Of Arabi*....hang on a flash. *Verulus. My* part. *Oh. Small wonder they hadn't called...*

'Yes, one hates to have to knock back a film part,' was one's version to the *Sun News-Pictorial.* 'But I mean, one has *all* these screenplays here awaiting one's pleasure,' I said into the phone, sweeping an arm at the empty coffee table before me. They fell for it. I think. FT's spirit glanced up from the Other Down Under and doffed his hat.

Sir Noel Coward was here. Directing his own *Sail Away* at Her Maj. At supper at Rylands, he admired one's skill with *bon mot.* Lovely of him to say so, but one already knew. You see, one's off-the-cuff epigrams kept popping up in his plays. Unattributed. Unremunerated. Yet one begrudged him not. His company reward enough. And he not the only one.

'Podge, Victor Borge is playing for us at Her Maj.'

McCallum, in his new JCWs boss hat. 'Likes to dine after the show.' Would I care to..? Alongside McCallum and Googie, one also invited Chilvers. Betty B. Little Paul Karo of course. *Antinous too.* Recall Victor, pixie? Maestro at the piano, acerbic humour with it. Huge in his day. Aren't we all?

GB Shaw's *Devil's Disciple* at the Union now. My man, General Burgoyne, played by Olivier in the film. Then Moliere's *The Happy Invalid* consumed one's September 1963. A fresh clash with Mr Closet over the boy Antinous, also cast here. We two suitors faced off in the cramped, tram-shaped dressing room.

'One of us will have to leave this play,' he said.

'I sell tickets, Butch. You don't.' Then one's last card. 'And I'll tell your wife.'

'You want to keep your place here, best smarten up your footwork, boy.'

The man was an ogre. One took Antinous under one's wing when Sumner turned on him, the fucking brute. A Black Jack special. Random humiliation, in front of the entire cast. To induce collective terror.

'To get their best out of them,' he snapped when I took him to task for it. Weary now too was young Anti of his semi-indigent status, he'd confided over pre-dawn omelette at Rylands – where be solace and protection from Sumner. And so it came to pass. His own room at Rylands. Meals. Services of one's twin crone housekeepers Edith and Margaret, gratis.

We dined out. Went to the pictures, the ballet. *Together.* Tired of hiding it and he was game. No fucker said a word. One taught him how to cheat at cards. He in and out of theatre and telly work, so one advanced him disbursements.

'To persist with your calling, lover,' I said. We grew entwined in symbiosis, beyond mere lust. Perhaps three months of unalloyed devotion.

But the boy suffered, one came to find, from causes baffling and unknowable. He'd seemed flighty but no more than that at first. Then, whatever he'd managed to suppress or disregard, began to take hold. Drank deep, *to stop the voices,* he said. Screamed, smashed things. On two occasions, assaulted me. Recalled it not when he awoke, broken and hollow. Edith and Margaret looked on, mute but alarmed. It worsened.

He attracted police attention with public outbursts. Then stopped coming home at night. When he did, hard to reason with. Echoes of poor, poor Viv Leigh. Yet one misses him still.

One Friday night, one was offered a lift home by Chilvers after a performance. Dear Antinous in the cast. By this time, the poor boy in some state of mind that rendered him tormented, seeking aught but oblivion. This night, as had become almost the norm, he had vanished right after line-up. The thing was, he could come rolling home at any time, in any condition, or not, so.....

'Yes,' one's reply to Simon's offer, 'thank you, dear boy, yes, I shall. But you can't come in when you drop me off. You *can't* come in. We have a matinee tomorr...'

But as we arrived, *oh, fuck it.* That bloody prodigal wouldn't be back till his money, sugar grannies and drugs were gone, and one so alone...

'Oh you will come in for just the one, won't you?'

Daybreak. *No more,* said Simon when I lifted the bottle. No sign of young Anti. One sloshed brandy into our coffees. At the front gates, *sorry you couldn't stay,* I said. To perish the lonelies, two Nembies, but, well, the caffeine. One couldn't sleep. So two more and then off one floated...

Jolted awake. That fucking *phone.*

'Frank? Silver Harris.' The stage manager. *Why the fuc...*'Can you get straight down here, please?'

Oh, *shit.* The *matinee.* Hmmm. Likely only half full. If that.

'I'll buy the house, darling. The tickets. The lot. Cancel. Give refunds.'

One sold a painting. One of Joy Hester's 9x5s, from memory, to pay for it. Plenty more where that came from. Should need arise, one need only to pluck one from one's walls of gold or black.

'Frank! Baby!'

Another bloody phone call, rousing one awake, deep in the long watches of the night. From LA. Sam Bronston, with new screenplays. *Night Riders Of Bengal,* of the Indian Mutiny; and no less than *The*

French Revolution. One asked not of *Fall Of* and what had gone tits up there. For Sam had cast me in both of these new pictures. All this as Antinous came home, seeking conciliation for his trespasses. We celebrated both, full well, Napoleon VSOP and Vallies. And then after all that, well, ...

'*Whothefuggizzit?*'

Two-fucking-thirty by the bedside clock. *I have Mr George Cukor on the line from Los Angeles, California. Will you hold?* The sound, like the operator was talking underwater. But *Cukor? Ye gods.* Directed *A Star Is Born* with Judy Garland.

'Vivien tells me great things about you, Frank.'

She'd put in a word. Darling Viv. 'Now, Frank, Henry Daniell. Did you know him?'

'Yes,' I lied. *Did?*

'Well, the most dreadful thing. Right after we shot his first scene.' A stifled sob. 'Passed away that night.'

'Oh, my God.' One's best thesp *Oh, my God.*

'Quite so. A fine man. Now, Frank, this means that...'

Invalid sold out its last week at the Union when one told the press of one's part in *My Fair Lady.* But Anti threw a fit when told he couldn't come. His madness, drug binges and rampages could get us deported. Or jailed. Or shot by the LAPD. Just not on. The iron had entered my soul.

CHAPTER TWENTY-TWO

I t was a Saturday, two days before one's flight. GTV 9 had recently started weekend morning broadcasts. I switched on the black-and-white Astor. As it warmed up, stills, blurry, wire-transmitted, emerged on the screen...*President Kennedy died at 5.30 AM Eastern Standard Time...*

I went anyway. Five thousand Brit actors who lived far closer than I to Hollywood, you see, agents forever sniffing round, so...

Stopovers in Fiji, Honolulu. LA International a daze, all redeyed zombies. At the Roosevelt Hotel on Hollywood Boulevard, one tried to doze...whooshing, colliding thoughts jerked out of orbit by jangle of bedside phone.

'Shooting in four days, Frank.' *Lady's* unit manager. 'To beat the Xmas shutdown.'

'Do you know where I can get my car serviced?'

The code as advised. A tip from Vidal. Scotty Bowers, LA's Mr Sex, operated out of this very hotel, opposite Grauman's Chinese Theatre. He sent up a surprise. Steve Reeves. Former Mr Universe. Failed star of sword 'n' sandal flicks. On the skids and on the game. Said three words to me. *Got the bread?* It was the best of sex, it was the worst of sex.

Scotty had amyl nitrate, too. Glass ampoules. Came in a yellow box. What a *rush,* baby. Over the next days, 'tween fucklings various and amyl poppers, one called Kirk's people, Wyler's, the lot. *Anything going?* Only one got back to me. I shall never forget him for it.

'*King Of Kings*, right?'

The man in Heston's booth at the Brown Derby rose, mitt extended. Crushed one's knuckles to shards. George Stevens had helmed *Shane*, among other classics.

'George has a screenplay,' said Chuck. 'Likes me for John The Baptist', *can you believe it?* in his chuckle.

'Chuck says you're our Herod.' Stevens. 'Tell me why.' *Chuck darling!*

'Well, Herod is no paint by numbers monster, George. Orders babies killed while smelling a flower. Speaks not in roars but lullabies. Your loud and livid tyrant brings one's blood to the boil. But this fellow induces it to freeze …'.

He liked it. Of course he did. Smiled. Gave me his card, and was gone. One quelled one's mad joy, that it look like this was an everyday bit of business for Thring. For our somewhat spartan and boozeless luncheon, one insisted on picking up the tab. Chuck, canny with his pennies, didn't object. And enjoyed talking about himself, so one asked him what he was up to.

'Just started a new one. Rex. Reed. Yourself?'

'Cukor. Rex and Audrey.'

Surnames only for directors, first names only for stars, never the name of the picture, Vidal had counselled.

'Frank, you know Diane Cilento, right? And Max Audley? They've told me a lot about you.'

Clearly not *that*, bless them, or I'd not be here with a swishphobe like Heston. 'They're both in this new picture,' he said. 'We have a table read at the Chat coming up. Why not drop by?'

It was all too easy. Stevens must have liked me for his Herod. He sent the script to one's hotel by courier. This called for a knees-up. *Hello, Scotty?*

Five fucking AM. A Warners car to Burbank. At one's fitting, in swept a pin-thin prancer. Wide-brimmed fedora. Mauve cravat. Purple suit.

'Oh. It's *you*.'

It was out of me before I could strangle it. Cecil fucking Beaton. Of *all* people. You see, one had clashed with Fair Cecily at one of Viv Leigh's parties during the *Titus* run back in '55. Pursuing the same stripling, you see. And here, one only now informed by the wardrobe people, he was *Lady's* costume designer.

'Oh, *no, no!* This won't do *at all!*' he squealed. His hands fluttered over one's British Ambassador's outfit as if a pair of white leghorns, spooked by a rat in a chookyard. '*Lipstick* on *elephants!*' he hissed as he flitted out. He and Cukor were feuding, one had learned from Michael Neuwirth, Fair Cecily's assistant *frou frou* wrangler here.

Beyond one's comprehension, pixie. I mean, whoever put two queens in joint charge of a musical should have been shot in a cellar...

'Frank! Darling, so sorry to have kept you...'

Cukor stood in the doorway. One had been bidden by Neuwirth to tarry after Fair Cecily's flounceout. *Not to worry, Frank, this happens every day.* Martell from Black Bag had made everything smooth and hazy. '...especially as I'm afraid to say we won't be proceeding with the shoot.'

He put his hands together as if for prayer, *will that be alright?*

'Perfectly alright, lover,' one managed, the booze keeping one afloat on ersatz lake of rapture. The shock yet to impact. 'Happens all the time.' A choke escaped one's throat on *time.* Damn.

'Look, Frank, I feel awful about this. Say, why not swing by my pad this Sunday, dear? You know, circulate. Pick up on *anything going.*'

Ah. Cukor's Sabbath *soirees.* The more, shall we say, colourful Tinseltown influential, and young lads seeking their favour. The *gobble 'n' go* as Hollywood insiders called such meetings. A feast of movers and shakers. Unmissable.

So the week not a total loss. An invite to this splendid party. A part in a Heston movie. Two shoots in Spain for Bronston, still to come. One would go home a conquering hero. If one needed to return at all.

The studios rented suites at the Chateau Marmont on Sunset. This, to sate the depravities of their stars and keep these hidden from the LA scandal sheets. And as a sideline, now and then, as a venue for script meetings. Today, for Heston as Michelangelo. Yes, pixie, I *know*. And Rex Harrison as Pope Julius II. *God help us.*

Couldn't contain one's joy at seeing galpals Max and Diane. Remembered just in time to keep it butch round Heston. Max and Dee Dee thoughtful in that regard, too. Peppered one with kisses, just short of went the grope, to allay any suspicions Chuck might harbour. After a quick drink at the Chat's bar, he had to go, he said. *For some acting classes, Chuck?* one managed to smother. Max and Dee Dee, one asked to dinner.

'Hey! I know him! It's that *guy!'*

Such is one's lot in LA. They've seen one in the movies but can't put their finger on where. And this pair of judies on one's arms really got 'em gabbing in the red booths at Musso and Frank Grill. Kicked on after that, the Boulevard and the Strip. Alas, one recalls but fragments...

A very pukka gent came over to our table at the Polo Lounge. Knew Diane. This fellow Terence Young had directed Connery in two Bonds, you see.

'And, yes, it is almost upon us, a third,' he said. '*Goldfinger.'*

'Ah, yes,' I said, garrulous from dust-dry martinis. 'One worked with Fleming on *Thunderball* in Jamaica. On Coward's estate.' Shook my head at the memory. 'Bugger at an impasse, I up to here with these bloody scripts to read, but he wouldn't take no for an answer...'

It felt like a shoal of stonefish had exploded in one's head. Last night; Ciro's, the Playboy Club, Come To The Party, the Largo. And a new joint, the Whisky-A-Go Go. The marvellous Johnny Rivers onstage there. Go go girls in white, in cages suspended above. Groping for aspirin now, one found Terence Young's card in a jacket pocket. Scrawl on the back. *BOND G FINGER CALL ME.* It came back through the bloodshot mist. *You'd make an awfully good Bond villain, Thring.*

'Frank? George Stevens,' said the phone. 'Frank, your take on Herod has really given me food for thought. Understated yet riveting.'

'Oh, George. No need to flatter, baby. It's what actors d...'

'Indeed. Thing is,' he chuckled, *they all do this chuckletalk thing,* 'United Artists feel that any links with an MGM picture like *King Of Kings* is, well,... Chuck asked me to pass on to you how sorry he is. As am I. Anyway, ...'

I fumbled for yellow subs. Fell back on the pillows. *Perchance to dream...*

Cukor's mansion, skyblue and alabaster. Swimming pool bobbing with balloons. Flowers everywhere. He'd serve brunch on Sundays to Simone Signoret, my chum Vivien or Hepburns Katy and Audrey. They were gone by three PM. Then, stars of the confirmed bachelor stripe. Fewer than usual today. A forlorn affair.

'JFK, Dallas, you see, dear,' said George. Vidal was here. Drawn, pale.

'I'm writing a rather good screenplay. *The Best Man* I've called it. Telemovie. Political drama. Henry. Cliff.'

Ah. Henry Fonda and Cliff Robertson.

'Well. *Rewriting,* given events.'

Vidal scoped the guests as he talked, for someone more useful to him than I.

'Forgive my disposition, my dear fellow,' he said. 'If you knew Jack Kennedy like I did,' his voice raised to be better heard by all, 'you'd understand.'

'So where to now for the nation?' I said.

'Oh, I've spoken to the family. Only one thing for it. Bobby must run in '68.'

'Mr Thing.' A secretarial type on the phone. 'Mr Young wants you to know that your proposals regarding the Bond villain are first rate.'

Oh, splendi...

'But regrettably, we've been taken off the picture. Thank you for your interest.'

To linger here beyond one's welcome, well, that's what FT did, pixie. And look what they did to him. But months yet before the Madrid shoots. One's decision not a difficult one.

'Frank! Run away from Orstralia again? Can't say I blame you, darling.'

One booked into the Algonquin. Then and always, the only hotel in New York.

And bumped into, off her chops on Stoli as per, Princess Margaret. You'll recall, pixie, that we'd met via Helpmann. *Ma'am darling,* as she made everyone address her, in the Apple on a goodwill Royal Tour of the States with newish husband Tony. Lord Snowdon to the rest of you.

Well, meeting munted Royals has its upside. One was invited to the reception for this most swinging of Royal couples, at Delmonico's in the Financial District. Near the all-white columns and cobbles of Wall Street. Smaller than one had imagined. Tony took some portraits of me. One still has them around here somewhere...

With companionable youths one met here and there, one took in the Broadway shows of '64. Like Carol Channing in *Hello Dolly* at the St James, West 44th. Ran into dear old Garnet Carroll here. We had supper at Frankie and Johnny's Steakhouse on West 45th. He went home to Melbourne full of bull about one's hectic moviemaking schedule.

'Yeah, well, it's kinda like the Addams Family house, but a grand view of Central Park West.'

It was a buzz to catch up with Robert Ryan. He and wife Jessica Cadwalader, the author, invited one to their home, Apartment 72 in the Dakota Building, the very same that would come to be occupied by John Lennon and Yoko Ono a decade hence. Ryan had just finished in *Mr President,* the Irving Berlin musical, on Broadway. And had tickets for a new show which couldn't be had for sex or money. At the Imperial, Zero Mostel in *Fiddler On The Roof* pushed us all three feet back in our seats.

'Frank! Frank Thring!'

And who should we run into at interval but Janet Leigh! Here with Robert Brandt. Married the day after she Mexican-divorced Tony

Curtis. She had free invites for a preview show, for a first timer who she insisted was it and a bit.

'You must come!'

The venue was the Winter Garden. The up and comer, one Barbara Streisand, the show, *Funny Girl*. Meeting La Streisand backstage a cherished memory. *I knew her when.*

And it just went from there. Recognised from one's films, one held court in theatre lobbies and at apres-show suppers to which one invited oneself. As bold as Orson Welles, from whom one had learned the art so well, with producers, directors, *anything going* here and there.

And I hit the Dizzy Club on 52nd Street, looking for hard liquor and hot romance. This the molly's bar where WH Auden had downed martinis as he penned *September 1, 1939*, on the day Hitler invaded Poland. On Vidal's tip, one also did the Everard Baths on West 28th. Known to all who knew as *the Everhard*. Quite.

'Wallaby!' Larry, returning one's call. So bouncy since he and Viv had called it quits. 'We're all on at the Pally tomorrow night! You must come, baby!'

On a whim, one had taken ship, to wit the Queen Mary, last of the Cunard Line. New York to Southampton via Cherbourg. Now ensconced in a suite at the Dorchester. At Larry's beck, one black-tied it for this midnight charity do. *The Night of 100 Stars.* In the presence of the Queen, Shirley Bassey, The Beatles. Poor Judy Garland choking *Over The Rainbow* to death. John Lennon stole the show with his bit about 'those in the cheap seats clap your hands,' and nodding to the Royal box, 'the rest of you just rattle your jewellery.'

One circled at the after-party. Every fucker there from Gloria Swanson to Zsa Zsa Gabor to Ringo Starr to Hayley Mills knew who one was by sunrise.

'Will you fight and drink for Thespis, Thring?' Including Peter O'Toole, star of *Lawrence Of Arabia*. Also a film *producer*, pixie, and knew of one's Pilate and Herod.

'I just wrapped on *Becket* with that mad fucker Burton at Shepparton,' he said. He meant the London film studios. 'I shall bear the scars for ever more.'

Here was surely *entre*. So, then, nothing else for it. One got into it with he and that unhinged Irishman Richard Harris. They knew all the early openers, holes in the wall and foyer bars in London. And one lived to tell the tale. If only one could recall it.

'The king must die so the country may live,' I muttered over and over. One's *moments* must blaze. Having such a jolly-up in London that one had only just now dipped into one's pages for *French Revolution*. My man here Robespierre, his Reign Of Terror and all.

'Something's amiss, old friend.'

Gregoire Aslan had me to dine on one's first night in Madrid. 'Sam and Yordan are here, but hiding behind closed doors.'

That was only the beginning. At Chamartin Studios, gigantic half-built sets for this flick loitered like chauffeurs at a funeral. The alleged leads, Sophia Loren, Ava Gardner, Chuck Heston and David Niven, nowhere to be seen.

'I've seen happier heads on stakes,' one whispered to Rita Gam as Phil Yordan stood before us. He'd called the cast together – what there was of one – and decreed we begin table reads. Albeit apprehensive, we, the support cast, Rip Torn, Gregoire, Genevieve Page, Rita, self, set to.

Three possible directors- Tony Mann, the eminent Brit Guy Green and, oh god no, Nick Ray – were mentioned by Bronston when he showed his face. But only Andrew Marton, first AD on *Ben Hur,* materialised. Marton had replaced mad Nick Ray, who'd almost dropped dead from a heart attack on Bronston's previous picture, *55 Days At Peking.* But at least Sophia, Ava, Chuck and David had turned up for that one.

You know how this one ends, pixie. Bronston was into Paramount for seven mill and Pierre DuPont, that most closeted billionaire, six more. *Fall Of The Roman Empire* had bombed, you see. *55 Days At Peking* took ten mill but cost fucking double that to make. And Sam's most recent fiasco, *Circus World* with John Wayne, well, need one say more? The news we knew was coming arrived via memo from Yordan, our hobgoblin ruinator.

Home then, from the ashes of this forever unmade picture, to Melbourne in July. Winter. Silver. Wild as a madman's hair.

CHAPTER TWENTY-THREE

I buried Lilith today. So many cats. She will be one's last. I mean, what might befall a pussy that outlives me? And I no longer watch *Midday With Ray Martin*. Ray has moved on to *A Current Affair*, known in telly circles as *A Cunt In A Chair*. In his place, Derryn Hinch, all the charm of a dog drinking from the toilet, will see this once fine program axed.

One thought about going to the cinema just the other day. It's been an age, you know. But the idea of oneself in a Hoyts or one of FT's old red velvet and gold-gilt palaces of marble – those few yet spared demolition– one cannot abide.

As for the films these days, well. What is Hollywood *doing* to itself? I mean you've got your *Jurassic Park,* where you've figured out the ending two reels before the film's numbskulled protagonists do. Then Robin Williams in a silly drag turn, *Mrs Doubtfire.* A predictable and unconvincing setup. And that lockjawed rumbledrone Sylvester Stallone defies the laws of physics in *Cliffhanger.*

Some of these pictures hint at intrigue. *Groundhog Day* one such. Yet one fears, as ever, that the denouement will endow enlightenment on all as they sail off on the last reel's sea of schmaltz. In one of my very favourite films, *Chinatown,* the villain gets away with it- all of it- in the last seconds of the final scene. Now *that's* an ending, pixie. Sudden. Brutal. As in life.

*

Home again, then, from Bronston's burning Troy. Got my skull on the telly. Blathered of one's 'Hollywood triumphs' in terms galaxies distant from the facts. But more or less the truth of the Bronston collapse.

Gra Gra Kennedy talked one into trad Japanese drag for our take of *I've Got A Little List* from *The Mikado* on *IMT*. Australia still found an 1885 Gilbert and Sullivan turn rendered butcher's shambles by two querulous queers quite the sensation in these 1960s.

Back but a week when Garnet Carroll died. Gone, the big walrus who took over the Prinny when FT's light went out. *Could've been mine to this day had Olive's brain not been so lonely,* one used to say. Often.

'So whose idea was *Channel 0?*' one queried of Ray Taylor when he called.

'That logo looks like a fucking glory hole.'

The jazzy jester from the Sydney breakfast show *Today* now compered a Saturday evening program in Melbourne- on a new channel, ATV0. On the *Ray Taylor Show,* one talked of one's 'overseas filmmaking jaunt' as conquest unrivalled by even Alexander. That led to requests from ghosts of telly past. On *Delo And Daly* at HSV7, Jon Daly asked me what I did in LA. One fibbed that one had knocked back the Herod offer from Chuck Heston, with no regrets.

'One doesn't want to become typecast, baby.' Up went the left eyebrow.

'I mean, look what's happened to *you two.*'

'Well,' I said, 'they don't call it Channel *0* for nothing.'

Ray Taylor not rating well, so he engaged self as his offsider. A wretched timeslot. Saturdays, ten PM. A no-budget talk show. Variety artistes and interviewees local only, as they came for free. As bad ideas go, in a class of its own. Not only Ray as compere, but as his accomplice, that flinty crank, mad nudist fitness fanatic Percy Cerutty. Okay as occasional guest on *DAN's* Panel People. He had provided that same attraction that sideshow freaks do. But here, Perce and all that goes with sports 'personalities', was co-host and off the chain. Ergo, a humourless bore.

Still, nothing like 'em for a razz. Like all snailbrained narcissists, too, too easy. You know, pixie, his dreary rants of being 69 years old yet 'fit as a fiddle' down to relentless exercise and inedible diet, *asking for it.*

'And what *kind* of *fiddle* would *that* be, Perce?'

The studio audience howled as his face caved in. His diet fair game too. Raw carrots, turnips, onions. One night, Ray munched at samples Percy had brought in. Made faces at the taste while one popped the tough questions.

'So, Perce.' I held up a huge carrot. 'How do you get your mouth around *that?*'

To give him his due, Ray was at least trying. No tired studio band and clumsy club dancers on this show, thank the lord of fuck. Rather, Dick Healy's jazz combo, or the Red Onions Band. Pretty snazzy for stitched-up Melbourne in 1964.

And ATV0 had an Outside Broadcast Unit. TV studio guts in a truck. Ray took it out around town. Did vox pops live to air with random squares on the streets. Just one snag. Ray thought himself funny but wasn't. Guffawed on camera at his own flat gags. Roved around the studio with no script, and never was a body in greater need of one.

'Look, I have absolutely no idea what's going on,' he'd say to camera. In sunnies, trench coat, or Panama hat. Wacky wardrobe apropos of nothing. Annoying, really.

As for Perce, well, one wearied of this most dull of marks. He'd complained to the network about me, this quote *fat poofter.* So he had to go. One night when he brought up for the bazillionth time his training camps where he'd hatched several Aussie Olympians, one took up one's halberd and swung.

'So, Perce. All these young chaps, in just shorts, bathers, or *less*, in a *camp* setting. Sounds like your idea of heaven, baby.'

'I'll knock your block off!' Ray got between us, a tussle of flailing. Floor managers had to intervene. All live to air. Made the papers. Perce was sacked. Off the back of the press coverage, we began to pull some viewers. Mission accomplished, baby.

'And so George Harrison says, 'you got us at the old price, didn't you?'

Perce was gone, but that still left Ray's idea of a good show. So one started inviting one's pals on. Kenn Brodziak, with tales of how he'd got the Beatles here on the cheap back in June. For their take on the Smirnoff and pills mess that was Judy Garland's tour in May, Noel Ferrier and Mary Hardy, *quid pro quo* all the free plugs they could cram in for their 3DB morning show.

'Judy couldn't recall the *Trolley Song*,' said Noel. 'Mary here was on her feet.'

'Shouting out the words, Frank, to try and help,' said Mary. How like one's predicament here.

'Don't you wish you could just kill them after you've fucked 'em?'

Yes, Bunney Brooke was here, growling of lost lovers. The good news; so was Simon Chilvers, and bibbly bubbly Adelaide gal Ellie Ballantyne. Sumner cast Ellie in everything he could. Smitten with her. But unlike other femmes of the company, one doubts they ever played trains and tunnels. The play, Ustinov's *Photo Finish*. *Photo's* Sam Kinsale is played by four actors. Self as Old Sam. And here's the bit. They recognised me not at first when I came on the stage. Given one's head and voice, an accomplishment, *c'est ne pas*, pixie?

Young Antinous in real straits now. Had to front his bail. In and out of mental hospitals. One sent money orders for his 'medical expenses' when he called. Couldn't have him at Rylands now. He'd stolen from me too many times, smashed things up, terrified poor Edith and Margaret. Brought home undesirables. Police had to be called. Best leave it at that.

But Paul Karo now a visitor in the midnight hour. Stopped the night as often as not. Near destitute, living, if one could call it that, in rusty caravan out the back of Noel Lane's pile on Kooyong Road. You recall Lane Motors, pixie. Sold luxury cars to Melbourne stars. Small wonder the boy embraced one's invitation.

'No, Frank. I'm happy with the way things are. Don't need all that,' he'd say when I ... Oh, well. His company, 'twould suffice. One retired alone as stars faded 'gainst first blue, that Dr Nembutal could do his vital work.

Back at *TV Week,* one critiqued GTV9's latest iteration of *IMT.* Bert Newton Mondays solo, Gra Gra and Bert midweek, Noel Ferrier with Tommy Hanlon Junior on Fridays. This last, surreal. Hanlon, former big top ringmaster, let all these acts from Ashton's Circus on the show! Yet one wrote that one preferred the Friday lineup. To annoy Kennedy, and to help Noel out, he weak in the ratings. Poor fellow. Forced by the boxheads at Nine to take on Hanlon as co-host. *Put the Yank on* the forever panacea. Such were the feeble minds of Frank Packer's board. Bloated from mixed grills, sole fare at the old muckworm's staff canteens, as he would feed on no other, they knew no better.

'From here on in, Hortense,' Ray told our viewers, this his unfunny name for them, 'no official ending time.'

TV stations closed at 11 PM back then, with an *Epilogue,* a smug homily from some insipid reverend. But ATV0 gave Ray license to go past twelve if things were swinging. Ideal for his new segment. Going out in the OB truck to target Melbourne's top restaurants, an ill-starred stab at a *Candid Camera* type of thing.

One night, a stripper hired by Ray was planted *incognito* at rooftop nosher Dolce Vita. Ray harangued diners. Last resort of bad comics, vilifying their audience. Then the stripper rose from her table. Started peeling off. The producer shat kittens and cut to a commercial. Ray was furious. Back from the ads. Camera on me, as ordered by Ray, one guzzled champagne from one of the gal's high heels while Ray railed to camera about Channel 0 being such prudes. The press gave us two full buckets.

'Well,' I said to the producer to palliate his fury, 'a faceful of ink beats the fuck out of none at all.'

But one was fatigued by Ray's antics oneself. I mean, he'd promised a show like *Daly At Night* had been before Seven turned it into a toad. Not this puerile maelstrom.

In December, one reviewed in *A Piece Of Thring* an ABC teleplay of *Othello*. Ray Westwell, with whom one would work many times, did for the Moor, did it well, but in blackface, which by then one had come to associate with the hideosity that was the *Black And White Minstrel Show. Were Shakespeare here in Melbourne today,* I wrote, *he'd cast an Aboriginal as his Moor, to really make his point.* Meant it, too. Readers wailed for one's hide. One's compatriots don't like reminders of our forebears' barbarity. Nor our own, come to that. Poor fella my country. Will we never learn?

'If you go upstairs,' I said to Paul, he agape at my rice-white face, 'you'll see the toilet is full of blood...'

He'd raused my GP out of bed at three in the morning after I collapsed, he told me later. Found the number on a list I kept by the phone. Of GPs, that is.

I came to in the Freemason's. A medico stood over me.

'Oesophageal varices,' he said. Throat haemorrhage. They cut me loose after several days, with dire prophecies should one not change one's ways. A terrifying prognosis. One had to have a drink at once.

1965 rode into town. The Seekers smarmed from Pye transistors between the few cracks left by the Beatles, midst jingles for *Things Go Better With Coke.* On the *Ray Taylor Show,* we now discussed issues of the day, at one's insistence. Or tried to.

'What's that monocle in aid of, Ray? Did someone *squirt* something in your eye?'

Yes, pixie. Ray's unfunny dressups persisted.

'Have you heard this, Frank? Menzies has decreed a conscription,' he said, ignoring one's jibe. 'This carry-on in Vietnam.'

'Yes,' I said. A *lottery.* An idiocy only an Australian government could concoct. Numbers in a *barrel.* On little *balls,* one imagines.'

'Where did you serve, Frank?'

Oh, for fuck's sake. I set you up for some ripping banter, and you...

'Oh, the Air Force, you know, Ray. Fancied oneself as a *rear gunner.'*

Helpmann came home now for good, to co-direct the Australian Ballet. Thank fuck, not to *act*. He did *Meet The Press on* Nine. Ripped the faces off Frank Packer's witless inquisitors with cheer and drollery. One had Bobby on Ray's show, of course. Afterwards, to Rylands with his retinue of becocked balletomaines. *Well.* As orgies go, top tier. It took one back to torrid nights back at Via Sistina. Edith and Margaret, the latter still living on the premises, disregarded it. As they should.

'I mean, look at these two axeheads,' I said to Bobby's boys as the stout pair served supper. 'Been an item since the emperor Domitian. No one else would have them.'

'If I were you, Frank,' said Edith, sounding just like her daughter Joan, 'I'd hire a food taster.'

Pop star Jimmy Hannan was a new part-time *IMT* host. One wrote in *TV Week* that he'd topple Gra Gra one day. While one was at it, blasted Ferrier and Hanlon as 'Fatty Ferrier' and 'Happiness Hanlon' for their Friday *IMT.* No offence, me hearties. It sold magazines, you see. Noel was in on it. One kept one's job and kept them in the news, that they keep theirs. The press turned it all into feuds between us. Just as one had planned.

'That OB unit,' I said to Ray. 'I have an idea.'

Ray's weekly restaurant invasions were turning off viewers and scaring off the eaters' customers. They'd complained to our third producer in eighteen months. 'How about I do the show from home?'

One went out live from Rylands that Saturday night, Ray in the studio at Nunawading. One wore a smoking jacket with a 'Sahara-dry martini, viewers.' Costume changes in the ad breaks. Back to me lounging on a couch in a black kaftan, stroking one's black cat, introduced to viewers as 'Black Pussy.'

One showed 'em one's statues of naked negro boys. Also goblets various and other souvenirs from the sets of *Ben Hur, The Vikings, El Cid.* Explained the twin stone lions at the front door, installed by FT. His nod to Chinese culture, these beasties symbols of security and protection. Spoke of one's fur toilet seat. Offered to show it to viewers but the floor manager went apeshit behind the cameras, cutting his own throat with a hand motion, *no, no.* Such were the times. One's other cat Puffkins got a look-in too. As did the drink stain left by Vivien Leigh on the rug, which one held up for all to see.

'Viv most embarrassed by her *faux pas,*' I told them. 'And quite mad by then. I mean, she went down on all fours and lapped it up.'

'Restaurant reviews? Me? Are you *mad?*'

The Melbourne *Truth* was a newspaper. Ran pics of 'nude romps', black bars across the eyes, crotches and nipples of the pudgy perpetrators. Tales of scandal. Ads for brothels. Men told their wives they bought it for its racing form guide. The editor had one to lunch at, er, Fanny's in Lonsdale Street.

'It's a top earn, Frank. And all you can eat.'

'That's what all the boys say, Butch.'

So there you have it. Paul Karo and self went forth to dine fine and defame. *Truth's* sales and lawsuits flourished.

'Well, Sir Noel once suggested to me that it's never too early for a *cock*tail,' I said. 'In any sense of the word.'

In February '65, a break from *The Ray Taylor Show* for a part in Coward's *Present Laughter* when Sumner asked. We opened in March at the Russell Street Theatre, the Union's newest ghastly home, next to the Rapallo Cinema. Oh, and the *Truth* food reviews ended after three months. 380,000 circulation, this rag. Cashed up. A magnet for defamation suits. One's column was bounced.

And this same year, one's first award. An 'Eric'. The Kuttners, for Aussie theatre.

One didn't go.

'Well,' I said when asked why, 'I don't believe them when they say I'm bad, so why do so when they say I'm good?'

It came by parcel post. One plonked it in the brasco, atop the cistern.

'This way one can't be labelled a poseur, displaying it like a fucking hunting trophy. But all will see it,' I explained to Paul, 'sooner or later.'

His bellyful of St Agnes proposed that they could cram their awards up their arse.

'Quite,' I said. The Eric resembled a dead tree. All spikes, horns and talons.

'Just the once?'

'But you have Wal Cherry, Moira, Ogilvi....'

'I'm off on a study trip, boy,' said Black Jack. 'And they're doing other plays. You've no choice.'

Thus my fate to direct, yes, *direct* Orton's *Entertaining Mr Sloane*. One's own fault, really. Saw it in London. Bought the Aussie rights. Gave it to Sumner for the Union. More fool me. *Sloane's* plot; sex addicts, a murder. Jealous nancy boy. Blackmail. An incestuous bisexual *menage a trois.*

'Think of it,' one said to the cast, 'as like a Saturday night in Adelaide.'

'Oh, fuck. You mean it's still not dead?'

One had enjoyed the break from Ray's program but was now reminded by the louts who ran Channel 0 that one had inked a contract and had obligations. The show hadn't improved, so one did what one could. Through one's painterly connections, an interview with Rosaleen Norton, self-proclaimed witch of Sydney's Kings Cross. She had an exhibition on in Melbourne. Just a bad painter, but a marvellous gimmick, one must concede.

'How did you get here from Sydney, dear? *By broom?*'

She played along. Certainly looked the part. A gap between prominent front teeth. Brows that arched up. A live toad as a prop.

'Now, if I wanted to turn that toad into a, er, *handsome prince*, what should I do?'

'Well, I'd say kiss it, Frank.'

'Kiss it.' I regarded the camera. Narrowed my eyes. '*Where?*' And braced for the inevitable. You see, every time one got a laugh, Ray would barge in and sabotage it. Couldn't keep his gob shut in an open sewer. *This means war*, I concluded. In my next column, I tagged him *Rebel without a pause,* to foment an imaginary feud between he and I. And for a bit of balance, gave the *Mavis Bramston Show* a serve. Touted by Seven as bold satire, the routines came from 1940s London revue, and 1920s Tiv Circuit stuff. *Someone's been robbing graves,* I wrote.

Ray persisted with his witless interjections, his unmentionables in a twist over one's column, you see. So I went to the producer. Teed up two solo segments; first, a bit from a stage part. One had seen Orson Welles do Shylock on the *Dean Martin Show*. Pure *ensorcelment*. Also, to read that week's *A Piece Of Thring* aloud each week. In a spotlit, darkened studio. *Alone.*

Speaking of one's column, one now railed at the *Ray Taylor Show's* rivals. To get them sputtering, to get us in the news. Socked it to *Sunnyside Up*. Compared it to turns one had seen in the 1930s at the Tivoli, *in one's first long-trousered suit.* Of compere Bill Collins, *when was the last time someone took his pulse?*

It did no good. It never does. It never will.

CHAPTER TWENTY-FOUR

'I always know when I'm home.'
Black Jack, back from his 'fact-finding tour' of British and American theatres. 'Customs confiscated one of my books.'

He got back Albee's *Tiny Alice* somehow and we ran it at the Prinny. Seduction and erotica, backdrop of the Church bilking the wealthy of their worldlies. But the sizzle of *Alice* in Sumner's cold blue hands summoned up necrophilia at best. Rough as guts Bunney Brooke in the lead, as a seductress, only reinforced this. Still, one had fun as my man the Cardinal. One night, Hoppy Hopgood, playing a butler, *not another fucking butler*, couldn't open a bottle of champagne onstage. In my full Cardinal's drag, I said *give it to me, darling*.

'Remind you of something, sweetie?' I said as it spurted high and mighty into the air. But our fusty subscribers weren't up for this sort of sport at all. It bombed.

'This is monu*mental* miscasting,' I said. 'Even for *you*.'

The play, Pinter's *The Homecoming*. 'I mean, *me*? As a Cockney *butcher* who rapes his *daughter* in law?'

Sumner was obdurate. *So.* One stabbed in the dark for one's man Max. Tried boilerplate South Londoner, but Black Jack was all over me like shit on a pig. One cursed him under cold half moon and reached for more Courvoisier. Then it came. Of *course*.

'I ain't bustin' my bollocks for no cunt.'

Mine host Bollocks the barman at the Coleherne Hotel, Earl's Court, in one's London days. Bollocks would serve nought but lager or ale. *A Prosecco in a long glass, if I may, tapster,* just asking for it. A voice deep as hell's basement, rough as sailor's breath.

I had my Max.

During rehearsals, the girl cast as Ruth fell ill. Her replacement, a new foxy doxie at the Union. Not without talent, indeed had trained in English rep, but one couldn't abide her. Jenny Claire well-cast as a prostitute here, given her no-knickers dress code. She inflicted upon us raw tales of wild youth whence she'd ridden squadrons of gallants to fountainous finish. Was married for a time to Clive Winmill, another Union stayer. Knew all these painters. Brett Whiteley's crowd. All bells and feathers, our Jenny. Lived in a loft in Carlton. Fell out of it once. Always injuring herself. Idiotic misadventures. Her wild red hair annoyed too, worn in outlandish styles.

'Who are you meant to be today? I'd bark.' Can't you do something about that mop? It's a fucking *fire* hazard!'

Yet she charmed some. Sumner for one. A known couch caster, albeit castees were said to be initiators as often as not. *This blackeyed martinet turned them on. Don't ask me.* And he never got rid of her, despite one's pleas, so one sometimes wondered...

''Ere, what 'ave you done with the scissors?'

One's Max, all flat cap and cardigan. First line, first scene, first night. But no sunshower of claps for a Thring entrance. Don't they recogn....? Then I saw. *No, they don't.* Actors dream of this. Muttering swept across the stalls as we proceeded.

'Is that...? It *can't* be, ...' Till as one, they rose. Banging their mitts together, cheering, whistling. A *standing O.* One of my best parts, pixie. Everyone said so. One was asked by the press why. In Australia, one must never bignote. One's man was required in one scene to rape Ruth, his daughter in law, on a butcher's block.

'Oh, that's easy,' I said. 'They actually believed *I* wanted to fuck Jenny *Claire.*'

On that absurd yobfest of Australia Day, in 1966, Menzies left office after several centuries as PM. His successor, Harold Holt. We were doomed. At the Union, *big cast,* said Sumner of *The Representative.* Including six children.

'Oh, god. Best bring net and trident,' one whispered to an unwell Antinous. He'd been cast here, albeit a small part. One had insisted. The boy needed work. One still gave him an envelope of the necessary now and then. To buy just one cold hour in his hell.

February 1966 brought decimal currency to our bold commonwealth. And back at the *Ray Taylor Show*, diners at the Top Of The Town were assailed live to air by Ray. One had long since refused to take part in these forays.

'What's the crab soufflé like? Enjoying it, are we?' They nodded, reluctant, mute, frozen. All Melbourne now wary of Ray's antics. 'Well, do you think these kids would enjoy it, too?'

He pulled out large photos - of starving African kiddies. One was watching at home, having taken the night off. The show was canned. Ray sacked. He hit the bottle. Had what is no longer called a nervous breakdown.

CHAPTER TWENTY-FIVE

'Frank, you should get out of the city more often.'
Oh do shut up, Paul.
'You know Lilydale?'
'Oh, fuck. Not that again. Go bush? I went once. It was *closed*.'
'This is different. There's a polo club. Friends of mine. Do you good...'

Perhaps some delusion that it might reap carnal reward. *Oh, very well, if we must.* One dressed now more or less all the time all in black. Had Edith run up ten shirts. Byronic puff to the sleeves. More jewellery now, too. And cravats. If nothing else, this foray a chance to mortify the squattocracy.

'To the countryside, driver.'

One drew a thick circle of the curious. Indeed rather more than for the charlies on horseback, *with their sticks and balls and arses in the air,* one observed. The grazier's wives loved me. A pleasant surprise. And then I saw. A scion of these barons of the bush. Young Hugh Rule. One constrained one's lust. They have Armalite rifles and earthmoving vehicles out there, you know.

'Hmmm,' I said when introduced, 'let's hope you're more than just a pretty face.'

He smiled, out of well-bred politeness. One made nice with all, but with one eye affixed on Huge Tool, as one would come to call him. Out of earshot of his parents, he told me, furtive and abashed, that he'd like to work in theatre.

'Well, then,' I said. Gave him my number. 'Dare to dream, boy.'

'It's time for me to move on, Frank.'

Oh, he had his reasons. One couldn't really help young Paul's career along, save snag him parts in plays from Sumner. And he'd grown testy at one's advances. He was gone from the guest room come the dawn.

His TV career blossomed not long after. So one served him most barbarous in *TV Week*. Yet proud of him. The apex of his career, the mid 1970s as Lee Whiteman in Channel Ten's steamy soapie *The Box*. His man a force ten flamboyant, a TV producer. One's favourite Aussie telly sex opera of all.

One met another young faun about now. Yes, pixie. He aspired to work on the boards and shall remain nameless. His story brief, as he wishes. One's escort for a time. First nights, fine dining, all that malarkey. One took him along on one's arm, that one be envied by one's rivals. Found him a job at the Union. Alas, he was dismissed when people with grudges sworn on skulls against me wailed nepotism to Sumner, and falsehoods of the boy's incompetence. This with half of them married to each other and fucking the other half on the side. Then he too was gone.

'*Speak.*'

'Frank?'

'State your fucking business.'

'It's Hugh Rule. From Lilydale...' Oh, yes. *Oh, yes.*

He came by next day. In school uniform. The neighbours could think what they liked.

'Drink?'

He kept coming back. For the firewater and one's collection of *Playboy, Harem, Dude* and other, well, rather more athletic stuff from certain city bookshops; *Loving Sweden,* you know. All stored in the room once Nanny's. One filled the biggest goblets one had and tutored him in the ways of the boards. One evening, one moved and sat at his feet, supplicant to this nascent Adonis. Under rising moon, patted his knee. He ached for sex, like all teens. But not with I. And never would.

'Whose crime was it to call you *Gloria?* Sounds like someone gargling something they shouldn't.'

One's agent, the relentless Gloria Payten, a busy bee. Back then TV and radio owners had to pay license fees for them. So, then. One was to be the face of this campaign for the government. Australians were going to lengths to defy and evade this Hobbesian imposition. As they do all such things.

One dressed oneself for the shoot. Velour jacket. Silk tie. Cufflinks as big as a fist, with ciggy and drinkie. First I, to camera, urging that the viewer go and check they had a license. If not, *there could be a knock at the door and you could be up for a very heavy fine. So embarrassing.* One turns to a second me on the telly one was watching, we fingerwaving to each other. *Most* camp. Then the me on the telly blows the other me a kiss. The other me buries face in hand. *Oh, no, the secret's out!* The viewer returns.

'Oh, you're back,' one says to camera. One comforts them. They can relax, enjoy their telly *with a clear conscience.* Meet a knock at the door, license in hand. Then in closeup, one's eyes narrowed to slits.

'Or *can* you?'

Viewer response? Mass resistance to this pernicious tax. One trousered the government shilling and laughed at the grey glow in the dark.

'A *ballet* is a dialogue of love. How can there be conversation if one's partners are so fucking dumb?'

Thus did Nureyev moan of his woes at our supper. Touring for Helpmann's Australian Ballet. One took Hugh, promenaded as boyfriend. Met up with Joan, still Rudy's tights wrangler against all odds. A disagreeable individual.

'Rudy,' said Joan, 'you can't kick and slap ballerinas just because they don't meet your impossible standards.'

'Fuck off,' said Rudy.

'I sometimes wonder why I keep doing this,' said Joan.

'Because I'm so handsome,' he said. A piece of work. Threw bread rolls at waiters to get their attention. Yelled at other diners if they stared.

'Poshel na khuy!'

'It's Russian,' said Joan, 'for *get fucked.*'

One's *TV Week* column wrote a eulogy in advance for Jimmy Hannan's awful new show on ATV0. *Anything to help. They'll need one sooner than they think,* I wrote. Next day, Jimmy's producer called.

'Frank?' The mind's eye surmised. Moustache, psychedelic tie, brown body shirt on the fuller figure. Enreddened by cab-sav from long lunch at some dark timber'd steak cave.

'About your column. Kennedy can't sing, can't dance. But he's a funny cunt. Jimmy isn't. As you've pointed out.' *Oh. Not the shellacking one had braced for.*

'Jimmy needs funny. You're a funny cunt.'

Thus did one become host's sidekick on the Thursday prime time *Jimmy Hannan Show.*

'Wipe off that gloomy mask of tragedy, it's not your styyyyle...'

Jimmy sang a number to open. *Put On A Happy Face* or other such goulash. One did punchlines to Jimmy's throws and read one's *TV Week* column to viewers. This scored other work; a few eps of an abomination called *Take The Hint* with Bobby Limb. Aired at two-thirty PM. Such dross met local program content rules, you see, so networks could run in prime time the Yank shows for which they paid so much. Oh, and Gloria scored me the odd voice-over. Radio and telly ads, you know.

'Fuck me dead,' I said at one such session. *'Continental Soup.* Sounds like a men-only Roman bathhouse.'

'I want interpretation, boy, not impersonation. Can you do that?'

At rehearsal, Sumner braced young Antinous, the boy in a dreadful state. Mild compared to Black Jack's usual bludgeons, yet set this lad to weeping in the brasco.

'Never mind him,' I said. 'His brother died in the war, you know.' Which was true, and explained a great deal. I rolled a bottle of Ben Ean under the stall door.

'Swig on that. Dry your eyes.'

Meanwhile, one's protégé Hugh Rule somehow got Black Jack to take him on. Don't ask me. One had had a word, but after what blew up with the other lad, well, Hugh certainly didn't get the job on my recommendation. Anyway, he gave Hugh to company co-director, Ogilvie.

'Can't do anything with him,' said George. So Sumner offered him an ASM's job.

'What do you think, Frank?' asked Hugh.

'Well,' I said, 'work in the theatre of any kind is as rare as happy marriages. The hours are horrendous, of course. Rehearsals ten AM to six PM, then show, eleven PM finish and famished. And tomorrow and tomorrow and tomorrow.'

He took the job. And, oh, Valhalla! Found himself bereft, friends abed, and poor Hugh half-starved after long days of toil, the cross of a thesp's fetchit. So now, a regular guest in the midnight hour, for one's omelettes with pimento and goblets of cheer in the still of the night. Our unspoken Platonic accord was a trial. But it would have to do.

'Yes, you heard me. Eighty thousand. In cash. *Now.*'

The second half of one's legacy now due and payable. But invested, said my accountant. Well, I'd none of it. 'You trying to rook me?'

'Cash out now, Frank, and you'll lose more than you dare dream.'

'Oh, fuck it then. How much *can* you give me?'

One was with Simon Chilvers, en route to St Kilda for dinner with his wife and their little son Sam. They lived around near Acland Street. Close by, the Palais Theatre and the Wattle Park buildings. The southernmost ruins of the First Thring Empire.

'Oh, why *me?*'

A musical. No way out. Beckoned by McCallum for JCWs, you see. It wouldn't do to snub a benefactor. A deplorable turn, *Robert And Elizabeth,* at the Prinny, with June Bronhill, then our *prima coloratura soprano*. With assorted castrati, baritoni and titanic-titted slappers. One's Union chum Finno was cast here, a lone kindred spirit, thank the god of fuck. Oh, the production numbers, pixie. The *waiting.* It was like a fucking film shoot. *Womens' Weekly* did a puff piece at June's place shortly before we opened.

'My task, to promote this gargantuan behemoth,' one sighed to the interviewer. 'The show, not *June*,' I clarified. She glared. The talk turned to diets.

'I shouldn't eat roast lamb and potatoes,' said June.

'Quite so,' I said. 'Especially not when one has to tote her all over the stage. It's like having to lug *me* around.'

Then I saw the set. All *stairs*. And tasked with lumping June, the singing baby elephant, up and down these fuckers. For the end of the first act, *exempli gratia*, one had to enter, bearing La Bronhill as she shrilled, down a staircase and out through French windows as the backdrop rose, replaced by a descending floral extravaganza. This as two white gazebos appeared and began to revolve. The customers went troppo, pixie.

But one night, we found the stagehand at the controls for all these doovalackeys out cold sidestage in a lakelet of vomit. One stomped on the buttons, jumped on the box. Somehow it kicked in. Dumped June onstage for her love duet and fled. Backstage, gulped down a stiff one. In a manner of speaking.

In May, a charity turn of *Rob And Liz*. For the Prince Henry Hospital. One was trapped in conversation with, well, let's call her Lady Biddy Fuck-Truffles. An emetic Tooraknik, calling forth memories of her sainted pal Olive. Enough was enough.

'Do you have children?' *Yes, three sons. Wh...* 'Then,' says I, '*one* of them must be queer. Is he free tonight?' *Beg yours, Frankie?* 'Well, what about hubby then? Is he here? *You* don't look like you're getting much.'

'Frank, so sorry, dear boy, but it's appalling,' said McCallum. 'All Melbourne is talking about it.'

'Precisely, John. I mean, you did ask me to promote this musical Hindenburg.'

The thing closed well before the end of its allotted span. As it fucking should have.

Disturbing times. US President Johnson flew in, to solicit more young Australians to die in Vietnam. Opponents to the war took to the streets. Riots. *All the way with LBJ,* smarmed PM Harold Holt. Karma awaited.

In November, we took *Rob And Liz* to the Tiv in Sydney. The crits called it 'routine.' But a fairy clap for me from the fairy critics of Fairy City stood out. And in the middle of all this, a federal election. For Holt, a huge victory. The nation seduced, and yet to wake in horror.

McCallum and Googie came to the show. Wanted to talk. Apres-show, we repaired to the Bourbon and Beefsteak up the Cross.

'It's a kids' show,' said McCallum. 'Well, family viewing. Focus on local fauna. Kangaroos, koalas and whatnot. For overseas sales.'

'Packer's ponied up six grand an episode,' said Googie.

'You smooth talking fucker,' I said to John.

'I had help.'

Sir Frank cared more for his dire newspapers than his telly network. So McCallum had pulled the coat of son Clyde, the somewhat more savvy prince regent of their TV division. 'Of course,' said McCallum, 'Clyde copped the usual monstering from Frank in the process. Says to get cracking on it, before the old man does his roll at the races and we lose our funding. So what I need from you, Frank, is...'

It became one of *the* timeless classics of Aussie telly. And to its story we shall return.

Oh, yes, and *that.* The year of Ronald Ryan. Well, the screws were all getting shickered at a Christmas party, so wouldn't you? He and a chum broke out of Pentridge. A most unhappy ending. A warder, stone dead. Shots fired from multiple carbines. Only one of them in Ryan's hands. For all that, he had Buckley's. You'll recall, pixie, that a state election was due. Our oleaginous Victorian premier, Henry Bolte, made his wishes clear. This despite proof that Ryan could not have been the slayer. His sentence, well... One sought shelter in sick humour, as we do at such times.

'Were FT still alive,' one said to Margaret as she fussed around the kitchen, 'he'd build the gallows at the Prinny and sell tickets.'

'And film it and run it at Hoyts,' she said. Smiling to mask her... we turned our blurred, flooding eyes from each other.

'Well, Butch, I told you so,' I said when the editor called. 'Kiss that censor's arse any harder, you'll get your tongue stuck in it.'

One was back at TV Week, after a blue over one's racy turns of phrase. Circulation plummeted in one's absence. Of course it had. And Jimmy asked me back on his show after a producer had canned me. The fellow himself punted just weeks later. Such is the magic of television.

One worked well with Jimmy. A good straight man. Example, of Aussie cop dramas:

'It was shot by Crawfords. Pity the director wasn't.'

'Oh, *Frank.* You've seen worse than that, haven't you?'

'Yes, I *have.*' Bared one's bottom teeth to smile at one's prey.

'Thought so. What's the worst show *you've* ever been on, Frank?'

'Oh, *that.* No contest. I'm on it right *now,* baby.'

For *The Right Honourable Gentleman,* one's co-stars were elfin Ellie Ballantyne, dashing Dennis Miller, Jenny bloody Claire. And that stealer of scenes second only to I, John Gregg. Also noxious Catholic Patricia Kennedy, for all our sins venial and mortal. Oh, and a new boy, Graeme Blundell. A Bambi-eyed youth, also ASM for this turn. Poor *Gay Gay Bundle,* as one called him. Half the day rehearsing, the second half performing; and the third half sourcing props, sweeping the stage, bumping in and out between scenes, and fetchworth to cast entire.

'To see if they are serious about their calling, boy,' said Sumner. Sounding, as he so often did, like a flogging captain. Gay Gay's man, a butler, *all these fucking plays with butlers,* had to bend over in front of me at one point, to place an envelope on a table. One's line here a coincidence too, too good.

'Watch out for the opening date!'

He served me as an ASM should. Uncorked one's Ben Ean Moselle. Kept one's goblets backstage refreshed. Yet begged off, citing exhaustion, when invited to one's home. 'Yes, Gay Gay,' I said, weeping inside. 'It's vampire's hours in this game. An actor's home is his *coffin.*'

All the theatres of London, it is said, without prompting or collusion, turned off their marquee lights for an hour that night in 1967. Our good Lady left us now.

TB and madness claimed credit with a smirk. One drank to Viv in soundless Rylands solitude. Such be the price of peace at last.

'People write to use about miseries inflicted on them. Crook tradesmen, banks,' I said. 'We get them on, *and* those complained about. We as ombudsman.'

Viewers were drifting off to other channels. So one pitched to Jimmy a new segment one had crafted. A TV-friendly one, I added. 'Doesn't cost a zack for the talent.'

Well, it worked for a time. But they canned it after phoned-in death threats. I recall it was all over the papers. Still, one had fun as the bods who made those calls.

'Textas, boy, two black, two red. And all the large white cards your arms will bear. Then write my lines onto them. Now chop chop, there's the chap.'

'Um, where do I find this stuf...'

'That,' I said, 'is an ASM's *job*. To *find* things. There's your starting point.'

A desirable but slow lad. Nameless he shall remain. Engaged him as one's factotum at one of Sheila F's shivoos. This for a trip to Sydney. A one-man ABC teleplay, *The Heat's On,* by the prolific Pat Flower. No rehearsal, so idiot sheets essential, held up by the floor crew aft of the cameras. Get it done in single takes, that we could all go home quick sticks.

One was pleasured by this boy, so took him on as valet for a tendril of time back in Melbourne. Alas, forced to dismiss him. Started stealing from me. Such a shame. Fairer to behold even than the Almighty judged Adam.

'Oh, anything for money.'

In fact, an obligation. One's ATV0 contract. One was a *network personality*, you see. The job, a part in a shitcom slapped together by

Jon-Michael Howson, writer, producer, actor of sorts. Another queenly institution of Aussie telly. *Hey You* it was called. Colin McEwan as Ocker Ramsey, career bludger. Ernie Bourne as the Major, patrician con man. Self as Mr Goodly, soup kitchen proprietor. The Major and Ocker make it over as a gentlemen's club. Playboy bunnies. Yes. *That* bad. *Hey You* was axed soon after. Isn't everything?

'Just the ticket, baby. Who's going to notice? I mean, those subscribers from the first run are all dead by now, with luck.'

For our *Moby* revival, we cast, among others, Gay Gay Bundle and a Union greensleeves, gimlet-eyed Helmut Bakaitis. One was captivated by his, shall we say, primal attributes. But then Hugh attached himself to this Helmut. As opposed to *me*. Helmut closer in age to the boy than I, you see. And a fucking judy magnet. Hence Hugh's attraction. One put Helmut through the customary pranks and trials, as per all new chums. He wore it well. And, for all one's resentment *vis a vis* Hugh, I liked the boy. In particular when at the prow of *Moby's* whaling boat of wicker skips. In a costume comprised of very little. One couldn't help but gravitate. At one point in the play, my Ahab cries 'Beach me, beach me, I'm the Great White Whale', with Helmut fore of me. Arm raised. Broom for harpoon in fist, as the cast pretends to row with imaginary oars. As one shouted, one grabbed Helmut around his arse. Every night. Well, he took it in good part but, it was plain, marched with that other regiment.

'I was away the day they handed out the faces, Frank. So the bastards gave me an arse instead.'

One beseeched Mary Hardy to reprise her Pip the cabin boy. She said she was too ugly. Having one of her turns. Poor child. She'd been sacked yet again from a radio job. Her ostensible crime, working blue. But in fact for being funnier than her male rivals. So one bid that Sumner cast Lyndel Rowe. A stout ensembler. Then, midst *Moby* rehearsals, a real monster emerged from the deep.

'Well, one was on his show once, touting one of your dreadful plays. Should have strangled him while I had the chance.'

One's explanation to Sumner when he asked what the hell was going on. One cloudclad afternoon, in the middle of a *Moby* run-through, one was served a summons. Damages for libel sought against self, ATV0 and *TV Week*. By just-sacked HSV7 compere Terry O'Neill. He of the appalling *Time For Terry*. The reason? *For all who fear that they watch too much telly, the antidote at last,* one's sentiments Terrywise in one's *TV Week* column. And more just like it, and repeated on *The Jimmy Hannan Show*. I mean, this clarinet-tooting Pom and his combover were finished when the only thing his turn had going for it, singing duo Olivia Newton-John and Pat Carroll, had the sense to bail and sail for England. Seven saw one's point and axed the fucker.

Time For Terry's other 'stars' were Vi Greenhalf, radio and TV fixture, loud, large. Partial to foursomes, it was said. Ian Turpie was, well, Ian Turpie. And Terry himself, well, he be Gra Gra Kennedy's take on a 'TV personality' as 'someone who hasn't got one.' Terry settled out of court. Some fuck off money from Channel 0 and *TV Week*.

'Now begone, Terry,' I said on Jimmy's show. 'We have our own TV stars here. The equal of any in the world. Like Jimmy here. Every bit as dreadful as you.'

Then McCallum called.

'Podge. That kids' show. *Skippy,* It's called. Can I send you a script?'

CHAPTER TWENTY-SIX

One is reading *The English Patient* by, what's his name, let's see here, Michael Oondaatje. It's just won the 1992 Booker Prize. Must finish it before they make a film and a mess of it. Speaking of which, a movie review caught one's eye in the *Age* TV guide. *Almost An Angel*, Paul Hogan's latest. Well, butter my buns and call me Slippery. Chuck Heston's in it. Cast as *God,* for fuck's sake. One also endured *Hook* on the telly, midst ads for hardware and dog food. Robin Williams as Peter Pan. Dustin Hoffman's Hook. Major, pricey stars, phoning it in. The cries of vultures aloft. Circling.

*

'A lunatic millionaire doctor. Simply made for you,' said McCallum. For *Skippy,* one's criminal mastermind Dr Alexander Stark, up against a marsupial with the smarts to foil the wiliest villain. *What's that, Skip?* Roos are in reality slower than slugs. But mine not to reason why.

Moby drew passable crowds at that old grey moll the Russell. Closing night's after party brinked on riotous affray. Up to Sydney for *Skippy* come sunup, aboard TAA The Friendly Way.

'Flat, stale and hostage to murderous hangover,' one's gruff rejoinder when a hostie asked how one was this morning. So, then. A handful of Nembutal in a windburned Travelodge on the Pacific Highway. Emerged come sunup, all showgal tits and smiles, for an RSL taxi to Duffy's Forest in Kuringai National Park.

It had rained all night. The fucking place was mudmired.

'Good morning, Mr Thring.' *Ooh, what have we here?* 'I'm Tony Bonner.'

'Thank you, Tony. Good morning to you too.' *I must have him, whatever it take....*

'Lee Robinson, Frank.' A slim bearded gent. 'We've met,' he smiled. He saw that one was nonplussed. '*The Flaming Sword*. Chips and I. You called it the worst movi...'

'Oh. *That* worst movie. Forgive me, Butch. I've been in so *many*.'

'Podge!' A voice at my back. McCallum.

'You sadistic turd.' I waved my arm at the muck. 'What *is* this goulash?'

'Language, old fellow.' A car pulled up. 'Boys, Mr Thring. Ken James and Garry Pankhurst.'

'Good morning, Mr Thring,' they chorused. Two of the best actors, despite their tender years, with whom one has ever worked. Did as told. Did it well.

'Exteriors today, Frank,' said McCallum.

'For what? The First Battle of the Somme?'

In the 'dressing room,' McCallum's euphemism for this cramped Sunliner caravan, Eddy Devereaux. Togged up in khaki as Ranger Matt Hammond. On his knees, clutching a rosary, the full Catholic bit. He crossed himself. Rose to greet me.

'How would you be, Frank. Remember when...'

'Ah, yes,' I said. 'That bloody Kangaroo Club. Sloane Square.' A booze billabong, refuge for destitute Aussie thesps in London. One had looked up Leo McKern in England in '55. He'd dragged me off to this pubful of the fuckers. Eddy, John Meillon, all that lot. Eddy grinned as he recalled.

'I think we drank it dry save the cleaning products.'

'Come off it, Frank. It's a kid's show. Not *World Championship Wrestling*.'

My man wore white suit, Panama hat, cravats. And toted a walking cane. One suggested using it, to belt one's nameless henchmen. Lee would have none of it.

Much of the first day wasted. Fake happy snaps for *TV Week* and the Packer papers. You know, pretending to consult a script with Lee. That sort of twaddle, to fool the mugs that we knew what the fuck we were doing. Then, one's first scene. Alighting from a vintage Rolls. For a showdown with Ed's Matt Hammond.

Outside, a hessian bag was bouncing around on the ground. One thought that one was having the dry horrors. Poked at it with my cane.

'Hello, Mr Thring.' The sound operator. 'That's Skip. We keep her in there so she stays calm.'

'Well,' I said. 'If that's the dressing room for the *star*, then what the fuck are they going to give *me?*'

'She'll be apples, Frank,' said Lee. 'Doesn't bite. Zonked anyway. We dropped some Valium down its gullet.'

A baby wombat placed in the crook of one's arm, to inform one's character somehow. Full of brandy too. Via nose dropper. One recalled Efftee Films and its koala. A detestable practice. We started to film. It started to rain. Hard.

'Ah,' I said inside their purpose-built Ranger HQ. 'That's it for today, I suppose.'

'No River Murrays,' said Lee. 'We'll do interiors.' Saw my dismay. Grinned.

'It's not *Ben Hur*, old fellow.'

'Fucking fleas and lice,' I said to McCallum. We were dotted in insect bites from cradling koalas, wombats, bandicoots. Scratching like stray dogs.

'What would you like me to do, Frank? I, er, ...'

'You could get some Fleatick powder from the vet's.'

'For all these animals? Oh, dear. That's a lot of money...'

'Oh, of course,' I said, 'that. Well, you could run us all through a *sheep dip!*'

'Tell me this is not delirium tremens.'

One almost trod on *three* jumping sacks.

'There's more than one Skip, Mr Thring.' Tony Bonner, laughing. 'We have JoJo, Stumpy and Wildy.' Lee appeared behind me.

'If one of 'em won't song and dance for us, we break out the others. Failing that, we've got a stuffed one.' He leaned in, lowered his voice. 'Wombats, too. The lot. Er, best not to ask, mate.'

'And what do you call *them?*' I said. '*Stiffy?*'

'Well,' I said to these two glums cast as one's henchdrones, 'the only way you'll get a hot lunch out of the Packers is...do those teeth of yours come out?'

They were whining about the catering. One had learned the hard way long ago. Bring a *cut lunch* or suffer the slop ladled out on location beatifying itself with the descriptor of food.

To Featherdale Wildlife Park at Doonside, deep in Sydney's west in pre-dawn murk went we. It stood in as Dr Stark's evil private zoo, you see. Here, Stark offers the abducted and imprisoned Skip a gourmet fruit platter. She 'jumps' him and 'escapes.' My man cops a faceful of fresh fruit. *The things one does.*

'It's on at the 729 if you want to be in it,' said Eddy. At week's end, to the 729 Club in St Leonards. Drinker of choice for the TV game. Red brick walls. Large logos of the networks on them. It behoves one to offer recall of wonderful nights there.

If only one could.

McCallum and Lee were liking my Stark. A villain full despisable to children despite Lee's wretched scripts. One saw an opportunity to help *Skippy's* media profile out, not to mention one's own. You see, for one scene, Skip gets caught in a cattle grid and is in peril from an oncoming truck. The crew jammed her leg through the bars to shoot this.

'Hello? RSPCA?'

Gave one's name as Dick Cockburn, *bush*walker. They raided the *Skippy* set next day.

'You're joking!' one was quoted in the *TV Week* cover story. 'That 'roo is treated better than *us*. Pampered like a Hollywood queen! After all,' I said, '*I should know.*'

That Friday, the 729. When they chucked us out, the Taxi Club at Darlinghurst was the go. Stairs almost vertical. But at the top, hold fast. The empyrean sphere.

Dim lights. Orange and red on black. *Frank!* boomed the cocks in frocks whose domain this was. One of them even sat on one's lap. Most agreeable. And a shickered Channel Niner took one home, he believing his catch to be, well,... an on-air personality, let's leave it at that.

Between *Skippy* shoots, back to Melbourne. A revival of Ionesco's *Rhinoceros*. At the Russell, enduring its backstage cramped and dark. Sumner called it 'The Submarine.' I had another name for it. The shared dressing room a thousand shortcomings, so one commandeered the shower recess adjacent as one's private suite.

'Want a shower? It's fucking *Melbourne*,' when people protested. 'Go outside and wait three minutes. Be *off* with you!'

My man in this turn, a brute of a boss. Values work above the health of his beleaguered staff.

'I shall model him on my other employer,' I told director George Whaley. 'Frank Packer.'

Young Blundell was in *Rhino*, as was languorous Dennis Olsen, a new recruit. Damn good, but needed his corners rubbed off. For *Rhino*, we all had to turn into one as we left the stage. Looking like one, as one does, helped. Dennis, a slim jim, did not.

'You're supposed to turn into a rhino, dear,' I said in front of the cast at line-up. 'Not a fucking *gazelle*.' A face-saving exercise. One had tried to get off with him. No sale. We became friends of course, in spite of that. Just like all the others. One was never alone. Yet, yes, always and forever, lonely.

She came in the stage door hobbling. A walking stick. Horseriding, she said.

'My mount threw me...'

'Middle of a run,' I said. 'You fetch up like this.' The cast stopped to watch. 'Pray tell, was your *mount* any good? Who was on *top?*'

To be fair, Jenny Claire kept coming back to an unrewarding job in money terms. Took parts as given. Even pulled her own ditzy crowd to our turns. Still, she must be punished. 'With all those lover boys of yours,' I said, 'how is it that you weren't *stuck fast* to the *saddle?*'

Ed Devereaux wrote the next *Skippy* ep. Stark hires an actor to impersonate Matt Hammond. To get him dismissed, that Stark might take over Waratah National Park. Ed played his man and the impostor.

'But,' said Lee, 'same face, same uniform, same car. How do we tell them apart?'

'What would you do without me?' I said. I stuck a lit cigarette in Eddy's mouth. 'See? *Bad* boy.' Pulled it out. '*Good* boy.'

A new cast member here too. The delightful Liz Goddard, as Clancy.

'To broaden our audience,' Lee told me. 'A *frisson* of romantic tension.'

'Ah,' I said. 'Beauteous ingenue amidst hub of princes.' He'd received a call.

'Packer here. *Skippy*. Put some tits in it.' *Clunk.*

This day no more bizarre than any other. One had to nurse a baby koala in the open back seat of this very expensive hired vintage Rolls Royce Phantom. Full of Tolleys TST and Vallies, the thing piddled and vomited all over me. McCallum almost soiled himself when he heard.

'Oh, dear. Is the car alright?'

For this ep, Skip had to once again 'attack' Stark. All three 'roos too thick to take direction this day, so they broke out Stiffy. Threw the thing at me from off-camera.

Got it in one take.

'Most efficient, these stuffed animals,' I said to McCallum. 'Why not do the same with your whole *cast?*'

'How would you be, Blue?'

Our location for this day, a grand pile on Fitzwilliam Road in Vaucluse. He cracked two two triangular holes each in steel cans with a kangaroo paw opener. Watched croc-eyed as I sculled mine. Chips Rafferty was at home. He'd loaned them his home for a scene, *quid pro quo* a part in a later ep.

'You call this hot?' said Chips on this sun-belted Sydney morning. 'Ah, you don't know hot till you've been opal mining. My word. I remember I was having a beer in a bloodhouse in Adelaide when this cove...'

Tight shooting schedule, so Lee rescued me lest I drown in these bloviations.

'We stuck it in the freezer for a bit,' said Lee. 'Cold-blooded. Went right off to beddy byes.'

A bluetongue lizard clung to one's lapel. It felt cold and comatose. Hideous. One's scene here, a demo of Dr Stark's spray-emitting camera. To paralyse animals and people. Enabling the Doctor to kidnap critters and disable pesky do-gooding humans. All done, McCallum asked for a quiet word.

'Er, this is awkward, old fellow. It's Sir Frank. Spitting chips.'

No need to spell it out. The old gila monster furious at John over one's being cast. A suspected *wally woofter* on his kids' show. One wasn't a bit surprised.

'I'm so sorry about this,' said McCallum. 'I mean, it's Packer. What can you do when he does his block?'

'Oh, that's easy, baby,' I said. 'Stick him in the freezer for a bit.'

CHAPTER TWENTY-SEVEN

'Oh, fuck. Not *again*.'

One had no choice. Oscar Whitbread from the ABC called. They were doing a four-parter, classic plays about greed. Jonson's *Volpone*, Chekhov's *The Proposal* as well as *The Bear*, and most avaricious of all, Oscar Wilde's *Salome*. Whitbread to direct. And I, Thring, dragooned to play, yes, that old pervert Herod.

Freddy Parslow fetched up well, one must concede, in nothing but a loincloth, as Jokaanan, or John The Baptist. Well, Freddy The Baptist. He never got out of Freddy enough to be anyone else, but the part so well written that even Freddy made it work. You know, the wrong side of babbling mad, as prophets tend to be. Freddy also had a spare, bony frame, just right for a clodpate who subsists on grasshoppers in the desert, *by choice*. And Monica Maughan did well as Herodias, all bitter scold and seething envy, despite her striking Celtic countenance, somewhat unconvincing in this Middle Eastern setting.

But then there was Buster Skeggs. My god, pixie, the girl was good. You see, Whitbread and producer David Goddard needed a bod who could dance as well as act, to do the seven veils bit. In those days, a bit thin on the ground. Actors acted and dancers danced and never the twain. Buster just twenty-one at the time, a Tivoli gal in a typical McCallum-wrangled JCWs turn, *Man Of La Mancha* at the Comedy Theatre.

'God, you're a looker. I so wish you were a boy.'

Buster took it as the compliment intended. We were friends at first sight, and while there was concern that a hoofer would make a hash of Wilde's lines, she was marvellous. One asked her how she did it.

'Showbiz parents, Frank. Both worked in theatre in the UK. Their advice, train up as a triple threat. Song, dance, acting. Never be out of work, they said.'

'You're supposed to be a madman, Freddy,' I said. 'A fanatic. Don't recite. Babble!'

Freddy, as ever, needed a push-start. Oscar concerned himself more with camerawork, circling around us, swooping in for closeups. So one felt obliged. The set design a bobby dazzler. Costumes after Aubrey Beardsley's original drawings. One's rococo headdress, more jewels than all the litany named in Herod's speech. And then there was Buster's striptease.

'This isn't the opera company. It's the dance of the seven veils, not the seven army blankets.'

So decreed bold Buster, and so it went with her daring costume. Choreographed by Joe Latona from *Daly At Night,* the gossamer and gauze bits came off in double quick time as she whirled her way down to a bikini of rags.

Salome ends with a long speech from the titular temptress, as she holds the severed head of the Baptist, and addresses it eye to eye.

'Thou wouldst not suffer me to kiss thy mouth, Jokanaan.'

The 'head' the ABC props people fashioned was covered in chocolate sauce, as this most resembled blood on a black and white TV screen. Buster had voiced her concerns to me about getting through this without fluffing it, and I assured her all would be well, that even the ABC would indulge a second or third take if the first she fumbled. Just at that moment, David Goddard appeared on the set.

'You'll never believe what's happened.'

One pictured our Prime Minister. Wind in the hair. Dick in the hand. With a floozy not his wife. Doing his Aquaman bit out in the wild surf of Cheviot Beach, that she surrender her charms back at the shack. Harold Holt had vanished.

'I'm afraid you only get one take, dear,' said Oscar to Buster. 'Every cameraman we have has been ordered down to Portsea to cover it.'

She did it too. Meanwhile, the nation entire went quite mad, wondering how such a thing could have happened. You see, they knew nothing of Harold's form, his secret life, his penchant for haring off in his Pontiac Parisienne with good time gals, his displays of marine machismo to bedazzle them. And the media, who did, were not about to let the peasants in on it. He'd gone swimming and spearfishing in wild surf before, and had already had two close calls. There was talk of up to six women with whom Harold had dallied. Those who knew him wondered not of how this end could come to pass, but why it hadn't happened sooner.

The strangest days. US president Johnson, British PM Harold Wilson, others, flew in for the memorial service. The Holts lived close by to Rylands, on St Georges Road. But one couldn't face Zara. Sent a telegram and flowers. Australia paid tribute as only it could. A new sports facility in Glen Iris was badged, perhaps in overmuch haste, as the Harold Holt Memorial Swimming Centre.

The Melbourne Uni trustees decided we weren't raking in enough lolly to keep them in mink and rubies. Kicked us out of the Union Theatre. Calling ourselves the Union Theatre company now, well, absurd. Henceforth, a new handle, the Melbourne Theatre Company. The MTC. Or *empty sea* as one called it, as in the stalls at any given show.

Sumner wanted a big launch for it. So we set to work on Arthur Miller's *The Crucible*. Even had the Russell's interior redecorated. Gold and crimson over its existing five shades, all hue of stained mattress.

January of 1968 was endured in the Les Williams Memorial Hall in Lennox Street, Richmond. A weatherboard and corrugated iron hotbox. Sweat fell from brows as if the blood from Christ's eyes. This now our rehearsal space and company workshop. Read-throughs were cut with saws, drills, and hammers. And other hells.

'Frank.' Sumner, hand on ulcer. Each word a wince. 'That stuff frightens kids at pantomimes. I want you to frighten adults, boy. Your man is a tyrant, convinced that he alone is always right.'

'Ah,' I said. 'You mean like a theatre director?'

Helmut was in the cast here. And one's lost chum Huge Tool was ASM for this turn. Still captivated by Helmut. It was like one had never existed. Oh, both of 'em paid one due deference, but... but...

For *Crucible's* dress, the much-welcome new aircon worked. All too well for Puritan veils, aprons and wimples, or the mens' cloaks and tall black hats. Veils flapped. Hats flew off. Mantles blew over heads. Opening night loomed and cackled. Enter wardrobe mistress batty Betty Druitt.

'Your spare change.' *At once,* said her face. She sewed the coins into hems and hatbands. One recalled for the cast something Olivier had told me.

'The Queen's people do this, you know. Stops her dress blowing up. And front page pics of the royal twangers.'

The Crucible opened with a blood-freezing scream offstage from nimble Annie Pendlebury. We all shone. But the best came from Monica Maughan, expecting at the time, but not yet showing, you see. One night, on trial for witchcraft as Elizabeth, she bolted from the dock to a prop wooden rain bucket, dropped to both knees and vomited. The customers thought it part of the act. Huge applause.

Sumner shipped us off to Wangaratta for its arts festival the day after *Crucible's* Melbourne run. We reeked of stale booze, heads ringing. In his past life a slave trader, surely.

'Best put Black Jack on suicide watch,' I said to Freddy Parslow. 'Besotted with his unfucked Elspeth, now nevermore attainable.'

Ellie Ballantyne and Dennis Miller, two of one's favourite colleagues, asked one to their wedding. But one of late disinclined to such things. Not very good at them. A sensation of anxiety and ... oh, I don't know. One wrote wishing them well. With a dozen fine wines and a card, dispatched in an Embassy taxi.

The phone trilled. Mary Hardy calling. Her tone bespoke tear-stained face. News of Martin Luther King, of Memphis and the Lorraine Motel. A spark for still deeper melancholy. Oh, and her marriage, to a musician, *what the fuck did you think was going to happen* one's unvoiced thought, had ended. Sent a taxi for her at once. Suicide watch, you see.

'You'll be with me. Imagine the fillip to your so far less than stellar career...'

One took reluctant Hugh to see *Mame*, a JCWs turn. Mary Hardy's Gooch, *Mame's* bumbling secretary, was sensational. At post-show drinks, one wheeled the boy around Her Maj to show him off. Truth to tell, selling oneself as much as he. The MTC stipend alone failing to service the second mortgage one had of late taken out on Rylands. Over time, one had sold one's slice of the Prinny, the Regent, 3XY. Plus the Portsea place, the family Roller, FT's Packard. Some paintings. This in lieu of film and telly work, scarce all too often.

Home alone, disconsolate, one tuned in to late night Boris Karloff movies. Woke up to morning cartoons. Cut short by a news flash.

'... Senator Robert Francis Kennedy died at 1.44 AM today...'

'A steer kicked me in the face.'

All black eyes and broken nose. A fetish for holidays in the Northern Territory had Black Jack. At the YWCA hall, opposite the Russell, we shaped GB Shaw's *Major Barbara*. The Les Williams Memorial Hellpit, meanwhile, had been commandeered by Ogilvie for Chekhov's *Three Sisters*. A huge cast. Even one's lost boy Hugh scored a part. *Damn. George will be gentle with the boy,* I mused. *I want him flayed.*

For *Barbara*, my man was Undershaft, 'cannon king.' Arms tycoon. The play involves the Salvation Army, as you know. He at one point pressed into service as a trombonist. Waiting the length of the Pliocene epoch at rehearsal for one's scenes, one worked up the skill on the thing to make *fart* noises when people sat down, or walked across the stage. One blew in time with their steps till Sumner served me his eyes that paralyse.

A twinge of sympathy for young Helmut here. As Stephen Undershaft, son to my man, a figure of ridicule in a costume dotty Betty Druitt thought splendid. Golfing attire. Baggy knee pants. Tam o'shanter, all that cobblers. Sumner was enraged.

'They'll laugh you off the stage, boy. Go and tell Betty you want a navy blazer, grey flannel strides. That sort of thing.'

Helmut did so and Betty blamed and cold shouldered him for ever more. Undeserved. No good saying anything. The woman was quite mad.

One had one's own trials. The *speeches*. Overlong, drab arias. Cut from the film of *Barbara* with Robert Morley and Syb Thorndike and should have been here. One chased one's lines through a dark Teutoburger Wood, struggling to recall them. A new, disturbing experience. One's enunciations full of holes punched by stutters, gaps and stumbles. And Sumner thought one was *acting* this.

'*Frank!* How much longer on this train to nowhere? Speed it up, sing it, *shout it,* boy! If I want relentless tedium I'll *ask* for it!'

Well. One collapsed in tears. In front of *everyone*. The wherefore, only I knew. My vanished. Dreamboat. Antinous. Paul, Hugh. Joanie. Others.

CHAPTER TWENTY-EIGHT

The zenith of Shakespearean glory, it is claimed, is to play the hangdog Prince of Denmark. Barred to many by unchangeables. But ye rough or bulbous to the eye, fret not. Make for the Boar's Head Tavern and ask for *Falstaff*.

'Perth Festival likes the idea of *Henry IV*.' Sumner. 'And then we run it here, for Moomba in February. A big play, so...we go al fresco.'

'We *what?*' said Ray Westwell.

'The Arts Centre. St Kilda Road.'

'But that's still a fucking building site,' said Annie Pendlebury.

'Precisely.'

For this be Black Jack's mad dream. To stage *Hal 4* midst quintessence of dust. Outdoors, in the unfinished eternal Arts Centre courtyard, the only bit of this Babelian fantasy they'd completed, the place most days an inert building site.

'Where are the customers going to sit?'

Well, one had to ask. With luck, to stir an uprising, to torpedo his deranged designs.

'We'll put 'em on planks, boy. The closest experience they'll ever get to the Globe Theatre.'

'If it rains?' Robin Ramsay. Here between filming eps of *Bellbird*, the ABC soapie, as one of Aussie TV's most loved-hated ever, real estate spiv Charlie Cousins.

'Umbrellas, boy. Parts of the Globe didn't have a roof.'

Sumner's face paled. His ulcer, you see. 'And it rains a lot in England, you know.'

He flinched, as if knifed in the gizzards. Dismissed us, a flick of his hand.

We began on *Hal* just after Xmas. Out of doors, we but huddled prey to the whips and scorns of the elements, on the Murdoch Court as it was called. A swathe of slate and concrete, those greys of battleships and misery. In winds burning. Boiling heat. Rain. Hail. Sometimes all in one fucking day. Melbourne, you see. The ABC filmed this trial by skygods. Ran it as a doco. *Rehearsal* they called it. *Why, there be method to his madness*, I conceded when the run sold out in advance because of it.

One day George Whaley, playing our Hotspur and behind the scenes our fight wrangler, gave out broadswords to all. Two each of the fuckers. No shields.

'Why, may I ask?'

'Twice the noise, twice the movement,' said Ray.

'Full of sound and fury,' said Sumner. Hand up against the sun, shielding his eyes, which had surely turned to those of a beast. 'Can we get on with it, please?'

After a turn on *IMT* one evening with Gra Gra Kennedy to plug *Hal 4*, one was invited by the marvellous Johnny Farnham's manager 'Sadie' Sambell to Xmas dinner at his South Yarra flat. Sadie handled, in at least one sense, the gorgeous Farnham, rock group the Masters Apprentices, and Darryl Somers, back before Channel Nine concluded that he was so insipid that Australians would love him. With depressing clairvoyance.

One had said to Farnham on *IMT* that night, apropos his debut single, *Sadie The Cleaning Lady*,' Johnny, you can be *my* cleaning lady any time!' One adores his work. His latest, *Age Of Reason* and *Chain Reaction* get a regular spin here at Fitzroy. One thinks of him often. In ways one shouldn't.

Xmas lunch, *chez* Sadie. Johnny. Glenn Wheatley from the Masters. Molly bloody Meldrum. It was I who gave Ian the 'Molly' nickname, you know. Back at ATV0 when he started out, on *Kommotion*. They hired Molly and others to mime to pop hits of the day. In lieu of film clips. Yes, pixie. Much to answer for.

Now, a disturbance at the door. *Sadie! Open up!* Glenn's bandmates. Sadie and Glenn went to answer.

'Take this and fuck off to the pie shop!' we heard Sadie shout. They returned. Glenn looking most put out. 'I gave them two bucks,' said Sadie to our stares.

'You can fuck off too if you don't like it,' he flung at Glenn, and closed his gob around a fluteful of Cristal. *My* Cristal, which one would have gladly shared with those waifs. Dreadful man.

New lads now pressed one for tutelage, seeking greatness on the boards. Their only obligations to one, as valet, to buttle as directed. On occasion this now meant helping one up the stairs at home or in and out of cars. Or to chauffeur one if they owned a vehicle. Should fortune favour, a bit of the other. Well, one could dream, but...

'Few fucks have flowed from all this free Frascati,' one confided to Freddy Parslow, he here at Rylands seeking sanctuary after a blue with his Joan. This happened often. Unhappiness in their union, its cause evident but unsayable.

One's agent Gloria had been busy. Film scripts came. The work of imbeciles, bar two. One to be directed by Britain's best ever, Michael Powell, James Mason to star. The other, *Ned Kelly*. Its director Tony Richardson, behind every second great British film since the late 50s. Here for Thring, perhaps portals back into cinema glory. In this case with Mick Jagger, no less, as Ned.

'Some people will do anything,' I said, 'to get at the best drugs.'

At the dress for our *Hal 4* at the Festival Of Perth, our Prince Hal, Robin Ramsay, sprained his ankle. The show must go on, decreed Sumner. They shot Ramsay so full of Pethidine it spurted from his ears.

'What fucking sadist cooked *this* up?' one roared as they herded us aboard, bussed in full *Hal 4* costume to ponce about at a swimming carnival for the TV news. This at the beck of the festival director, an idiot. So *Perth*...

Swordplay. Hot work in balaclava, rubberized armour, mittens. And 'chain mail,' knitted wool spraypainted silver. At the dress, one clashed on as best one could...

'*Frank?*'

From far away. Margaret, Sumner's latest wife. One was flat on one's back. Above me, spotlights and acoustic fins.

'Get rid of the balaclava and mittens.' Betty Druitt. 'The padding, too.' She looked me over. 'You don't need it to convince as a fat drunk.'

Yes. Thanks to giddy Betty's costume, one had fainted. She slit the legs of one's outfit. Put press studs on 'em, to open up and get cool air in while offstage. And Margaret thrust a jug of iced water at me. *Seven pints a day,* she insisted.

'But I *have* been drinking,' I protested.

'Alcohol doesn't count, Frank.' She produced white pills. 'Salt tablets. Twice a day.' She shifted her deathglare to the cast members and stage managers gathered about. 'And *no booze.*'

'Quite deranged,' one explained out of Margaret's earshot. No doubt posted as spy by Black Jack, she rooted out one's stageside stashes and confiscated them. One informed the SM, the errant Huge Tool, that her orders were countermanded.

'One's stage fright be passing greater malady. And wine its only salve.'

Ah, Sumner's big turns. These TV lifers he cast. Dross on legs from *Homicide, Division 4* or those loathsome kiddies' shows. All on the basis of their profile. Certainly not their merit. To pull telly addicts to our box office. At *Hal 4's* first night after-show jolly-up, one such in our cast appeared in an outfit that should never have been created, let alone sold to an idiot. She shall remain nameless is all the mercy one can extend. Her idea of *haute couture,* this gold and silver taffeta creation. Twisted, puffed silk type of deal.

'Not a triumph on the fuller figure.' One's assessment to cast and crew, as one circled her, eyeing her up and down. The company fell silent.

'Well, from where I'm standing,' I said, 'it looks like a badly opened *can.*'

We knew our play was good when my Falstaff raised dagger to stab dead Hotspur, to claim credit for the slaying. The customers *gasped*. Almost sucked me off the fucking *stage*. One of them screamed, *Oh no! Don't do that!* Huge laughs. Then mighty applause. Yes. We had enfolded them into our place and time. In fact, one thought one had popped Betty's press studs on one's strides. Now that *would* have scored a standing O.

'It's too slippery,' said Whaley. 'For the fights. We'll go arse over.'

Melbourne. Opening night. Sumner's fucking outdoor stage. Life-size replica of the original Globe Theatre. All platforms and stairs. Now rendered a banana-skin minefield, shinywet timber, by scattered showers and drizzle. So nutty Betty, not altogether useless, had us rub our bootsoles in boxes of sand. The rain ceased. Right up to *Hal's* final line, the very last of the play:

Let us not leave till all our own be won.

On *won*, down crashed the night sky, celestial whitewater oceans. The roar of divine acclamation.

One did a piece in the *Age* to spruik *Hal*. And a pic for their snapper, of one's Falstaff swinging sword, *I do love a swinging sword,* I said to journo and shooter, as one's co-star, radiant Annie Pendlebury, also in costume, looked on and smiled.

Our *Hal* wasn't perfect. Moomba fireworks went off in quiet moments, but not during battles. We had to shout like sailors in a storm over the snarl and roar of traffic on St Kilda Road. And one's Falstaff, informed perhaps too well by one's own health challenges. Didn't have to pretend to be out of breath, i'faith, not after mounting that platform atop those staircases. Nor did one need to wear much slap for florid complexion. Yet, unlike Plump Jack, one was now and then lost for words. Helpful colleagues whispered or mouthed Falstaff's lines at me. One couldn't hear the little bird in prompt corner for all the semi-trailers rumbling by. Stage fright surely the cause of one's dries. Ben Ean at hand for solace and succour. But for a'that, we maintained our *sangfroid*. Made magic on the stage of Sumner, a madman.

'Well, he's a man in scarlet satin, white lace blouses and petticoats, with matching millinery. How d'you *think* one should play the fucker?'

A Harry M. Miller turn was *Hadrian VII, for JCWs* at Her Maj. First night imminent. They'd already printed the programmes when one of the cast dropped out and McCallum roped me into it. One was at a loose end, so why not?

The lead, as ever for such productions, a foreign star. Well, the cheapest also-ran or has-been slumped dusty in the shop window, to tell it full and frank. Barry Morse in this case. One recalled Barry's turn in *The Fugitive* TV series, but not, er, *Space 1999*. Did anyone *notice?* Ray Westwell directed. In a style from guess where.

'We've seen that, Frank,' to one's high camp Vatican Secretary Of State.

'The customers haven't.'

'And they never will.'

'Barry's threatened to sue and fly home.'

Ray asked me to ease it down a notch, that Barry The Sook be the only colour on a sepia stage. So for the second of only two rehearsals possible, one drained my man of blood. But come first night, not a chance, baby. Enter roaring.

'*Poor Barry.* Came to a *cock* fight with a *feather,*' when Ray remonstrated. And why stop there? Each night Barry found his props glued or nailed down, as if the japes of phantoms. Opened his prop bible onstage to hardcore porn snaps from *Ribald* magazine pasted on its pages. And one got up good and close that one might dish up facefuls of Thring spitshower. *The stage was mine. Hadrian* ran four weeks at the Maj in Melbourne. Then to Sydney's Tivoli, sellout season from May. One only learned years later the real reason McCallum had asked one on board at such short notice. You see, Barry had sold them so few tickets that the show was unlikely to make it past opening night. So they saved their bacon by dropping *me* in, bumping the poor bugger who'd been hired as one's man Cardinal Ragna. You get no thanks. Be mad to expect it.

Ah, the Sebel Town House. Sydney in a bottle, amid the deranged swirl of Darlinghurst. One's sorties beyond this hotel's tiny but marvellous bar were selective. Toney eaters like Pruniers, or after-parties for other people's shows. Siblings in Thespis, we shared our troubles.

'One ventures out in public less and less,' I said to my companions one post-show evening. 'It's all these hobyahs in passing cars. Bellowing whether one has one's telly and radio license. Funny in its own way. The first five hundred times'.

Yet one's trials nothing compared to some. Far more beset by braying hooligans than I was a gal who had done a TV ad for a chocolate bar. Directed to slurp on it like a, well, pixie, you can conjure it up from there,...

Nureyev was in town. *Swan Lake*. One met with Joan and friends, no Rudy, thank fuck. Supper, at Beppi's. Here one heard about *Hair*, the rock opera. Its Australian premiere here in Sydney imminent.

Line-up curtain fell on *Hadrian*. One made fast out of there and into a Legion cab up William Street to the Metro Theatre on Orwell Street, where *Hair* was on. One just made it as the customers spilled out at show's end, honking and babbling, Sydney's crass and rubicund C-listers. To the press shooter's flashbulbs, one blew kisses. To assure one's piccy in the papers, you see, in the glossy mags, a run on the telly. Helpmann here in a fringed buckskin jacket. He somehow got away with it.

'Podge'! One about-faced. Gra Gra. With a boy in tow, this lad with a huge perm.

'*Well*,' one addressed the lad. 'Cock a poodle *doo!*' Liked what I saw. 'I think I'll call you *Fifi*.'

One of the stars of *Hair*, he be. One followed them to the best after-bash. Well, *they* followed *me*.

'You're a long way from home, baby,' said I. 'You need someone to show you *around.*'

Midst cheesecloth, headbands, flagon wine and pot smoke, one fell upon the swish from among the imported African Americans in the Hair troupe.

'Well, ain't *you* the one,' says he. And then, oh fuck, no. Bernard fucking King. He and *my* boy embraced. Air-kissed. *Mwah mwah. King, TV whore!* You remember Bernard, pixie. Talent shows. Cooking shows. Stealing one's crown as Australia's Idiot Box Queen. *Asking for it.*

'Bernard wets the bed, you know,' I said to our common prospect. 'And worse.'

Got nowhere with the little imp. But went back to *Hair* every night, made the scene backstage. This was where it was *at,* pixie. Fabulous boho parties at Gipps Street, Paddington, where some of the *Hair* cast lived. Expeditions to the Chevron at the Cross. The Pink Pussycat had just burned down, *best not ask,* but the Bourbon and Beefsteak thrived still. So too the Venus Room, Texas Tavern, the Bottoms Up bar at the Rex. A moveable feast.

'Where to tonight, darlings?' was all one had to say.

One night we caught Billy Preston's show at Chequers, in Goulburn Street in the city. Billy had just come from working with the Beatles, he said. *And* was of the tribe. Yes, one tried, but...So, then. Nothing else for it but Rent-A-Sprite. Whisked up to Sebel suite in the sky, from the Gomorrah bubbling below.

'Frank!' David Goddard from the ABC, at a jammed backstage post-*Hair.*

'I'm glad you're here, old man...'

We shot at Appin, south of Sydney. Site of a massacre of Aboriginals, one learned. Well. Where *hasn't* there been one? The show, an ABC police drama series, *Delta.* My man, that week's guest ubervillain, evil anthropologist Dr Spencer, back from Papua New Guinea, with voodoo bibs and bobs for sinister purpose. Horrors ensue but flatfoots triumph. Justice is served, full brutal. Oh, *anything for money.*

Speaking of which, one met with Gloria Payten while up in Sin City. A pile of TV work had she snared for me. Ads and such. I could have kissed her. Or killed her.

'The fire,' said the director to the boy on the crew. 'A bit pissweak. Siphon some juice from my car. No, wait on. Your car.'

In skintight red devil costume, cape, horns, tail, the whole *nine inches*, baby, one stoked a patio barbecue with Little Lucifer fire starters. Yon fetchit, the great taste of Golden Fleece in his gob, had to pour it on the barbie between takes, to make it go whooshka.

'*Cut*. Nah. Bit more,' says Herr Direktor. *Cut*. 'Bit more.' Whoosh*kablooey!* One was blown back, arse over.

'Well,' I said, tang of singed brows and beard in the air. 'How do you want me, Butch? Rare, medium or well fucking *done?*'

I looked up. Pointed with green Ben Ean bottle.

'Oh, and your verandah is on fire.'

'Take it from me,' said my Satan of his product. 'I've had a *million years in the business.*'

Yes. It worked. People watched this muck rather than go for a cuppa or to the brasco. Kept 'em on the couch, channel unchanged. In an ad for this 'leather look' furniture, Ferrier and self in a word association game. One's answer to his every question, the name of this product. The script, as funny as tetanus. At one point one had to pour a glass of champers over an armchair, then click one's fingers for a gal in French maid's outfit to wipe it up. *Yet it gets worse.*

'You're out of your mind. What am I selling? A swingers' club?'

One had been costumed in a cape, mask and tights. To save the world from colds and 'flu. Yet one gave it one's all. I mean, cough sweets resembling urinal deodorizer blocks dunked in wood varnish needed all the help they could get.

But now, a movie shoot. For British legend Michael Powell. A vilified genius, blacklisted in the UK for his 1960 slasher classic *Peeping Tom*, starring one's galpal Max Audley. Now the poor man was reduced to anything, anywhere that would have him. Yes. Even unto Australia. Gloria was casting director on this film of Norman Lindsay's novel *Age Of Consent*. James Mason the male lead, an alleged painter, as well as co-producer. My man, Godfrey, a New York art dealer.

Well, one's scenes were set in New York, but shot in Sydney, in empty streets 'tween twelve bells and blue dawn. Yet featured a dubbed babel of car horns at rush hour, the sonic spooks of a million ethereal Yellow Cabs. Fucking surreal.

My man's gallery no Guggenheim either. In its stead, Ajax Film Centre in Bondi Junction, a set threadbare and people-bereft. The budget ran to pricey locations on the Barrier Reef, but not extras. Every room in this 'celebrated New York gallery' looked as if someone had just squatted and dropped a nugget on the floor.

'We bear the same scars, Thring,' he said over dinner with self and Powell at Diethnes in Pitt Street. James Mason and I had both filmed epics ancient, and survived British theatre. One talked through a two-hander one had with Mason. And another scene with Tommy Hanlon Junior as a crass American tourist. Well. Who better? One had given Tommy so much grief over the years in *TV Week*. Example, *this former ringmaster's performance has one wondering whether the circus ran away from HIM.* No wonder he kept his distance. Mason feigned the Aussie accent of his character with cod South London. You can imagine, pixie. Mason's Strine was even worse, if this be possible, than Dick Van Dyke's Cockney chimney sweep in *Mary* fucking *Poppins.*

Age Of Consent was a hit in Australia. You see, it offered all the skin of a very young Helen Mirren that was there to see. Globewise? Into yon pit of oblivion, begone.

Ned Kelly? Could have been worse. I mean, there'd been talk of Chips Rafferty in the part. The young Ian McKellen screen-tested for it too. Now *he* would have been splendid, but at that time, 1969, he was neither Sir nor star. Mick Jagger, as famous as they make 'em, you see. On the unconsecrated grounds of Old Melbourne Gaol, Ned's headless body whirled in its grave.

It was just after Apollo 11's moonwaltz. Mick and consort Marianne Faithfull landed in Sydney. Straight from a Rolling Stones concert in London's Hyde Park, this just days after the death of their co-founder Brian Jones. Pilloried by the embarrassing Aussie media, *which one's the girl,* all that drivel.

Then Marianne took 150 Tuinal. She'd walked in on Mick servicing a gal of the press at their hotel the Chevron, they say. Rushed to St Vincents in a coma. Mick, ever the showman, baulked not when director Tony Richardson wrenched him from her bedside to a media conference, then to the southern NSW town of Braidwood for location shooting.

It did not go well. Hobyahs and hippies invaded the set. Mick's clumsy Irish accent made the crew snigger during takes. Then he injured himself with a prop pistol.

'Richardson's re-writing as they shoot,' a pal with a small part on the film told me. Sure sign of a script beyond saving. For my man Justice Redmond Barry, who sent Ned to the hangman, we used the Supreme Court, down from where he had swung at the Old Melbourne Gaol. The undemolished remainder of this place a museum now. Ghosts may be heard.

'My dear boy. Where to begin?' I sighed at our table read. 'Your man must win our tussle. But *my* man must *think* he has. Think you can manage that?'

One pictured oneself buggering the lad into grunting submission as one continued.

'And don't snarl like a circus dog. Say it with a smile. Ned would have.'

Here to help. Don't mention it, Mick. Our scene together, at the close of Ned's trial and his sentencing, the best thing in it. But the film was condemned on release. To hope otherwise, delusional.

'It's a cop show, Frank,' said someone from Channel Nine in Sydney. Ordered into existence by Frank Packer. To take on Crawford Productions, you see, they winning ratings for Seven with *Homicide* and *Division Four.*

The Link Men was doomed from the off. Packer rejected the pilot. It never aired. Then the old razorback fetched up, unasked and interfering, at every shoot. For one scene, he took it a step further.

'That's not how you fight!'

He peeled off his jacket to show actor Jack Fegan how. Jack dropped him with ease. Packer ordered him sacked. Son Clyde had to explain that the shoot was already half in the can. To start over, costly. He relented. Just.

For ep five, *See Amsterdam And Die,* one played Bruce Crane. A diamond thief in a swank townhouse. Here, a cage full of birds. Critter accessories *de rigeur* for 1960s criminal masterminds, you see. But we couldn't shut the fuckers up for takes. One recalled *Skippy* and suggested Tolleys and a nose dropper. The show? Canned after twelve episodes. Another triumph.

'Two boyfriends. Talk about having your cock and eating it too,' I said to the cast. My man here Irrugia, a fruity Spanish general, one of two lovers of a lady in Feydeau's *Cat Among The Pigeons.* Old-fashioned sex farce. In desperate need of media coverage for this unloved play, one told the press that one should rightwise be crowned King Of Moomba. This, Melbourne's strange annual carnival. Conceived in the 1950s to dispossess the Labour Day workers' march, wouldn't you know.

'What I need is colour,' I said. 'One's costumes in this play aren't the brightest. So the Moomba King's robes perhaps, to cheer up you wretched miserables. Melbourne has become such a dull city.'

'How long have you enjoyed doing dressups, Frank?'

'Ever since that purple toga in *Ben Hur.'*

'You always wear black. Isn't that dull too?'

'I own twenty-four gaily shaded smoking jackets and dressing downs. Come back to my place, baby. I'll model them for you.'

The things one does.

'But McCallum gives us all a lot of work,' I said to Sumner. You see, Googie and John had put the arm on me to winkle from Black Jack a front stage part for their daughter, Johanna. She'd been with us for a while but Sumner had to date consigned her to walk-ons and ASM drudgery. Black Jack not keen, but gave in. Cast her in Brecht's *Caucasian Chalk Circle.* As Grusha, the lead.

'That the best you've got? Of course not. So where is that?'

Johanna opened her mouth. Sumner's hand went up. 'Who told you that you were ready for this?'

'N-no-one told me, Mr Sumner. I...'

'No, they didn't. I can see why, too.' The fucker just couldn't help himself. One pulled him aside later.

'How could you *do* that to her?'

'To see if she comes back tomorrow, boy.' She did, too. That's my girl.

My man in *CCC* was Adzak, a drunk made a judge as a joke. Rather like Australian governments do. Only featured in the last act. So at rehearsal, they didn't get to me until one's third green bottle for the day. Well, they did say *drunk*. An actor prepares, pixie.

Ah, Brecht. Could be so Teutonic. So grim. So one played it for laughs, one's Azdak a comic bibulous. *The Age* came to rehearsal one day and took a pic of one's head being shaved for the part. One attacked one's own skull with scissors. Mugged like the Three Stooges. Well, it sold seats, did it not?

One's errant young companion Hugh Rule had seen a house in Richmond. But had insufficient for a deposit, he told me. He didn't ask for it, wasn't dropping hints, but one gave him a swag of the necessary anyway. When he didn't get the place, one didn't ask for it back. He was trying to get somewhere as a producer now, so perhaps one's bounty could serve this cause... and so to bed, clutching a black SM's t-shirt he'd left at Rylands. Handy to wipe away one's tears, like so much spilled wine.

In the rat's nest of the MTC's props bay, one found my Azdak a judges' gavel. Banged it over other people's lines. *My scene, baby.* Johanna sought one out at the first night after-party, plaintive eyes imploring critique.

'You were appalling,' I said. She was brilliant for the rest of the run.

CHAPTER TWENTY-NINE

'He feels Hollywood and Broadway to be the instrument of the devil,' said Sumner. Hallowed Shakespearean Sir Tyrone Guthrie had descended on a cloud or something to direct our *All's Well That Ends Well*. My man, Lafew. A jealous, lonely, shopworn queen. Well. One found one's moments with ease.

'Begin', he said. This Guthrie walked among us in the squalid rehearsal space above the Russell's foyer. Saying nought, shaking his man in the moon head. Hmmm. Ominous. When we moved across the road to the YWCA hall, he insisted we put down the book. This after just one week. Several of the cast doomed themselves for the crime of addressing the sour old glodd as 'Tyrone' or 'Mr Guthrie.'

'*Sir* Tyrone,' they were corrected. What a fucking nonce.

All's Well has supers in the cast, extras with no lines. Servants and such. But this Guthrie started taking lines off us if we fluffed them, and giving them to these peripherals. A ruthless fucker. Cold as charity. His response to any problem, a Geilgudesque 'rise above it.' A voice of rust and dust, as if sourced from a crypt.

Nose aloft, like an indignant camel.

'I don't like the way you look, boy. Not right for this play. Just won't do.'

Poor Helmut. This grey iniquity Guthrie exacted from the boy not one but several pounds of flesh. Forced him to get this ridiculous haircut. Shaved sides and back. It rendered him the countenance of a hillbilly simpleton.

'You're not a very good actor, are you, boy?'

This to Helmut, the cast entire as witness. To invoke the Bard of Avon, this Guthrie was a parcel of dropsies. And perhaps even worse, one of these *Shakespeare didn't write Shakespeare* mouldies.

'But what if it emerges, as well it might, evidence, quite feasibly to one day be unearthed, not beyond the realms of the possible, which deems that, and one is but one of many, is one not, who contends thus, that Shakespeare, he of Stratford, is not in fact the author of the works which, by dubious popular consensus, he has been awarded title?'

What bilge. Of course, one nodded assent, like all of his downtrodden herd here, lest one lose the few lines one still had.

Others had it worse. I mean, she was so *sweet,* our Diedre Rubinstein. Oblivious to how annoying these were, her breathless responses to everything anyone said.

'I put out the bins last night.'

'Oh! Did you?'

'I've brought some Vita Weets for lunch.'

'Oh really? Have you? Gosh!'

Guthrie didn't much care for it either. At the dress, Dieidre was in a crinoline. You know, those hooped petticoat thingies.

'When you reach the bottom of those stairs, drop to your knees and slide across the floor, do,' said Guthrie. Deidre, for all of her ditzy ways, a trouper. Not one to baulk at a directive. Did as bid. Slid across a sheet of Masonite painted to fake it as marble. Squeaked to a halt at one metre.

'No,' he said. 'More slide.' She obliged. 'No. That won't do.' Many more tries.

'But this dress, darling,' she said. 'It slows me down.'

But the old bastard was immutable. So this time, she clumped down the stairs, a runup like a fast bowler. Dropped, slid across the sheet. All the way across it, and off the edge of the stage. Into the orchestra pit. *Crashtinklethump.*

I peered down, she sprawled in jumble of music stands. One couldn't resist.

'Rise above it.'

'I've always admired Jesus,' I said. Patricia Kennedy and her Catholic fetish were also in *All's Well*, you see.

'Our *Lord*, if you don't *mind*,' she huffed. The fixated devout *hate* we mocking apostates *saying the bless'd name*. Another castee, a self-described recovering Catholic, had told me this.

'Yes, of course,' I said. 'Funny, you know. That he never *married*.'

Some purse their lips. Patricia, her whole face. The most amazing sight. Perhaps what followed, divine retribution. One night, as she and I went on, one groped around within one's skull for one's line. Nothing. So one made it look as if the first line was hers. Gestured at her, *come on, out with it*. She fetched me a glare. So I sighed. Turned to the footlights, fists on hips.

'Look, I'm sorry, everyone,' I said, 'but this,' pointing at her, '*this* has been a complete waste of *time!*' Flounced off.

It did not go unnoticed. Guthrie was talking of replacing me, warned Sumner. So one had the SM write out the first line of one's scenes and tape them up in the wings. Propped one's Ben Ean there too. To quell one's stage fright. The cause, without question, of one's lapse.

From the Prinny run, to Canberra. Three shows. That execrable theatre.

'Why that awful place?' I once asked Sumner. His response, that the MTC had the arse out of its tights and were able to rent this brutalist pile cheap, precisely because it wasn't very good.

'One could say,' he added, 'not unlike the reason *you* lot are paid as you are.'

What a fucking charmer. Helmut said it best.

'Those white seats. It's like playing to a graveyard.' Indeed. In the dark, these, as if rows of tombstones, were all one could see. 'A complete dog, this fucking playbox.'

'It's a shambles, Podge.'

Ferrier on the blower, calling one's hotel suite. 'I'm here to host the AFI Awards. You free Friday afternoon? Helpmann's in town, too, so...'

January 1971. We'd been herded onto a TAA jet. *All's Well* at the Octagon for the Festival Of Perth.

Well, *noblesse oblige,* pixie. But at the TV studio, the producer was in a catfight with the floor manager, a queen of bones squealing that nothing Ferrier had asked for was available. One left them to it.

Ah. In the Green Room, champagne. Not from flutes, but those hideous glasses fit only for that singular horror that is prawn cocktails. So Perth. Or Brisbane. Or Sydney. Or...

'Will Sir be dining today?' One held out some Mandies to Helpmann.

'Oh, fuck off, Podge. Last time I woke up with a gobful of sailor's cock.'

'Oh, Bobby. Anything for a free feed. You haven't changed.'

'Look who'd talking. You old bitch.'

'Not as old as *you,* lover.'

We went *campus maximus* at the AFIs. Scared the tripes out of the squares.

'We're all going to *die* here,' I said.

Sumner had found a new home for the MTC. A warehouse in Farrars Street, South Melbourne. Full of rats. Leaked when it rained. Here we shaped Brecht's *Galileo.* Self in the title part. A big one. One was grateful for Sumner's restored faith. But *so many lines.* Interminable speeches to open each scene.

'The customers will *expire* in their *seats.* How about we project these fucking litanies onto a screen? With old black and white science fiction movies. You know, Buck Rogers, that sort of thing, as background?'

Of course he went for it. A good job, too, for it cut one's lines in half. So thus spake one's Galileo to backdrop of flickering black and white, Flash Gordon's *Purple Death From Outer Space.* Above us hung a 3D model of the Ptolemaic universe. Earth at its centre, like one of the old gods.

This new MTC shedcave was on the corner of two main roads. Traffic roar relentless. When it rained, puddles on the floor. Birds nested in the crossbeams. Droppings fell on us in kilos. Came here now, Roland

Rocciccioli, stage manager for Harry M. Miller, from *Hadrian VII*. Poached by Sumner as our new SM.

'Welcome aboard ye sinking ship, matey!' I shouted. It was raining outside.

And inside.

For *Galileo's* carnival scene, Sumner had people dance, twirling lit sparklers. At the dress, yes, guess who, poor Deidre set her costume on fire. *Aaarrrgghhh!*

'Quick!' I shouted. 'Roll her in the puddles!'

No burns to her person, praise be. What else could one say?

'I *love* Deidre when she *sizzles.*'

Oh. And in the middle of all this, Lola passed away. One's vivacious half sister who'd somehow evaded the family black dog. For a time there, one was closer to her than to FT or Olive. But we'd fallen out of touch. One repented at leisure, desolation cloaked in regret. *I now the last of us.*

There I sat, pixie. In a fucking bathtub. Shirtless. As autumn shivered into winter, quivering like pink jelly.

'This isn't fucking working. It needs something.'

'Such as, Frank?' Sumner. Not even looking up from his script.

'Oh, I don't *know*. Some tassels on my tits so that I can swing them around, perhaps. *Why a fucking bathtub?*'

'To establish change of scene without having to build a set,' said Roland.

'Yes. All the best bankrupt theatre companies do it.' Sumner.

'Oh, for fuck's sake!' I said. Pointed at Roland. 'Guards! Seize him! Will this never *end?*'

'Yes, it will. Eventually,' he said. Unmoved. Now, twenty winters on, a litany of mortal pangs I be. The Reaper hovers at the gate. One would sit in yon tub forever if it meant that...

Roland prompted me. I said nothing. Prompted me again. I stayed mute. Then he gave me the full line. Yes. One had *dried*. But no-one must know. I raised my head.

'*I know.*' Pause for effect. 'I'm *acting.*'

I think I fooled them. The first few times.

Kathryn Denniss, MTC wig wrangler, made me a red hairpiece, beard, brows. I didn't look like *me* anymore. *Inhabited* one's Galileo. Like Max, one's Cockney butcher, or Ahab in *Moby*. Four sold-out weeks. Ten curtains at line-up. *Was FT watching?*

'I have Mr Sam Bronston here for Mr Frank Thring.'

'Frank! Who's your daddy, boychik? Sam, that's who!'

'Oh. Sam. This is unexpec...'

'Making a new picture, baby. With Charlie.' He meant Bronson. 'And Sophia. About Columbus.' One's bedside clock said three AM. 'And I need a Torquemada.'

'Scenic, baby.'

One's news scored a big run in the papers, wireless, telly. The script came airmail, from the gelid hand of Phil Yordan, all the *vita* of a Paleolithic hunter-gatherer exhumed from a glacier. No matter. He'd no doubt shanghai scribeslaves far more able than he to slap it into life.

'We're still in talks with Charlie Bronson's people.'

One should have fled Madrid that instant. But didn't. Nor did Rip Torn, Herbie Lom, Genevieve Page nor Hurd Hatfield. Hurdy not so lovely now. More sideshow skull on a stick. Rip stopped drinking long enough to speak.

'Fuck *Bronson. I'll* play Columbus.' Bared his teeth at the Wild Turkey's erubescent throatburn.

'No, Rip. You are King Ferdinand. That's that,' said Sam. He swerved from Rip and scanned us all, *oh, by the way...*

'Oh, and Miss Loren sends her regrets. But we have our director.'

Nick Ray had to be carried down the jetstair. An eyepatch these days. *One thought it prudent not to ask.* His hair a Harpo Marx frizzmop, in his fist a doctor's bag of drugs.

'Nick,' said Rip, indicating me, 'would this mere Dominican friar have the nerve to say what he just said to *I, King Ferdinand?*'

The table reads were blood sport.

'Torquemada, cut that line,' said Nick. Swigging wine from the bottle, he hoisted it like Lady Liberty's torch.

'Great for Vitamin C, people.' Fumbling in his bag, he dropped the thing. Syringes, ampoules, bottles of pills bounced and rolled. He waved his bottle at it.

'You boys had breakfast?'

'Charlie Bronson says no,' said Sam, a week into table reads. 'But we have a great actor for the part.'

Stephen Boyd was no longer the peach of yore. He lived in Spain now, pursuant to his only work these days, spaghetti westerns. Worse, he'd embraced Scientology. A zealot. Spared no-one his delusions.

'Frank. You gotta read this.' He pressed upon me a slim volume. *Dianetics.* Poor man. His fall, long and slow. Dropped dead five years later. On a golf course.

One looked out the plane's window as we banked. The last time one would see Spain. Left a note for Bronston, with thanks and regrets. *Isabella* was never made.

'Best buried. Dead or alive.'

One said the only thing one could about the lost film. The MTC still no less broke than before, so we did a return run of *Galileo* in Melbourne. Then, that fucking Canberra Theatre.

'Those white seats. Like rows of teeth,' I said to Roland, 'waiting to tear you apart.'

And that stench. When the pinchbeck Canberra glitterati took their seats, one's eyes would water and sting from the naphthalene. You know, mothballs. From the dowagers' furs, in storage since the last fucking opening night. Come to think of it, those biddies looked like they were packed away in camphor between first nights themselves. You might well ask why we bothered with the nation's capital at all, pixie. But you see, these runs were our *grazie mille* for occasional bones tossed from the Federal Government's table. These, possibly human.

CHAPTER THIRTY

'The web of our life is of a mingled yarn, good and ill together,' one recalls from *All's Well* as one reads the papers to Edith, she fiddle-faddling about as housekeepers do. Seems Czechoslovakia is to become the twin nationettes of the Czech Republic and Slovakia. A transition attained without bloodshed.

'Must be a first in those parts,' she says. The Velvet Revolution, they're calling it.

'Oh, and Bill Wyman is leaving the Rolling Stones,' one notes. 'One presumes, to spend more time with his bandmates' granddaughters.'

And there's more Royal marriage chaos. *Squidgygate* the label the press have tagged these secretly taped phone conversations. 'Squidgy' being the nickname bestowed on Princess Diana by one of her lovers.

'Sounds like a noise made *on the job*,' one says to Edith. The Royals have rallied round the jug-eared Prince Regent.

'Well, this won't do at all,' one says. 'I mean, for some good telly, Her Maj might at least have Diana and swains beheaded live via satellite. With chainsaws, for a modern touch.'

As for Charles, he wishes he were a tampon, these tapes betray. To full enjoy the enfolding ambrosials of paramour Camilla.

'Round the *twist*, the lot of 'em.'

'Compared to whom, Frank?' This Edith. So like her daughter. My Joanie. My lost Flowergirl.

One's foot throbs. One's surviving toes sting. But one must disregard this. For this day, a job. Only a voice-over, but *Hercules Returns* sounds like a lark. Some Melbourne comedians are shooting a feature film, you see. Its absurd premise, that a cinema owner must do live dubbing of a script onto an Italian sword 'n' sandal epic which has arrived for its screening without a soundtrack. My man, Zeus, no less. See, the young'uns remember me...

*

'Alcoholic, corrupt, closet queen, keen on the noose and the lash,' said Roland of my man Judge-Advocate Atkins.

'Well, then,' I said. 'Not much of a stretch.'

In the early 1970s, we took on Ray Lawler's new play, *The Man Who Shot The Albatross*. Of William Bligh, and his brief tenure as Governor of New South Wales. One was not Sumner's pick for the Bligh part. The fucker's treachery a stalactite snapped off and deployed as knife of ice in the back. One's resentment was leavened a skerrick when one beheld Bligh's blizzard of lines. And his choice for the role, inspired, for all his cuntery.

'Don't know how you can keep that paint stripper down, Thring,' he said, eyeing one's Ben Ean. Leo McKern drank all day. Two-litre flagons of Kaiser Stuhl bold reds. One's smaller part had bile enough to drown all others about me. One now set about making it so. Other distractions pleasant here, too. *Per esempio,* young Gary Day, a thesplet new among us. Wore leather pants to rehearsals. One didn't know where to look. Nor did Mr Closet.

'You haven't had a single line yet, Butch,' one said to this Gary, one's tone gossamer, in overture.

'Well, Mr Thring, I have none. I'm a super. Soldiers and drunkards various and a Hawaiian native.'

'Don't mind Frank,' says Mr Closet.' Got up on the wrong side of his park bench this morning.' *Oh, ho ho.* One disregarded this witless desperate. Waved one's hip flask of brandy at Gary.

'Ignore him. Married.' Fixed *his* cheese. 'Something with your Bushell's?'

'Where do you live, boy?'

Waiting for one's Arrow taxi, one saw Gary making off down the street.

'Toorak, Mr Thring.' *Glorious happenstance!*

I unchained the gates of Rylands, garlanded with spikes and barbed wire now after an assault by a youth one had in careless inebriation invited home. Plump Edith was headed for the huge laundry and ironing room behind the kitchen.

'Stealing the silver again, eh?'

'No, Frank, that was you,' she said.

'Senile,' I said to Gary, as one's cats ran to greet me. 'Oooh, Furry Pussy! Tai-Tai!' I scooped them up. Dark now, so one had Gary open the drapes as one served brandy and dry. An agreeable evening. Regaled the lad with chronicles of Oliviers, Tony Curtis, Kirk Douglas, Chuck, Jagger. Later, patted his thigh. No response. *Ah, well...*

As we worked through the Bligh play, dull abdominal ache, nausea, tiredness came to haunt one's temporal frame. Inconsequential at first. Then worsenings. One ignored them. *Then they did smite me.* Pain acute. Stomach and back. Blood in the whatsit. One's game was tumbled when one fainted at the dress.

'Just until you're back on your feet, Frank.'

Sumner cast James Condon, a Sydney thesp, in my part. He and Roland refused, at one's bedside at the Epworth Hospital, one's pleas for smuggled refreshment. Yes. Hard gods.

'Behold, for he is *risen*,' one announced to the dressing room. Took 'em a moment to jerry who the fuck I was. Now two stone lighter in the old money, you see. One made the Adelaide Festival run of *Albatross* there in February. One had missed Melbourne, Sydney, Canberra, Brisbane.

'Have a butcher's at this, Thring.'

One dined with McKern in Adelaide, at one of its newer and more pretentious *trattorie*. You'll recall, pixie, that he had a glass eye. So anyway, mid-meal, the mad bastard took it out. Pushed it into his *ragu alla Bolognese,* well, spag bol, then clicked thumb and finger at the pony-tailed waiter.

'What's the meaning of this?' Pointed at his plate. The *garcon* blanched at the eye glaring up at him. One played along with one's reactions. Wasn't until the manager came, the whole place watching, that McKern plucked it from the plate, sucked it clean and crammed it back into its socket. Looked round the room. And winked.

The MTC's big play for 1972, *Danton's Death,* in April. Huge cast. A tale of the French Revolution. One's part, but a spit and a cough. Had Sumner written me off? Mine just one of many walk-ons. All of these flaky fuckers out to prevail with one line of glory. *So. Sabotage it must be.* Gary Day had one such partlet. Fortune smiled with yellow fangs. For his wig was a brunette helmet.

'You can't go on in *that,*' I said, just as he went on. 'You look like Prince *Valiant* fucked Mary *Hardy.*'

It worked all too well. Unmanned him. A customer yelled '*Your acting is dreadful!*'

My man Simon, pronounced *Seemon,* a 'tough citizen,' had to stomp around under the set, a giant clockwork wheel. Symbolising, well, fuck knows. *Oh, for a bucket of fuck it.*

'Frank? McCallum here.'

Chekhov's *Cherry Orchard* and Wilde's *An Ideal Husband* was the brief. A run at that old hussy the Comedy in Melbourne, then a three-city tour. Googie starred. Sumner to direct *Cherry.* The kinder, gentler Ogilvie, *Husband.* One prefers Wilde, and said so to Roland, who, given his unpronounceable Italian surname, one had taken to calling Vera Vermicelli.

'One likes one's toffs in the strangling hands of Wilde, Vera. Not Chekhov's tubercular shoulder for the fuckers to cry on.'

But duty called. And Googie as Madam Ravensky, with self as her brother George, would pull more crowds than a road smash.

The man was insufferable. Black Jack, all morning at rehearsal. *I don't think so, Frank.* Then at the break, one had a brainwave, remedy to the fucker's truculence. Re-energised, one swept into the tea room to tell him. Oh. Not here.

'Where's the sadistic shit *got* to?' I bellowed. Then, astern, at one's shoulder;

'Looking for me, Frank?'

To the ABC rolled plump Thring, to plug *Cherry*, with Googie, on one of those arts programs no fucker watches. Another guest here took me aside. Phillip Adams. These days an ad man, columnist, film producer, radio broadcaster. Quite the genius. By his own acclamation, no less.

'A thought, Frank. How would you feel about coming out? I've asked Kennedy. A few others. Get the pink vote out for Labor. So...'

'Are you *mad?* Frank Packer would sack the lot of us. Ban our ads too. Fitzroy Gardens would fill up with filthy old queens. Full of Yalumba Four Crown Port, abusing and flashing passers-by.'

The *cheek* of the fucker. *And* he stole one's all-black dress code. One wonders where he'd be had he made this proposal to any of the confirmed bachelors of *TV Ringside* or *World Championship Wrestling*.

The opening night of *Cherry* was going too, too well. Something had to go south. Always does. Then *crash!* Wendy Hughes, as Anya, leaned on a pillar not tacked on to anything. Went arse over. One led the applause from the stage. *Brava Signora!*

Googie and self took our exit each night to massive applause. We were as gods.

'That is, if you fancy worship by cloudgrey frumps,' I grumbled to Roland.

'The customer is always right, Frank,' he said.

'Yes,' I said. 'They like it soft and mushy. Still warm from pre-mastication.'

One had but one, yes, one scene in *Husband*. A dreadful impost. Hours of hanging about. But Googie had asked, you see. *Need you there to thicken up the crowds, darling.* To refuse, just not on. My man, the Earl Of Caversham. Some nights one slipped out to nearby parties, in full costume, weary of waiting backstage for one's cue. Gave poor Googie the dry runs. But one was always back in time to strut and fret one's five seconds upon the stage.

'I shall wear it thus, till you see reason.'

At the dress for *Husband,* one looked like Wolfman fucking Jack. So one stuck one's moustache on over one's eyebrows, the brows under one's nose. Pulled the wig down low over one's forehead. Hideous. Humpty Dumpty bitten by a werewolf. The hairpieces did not survive the day. I somehow did.

'Dame Sybil's 90th, Frank.' Reeny calling. 'Thought you might like to go with me.'

Well, why not? The timing apposite, one somewhat less than encumbered with work. And Dennis Olsen and Teddy Hodgeman, Adelaide boys, were en route to Melbourne for *The Tavern* at Russell Street. Thesps from interstate rarely had the necessary for hotels. Had to crash with friends.

'You can *camp* at Rylands,' one told Olsen. One's custom for some time now. Open house to travelling players, when one was out of town. Many took up the offer. John Jarratt, gorgeous Harold Hopkins, John Waters, Bryan Brown, Mel Gibson. One's pantry well-stocked. Grog, enough to fell swarms of Vikings. Yes, a glimmer of an ulterior motive. Flimsy hope that one of them might, you know, but...

'Wallaby! So good to see you!'

Larry, dear Larry. At the Haymarket. With Richardson, Geilgud, Edith Evans, Ustinov. Pals from Stratford. Max Audley, Butch Quayle. JB Priestley did the testimonial. Birthday gal Syb was frail. Made only a brief appearance.

One stayed on in London. Looked up some old co-stars. Terry Longdon from *Ben Hur* was out of work. *Resting,* as the euphemism has it. At lunch, Wiltons in Jermyn Street, our post-prandial ports proposed a reunion of the *Ben Hur* support cast.

The dinner at Rules in Maiden Lane, well, ...Taffy Griffith was by now sick from the booze. Very little work of late. Naught but a cameo, a grotesque in a Vincent Price film, *Dr Phibes Rises Again*. Hawkins no longer possessed a voice. Throat cancer from all those Rothmans. He had a part in a Price film too, *Theatre Of Blood*. Others dubbed his lines. One asked about anything going. With Vincent Price.

A train up from London to see Hugh Rule, now with Birmingham Rep. He'd found an ancient poster there of Olivier's stage debut, which he gave me. One put it in a Royal Mail tube to Sir Laurence, asking him to sign it. Came back ascribed, *Dear Frank, with love, Larry*. One hung it in one's fur-throned brasco.

Hugh was a producer now. Running here the Australian Jack Hibberd's first and worst play, *White With Wire Wheels*. It neither enlightened nor amused, said I loud and clear at the first night party. The crits next day concurred. One's work here was done.

'Huge Tool,' I said, 'these provincials don't deserve you.'

One invited him back to London. We saw *Twelfth Night* at the Old Vic. Dreadful, save for Sir Toby Belch, played by Michael Blakemore from our 1957 *Titus*. One's wine at supper told him that the MTC ran rings around this mob. All this talk made Hugh homesick. Declared he wanted to work for us again. He didn't. Our loss.

'I had to talk them out of pressing charges, these two ballerinas he kicked in the arse at rehearsals.'

Dinner with my Joan and Hugh at the Criterion in Piccadilly. More tales of Nureyev. He'd sacked Joan many times, she revealed. He sent gifts later, but never apologised. A global star now thanks to her. She'd done alright out of it, too. Indeed, now more successful than I. One felt no envy. If anything, joy. One had, for once, done something good for someone in this life.

On one's last day in England, melancholy at the prospect, one went out and bought zebra skin rugs. Fresh off the boat from Africa, they lied. For one's reception room. A Hemingway feature, should a body meet a body and...

One of my hand-blown Venetian wine glasses was gone. Edith folded under questioning. Olsen and Hodgeman had invited Chilvers over.

Olsen had smashed the glass during a drunken game of bridge on one's gilt Louis XV table. Edith found a spare somewhere. But then I came upon a curved shard of blue crystal on the rug near one's cabinet full of such pieces. Poor Margaret. Now frail, near blind, had dropped a crystal ball while polishing it. Olive had started this collection. One had continued to add to it over the years. For some reason, I wept.

December '72. The behemoth Whitlam became Prime Minister. We took our *Cherry* and *Husband* to Perth. The aircon at the theatre failed. Here we be, in heavy wigs, dressed for Russian winter. In a city baked by solar fire. Peopled by grogans.

'Sorry, folks. Dress code.'

We, this Perth Festival's stars, made for the theatre bar after *Cherry* one night. La Goog in blouse and slacks.

'A dress is required, madam.'

'Well, this *is* a fucking *dress*,' I said, flapping one's black kaftan at him.

'Come on, Googie.' I gestured at the oaf, *clear a path*.

'Oh, fuck it, Frank.' More security was headed our way. 'Let's go.' She could see it ending badly for me.

We shared glugs from one's bottle of Martell from Black Bag on a bench outside the theatre, under Indian Ocean stars. Rather like a pair of derros, one mused.

'I suppose one should start getting used to this.'

On to Brizzie, Canberra. In Sydney, HG Kippax from the *Herald* was enraptured by our turn. I, less so.

In March, *Jesus Christ Superstar* ended its Sydney run and made for the Palais in St Kilda, built by FT in 1927. One had tickets to the prem. But then...this theatre, once mine...one blinked away tears. Called Chilvers. Sent over the tickets in a taxi. And for I, one's nocturnal factotum, Nembutal. To make this, the new world, go away.

'From the Berliner Ensemble. Knew Brecht personally, boy.'

For Brecht's *Mother Courage,* at the Princess, our director lured here by Black Jack from East Berlin, one imagines, with promise of edible food. Joachim Tenschert, the greatest Brechtian alive. Fresh from directing Anthony Hopkins in *Coriolanus* for the Old Vic. He was trouble from the off.

'This *theatre. No.* Too *big.* Is not *right* for Brecht.'

'No other available,' Sumner lied. 'And Brecht deserves a larger audience; to spread his message, Herr Tenschert.'

A smooth talking fucker when needed, was Black Jack. We needed to go big on this one, to *make some fucking money* for a change. And to that end, some canny casting. Black Jack's pick for the title part, Gloria Dawn, was a Tivoli all-rounder, lifer showie and revue singer loved all over the land.

'I don't work blue or nude, John,' her only caveat. He flew up to Sydney with Tenschert, that the latter might meet her and give his imprimatur. Lobbed at her flat just as she did, she with a carful of groceries. She whistled with her fingers.

'Oi! Give us a hand, boys! Thirsty?'

She tossed cans of Toohey's New at them. Teetotaler Sumner caught them both. Cracked Tenschert's open for him. Spurted beer suds over him. Black Jack turned to bluestone, but Gloria just cackled. Tenschert wiped at himself. He asked her how she might play the part, a woman profiteering from war, at the price of her children's deaths. Yet a victim, as much as them, prey to vile demons of survival instinct.

'Well, she talks a lot, Mr Tennison,' said Gloria. 'But I've never dropped a line or missed a cue yet. She'll be apples.' And winked. 'Eh?'

Tenschert's brown leather jacket creaked. His face a mantle of misery, this man from the Stasi brutocracy of East Germany.

'No no *no*, zis vill not *do*. You.'

To a rookie here, Jenny Hagan, at rehearsals. 'Like zis.' He demonstrated. 'Your son,' *two steps forward*, 'Sviss Cheese,' *two steps forward*, 'is dead.'

Did the same to me. Well, tried to.

'Oh, well, I don't think so, Joachim,' came one's response, tart and immovable.

He shrugged.

'Perhaps another actor is bedder for zis part,' he said to Roland. 'Zat is how it vass done in Berlin. For fordy *years*!'

'Oh, very well,' I sighed. We were creatures of Sumner. We did as bid.

Gloria's songs for *Courage* were showstoppers. She shimmied, winked, fell to her knees. Whistled solo breaks, to Tenschert's horror, but grudging capitulation. Tiny, plump Gloria wore kaftans to rehearsals, so one followed suit.

'Nothing underneath but Fidji eau de cologne, *baby*,' I said. 'What about *you?*'

She was aghast. Devout Catholic, you see. Practically a daily communicant, young Jenny Hagan told me. Indeed. Gloria also asked one to stop the swearies, so much a part of one's lexicon. So instead, one wore an iron pyrites medallion one had made by Dunklings the jeweller. The word *FUCK* engraved on it. Every day.

And then there was Jenny Claire. Holding up MTC canteen queues with her interrogations of the staff. One day, no fresh milk, only the longlife gear.

'Well, dear,' was all one could say after enduring her gibbering at the poor caterers. 'You've got a pair of tits. Why don't you fucking *use* them?'

One likes to be noticed, so one's man in *Courage,* The Chaplain, chopped real wood onstage. Noise, chips flying. One night the axehead flew off the handle in mid-air- and embedded itself in the stage! *Well,* I bawled at Roland, *you're the fucking SM. You should've checked the bloody thing.*

'Piss off!' he said. Arm out, pointing. 'On your way!' Not a fellow to take a backward step.

Unaccustomed to that kind of lip from an SM, one pondered springing a surprise that night. But alas, Myers does not stock chainsaws. The axe came back, the head taped and glued solid onto the handle- and the edge blunted by hammer blows. *Bastards.* A major disadvantage up against

308

Freddy Parslow. The louder one's woodsplitting, you see, the more noisome his Cook's vegetable chopping had grown. He went at it even louder now. It had to happen. The very next night, he nearly lopped his finger off mid-scene. A gushing wound. Fucking scene stealer.

They had to drop the curtain. One of the ASMs, a first aider, jumped in. At interval, a medico sutured it and pumped in painkillers. Bold Freddy boxed on. Playing Freddy Parslow as only he could.

'More thought could have gone into that title,' one said to Roland of *Batman's Beach Head.* One had a small part in this turn by a local, Alex Buzo. As ever, one had been cast by Sumner only to get someone, anyone, to come see it. In vain.

The MTC, running three theatres now, shoehorned one into a play at St Martins, the former Little. The job, *The Play's The Thing.* The cast, older males. Rough types. One feared for sole female castee Jenny Hagan's safety.

'You stay away from those men,' I told her. 'They're all ratbags.'

When we toured *Play,* one bade her travel with me, my car and driver. She had her own dressing room, so one invited oneself to share it.

'But, er, Mr Thring...'

'Animals they be, my dear. I can do no other.'

On the road, we had to sing for our slops at Rotary and Lions clubs. You know, give talks, try to pull a few fudds to the shows. One fed the twilight zoners yarns of *Ben Hur, The Vikings, El Cid.* Selected ones, lest one trigger coronaries.

One rarely left one's Travelodge before or after shows, unless invited. Jenny most kind in this regard. She had me to the world's smallest hotel pools for drinks out in the mulga whenever her hubby joined us with their little son. Deep in conversation one afternoon, one left Black Bag unwatched.

'What's this, Uncle Thing?' one heard tiny Gus asking. I swerved. He held up one's new Bowie knife. Still ensheathed, thank fuck.

'Oh,' I said, gently disarming him. 'That's my knife.' Winked. 'Just in case.'

One tried to be more careful with one's dilly bag after that. And its many successors.

'Knickers, knackers and the old piss flappers,' went an old Kings Cross stripperama spruik. Said it all about Sydney. One knew what was coming when local film producer Al Finney called. There are worse Aussie flicks than *Alvin Rides Again*, sequel to *Alvin Purple*. It wouldn't even run a place in that Melbourne Cup field. One knows this to be true, for one is in most of those too.

'Oh, anything for money, baby.' It was out of me before he finished his pitch.

And one couldn't refuse John Cornell, AKA Strop, producer of Paul Hogan's TV show of the time. For a sketch, one's Little Lucifer's devil went toe to toe with Hoges in shorts and Delvene Delaney in somewhat less. That one earn, to have wine, that one earn, to have wine, that one...

Ah, yes. 1974. Shifty 'Tricky Dick' Nixon fell on his sword.

'Fifty times by the look of him,' I said to Freddy P as we watched this doomed US President, ensnared by Watergate, resign on telly, over Tanqueray and tonics. Oh, yes. And Sinatra toured Australia. What a catfight *that* was. Stranded here by trade unions after he called journalists 'bums and hookers' onstage at Festival Hall. Concerts cancelled. His plane unfuelled. Room service cut off. He'd lobbed here crabby. His comeback world tour tanking, you see. Now, worldwide news, this fracas. Shoved Watergate off the front pages. Result, the tour sold out all over the globe and his new flop album started to sell. The wily fucker played us all. What a showman.

And so to *Alvin Rides Again*. My man, Fingers. A gentleman crook in a gold lame skivvy. A gangster queen. Target audience, teenage boys, fists to the pump at the female nudes. For every scene he was in, Fingers was directed to take Ross Bova, one's diminutive co-star, pick him up and throw him around. I refused.

'It's okay, Frank,' he said. 'I'm used to it. From the dwarf-tossing.'

'The *what?*'

'At the pubs. Winner's the one who can chuck me furthest.'

He saw my face. 'You'd do it if you were me.' He was right, of course.

Annabels, all stained glass, red felt walls, dark wood bar. The set this day, in Alfred Place, off Collins Street. As the Naval And Military Club in the 1940s, Olive had hosted wingdings here. Now, a night club. Second home to my hometown's homos. Brian Cadd's Bootleg Family Band onstage. My man Fingers facing off Gay Gay Blundell as Alvin, he forced to impersonate gangster Balls McGee... oh, never mind. The script should have been drowned in a bucket of muck. Finno was here too, as a magician, all turban and robes.

'Same as you, Frank,' he said before one uttered a word. 'Need the fucking money.'

We shot other scenes at Noah's Hotel and the Motel Palm Lake on Queens Road. Fingers dies early. Rather like the film itself.

CHAPTER THIRTY-ONE

I think it was last year. One purchased a Betamax video machine on the advice of others. Far surpassed the other mob, VHS, it was averred. But one's Beta has now whirred its last. Cannot be repaired nor replaced. They laughed at the RetraVision store when one asked. And there's fuckall on Beta at Video Ezy, that maze of a thousand disappointments. So one has bought a VHS machine, under protest. *No choice, mate,* says a smirking hobyah at the store.

Then there's my new telly. Several remote control devices. Each studded with buttons, alien hieroglyphics. I can see them now, pixie. At the Alfred's casualty. Rueful, ashamed. *I sat on it.*

*

Congreve's *The Double Dealer* was not the MTC's finest hour. My man, a small part, *yet another,* Lord Touchwood. Met a delightful boy in the cast here, Stephen Oldfield. To Rylands we went, for goblets of cheer, card games, one's fab fables of the stars. Alas, none of *the other* did it yield. Gloria Payten called. Two jobs in Sydney.

'Trenchard-Smith here.'

'*Oh.* Brian,' I said. At ATV0, he'd been the news editor. My man 'Willard' had just two scenes in Brian's debut screenplay *The Man From Hong Kong,* so one must make the most of 'em. One's co-stars the erstwhile one-film James Bond, George Lazenby, and a fellow Brian called the next Bruce Lee, one Jimmy Wang Yu. Kung Fu was now a huge, global fad. This would make a motza, Brian believed. And be just the first film of many such.

'Frank, if Jimmy asks you for anything, just refuse, okay?' said Brian as we drove to Pruniers' in Woollahra to meet the cast for lunch.

'You have my word, Butch. Er, what *kind* of anything?'

'Where I can buy gun?'

A hard-faced Chinese chap with Beatle coiffure picked up his steak knife. Pointed it at me.

'I fight a'yone, no p'oblem. Hong Kong, I know many of ga'ster.'

'Don't do that, you hear? Put it *down.*'

'One time I kill man.' Pointed the thing at me again.

'I *told* you not to *do* that.'

Nothing else for it. I grabbed his wrist. Twisted hard. He dropped the knife, gasped. The others were shocked. Well, one may be a fairy, pixie, but one is a big one.

Jimmy played a Hong Kong cop in Sydney, chasing Lazenby's man, Aussie crime lord Wilton. My man Willard gatekeeps at Wilton's lair in Sydney. The set, a conference room at the Esso Building in Kent Street. Jimmy's offsider, Roger Ward, a local TV and film fixture, played an Aussie cop. Hugh Keays-Byrne, you know the one, Toecutter from the first *Mad Max,* as *his* offsider. Brian, new to feature films, gave odd directions to say the least.

'Frank, when Roger and Jimmy come through the door, don't do anything. Wait until Roger starts acting.'

'My dear boy. If we have to wait until *Roger* starts *acting,* we could be here for*ever.*'

Put him off his game, that one steal the scene. Some producer with a job going might see this flick, you see. One of late more needy than in the crowded days of fame, now surely passed.

Same set, next day. Lazenby berates my man. One sat immobile. Expressionless. Never shifted one's gaze from him. An Olivier tip. The scene was mine before we even shot it, baby.

'*This-* is a *commercial-*as you may have gathered.'

One descends a set of steps and lights up a gasper. One is embraced by a blonde, clothed - up to a point- in gold. This set, for Martins King Size

Cigarettes, a Busby Berkeley staircase lined with leggy lulus in gold satin gowns. Wigs to match. My idea. To take the mick out of Wagstaff, his supercilious Benson and Hedges ads and the product's gold packaging, you see. Self in gold lame frock coat, gold bow tie.

'*Must* we dance?'I sigh. Roll my eyes. A pianist, yes, clad in gold, plays a gold grand piano as we tango. Of course, all that could go wrong did. Aeons and fortunes were squandered.

Martins had a second variety, so a second shoot was required. The setup as for the first. But this time I with a brace of Dobermans. Diamante collars, on gold leashes. They tracked up to me, past the lulus, the dogs, to my face. One turned to camera.

'Have you tried Martins' *Extra Length?*'

$40,000 in 1974 money for this. One's reward to self, from a discreet Sydney men and boys' emporium. Talk about dinner and a show.

And then yet another 'head job', as one calls them, while in Sydney. Worst concept ever devised. Even for Channel Nine. *You've Got To Be Joking* comprised a season of risible vintage Aussie cinema. Ken G Hall's early talkies and such. A ruse to meet local content quota rules. One topped and tailed these old grey films, that this pass as a real show. One's task, desecrate the flicks, bow to stern, pre and post screening. There was no second season.

'Sure. Splendid. Shakespeare.'

'So what do you want to do?' I said.

'*Merchant*,' he said. 'You ready for Shylock?'

Ogilvie calling. He now director of the SA Theatre Company. One had pined for a signature part. Sumner would not indulge. So one wrote to George. Hmm. Shylock. Marvellous part, but one knew not a syllable of it.

'What about *Othello,* George?'

Now the Moor I knew well. There was a clumsy moment's silence.

'Um, it's a hard play, Frank. Not that good, you know. Boring in parts. So many people, bits and pieces going on.'

But I *knew* it. And all those lines for Shylock...

'It's my favourite, George,' I lied. 'It's that or nothing.'

An unselfish man, he didn't object. Perhaps he should have.

Well, rehearsals started off alright. But George was given to writing down notes as he watched us at it, as it were. *Irksome.* One day, couldn't bear it anymore. I stopped. Glared at him. *What?* I barked. From then on, if I objected to anything, he'd tell me to go to hell or get on with it. We seemed no longer friends.

One's Moor *faux*-strangling Barbara Stephens' Desdemona wasn't working. So on opening night, no forewarning, one stuck a pillow over her face – and held it down.

'*Mpppphhhhh! Grrrrpphhhhh!*'

She flailed, kicked. Then realised that one would only release it if she feigned death. Backstage, she was livid.

'Fuck, Frank! You nearly killed me!'

'Barbara, darling!' Ogilvie materialised. 'Magic! Best death scene I have ever...'

'Just like the real thing, baby,' I said. 'What a gal. I don't know how she does it.'

This *Othello* recalled The British Raj in India or French colonial Africa. The Adelaide press called one's makeup a 'cappuccino Othello.' Fuckers. The set, all these vast staircases. Getting on and off stage took a fucking week. And Ogilvie loved Teddy Hodgeman's Iago. *Too* much. So one went front stage all the way, even after his man has reduced mine to jelly.

'Stop squashing Teddy, Frank,' said Ogilvie, but fuck that. Critics called Teddy a 'bantamweight.' Perhaps unfair. But one didn't give a continental. One despised Adelaide anyway. Nothing ever good enough for them. Neurotic envy of the *eastern states* as they called us. As if speaking of sex offenders.

'I'm not competing with *that!* Talk amongst yourselves!'

Exit Othello, livid. Great noise from a box at Festival Theatre this night. Right in the middle of one's man doing murder. From up in the gods, gasps of air, gurgling sounds, wailing. The customers shifted their gaze to it. *Away from me.*

In the dressing room, one poured Ben Ean to get down some Mylanta. Splendid solitude for several minutes. Then the SM, in state of high alarm, as these floozies are.

'Frank, I'm terribly sorr...'

'Have you removed that noisy fucker? Because if not, ...'

'Frank, she was having a seizure. Not putting on a turn.'

Oh. Anyway, an ambulance had been called, one was informed, and that poor wretch ferried to whatever care was required. So order restored. On with the show.

'Ladies and gentlemen,' I said to the house, 'we will now resume the play.'

Barbara had lain there all this time, feigning sleep. I shook her shoulder. 'Wake up, dear,' I said. 'They've been looking at you long enough. Go into the handkerchief bit.' Barbara rose on her bed.

'My lord?' Right on cue. I turned to the customers.

'You *see?*' I roared. 'You see how *easy* acting is?'

They took the roof off with their applause. Yes, pixie. They hadn't come to see *Othello.*

They'd come to see *me.*

George bailed me up in the Festival Theatre car park after the show.

'Frank, about tonight...'

'We should bung that woman on every night. Wake up these fuckers a smidge.'

'Well, Frank, about that. I'm told that her sister was murdered some years back. The death scene triggered the memory and the fit this poor lady had.'

'Oh,' I said. 'Was *she* strangled by a blackamoor *too?*'

CHAPTER THIRTY-TWO

'You as Superintendent Cobham, Frank. Demands Mad Dog's severed body parts...'

'Well, that's me to a tee, Butch.'

Philippe Mora was son to Mirka. Her Mirka's Café a refuge to Melbourne's beatniks, jazzers, painters, thesps and all back in the 50s. One had known Philippe since he was a tot, via the café and Mirka's restaurant, Balzac, or as one pronounced it, *Balls Ache*. Now at Rylands, he sketched out his first go as a features director, *Mad Dog Morgan*.

'So who's our Morgan, then?'

He told me. So. Out in the scrub with a madman. We know how that one ends...

Dennis Hopper flew into Sydney, jet lagged, booze and other brainmelters on board. Hoved off to Kings Cross. His fame here legion, as director and co-star of *Easy Rider*. Back then to the Hilton with a mob about him. Chaos in the bar and up in his suite. Police. Come sunrise, some of Sydney's less relaxed drug dealers in the foyer. Wanting large sums settled. All this, mere prelude to what did betide.

In Melbourne, table reads. Self, Bill Hunter, John Hargreaves, David Gulpilil, Kurt Beimel, and Jack Thompson. Graeme Blundell and Robin Ramsay had small parts too, er, in a manner of speaking.

'Top of the feckin' mornin' to alla youse!'

Hopper. Bundaberg OP Rum and jazz cigarette in one hand, can of Fosters in the other. Some joker had told him that the real Mad Dog had drunk OP rum daily and in quantity. So here he was, deep in character.

'We better be after learnin' dem lines then, to be sure, to be sure!'

And get this. He was terrified of *me*. Swerved to Philippe whenever he saw me.

'Tell him not to fuckin' *look* at me, man!'

Let me guess. Some fucker here had made up some story about one's proclivities and intentions in regard to our star's virtue.

'What's the matter with that boy?' I said to Philippe. 'I wouldn't harm a hair on his head.' One invoked Jeffrey Hunter from *King Of Kings*. 'Doesn't he know I fucked Jesus in Hollywood?'

Our last night in Melbourne, Dennis invited the cast and their squeezes to join him in his suite. As they arrived, he shoved the men away. Grabbed the women and yanked them in, locking the door. The cuckolds, enraged, ran riot. Police.

One stayed in Albury, thirty minutes' drive from the shoot's ground zero, Culcairn. Most of the cast, madmen. A safe distance essential. And Albury had a Travelodge. One's preference. All identical, you see. A minimum of fuss. Car and driver provided, and a youth along as one's valet. An aspirant thesp. Served needs unmet for too, too long. Well, did his best. One's spirit willing, but the flesh, well. Weak as last light from a star already dead.

'I want his spleen on my desk by sundown.' Or 'Cut off his scrotum. It might make an interesting *tobacco* pouch.'

Such be one's man Cobham. One's only scene with Hopper was over his man Morgan's corpse. One wondered how the fuck Philippe would get him to do it. You see, his mortal fear of Cobham, of *me,* was the product of Dennis submerging himself in his Stanislavski Method delusion that he really was Mad Dog, and I his eviscerator. Too good to resist, pixie. When one ran into him on the set, one would stop dead and stare at his crotch, one brow raised, just to watch him dissolve into terror. Yet he need not have worried. I mean, we couldn't go near Dennis. He reeked. Stayed in filthy costume, you see, in character.

'Mad Dog didn't take showers, man.'

So in desperation, Philippe told him that bushrangers washed in the river. 'Far out, man.' He leapt fully clothed into the Murray.

And then, invaders. Po-faced hippies, clots of inert misery. Drug dealers drove in and lurked on the perimeter as well. Bikies, too. So at

Philippe's direction, the crew reversed all the road signs hereabouts, to confuse and deter further pilgrims. Some perhaps still out there, wandering, lost. Subsisting on their weakest as they fall.

'Old Spice,' I explained to Peter Collingwood in the makeup caravan. Hopper and some of the crew looked as if they'd been poisoned.

'Philippe heard yodelling from Hopper's room this morning at five or so,' I said. 'Found Dennis and sundry crew there. The rum and beer had run out, so, well... and when *that* ran out, someone's Eau Savage cologne.'

Peter and I had one scene together. A stroll in the bush, a chat about birdcalls.

The subtext, that his man Justice Redmond Barry and one's Inspector Cobham, were cobbers in more ways than one as we discussed *willy wagtails*. It went well. As did my man's scene with Dobbyn the coroner, played by Kurt Beimel. Cobham has a bull terrier. In this scene, he ponders the lower orders.

'The more I see of *men*,' I rumbled, 'the more I like *dogs*.'

Philippe also had me play a second character, Edwin Booth. A nineteenth century actor, huge in his day, who had toured out here. And was brother to John Wilkes Booth, who went on to star as Lincoln's assassin at Ford's Theatre in Washington.

So we shot a scene, self out in the scrub, reciting Shakespeare. Didn't make the cut. Fuckers.

'Well, he was quite taken with Dennis at first,' said Philippe, 'but now he's freaked him right out...'

A disaster. One day Gulpilil shot through. His part, Mad Dog's offsider, a big one. Shooting couldn't proceed. The local police brought in trackers, 'Aboriginaries' as Hopper called them, to find David. On his return, Gulpilil explained that he was in a flat spin about Hopper and his excesses. So he'd gone bush to consult the koalas, kookaburras and such.

'And what did they decide?' I asked.

'Same as me,' he said. 'He's crazy.'

They called a wrap. It was just noon.

'*What?* Why, may I ask? Been sitting here all morning in costu...'

'You've not heard, Frank? The sacking?'

'What? Hopper? About bloody tim...'

'No. Whitlam. The government.'

Cast and crew got angry drunk. Back at Albury Travelodge, one watched our nation tear its own heart out in these first days of colour television and stolen crown.

'I have a vision of you riding along, Dennis. You look up. See your own face. And then it explodes!'

One thought Philippe had gone as mad as Hopper, but this was the only way he could get our star to co-operate. You see, Philippe had concluded that Dennis, given his intake of Bundaberg Rum, ganja, amphetamines, not to mention Fosters Lager and after shave lotion, might not make it to the wrap alive. So, a contingency plan. Philippe thus convinced Dennis to allow an artist to cover his face with gelatin and fashion a face mask with plaster and paint.

Dennis did not expire, but the mask came in handy all the same. One's scene with Mad Dog, laid out after he's been shot to shreds by police, was completed using it after he had left the picture. It was easy, pixie. I mean, one has worked with so many actors more dead than alive.

'He's *what?*'

At shoot's end, Hopper swiped a car from the set's motor pool. Still in costume, with Philippe's adventurous mama Mirka on board, he made for the real Mad Dog's grave at Wangaratta Cemetery. Poured a bottle of Bundy OP over it. Drank another himself before the cops nabbed him.

The judge said that his blood-alcohol level meant he should be clinically dead. Forbidden by the beak to drive a car, or even be a passenger in one, it was said, and deported. They got him to the airport in the boot of a Torana, was the whisper, for a flight to the Philippines. This for his next film. A thing called *Apocalypse Now*.

'It was a gift from Richard Burton, ducky.'

Frankie Howerd had a walking stick. A secret hollow in it, as a rule full of Stoli or Gordon's. One was now cast in *Up The Convicts*, a humour-deprived comedy of early Sydney Town, for Channel Seven. The star, Howerd, in a retread of his Brit series *Up Pompeii*. Co-stars included Abgail, a 1970s Aussie sex symbol who'd jiggled naked on *Number 96*, Channel 10's sex opera. Good thesps wasted here too. Jacki Weaver, for one. Howerd played Shirk, a convict servant. My man, Sgt Bastion, his overseer.

Frankie brought out his catamite, Dennis Heymer. Not allowed out in public, except for filming on the set or locations. Shanghaied by Frankie as his dresser.

'And, one presumes,' I said to co-star Carol Raye, 'kept in a dogbox and fed with fish heads.'

The Channel Seven people took Frankie out on the town. More fool them. You see, he insisted on going to strip clubs up the Cross - and chatting up young men. They, of course, lagered up. Spoiling for *poofters* to bash.

'You don't know what you're missing!' he shouted as Seven's mob dragged him out, lest their heads all be ripped off.

'How *dare* you! That's it, I'm off!'

But Frankie's wig *did* look different this day. It created a continuity problem, you see.

'Frank, can you...'

One had no choice, as the show's whoopsy calmer by appointment.

'I steam it to give it a bit of body,' he snarled. In his dressing room, he sucked on his walking stick. 'Bette Davis told me about it. Hang your wig over a hot teapot and it fluffs up a bit, she said. Fucking fish-eyed bitch.'

Convicts bombed, and was axed. Well, what did you *think* was going to happen?

All shudders and sobs, one ventured by sun and moon down the River Moselle to the sea of same, stopping only to take on fresh Armagnac. For dear Margaret was gone forever. One had paid her specialist's bills, but no physic is infallible. No surviving family. The least one could do was cough up for her funeral service.

Rex Reed, the great American critic, raved about one's Cobham in *Mad Dog*, but no fucker noticed. Brandy-numbed, one rounded up all the sleeping pills one had.

Just as Sumner called. Saved my life. Bastard.

CHAPTER THIRTY-THREE

'Ben Ean and St Agnes in the wings,' I said. 'Kept topped up. See to it.'

Problems with a new SM, neglecting his duties. Perhaps at Sumner's directive. Insolent jackanapes. So, one took care of it oneself. For *The Nuns*, by Manet, Teddy Hepple gave good grotesque. Also here, scrummy Stephen Oldfield, and spry Jenny Hagan. Young Stephen, Sister Ines to one's Mother Superior in *Nuns*, joined one at Rylands some nights. We drank, talked latemost. Dined out, did opening nights.

At Toorak Village, one taught him some shoplifting moves. To impress, one supposes.

'An essential skill for young broke actors, Butch. And going by your efforts of late, you could be in such straits sooner than you think.'

One was not as swift these days, but well-liked. Shopkeeps who saw one at it just added the hot gear to one's bill.

One's other advice to this stripling was to try his luck overseas. At acting, not shoplifting. Alack, he did. One's last sorcerer's apprentice. From here, naught but lads at call. Cash up front. Remorse at leisure, betimes danger.

'Brigands used to robe up as Catholic clergy to rob, rape or murder the unsuspecting,' one explained to one's co-stars. 'A top rort. Wish I'd thought of it.'

Ah, *The Nuns*. We males in Sisters Of Mercy drag. Looked like a bad taste camp gag, but was based on precisely that practice in Haiti during a slave revolt in the early 19th century, whence this play was set.

'They should stick to who's fisting who in the social pages.'

One's retort to young Stephen when the critics called one's casting *strange* and *inexplicable*. Still, one got off lightly. Poor Jenny Hagan had to spend the entire second act playing dead onstage after we 'nuns' kill her for her baubles. A kind soul. Gave me lifts home after shows. In the kitchen, we'd wind down. Gas jets on the stove kept us warm till one's yellow sleepers, popped at interval and after the show, started to come on. Then one would relieve her.

'You can go now.'

One night, bored, one took a Rohypnol, these quite the fad among the younger set. Spent the second act leaning on the proscenium to hold oneself up. One braced for castigation. But Sumner didn't hear of it, or chose to disregard it. For he now cast me in *School For Scandal* and *Merchant Of Venice* for the first 1977 season, both at that hoary old slut the Athanaeum, in Collins Street.

One had just a small part, Oliver Surface, in *School*. But, praise be, Shylock in *Merchant*. One had regretted refusing Ogilvie. Now could redeem oneself. And other marvellous news.

'I have asked Diane Cilento to do both plays,' said Sumner. 'She has agreed, paperwork pending.'

Then, as fast as Diane had said yes, she said no. That said, a top cast for *School*.

But the stage too small for all of us to fit on the thing. Many entrances, few exits, you see. Filled up like a bloody tram at peak hour.

'Write in more exits,' I said. We did. But now had people coming and going like house cats. And the roof of the Ath was old. Part of it blown off in a storm. Pigeons nested above the fly tower. Dropped shit on our powdered periwigs and frock coats. We boxed on, feigning oblivion. You get more laughs that way, you see.

Then, my Culloden. Last night of the run. Forgot not just what to say, but who one was and to whom one was talking. A two-hander with Chilvers. He looked sidestage, for someone to come on, help him improv our way out of it. Then BANG! Turned to see Thring, out cold, on his back. Yes. I threw a faint.

'Is there a doctor in the house?'

Yes, pixie. Simon actually said that. Bruce Myles, still in costume, ambled on, to whispered confusion among the customers.

'Pick him up and get him off, for fuck's sake,' he hissed. But one had grown portly, so the two men not equal to this. The stage had a revolve, so Bruce signalled the techs. 'Revolve him off! Revolve him off!'

They stood mute over me as we rolled comical slow round to the dark side. Yes, the dark side. There's no place like home. There, one waited for Nembutal to overcome. Whispered four words as pre-dawn birds sang in colours that no longer pleased me. *You can go now.*

We started run-throughs for *Merchant* in June at a new add to the MTC's condemned property portfolio, in Ferrars Street, South Melbourne. Vermin-ridden. Once factory or warehouse. Sumner cast his best, his *full house* he called it. Among them, young Oldfield. One's lust stirred as kraken on ocean bed, but his interest in one's company now dwindling. The usual.

Fresh hells here, too. Like Natalie Bate, a rookie Sumner adored. Dedicated, gifted, punctual, imaginative. But the gal had halitosis. Vulture's breath. And one has worked with a lot of Englishmen.

'A Bate worse than death', one would say. And 'Oh, no,' after a scene one day. 'She's been eating *rats* again.'

'You look like bloody Nelson at Trafalgar,' I said.

'And you look like the bloody French navy, same place,' Sumner, one hand each on forehead and ulcer. '*I am not bound to please thee with my answers,*' he said, one's line unrecalled. 'Again, please, Frank. With dialogue this time, if you would be so kind.'

'I put you on propranolol,' said the sawbones at one's hospital cot. 'Lowers blood pressure, so stops the bleeding.'

Cars had roared by as the big gent in black on all fours vomited blood on the footpath. The brasco too far, you see. One's Shylock thus felled. The part, to Robin Ramsay, full deserving. One lay in the Epworth, full despondent. On one's Radio Rentals telly, news that Don McKay, an anti-drug wowser in Griffith, NSW, had gone missing. As had I.

'Ah, Podge.' Noel Ferrier. 'You know *Blankety Blanks*?'

'The misfortune is all mine, yes.'

'One is busy elsewhere for a week. *Tickled Pink*, it's called. An ABC comedy.'

'ABC comedy. A contradiction in terms,' I sighed. 'Oh, if one must.'

To Sydney for this tribulation. Gra Gra Kennedy, the host of this smut-caked and top-rating game show, had moved there, you see.

'Podge, you big poofter. You know the drill, I'm sure.'

Gra Gra loved calling other poofters poofters.

'Yes. Take me now, Lord.'

'Can it wait till after this, Frank?'

While here, one was prevailed upon to shoot a single scene for a miniseries, *Against The Wind*. Jon English, the singer, as convict. Self, the judge who banishes him to the prison beyond the sea. In red gown and mantle. Eyes and nose to match.

'Ask for Walter.' *Valter.*

Hugh Rule had made some kids' films with Gulpilil. Told me at a new Cantonese nosher, Flower Drum in Little Bourke Street, that he was off to Cannes and another film festival in Munich. One recalled *The Vikings* shoot and from Black Bag reefed an envelope. Five hundred or so in it. Told Hugh he must dine at the Walterspiel restaurant at the Four Seasons there.

'Yes, Walter. Probably dead by now, and if he isn't, ...he fucking should be, but anyway, take it, take it...'

Yes. Walter perhaps better off dead. And he not the only one.

CHAPTER THIRTY-FOUR

'The answer is yes.'

One's second mortgage needed satisfying. One thus roped into *The Kingfisher* with Googie and McCallum. My man, Hawkins, butler, *not another fucking butler,* to Cecil, 70. Cecil fancies Evelyn, just widowed. By he who stole her decades prior.

'At their age,' I said to Googie. 'Far too old to fuck.'

'Speak for yourself, darling.'

'I'm doing *Kingfisher* with Frank and John,' La Goog told Ogilvie when she asked him to direct. He was appalled. I mean, McCallum is a kind and gentle man. Takes that with him when he goes onstage. Cecil, however, is nasty – and in the closet. Now John could never play a gay man. Saw not the signposts that demanded it. So, one wasn't much looking forward to it at first day read-throughs. Saw Ogilvie there and stopped. Heard oneself say what one was thinking. About oneself. Perhaps time to...

'Coming to the end. Coming to the end.'

'What the fuck is *this*? I've been this fucker's valet since the Bronze Age! This clobber should be old and worn out, like, like *me!* I can't *play* this part!'

I couldn't believe it. My butler's outfit. Fresh from the tailors! McCallum tried to hide his smile. I rounded on him. 'And I'm not the *only* one with *that* problem, Butch!'

Yes, pixie. Over the top. But couldn't stop myself. What had become of me?

'This play is like paying to watch your grandparents fuck.'

This to Roland, he stage-managing this turn. January in Melbourne. Hot and windy. Disappointing houses. Onstage, one could almost hear the boiling within Googie's skull when one dried yet again. Of late, one had taken to wearing a large bauble round one's neck. Cut like a diamond. Synthetic, yet I called it one anyway. It was talk of 'my diamond' that set her off.

'Oh, for fuck's sake, Frank! If that *were* a diamond and that big, it would be in the Queen's collection.'

'Well,' I said. '*Isn't* it?'

McCallum cavilled at one's drinking, to others. Too much the gentleman to shirt-front me himself. But one needed the Dutch gumption. John's man he'd made a bore. So one had to front stage it, loud. Keep the customers awake. When one could bring one's lines to mind, that is. Googie and John had to improv their way out of these quagmires. So after line-up one night, to their dressing room went I, to repent.

In the doorway, I heard Googie's voice...*a fucking amateur, darling, he's just a fucking...* Then McCallum's. *It's the rivers of Ben Ean...* They saw me in their doorway.

'Oh,' I said. 'I came to apologise, but you can just go and get *fucked!*'

Midst no speaks offstage, to Brisbane, then Canberra. For Perth, Ron Frazer was shipped in. One was discharged, Ron's Hawkins deemed less of a nightly adventure than mine. Somewhere in there, one was a guest on *Parkinson In Australia*, for one's sins. Greater and further penance awaited.

CHAPTER THIRTY-FIVE

One's mortgage debt, unserviced. The bank, shouty now. One's accountant warned that one might have to sell. Inconceivable. Well, one could still pull in the provinces, so I called a former protégé now with the QTC in Brisbane, to reef *The Man Who Came To Dinner* out of its cryogenic chamber.

The director, John Kummel. Very capable. But his stabs at jolly banter irritated. There's a line in *Man* about the Sherry-Netherlands Hotel.

'Do you drink sherry, Frank?'

'It's a *hotel,* you stupid berk! One of the finest hotels in New *York!*'

I turned on my young chum. 'This is fucking absurd. What am I doing in this place? Get me *out* of here!'

Out of the question, of course. Opening night imminent. So they had the SMs place one's pages for each scene on my man's wheelchair tray. Large sheets with one's first lines taped up in the wings. Co-players to feed me these aloud just before one went on. One got there in the end. But then, so did Scott of the Antarctic.

'Well,' I said, 'buggers can't be choosers.'

The Sydney Theatre Company's director Richard Wherrett was the son of a violent drunk given to transvestism. The boy had suffered in ways one couldn't envisage.

The turn here was *Close Of Play* by Simon Gray. Opera House Theatre. Co-star, Ruth Cracknell.

'Crackers and I will put more bums on seats than Central fucking Park,' I assured Wherrett. And about my lines, pixie. *There were none to speak of.* My man has had a stroke, you see. So just one word at the end of Act One and a sentence to close the second. *Someone must have told them.*

The accommodation inflicted upon one by the parsimonious powers that be at the STC was quite dreadful. They'd only spring for the Chevron, not one's stated preference, the Sebel. One compensated in other ways. Mandrax, Tuinal and Rohypnol there be in abundance Sydneyside. From stagehands to celebrity physicians. Parties, premieres galore. Sydney's so-called 'society.' Rough, scathing, obnoxious. Yet mesmeric. One's hotel did have one small benefit. Located right in Kings Cross. Lads for lease a phone call away, should one feel inclined. The sad but true of it, less and less so now.

One evening, a night off, one watched the ABC's *Countdown.* You know, to deride out loud its mumbling, scatterbrained compere Molly Meldrum, this something of a national pastime. Saw a new group called ACDC. The school uniform one of them wore stirred urges within. I called Brett's Boys.

'You're not a schoolboy. I asked for a schoolboy!'

The surly lad shrugged. But a bit of alright, one had to concede. 'Oh, come on then. You'll have to do.'

To plug *Close Of Play,* one endured birdbrained Mike Gibson from a Sydney tabloid. He pointed out to readers one's bleached blonde remnant up top. This from a man who thought his own receding Prince Valiant cut and Village People moustache a jazzy look. He asked, fuck knows why, if one had ever pondered moving to Sydney.

'No, not really, Mike. I have a delightful house in Melbourne, my own Siamese cat. And a Siamese houseboy.'

He choked on his Reschs but recovered to ask if the cat was desexed.

'No. Neither is the houseboy. You know, Mike, last night, well... this lad one engaged was screaming. So I called his, er, agent. *Bring me another boy, will you? This one's bum's burst!'*

It would be all over Australia within hours. One must service one's profile, pixie.

Broke was I, so called *Womens' Weekly*. Suggested a feature on Rylands, this to showcase its as yet unsold antiquities, paintings and curios. Among them, altar lamps and antique silver candlesticks one had salvaged from a cathedral demolition in Roma. And a green and pink tapestry cushion Googie had sewed onstage throughout the *Kingfisher* run. The idea, not revealed to the *Weekly,* was to attract moneyed collectors. One item one couldn't part with was a Donald Friend *Balinese Boy* sketch, of a lad bare and irresistible. He hung, so to speak, over the fireplace in the reception room.

'One's last houseboy,' I'd say to guests. 'Have you *eaten?*'

Yet offers came there none. So it was *oh, yes, if one must* in May to a *Close Of Play* return run. Theatre Royal. Twelve shows. Oh, and the ABC cast one in a period drama, *Outbreak Of Love*. One's man, a rogue of the squattocracy. Stank to the ionosphere, but, well, needs must. Then the bank called again.

I dried my eyes.

'So a swag of cash from the sale, one presumes,' I said to my accountant.

'Well, yes and no. That foreclosed mortgage must be paid off. Won't leave a lot...'

It all went black as down I went in a faint. From a hole in space, one heard a tram's bell. *Ding.*

Outbreak Of Love was a novel by Martin Boyd. The *Age* would come to call this TV series the latest assault on Boyd's work. *Too kind,* in my view. Featured Rowena Wallace, Tony Bonner, one's *Skippy* co-star, Sigrid Thornton, and Val Lehmann. This last playing Queen Bea in a new and marvellous TV show, *Prisoner*. Sheila Florance, Ellie Ballantyne, Betty Bobbitt and more from one's faded triumphs of yore also starred in this fang and claw series of women behind bars.

'Oh, fuck. How *could* you?'

'Well, it sells, boy,' said Sumner. 'And you've just done it up north.' *So a slim chance you might recall some of your lines,* he meant. Simon Chilvers would direct *The Man Who Came* for the MTC. He cast Rosie

Sturgess, a good choice. Great comic timing, and a face about the place on the telly cop operas of the day.

But Freddy Parslow, well, not ideal. You see, he was at that time doing a one man play at the Universal in Fitzroy, *A Man Of Many Parts,* by that bloody Jack Hibberd. Freddy playing an actor, Noah Hope. Black tights, lurid waistcoat. Talks to a pet tadpole of impressing King Farouk in his *Faust* for Cairo's Goethe Society back in the times. Yes, pixie. The bastard was doing *me.* Justice was served as if boiling water poured upon attackers in a mediaeval siege when it closed after just three nights. But Freddy had transgressed in manner most treacherous. One lay in wait with further and greater punishments.

Elsewhere, the wedding of Prince Charles and Diana Spencer turned heads from IRA prisoners hunger striking to expiration. Satellites and computers brought news of frogs and princesses and bring out your dead.

'Where can I *hide?*'

Mad biddies were about, screeching like jungles on fire. Sumner, penniless, had started charging for guided tours of the MTC.

'Oh. Mr Thring.' The SM saw the cask in one's dilly bag. 'Would you like me to put that in the fridge?'

'No! *Leave* it! Just get me away from these...'

'Oh. Here they are. They want your autograph, sir. Hello, ladies!'

One waved them away and fled. No easy matter. Black Bag this day held four litres of Lindemans Cellar Park Moselle. My doctor in the house.

CHAPTER THIRTY-SIX

'I could *kill* him.'

Man's first night was good. But the second...a Rohypnol at interval. The previous night sleepless, you see. That and one's wingside refreshers, well, one drifted. Sumner in the front row with Simon as those four words came at me, bandits in the dark.

'Hear about John Lennon?'

One was asked a hundred times on that dreadful day. I fixed Freddy's cheese for that Hibberd play. In our scenes together in *Man,* one coughed, sneezed, blew one's nose over his lines. Rolled one's wheelchair over his foot, you name it, baby. At post-show drinks at Rylands with Jenny Hagan, Simon, and others, Freddy, quite shickered, tried to set one's foot alight. Yet there were other reasons for his madness. He and wife Joan hadn't spoken for years. Had their son pass messages, one had heard. A woebegone impasse. That poor lad.

'I'll buy the house!'

Too, too ill for this day's matinee. 'I shall just have to sell a painting or somethi...'

The fuckers refused. Sent a taxi for me.

No surprise that the *Man* run wound up before its time. And *Outbreak Of Love* aired in March on the ABC. The critics' cardigan club raved joyous at this lumpy swill.

I howled at the moon for more wine.

Dishy Keith Michell came home from England after half a lifetime there. He'd made good in films, BBC telly, theatre. Brought with him his flatulent Aussie take on *Peer Gynt,* the quite awful *Pete McGynty And The Dreamtime.* Still, two parts for me in a cooee cobber rendition of this Nordic fable.

'So one needs no convincing,' one said to Sumner, 'of its, shall we say, vast potential for greatness.'

You see, Black Jack needed a big name like Michell's to restore the MTC's tattered fortunes. The only way to get him was allow his vanity project to come, too.

One's Bunyip costume was ghastly. A rainbow stocking cap and body stocking. Blue tail and moustache. Tea strainers for eyes. Not so much mythic monster as king-sized blue-arsed fly. One posed with Michell for the press. He held my tail, gasping wide-eyed at its length, as if it were a huge...yes. *The things one does.*

In the middle of all this, a TV ad. Hutton's Smallgoods. A two-hander, Ferrier and self. And the script, O happy day. *They knew.* For one had *no lines.* One's task, to react, *mute,* to Noel's. A masterful performance, if I do mime so myself.

Back at *Pete McGynty* at the Prinny, smoke machines and strobe lights made it hard to navigate the stage. One's costume too hot. I passed out. Bunyips various hauled me off. One night, as the Old Swaggie, one dried right up. *Fuck it,* I decided, and looked straight at the customers.

'Look,' I said, breaking character, 'I'm sorry, but I forgot what to say here.' Doffed my hat. 'I'll collect my thoughts and we'll get on with it. That be alright?'

Applause roared as rainstorm on rusty tin. One dropped one's head, a bow from the neck. Signalled for shoosh with my hat. Sat down, resumed. Yet I swear Sumner, out in the sweep of seats, reached for my death warrant.

I've always been a Myers kind of gal, but only David Jones ever called with a paying job, namely to launch a Sydney branch of DJs high-end Melbourne offshoot Georges. The cheapest Melbourne celebs to be had, society hairdresser Lillian Frank and self, did the honours. The opening, at DJs in Sydney's Market Street. All Sydney C-list *lumpens.* Wagstaff was MC. I turned to he and Lillian.

'We are among cave dwellers and she-dogs.' Wagstaff's speech, suave and short.

'Georges has been in Melbourne for over a hundred years,' he said. 'That's a long time to rehearse the provinces.' Hoots from the Sydburgers, surely descended from dinosaurs. I caught up with Waggers in the brasco.

'Don't say I didn't warn you, baby. Those trollops out there will start laying green eggs any minute.'

One roamed about Rylands. Whispered to spirits of Grandma Harriet. Nanny, Margaret, Ernest. To FT, Lola. Even Olive. Yes, I missed her. Far, far too late.

Out beyond one's haunted mansion, Sumner and the MTC were little shy of destitute. So one proposed a one-man show, *Frankly Thring.* Roland helped with a script. Well, with prompts to trigger recollection when *that* all went to buggery. For example, boyhood recalled via poems learned by heart at Grammar which one recited. Wilfrid Wilson Gibson's *Flannan Isle,* or *The Pigtail Of Li Fang Fu.* To prod memory of *King Of Kings,* one read aloud some Wilde, the same volume of works which one had read during the hatcheries of disasters that shoot comprised. From one's days on the *Ben Hur* set, a selection from *The Portable Dorothy Parker.*

We screened footage of one's childhood Efftee turns, in *Diggers* and *The Sentimental Bloke.* Elsewhere, scenes from *The Vikings, Ben Hur,* one's TV ads. One's movie costumes, the purple togas, kingly robes, in fact MTC-made facsimilies, we draped on mannequins. Dressed the stage with them, these Ghosts of Thring Past.

'Lifeless dummies,' I said to the audience, 'that uncannily recall Chuck Heston.'

One's stories of co-stars were all true, one insisted. 'Depending on how dead they are.'

'Well, Melbourne, you took your bloody time about it.'

One's first response when off the back of *Frankly,* one was asked, at last, to be King Of Moomba. Mine now the sceptre and orb ere clutched in the clammies of repulsive Rolf Harris, boxer Johnny Famechon, Bobby Helpmann, Barry Crocker and Graham Kennedy.

One's investiture was at Melbourne Town Hall. January of 1982. One proclaimed that one would 'rule with a rod of iron.' The MTC created for me a crown and robes. The crown, of crucifixes. Did breakfast telly with that imbecile Gordon Elliott. Told him I would reign with 'my sceptre firmly in my hand.'

'Cease! I command thee!'

One bellowed at the downpour, cold teardrops of a million weeping angels. A hard rain on one's parade. The procession was long, so from the MTC, a junior thesp, one Stephen Pierce, with a bucket. A piss boy fit for King Thring. One waved at the crowds. Well, waved them away. Halfway through, drenched, one declared one's abdication. *'Fuck this!'* Made off in a Silver Top.

The nation sank into recession. Stayed the hand of those slobbering to buy Rylands and demolish it. To balance the karmic ledger, one collapsed outside Ford's the Chemist at Toorak Village. Somebody called an ambulance. Fuck knows why.

One had seen oneself on the telly doing Moomba duty, and was revolted. A wobbling turkey neck had to go. Surgery. They sucked or gouged it all out. But it returned like bloody salvation jane within a matter of months.

'The fucking thing's back!' I raved at Freddy P when he dropped by. Yes, we had beaten our swords if not into ploughshares, then drinking vessels. Mine the bigger.

As with all things.

CHAPTER THIRTY-SEVEN

An idle year, '83. Save a return to *TV Week*. One gave the wartime series *The Sullivans* the old one-two. Well, every fucker loved it, so it had to be done. All it did, one wrote, was to show what a dismal city Melbourne had been back then. On happier note, short-lived soapie *Starting Out* was axed in the wake of one's column devoted to its shortcomings. It felt good to kill something.

The pea-green Telecom Touchfone tingled. Oh, dear. *At Last: Bullamakanka The Motion Picture.* Where does one begin? Boy Scouts running an SP betting ring and a whisky still. Molly Meldrum a priest in charge of them. Yes, I *know*. Derryn Hinch, a gangster. TV wrestler Steve Rackman a corrupt mayor. And who else but Angry Anderson as a senator's staffer? Farnham a *cop*. And my man, a TV producer. A very Channel Nine affair. And for no purpose but to lose money. You see, the government of the day begat a rort whereby any business that invested in any film could claim a hundred and fifty percent of that sum as a tax concession.

The plot, oh, why bother? My man directed to speedgobble fistfuls of pills when things went wrong. Not funny in 1920s silents and hadn't improved. *Yes,* murmured the walls of Rylands. *It's come to this.*

Chuck Heston was out here spruiking the hit TV series *Dynasty,* in which he had a part. For the *Mike Walsh Show,* one was a surprise guest for Chuck. Our shared recall of *Ben Hur* and *El Cid* was champagne telly. But Chuck had changed. Once civil rights activist, now Reagan Republican. He bolted like a taipan from a burning canefield the instant the segment was done. I knew I'd not see him again.

For the mini-series *Eureka Stockade,* one was cast, yet again, as a judge. A script beyond rescuscitation. Our nation's tangled and ugly past as fruity melodrama. Its villains, of two dimensions. Its heroes, one fewer.

'Where did you get all these fake beards?' I asked on the set. 'Brazilian waxes?'

'How cunty do you want me?'

Gloria, who got me into that *Eureka* sludgefest, redeemed herself with *Bodyline,* casting me as the loathsome Lord Harris. And Sumner called. It never bloody rains...

'Are you well, boy? Do you know *Loot?*'

'Yes. The Orton play.'

'Lawler is directing.'

'But he doesn't like me.'

'Well, Podge. There's your starting point.'

The Melbourne *Herald* had a series called *My Favourite Room.* One chose one's kitchen. Their scribe Dorothy Goodwin quite taken by all the newspaper caricatures of me, the originals framed and hung on the pantry door.

'Yes,' I said. 'They're *always* doing me. They know I'll buy the fuckers, you see.'

One introduced old Edith as *one's surviving servant,* as she re-stocked. Ben Ean, Hennessys. Smoked oysters, pressed chicken. Cartons of Marlboro. Water crackers, quince paste. Dorothy wrote that it was *like a supermarket in there.* Well, it got my name in the papers. It was that or kill myself. Or someone else.

The subs at *TV Week* ghostwrote *A Piece Of Thring* when one was indisposed now. You know, in meetings with Stanley Leasingham and Black Bottle. They also had to rewrite it even when one did file. Whether one fell or was pushed must remain conjecture.

At home, one filled teardrop-spattered pages, handscrawled slanders of *Sale Of The Century* and *Sixty Minutes.* To try and win one's column back, with a jazzy show reel as it were. But couldn't get it down as it was in one's mind. Then *Bodyline* bid one get back to work.

'They bugger them silly at Eton. That's how it starts,' I said to Ogilvie, one of *Bodyline's* directors. This while discussing my man Lord Harris, who claimed credit for having brought cricket to India. This a bloviation, as the game was well-established prior to his arrival there. The worst governor of Bombay in the history of the Raj, and it was he who later ordered England's bowlers to aim for Aussie batsmen's heads. *I know the type.* Self-loathing, closet queens trying to make it go away. 'A lot of it about, George.'

'It's a bit dark in here with the drapes drawn at midday, Frank. Could we open them so...'

He knew one's answer by the eyes one gave him. Even behind VYI sunnies. Ogilvie had come to Rylands with the script. Without ever saying *he knew*, Ogilvie suggested a little pre-production prep. We did some good work and he stopped the night. One's last ever house guest there.

The RSL taxi pulled into the car park. There, a TV, smashed on the ground. Ah, the Sebel. Late night suppers, and John the barman open all hours of the moon. In the foyer, a fellow in white suit, red carnation and black eyepatch, played a white piano in the evenings. There was a wedding reception there next day. Elton John's, no less. It would fool no-one.

'It never *has*,' one murmured to oneself, unpacking Ben Ean and Mylanta from Black Bag. One recalled Joan and self's wedding day so long ago and dropped a tear.

One's Lord Harris makeup for *Bodyline* astounded. Muttonchop whiskers. Eyebrows that reached for the sky. Handlebar moustache. An Oscar Wilde wig, at one's suggestion, to imply a fellow of moonlit hue. Sitting there being made up, one felt strange all of a sudden. Then realised. It was *elation,* so long lost, at being a part of all this carry-on. Ogilivie came in. Noisy in there. I turned to him. Mouthed two silent words. *Thank you.*

We used Sydney Uni, or Rawson Oval in Mosman, doubling for Eton or Winchester. In a marquee on the oval there, one played out scenes with Hugo Weaving, John Gregg and others. We rehearsed before we shot. Producer George Miller, a movie and TV man, was full bamboozled.

'They'll know the lines. It won't seem spontaneous.'

Ogilvie looked at us, then back at Miller. Smiled.

'They're fuckin' *actors!*'

Elton was touring NZ but flying back to Sydney most nights. Huge parties at the Sebel. One sang for one's bubbles. Stories of Stratford and Hollywood co-stars.

Some of them true.

Back at the *Bodyline* shoot, a plethora of scenes. First, with a child actor playing English skipper Douglas Jardine as a kiddie. Then on to Lord Harris and confederates, plotting. And Hugo Weaving and I, for Harris on his deathbed. This last, closer than one cared to ponder, to one's own reality.

'A baddie to make your flesh crawl, this one.'

Back in Melbourne, George Miller called with a job in his next project, *Mad Max III*. But Sumner had cast one in *Loot*. The two clashed and Black Jack had asked first.

'Righto,' said director Lawler. We were two weeks into rehearsals for *Loot*. 'Books down today, everybody, please.' *But I knew not a line.* I waved at the empty stalls before us.

'Do you see customers here, Ray?'

'No. But that's not the poin...'

'Very well, then,' I said. 'Shall we continue?'

'Yes, Frank. When you put down the book.'

'I can't *do* this fucking play!'

He took me out into the foyer. It was threatening to rain.

'Frank, I think you're right.' It started to rain.

'Of course I am. I just need a little more ti...'

'No, the other right. You can't do this part.'

Forked lightning cracked the skies. Then thunder. That night, the rain turned to hail, one steeped in piteous remorse. The phone jangled over the roar. George Miller. Would one reconsider for *Mad Max*?

'Very well,' said Lawler.' What are your plans now?'

I hoisted a brown coffee mug abrim with Ben Ean.

'Breakfast. *Benediximus* with the play, baby.'

One didn't tell him why one was leaving. He would hear of it soon enough.

'Hi. I'm Tina.'

As in Turner. I was spellbound. Someone called my name.

'Excuse me, my dear,' as I wheeled around. '*Ah*. Mel bloody Gibson.'

'Tina, do you know this guy? I've wanted to work with Frank forever.'

My God. *I was back.* Oh, yes. And one met Mr Angry Anderson. Rock singer. Shinybald, like me. Black-clad. Like me. But Angry not, well, lofty. In our unfortunate scenes together, he resembled a Frank Thring action figure.

Then there was Angelo Rossitto as Master. He'd played in flickering silents with John Barrymore. In *Freaks,* that grotesque film, in 1932. Then, in Bela Lugosi's last movies. Two foot ten inches tall in the old money. Eighty summers now. Almost blind. So one helped him about the set.

'You're a prince, you know dat, Frank?'

The most wonderful compliment. And yes. If he thought that, with one's appearance these days, he surely was sightless.

'Splendid. Thank you all.'

Ogilvie's words at our final rehearsal the green after the rain. 'Start on the set Monday, first thing in the evening.'

Yes, pixie. *Night shoots.* The horror. January in Sydney. Yet freezing out at Homebush, abetted by rain. One clad in a sleeveless leather jerkin, patina of baby oil and little else. We in an open-air quarry, clustered around a huge thing of junkyard scaffolding, the Thunderdome. Overcoats and brandy between takes, no match for this blood-freezing tempest. Ogilvie honked tinny inspiritment through a megaphone. But in such context, these as if a demon's taunts to the damned.

'Mary Hardy, one of Melbourne's best-known...'
ABC radio news, in a taxi en route to the shoot. Home alone, she was. In the bathtub. Shotgun. I fell into a pit of tears. Cared not if I be drowned.

Now to 'Bartertown', another set at Homebush Brickworks. In a fucking quarry, a post-nukes frontier fleshpot. Wrecker's yard junk as dwellings, marketplace and so on. A tower of jetsam in its midst. From here, Tina's Aunty Entity policed goings-on down below. I, The Collector, her dead-eyed consigliere and gatekeeper. My one two-hander scene with Mel was upon us. His Max seeking work, and my man's assessment of his worth.
'The brothel's *full.*'
Solid gold, baby. And for one's scenes with Tina, great relief. One's lines, mostpart repeats of what she has just said. So. They knew of one's *un petite maladie.* Ogilvie's intercession, most likely. One said nothing. One's gratitude, heartfelt.

We both liked a cold drink. But he didn't want people to see him at it. So Mel suggested Tina's Tower, as we had taken to calling it. Angelo joined us. Teetotal, but impressed.
'Frank, you're the only guy I know can drink more than Mel and still remain a gentleman.'
But Tina, once Baptist, now Buddhist, wrote Mel a letter upbraiding him for this. One's name was mentioned. Not in favourable light.

'Thank you so much, Frank. Great, great performance. Lawler was right.'
One's last day on the set. Miller had taken me aside.
'Eh? Beg yours?' What the fuck was he on abou..?
'Ray Lawler. Called me. Said you were free from that play, so I should give you a call and...'

Oh. I *see.* Yes, perhaps one should have been thankful. But the subterfuge enraged me. I slid into my taxi. Made for the airport without saying goodbye.

CHAPTER THIRTY-EIGHT

'We'd be better off under the *Japs*.'

One scene in the whole film. As a street speaker. Dear Philippe had written it in, just for me. His new film, *Death Of A Soldier*, a true story of an American GI in wartime Melbourne. Murdered three women before being caught and hanged. They filmed an establishment shot of Parly House in Spring Street. But for the scene proper, we used the steps of Collingwood Town Hall. Here, one's maternal Grandpa Max Kreitmayer had once been mayor. My man rails at Yank soldiers. One of those parts where I became someone other than me. And wished I could stay there.

One could repel the Visigoths no longer. Massing in navy blazers and fawn flannel strides at the gates of Rylands, hung with FOR SALE signs. These barbarians without, come now for the dirt upon which stood one's home. Hugh came almost every day. To help one pack, to eat, to decide which of one's possessions would be coming with me. And which not. He, Roland, others, bless them all. Ministered as best they could to the hollow shadow they beheld.

'The Ming stauettes, the Louis XV pieces, the precious stones, the crystal. Auction it all,' they said. One did as told. Sold one's collection of several thousands of Penguin paperbacks. Some bear moselle-infused tearblots to this day, where'er they be. The press called. A dutiful thesp, one clowned and entertained, tossed them *bons mot*. Comedy mask in place, to neutralise their predatory instincts.

'Oh, you just have to have it put down,' one joshed of Rylands. 'Like a pet grown feeble and infirm. Or a *parent*.'

This coincided with the prem of *Mad Max III,* so one put in a massive plug for the film. One could still play the newsdogs. Even with the arse out of one's kaftan.

'What about open inspections?'

One begged a final hour reprieve. That at least Rylands could remain standing. *Nah, mate, no point,* said this realtor. Henna hair dye, moustache. Grey vinyl shoes. *With zippers.* Other crimes.

'Nobody wants this old dump, mate. Just the land.'

Well, that did it. Sorting and packing, one had found some interesting items about. So now, one reefed out FT's old Winchester rifle from behind the front door. Ran the fucker off. Word got back to one's carers.

'Best get you out of here, Podge.'

Roland now did PR work. The Rockman Regency a client. One stayed in a suite there for two weeks. Gratis, one was told, inert in one's distress. Others prepared one's just-purchased cottage in Mahoney Street, Fitzroy. One tried to get out of bed, but the doctors had one quite sedated. Hugh, Roland and others supervised the move. Painters did it out in white. Some of the windows, one had refitted. Stained glass, after drawings by Aubrey Beardsley. And one had a Jacuzzi installed. *Just in case.* One's bedroom here, repainted. Two coats. Windows too. Black.

'Take your time in bed in the morning.'

A line from one's new telly ad for the new, faster trams. But the usual witch-burners put the Minister who'd commissioned these ads on trial by fire. He swore he'd been told that the drink one had used to toast viewers on the tram in the ad was water. Well, he had. By me. Then they whined about the sexual allusions, as just described.

'Well, you don't have to watch it if you don't like it,' one told the press when they called. 'That's what I tell my houseboys.'

Fitzroy not so bad. Walking distance to Coles, ergo Liquorland. A Bottlemart too. A reliable chemist. One had lost the latest incarnation of Black Bag in the move, so purchased a blue TAA flight bag.

348

And something else. One couldn't resist this place, being an old wireless man. A radio station at the end of one's street. 3RRR by name. And what luck! The station manager, lovely Lucille Rogers, Hugh Rule's spouse for a time. She asked me to do a voiceover for the Wilderness Society. One was only too happy to oblige.

'Don't muck about with your knob!'

One went back, almost daily. Did station promos. Stay tuned to RRR was the message. Or *'Subscribe or die!'* A public radio sort of deal, so no revenue from paid ads, you see. For subscriber drives or radiothons, one recited filthy limericks on air, in return for listeners' donation pledges. *There once was a woman from Kew, Who filled her vagina with glue,* that sort of thing. *They'll pay to get out of it too,* the punchline.

One day a DJ there, Arch Cuthbertson, had one on air to play one's choices from the record library. *Everybody's Talking* by Harry Nilsson, *Galveston* from Glen Campbell. Bobbie Gentry's *Ode To Billy Joe.* Yes, pixie. I adore that stuff. Not many people know that. Archie asked about one's penchant for basic black, and one's chunky accessories.

'Well, you see, Archie, I am the original *rapper.*' And more. 'But when *I* speak of *bitches,* well, ...'

Someone called Rob Wellington was directing a video. For a song from Farnham's new album *Whispering Jack.* An offer via phone at RRR one day. One played oneself. Rolled like a rapper. Feigned a heart attack. Fell down dead. Just one line to camera at the start of the clip for *Take The Pressure Down.*

'There's only one step left to overcome your quest for success.' Dropped to a whisper. *'Pressure.'*

The Howling III: Marsupials is not a film one has seen, nor wishes to. Still, it was kind of director Philippe to ask. Off to Sydney for this job. My man Jack Citron, film producer, versus marsupial werewolves. *Yes, I know.* A young AD working on a film one's man is shooting is cuntstruck by a female from this pack. As is one's Jack Citron. In one scene, one danced in a disco. In a cape. Watch it if you dare.

No work now. One drifted in the stunned grey exile of the unwanted...

One was watching the Queen open the new Parly House in Canberra when Gloria called. For *The Bayou,* enter my Jake Morgan. White sex slaver based in New Orleans. They'd revived the 1960s TV show *Mission Impossible.* Peter Graves once again as Jim Phelps. But two decades and too many facelifts on, he wore that eerie cast, of an alien held too long in custody. The director, to one's delight, Don Chaffey from *A Question Of Adultery* a lifetime ago in London.

The shoot, at Village Roadshow on the Gold Coast. Machine snarl and dust of building sites surrounded us, these festooned with billboard promises of wonders to come, Movie World and Wet'n' Wild World. One flew home as if from the moon.

Kids who'd grown up on one's telly ads had become a staunch cohort of fans in adulthood. One of these, the excellent Gerry Connolly, had me on his new ABC show. But I couldn't get my bit right. As one opened the last of one's Ben Eans for the day, one swears one heard the exasperated floor manager whistling *Ten Green Bottles.*

A protégé from one's days gone by saw one on Gerry's show. One was asked to be guest of honour at the NIDA awards for 1988. Drama school graduates. *Oh, alright.* Noblesse oblige, one supposes.

One arrived in Sydney quite merry. Perhaps overmuch. Nerves, you see. Asked to deliver a speech, one had reached for a settler. Couldn't muster the oration one would have been delighted to create, had it not been for...

'Terribly sorry, Butch,' one managed to one's host. The kids were astounding. And yes, I wept. For one award was posthumous. A youngster who hadn't lived to collect it. Some called it a spectacle unbecoming. But who could not be overcome? Then and there, one willed one's earthlies entire, such as they were, to a new NIDA scholarship.

'Baby, I'm the well *before* the *then* part.'

The *Sunday Age* called. For a story on the MTC, then and now. 'You must have found me via fucking ouija board.' They asked if people came to see *Othello* or to see Frank Thring. I sighed. 'They come to see Frank Thring *fail* as Othello.'

I hung up. Fuck 'em all.

I stood shouting and crying. Neighbours called the police. Coming home from the shops, one forgot where one lived, you see. The young wallopers knew not who Thring was. Set to cuff me when darling Lucille happened along and told them.

Visitors came. Banged on the door till they gave up. Joanna McCallum slid a note under it. Roland too. One disregarded them. When friends phoned, *fuck off*. Then one stopped answering altogether. That it might stop ringing.

Then one saw in the papers that Joanie was in town. We went out, dinner and drinks, but one had a sort of blackout when we got back to Fitzroy. Thought Joanie was a stranger come to rob me. Pushed her out through the open front door. Her shoes and suitcase still inside, so she had to come back. One was waiting, arms wide, *so sorry*. What the fuck was wrong with me?

CHAPTER THIRTY-NINE

D ischarged today from St Vincents. Fortunate that it's located in one's home suburb of Fitzroy. One has crutches. But stairs at the main entrance. One good leg, t'other bandaged, toeless. To walk on, pain beyond articulation. One's taxi waits, but one can't lower oneself into the seat. The driver stares ahead, no help. I sigh and kneel on the back seat from the passenger side. Crawl across to swivel into a sitting position. The radio tells us that someone from a rock group, Nirvana, Kurt someone, has shot himself. *My dear fellow. I quite understand.*

*

'Frank? It's Simon Phillips. From the MTC. We're staging the Wilde play...'

Black Jack had retired. One would never perform in the MTC's new Playhouse on St Kilda Rd with its circumcised Eiffel Tower thingy.

'Oh, yes. I suppose you want some free pre-match *entertainment* for the first night reception...'

About all one was offered these days. By anyone. Well, they could go to buggery.

'Well, ...'

'Don't *interrupt*. I'm not *finished*.'

'Sorry.'

'Fuck off.'

'Frank, I...'

'I'm finished.' *Clang.*

Then a *letter.* Might one want to play the parts of Lane and Merriman, the butlers in *The Importance Of Being Earnest* ? *Not another fucking butler. Two, even worse.* One chose not to reply.

'Let's see what this greensleeves is made of,' one addressed the bathroom mirror.

'Who is it? I have a gun!'

I gripped the Winchester. From without, the reply, muffled by the door between us.

'Frank, it's Simon from the MTC. Can we talk?'

Well, what can you *do* with them? One hid the rifle back behind the door. Unlocked the chain, the deadlock and the bolt. All installed to pre-empt robbery or worse, you see. Saw it was a fine and mild morning. Offered refreshment. He held his goblet like a severed body part.

'Frank, do you know Ruth Cracknell?'

'No, Butch. *She* knows *me.*'

'Well, she's Lady Bracknell in our *Earnest.* And, Frank, the cast have asked after you. There's a strong consensus that you'd make a marvellou...'

'All very touching,' I said. 'But...'

'Well, if you change your mind, I have a script...' He fumbled in his satchel.

Oh, fuck it, I thought.

'Don't bother, darling boy,' I said. 'Got my own, you see.'

'Podge!' Dear Monica Maughan. 'I'm so glad you said yes.'

'I thought the fuckers would never *ask,*' I said.

'So, *Thring.*' Crackers.

'Cracknell as Bracknell,' I said. 'Wait till the buggers get a hold of that.'

The cast lined up. Self as minor royalty reviewing the troops. First, a fellow here a spit for Ian Fleming.

'Frank,' said Simon, 'Geoffrey Rush. And his wife, Jane Menelaus.'

'Dear boy. You've brought your other half. Oh. What might have *been.*'

Then I saw Bob Hornery. *Fucker.* One had lost parts to this bastard. I was *sure* of it. But luck was in. No-one else there one despised. The lovely Helen Buday from *Mad Max III.* Andrew Barker a competent thesp. And this other chap, fresh from the UK. Had no idea who one was. Refreshing, truth be told.

'Richard Piper's the name.'

He looked askance but not without admiration at one's brown coffee mug of Ben Ean at ten AM. One had found one's chum for the run. Whether he liked it or not.

The set was like being enveloped in a huge Aubrey Beardsley diorama. Aesthetic balm to one's inner Noel Coward. It featured a huge book on a lectern, its pages facing the customers. For one's butlers, between scenes, one's task was to turn a big page to announce via display the next one. One played it as if it took all of one's strength to budge. Great mirth did I enchant from the customers.

For one of my two men, one suggested an Oscar Wilde wig. Its entrance pulled a laugh every night. But, pixie, the *lines.* At one point one must announce Mr Earnest Worthing. One even held a card in one's palm with his name in it, supplied by the SM. And Andrew Barker as Earnest took to whispering *Mr Earnest Worthing* one's way as he entered. Yes, one should have been thankful. But it grated.

'Mr Hugo Weavi...' I looked at the card. A blur. 'Mr Edward Worthi...'

Andrew stagemuttered *Earnest Worthing.*

'Yes, I *know that,* Andrew!' I shouted. 'Mr Andrew *Worthing!*'

Ah, well. Helen Buday, in character, sometimes whipped the card from me.

'No, no. It's Mr Earnest *Worthing!*' she'd scold, to make it look like part of the show.

Well. If one's idea of entertainment is a mad circus elephant stomping the clowns and acrobats to death, this was all that and more.

One night, Geoffrey Rush was too ill to go on. Director Simon stepped in.

'The most amazing thing I've ever seen,' went one's herogram to the *Age.* But the customers were coming to see *me,* not the show. Some of the cast grew miffed at this.

'*Help* me, Butch!' one wailed at Richard.' It's like the Old Testament!'

One had also said yes to a tour for *Earnest,* of rural Victoria. And one now reaped that firestorm. Oh, baby. Hot wind at Bendigo. And a plague. Grasshoppers. The *noise* the fuckers made. Got into food, clothes, cars. And the *heat!* About to faint, one plonked oneself in a chair in the dressing room. The wicker seat caved in under my bulk. Arse wedged in. Couldn't fucking budge. Richard and others had to haul me out.

The hoppers crunched underfoot onstage. And they'd get stuck in Jane's and Crackers' horsehair wigs. A most amazing sight.

'If they're that thick up top, Madam,' said one's Merriman to Crackers' Lady Bracknell one night, 'one would hate to see *down*stairs.'

To Ararat. Here, no grasshoppers. Instead, moths. Millions of them. And no aircon in road-melting heat. Helen Buday somehow found me two fans. A living saint, as Olive used to say of far less deserving candidates. In Nhill, as in *nil,* we couldn't find our hotel, wait for it, the Zero Inn. One couldn't resist.

'And I suppose that's located on Fuckall Street?'

Thence to Warrnambool. One thought of grandfather Max and FT on this road. Of Max Kreitmayer's waxes, boxing kangaroos, dwarfs and burlesques. Of FT's kinescope, his Great Dexter turns. And now me.

'*The last of us,*' one whispered aloud in one's room.

Now to Geelong. The Arts Centre. Then Wonthaggi. Warragul. One said yes to any proffered marijuana from cast members thus inclined when gathered by hotel pools. One drank to ward off the dry horrors. *One knew they knew but dared not say.* Thring now infirm, a lame dog. The shotgun not yet racked. Kept alive for sake of sentiment, to yet lure custom. Such shallow purpose must suffice.

'Hope you don't mind a bit of speed, Frank.'

Back in Melbourne, Dennis Olsen was in town for a show he was in, camping at Rylands. Drove me to our next stop, Wangaratta. At the wheel, he had Hawkins and Quayle qualities, I remarked. Tony had breathed his last just a couple of months back. One recalled to Olsen one's hand-blown wine glasses surviving a prang in Quayle's Aston Martin in the Serbian countryside.

'But only you and fucking Chilvers and bloody Teddy Hodgeman could have destroyed one of them in a game of bridge.'

Albury. Our last night. Just one sleep and three hour drive home come morning. Roland here with a film crew. A kerfuffle. He'd been greenlighted to video one's last ever show. But someone had objected. Mattered not who. Message received.

One slipped out after curtain and line-up without a word. And saw a taxi waiting there under bright moon.

'Where to, mate?'

'Melbourne.'

One supposes it must come to this. The last of FT's legacy now bequeathed. Oesophageal cancer, say the whitecoats. One has asked Hugh and Lucille to burn the body and scatter one's mortals off Queenscliff. That the waves may declaim, like Titus Andronicus, that *I am the sea.*

So then. Joan. Yes, pixie. This is for you. This tale, a last unworthy gift to one's first and true love. Upon me that hour, to bow and exit. Mayhap to catch an eye somewhere anon, one gone to become but a dim and feeble twinkle among these countless in the ink of memory.

You can go now.

ACKNOWLEDGEMENTS

The list is endless. My way better half Ali Rose and my son Paddy for staunch and formidable support. My sisters Jenny and Louise for an academic historian's guidance and toil, and a gun graphic designer respectively. Meredith Rose, for many hours and invaluable advice as an editor. Michael Fitzjames for the cover art. Charlie Maclean for inspiration. All those who agreed to be interviewed for this, the many who volunteered information via social media, as well as those who provided contact details for others believed unreachable. And friends and workmates who encouraged and abetted, who listened patiently to endless anecdotes on the subject of Frank, who grew to be something of an unhealthy obsession with this writer. You know who you are. Couldn't have done any of this at all without all of you. Thank you.

SELECTED BIBLIOGRAPHY

THE ACTOR WHO LAUGHED Frank Thring and Roland Rocciccioli (Hutchinson)

THE TWO FRANK THRINGS Peter Fitzpatrick (Monash University Publishing)

RECOLLECTIONS AT PLAY John Sumner (Melbourne University Press)

THE FLOOR OF HEAVEN Richard Wherrett (Hodder)

THE NAKED TRUTH Graeme Blundell (Hachette)

MY STORY Harry M Miller (MacMillan)

LEO 'RUMPOLE' McKERN: THE ACCIDENTAL ACTOR George Whaley (New South)

THE RAGMAN'S SON Kirk Douglas (Simon and Schuster)

IN THE ARENA Charlton Heston (Harper Collins)

THE ANCIENT WORLD IN THE CINEMA Jon Solomon (Yale University Press)

ORSON WELLES Ben Walters (Haus)

LITTLE BLACK BASTARD Noel Tovey (Hodder)

A BIASED MEMOIR Ruth Cracknell (Penguin)

MAVIS BRAMSTON, NUMBER 96 AND ME David Sale (Vivid)

MEL GIBSON Roland Perry (MacMillan)

THERE GOES WHATSISNAME Noel Ferrier (MacMillan)

TONY CURTIS: AMERICAN PRINCE Tony Curtis (Virgin)

JOHN GEILGUD Gyles Brandreth (Sutton)

SCREW LOOSE Peter Blazey (Picador)

DAMN YOU, SCARLETT O'HARA! THE PRIVATE LIVES OF VIVIEN LEIGH AND LAURENCE OLIVIER Darwin Porter and Rose Mosely (Blood Moon)

OLIVIER Philip Ziegler (Maclehoe Press)

OLIVIER Terry Coleman (Bloomsbury)

LAURENCE OLIVIER: CONFESSIONS OF AN ACTOR
Laurence Olivier (Simon and Schuster)

ANYTHING FOR A QUIET LIFE Jack Hawkins (Coronet)

ON THE INSIDE: AN INTIMATE PORTRAIT OF SHEILA
FLORANCE Helen Martineau (Australian Scholarly Publishing)

RATBAGS Keith Dunstan (Golden Press)

IT WON'T LAST A WEEK! THE FIRST TWENTY YEARS OF
THE MELBOURNE THEATRE COMPANY Geoffrey Hutton
(Sun Books)

INSIDE TRADER Trader Faulkner (Scribe)

THE ROYAL SHAKESPEARE COMPANY: A HISTORY OF TEN
DECADES Sally Beauman (Oxford)

NICHOLAS RAY: THE GLORIOUS FAILURE OF AN
AMERICAN DIRECTOR Patrick McGilligan (itbooks)

CLOSE UP: 28 LIVES OF EXTRAORDINARY AUSTRALIANS
Peter Wilmoth (MacMillan)

SIMPLE GIFTS: A LIFE IN THE THEATRE George Ogilvie
(Currency Press)

STAGES Reg Livermore (Hardie Grant)

SELECTED ONLINE RESOURCES

AUSTRALIAN DICTIONARY OF BIOGRAPHY Frank Thring
by JP Holroyd, Max Kreitmayer by Mimi Colligan (Australian
National University)

'FRANK THRING INTRODUCES THE STARS' (1931)
Australian Screen An NFSA website

FRANK THRING RADIO AND TV LICENSE AD Australian TV
Commercials website

FRANK THRING MARTINS' CIGARETTES AD Belinda
Darlington website

FRANK THRING NYLEX MOCCASIN AD kurvapicsa website

GARY DAY unpublished online memoir

ALAN ANDREWS unpublished online memoir

ORAL HISTORIES

Interviews conducted face to face, via phone or email: special thanks to
Jenny Cornwall for her interviews with Noel Tovey, Ellie Ballantyne,
Simon Chilvers, Trader Faulkner and Kevin Miles; to Gayle Kennedy
for her interview with Tony Bonner, and to Jay Katz (Jaimie Leonarder)
for his interview with Roger Ward.

GEORGE OGILVIE
ROLAND ROCCICCIOLI
HUGH RULE
NOEL LANE
RAY LAWLER
LUCILLE ROGERS
ARCH CUTHBERTSON
KEVIN MILES
BOB HORNERY
TRADER FAULKNER
SIMON CHILVERS
ELSPETH BALLANTYNE
BETTY BOBBITT
TONY BONNER
JENNY HAGAN

JOHN SUMNER
ALAN HOPGOOD
ROGER WARD
NOEL TOVEY
PHILIPPE MORA
PAUL KARO
RICHARD PIPER
DENNIS OLSEN
DAVE BARRY
HELMUT BAKAITIS
REG LIVERMORE

SELECTED BIBLIOGRAPHY: NEWSPAPERS AND MAGAZINES

The news stories, colour pieces, critical reviews pertaining to Frank Thring, interviews with Frank, not to mention columns and opinion pieces by Frank himself in Australian periodicals are almost innumerable. The writer is indebted to the following publications, some now gone, others persevering.

The *Argus* (Melbourne)

The *Age* (Melbourne)

The *Sunday Age*

The *Sun News-Pictorial* (Melbourne)

The *Truth* (Melbourne)

The *Advertiser* (Adelaide)

TV Week

The *Sydney Morning Herald*

The *Daily Mirror* (Sydney)

The *Daily Telegraph* (Sydney)
The *Daily Express* (UK)
The *Australian*
Womens' Weekly
The Bulletin
Everyone's magazine
Listener-In magazine
Plays And Players magazine (UK)

ARCHIVAL RESOURCES

FW Thring Collection, Performing Arts Museum, Melbourne
Public Records Office, Victoria
National Film And Sound Archive of Australia

www.ingramcontent.com/pod-product-compliance
Lightning Source LLC
Chambersburg PA
CBHW050918030726
47503CB00007BB/2356